HIS FRIEND INSERTED his body between Rodney and the only door, and now looked down at him from that scarecrow-tall, somehow *creepy* height of his.

Rodney had forgotten just how tall his friend was.

Jacob blinked into those large brown eyes, eyes that used to get him stuffed into lockers back when they were in school.

"Wait," Jacob said.

He held up one of his gloved hands, expressionless.

"I have a birthday present for you, Roddo."

"Don't call me that." It came out angrily, without thought. "Don't call me Roddo, Jacob. No one calls me that anymore. They haven't called me that for about twenty years."

Jacob didn't seem to hear him.

"Just stay for one more minute. I have something for you. Just wait right here."

Rodney frowned, but didn't move.

When Jacob didn't either, Rodney made an impatient wave with one hand.

"Well?" he said, annoyed. "What is it? I really have to go, Jakey—"

Something stung his neck.

He didn't feel any pain.

He didn't feel anything at all.

He also didn't see his friend move, not until it was too late.

He felt the pressure, realized one of those gloved hands was by his neck—

"Happy birthday, Roddo," Jacob breathed.

His mouth hung by Rod's ear.

He moved his face back, and Jacob's too-red mouth was smiling at him.

"Don't worry, Roddo," he whispered softly. "You're going to like this..."

His lips pulled higher in that upsid͏e-d͏o͏w͏n͏ ͏s͏c͏r͏e͏a͏m͏, ͏h͏i͏s͏ ͏d͏a͏r͏k͏ eyes blank as mirrors.

"...You're really going to like this a l͏o͏

G000065543

BLACK IS MAGIC

Quentin Black Mystery #15

JC ANDRIJESKI

BLACK IS MAGIC: A Quentin Black Paranormal
Mystery Romance (Book #15)

Copyright 2022 by JC Andrijeski

Published by White Sun Press

First Edition

ISBN: 9798425948328

Cover Art & Design by Damonza http://damonza.com (2022)

Link with me at: https://www.jcandrijeski.com

Or at: https://www.patreon.com/jcandrijeski

Mailing List: https://www.jcandrijeski.com/sign-up

White Sun Press

Printed in the United States of America 2022

Dedicated to all those who had a tough time in high school... and anyone who lost themselves along the way

THE CHOSEN

Jacob Mulden sat on a ratty, cigarette-burned, red-satin chair.

The chair lived in a closet-sized dressing room, a room smelling of cheap flower air freshener, pot smoke, and even cheaper perfume. The alcove lived behind a slanted wooden door, and formed the only backstage to a theater called *The Blue Cat* on First Street in downtown San Jose.

Jake didn't mind the smells.

He didn't even mind the faint hint of vomit behind the odor of stale beer.

He'd been here before.

They were mostly good to him here.

He checked his watch.

Twenty minutes. Then Rodney would be here.

Plenty of time to get ready for his act.

Jake smiled at the photograph-plastered box he'd made for his friend. It sat on the glass-covered dressing table, a wooden cube of smiling faces, seventies bell bottoms and tight T-shirts, faded peace-signs, rollercoaster hills, sunsets, old Halloween costumes.

Jake smiled, turning the box over in his hands.

It wasn't even really about Roddo, not anymore.

It was about a whole life... a whole version of himself.

He'd dug through two garbage bags of photos in his closet to find and cut out all the memories of his youth. He'd flipped through scrapbooks to find the newspaper articles he'd saved, carefully un-taping them from the old pages.

He'd gone through the attic of his house, hunting down keepsakes and warped videotapes, time capsules from what was now a bygone era.

Inside the box, which he'd painstakingly decorated with all of those photos and film fragments and paragraphs of text, Jacob placed one of those old videotapes from those years. He'd picked out the exact one with the utmost care, along with action figures from their favorite movies, drawings they'd scribbled out in class, notes they'd passed, shells they'd collected, sets pieces from their home-made movies, odd keepsakes, things they'd brought back from camping trips and trips to the Santa Cruz Beach Boardwalk.

He even had an old arrowhead he'd found hiking with his friend.

He was ridiculously proud of what he'd made.

Nothing in it would ever be forgotten.

Wherever his life took him, he would never forget his roots.

"You only turn forty once," he said fondly, patting the top of the decorated box.

That's true, a familiar voice murmured. *That's very true, Jacob.*

The voice had been with him for years now.

Encouraging. Teaching.

Telling Jacob why he mattered.

Telling Jacob his true purpose.

...Still, the creature mused. *One wonders if he really deserves it.*

His heart now lodged into his throat, Jake only nodded.

"It's okay," he said. "He can't help what he is."

Jacob felt the being approve of these words.

That's very true, Jacob. Very wise.

"Will you be here?" Jacob said. "For this, I mean. Will you come to me, when it is done?"

Soon, the presence promised. *Very soon, Jacob. There's something I must do first. There is some clearing of the path that needs to happen. Some making ready of the ground. Now is not the time to get impatient. We are, after all, so very close now, Jacob.*

Jake nodded, feeling his shoulders relax.

"Yes," he said out loud. "Yes. I understand."

You will do your part? the voice asked. *You don't need me for this?*

"I will do my part," Jacob said, still nodding. "Just as you have said, father. I can do this. I don't need anyone's help."

Good, the presence murmured. *That is very good, my boy. I am pleased.*

The dense, deep, disconcertingly melodic voice whispered it in his ear. The words pulled at him, lulling, made of silence and starlight.

Jacob didn't mind.

He smiled into the worn mirror with its blackened edges.

There was no one there.

Even the man looking back at him wasn't really there, Jacob thought to himself.

Jacob wasn't Jacob anymore.

Not really... and never again.

He faced the one and only door into the cramped space.

He settled in to wait.

It wouldn't be long now.

It wouldn't be long at all.

Rodney Gallows banged his head on the low ceiling when he walked too quickly through the slanted door to the backstage room.

Wincing, biting his lip to keep from cursing up a blue streak, he pressed a hand to his forehead. He forced one eye open, glaring at the man watching him by the dressing room mirror. When that man didn't look remotely concerned about Rodney's banged head, Rodney dropped his hand, scowling harder.

"All right," he grumbled. "I'm here. What am I doing here, Jakey?"

Rodney Gallows stared at the face of his oldest friend.

Jacob Mulden sat on a blood red, threadbare, used-to-be satin chair, peering into a blackened mirror that looked like something from a carnival funhouse.

Rodney watched, half-disturbed, half-fascinated, as Jacob carefully pulled on pristine white gloves to go with his cheap, stage-style tuxedo and moth-eaten frilly shirt. Rodney's annoyance turned into numb disbelief as his friend tilted his face back and forth, staring at his makeup in the mirror intently, as if he were about to walk out onto the stage at Carnegie Hall.

Jacob Mulden adjusted the collar of his cape next.

It was long and black, a satin thing with red lining that belonged in one of those cheesy, late-night horror movies they used to watch as kids, those super-lame eighties flicks with the fake blood and the ridiculous dialogue that were about as scary as his mother's daytime soaps.

Jacob started combing his thinning brown hair next, examining his part carefully as he peered into the stained and warped glass with deer-like brown eyes.

Rodney wasn't sure what Jake was on, but the whole ritual was damned weird.

None of this was necessary for a show at a place like this.

Rodney had only seen maybe three tables of drunk, tech-bro, frat-boy types when he walked through the bar on his way back here.

Really, Rodney would be shocked if any of them watched even a minute of Jake's act.

No one came to a place like this to watch magic tricks.

They came to look at the naked breasts and asses of (cough) eighteen-year-old girls.

Like the girl out there now, currently writhing and gyrating on the tiny stage to thumping bass music, who Rodney swore attended classes with his high school aged daughter.

Remembering that, Rodney scowled.

I don't give a good goddamn what Liana says, he thought angrily. *Dee's not spending another fucking minute in public school. Not in San Jose. Not in Cupertino. Not even in Palo Alto. If I found her in a place like this, I'd kill her mother with my bare hands. I swear to God, I'd murder that whore...*

Yeah, he was done.

He couldn't trust his New Age, faux-hippy, cunt of an ex-wife to do the right thing by either of their kids, but especially not their eldest daughter.

Liana seemed to have no comprehension of the dangers out there.

He wanted full custody.

He could raise both of his kids better without Liana's constant interference and idiotic ideas. The last thing he wanted was for *either* of his daughters to end up like their mother. She could have them a few weekends a year. A few holidays, maybe.

That was more than enough.

Really, even that might be too much.

He would put his lawyers on it, first thing in the morning.

It would be his birthday present to himself.

Folding his arms, Rodney exhaled. He couldn't stop himself from looking at his watch, even knowing Jake likely caught it in the mirror.

This place was a shithole.

He didn't want to be here.

At all.

Especially not tonight.

"Jake... man. Tell me what I'm doing here." Rodney's impatience leaked into his voice. "You know I can't stay for the show. I told you that already. I have plans tonight. Long-standing plans. People are waiting for me..."

His childhood friend didn't look up.

He didn't nod.

He didn't acknowledge Rodney at all.

He continued staring intently into that fucking mirror, like Rodney wasn't even there.

Half the round lights bordering the mirror were burned out in the dingy backstage room. The tray resting on the cracked and dirty glass tabletop held a few tubes of face cream, some eyeliner, a couple shades of too-dark rouge definitely kept around for and used by the burlesque dancers, and about twenty tubes of lipstick in various stages of depletion.

Hanging on the open clothes rack on Jacob's other side, Rodney saw sparkly bikini tops, feather boas, cowgirl outfits, nurse costumes, a dominatrix-type thing with a dog collar...

His eyes drifted away, already bored.

When he hired call girls, it wasn't from a place like this.

He had the money to do it right.

Rodney was pretty sure the white and brown powder he saw all over the glass and sagging satin chair wasn't all make-up, too.

Cocaine. Heroin, maybe.

Maybe something worse.

The drugs people used these days made the stuff he'd done in college and his first years of working seem like aspirin in comparison.

An overflowing ashtray squatted on one end of the cracked glass tabletop, smelling up the broom-closet-sized room even more. Every surface was dirty, smudged, covered in fingerprints.

The place was disgusting.

It needed a once-over with a pressure-washer.

Rodney, who'd hadn't seen Jacob in the flesh since forever ago, looked at his friend and wondered if he'd cracked for real.

"What's with all this?" Rodney motioned around the claustrophobic dressing area. "Why are you even doing this, man? At our age? I mean, seriously, Jake. This is nuts."

When Jacob didn't answer, Rodney's tone sharpened more.

"Is this a midlife crisis?" he asked. "I hope you're not sleeping with any of those girls out there, man. Because you'll end up with a venereal disease... or in jail... or both."

His lip curled in distaste as he noted the smear of what looked like blood on one segment of the dingy gray wall—a wall that likely started off white but hadn't been that color since the last time he and Jake walked to class together at Saratoga High School.

Rodney, who now worked as a business consultant, angel investor, and all-around "idea guy" in Silicon Valley, land of the monetization of crazy ideas, stared at his grade school best friend, and had to remind himself the two of them used to compete for the top GPA in their class.

They used to make movies together in Jacob's garage.

They used to fantasize about what they'd do to the jocks if they ever had the nerve... or the right circumstances... or the nerve... to act on any of their pent-up anger.

In the end, Rodney decided to get them back by buying and selling all of their asses, hopefully a few times over before he was done.

Rolling up to the first of those stupid school reunions with a supermodel on his arm, wearing a thirty-thousand-dollar suit, smirking right into their stupid, already alcohol-ruined, fat, ex-jock faces... that healed a *lot* from those early years.

It healed a fuck of a lot.

Looking at Jacob now brought it all back.

And not in a good, coming-of-age-movie kind of way.

"I'm going to go, Jake," he said.

His voice came out businesslike, brusque.

He didn't want to leave any room for Jake to argue.

"I'm sorry," Rod said, in a tone that made it clear he wasn't. "I'll have to catch the show another time. Hope it goes well... and good luck..."

He turned to leave, but Jacob moved.

He moved so fast, Rodney came to a startled halt.

He found himself too close to that middle-aged face—a face now lightly sweating under a pancake layer of clown-white make-up. Rodney stared into those doe-like eyes, suddenly unnerved by the blankness there.

His friend had inserted his body between Rodney and the only door, and now looked down at him from that scarecrow-tall, somehow *creepy* height of his.

Rodney had forgotten just how tall his friend was.

Jacob blinked into those large brown eyes, eyes that used to get him stuffed into lockers back when they were in school.

"Wait," Jacob said.

He held up one of his gloved hands, expressionless.

"I have a birthday present for you, Roddo."

"Don't call me that." It came out angrily, without thought. "Don't call me Roddo, Jacob. No one calls me that anymore. They haven't called me that for about twenty years."

Jacob didn't seem to hear him.

"Just stay for one more minute. I have something for you. Just wait right here."

Rodney frowned, but didn't move.

When Jacob didn't either, Rodney made an impatient wave with one hand.

"Well?" he said, annoyed. "What is it? I really have to go, Jakey—"

Something stung his neck.

He didn't feel any pain.

He didn't feel anything at all.

He also didn't see his friend move, not until it was too late.

He felt the pressure, realized one of those gloved hands was by his neck—

"Happy birthday, Roddo," Jacob breathed.

His mouth hung by Rod's ear.

He moved his face back, and Jacob's too-red mouth smiling at him.

"Don't worry, Roddo," he whispered softly. "You're going to like this..."

His lips pulled higher in that upside-down scream, his dark eyes blank as mirrors.

"...You're really going to like this a lot."

2

REGULAR OLD HUMAN-MURDER

"Hey, so I know the timing sucks." Cal's full mouth pulled down in a frown. "I get it, man. I really get it. I just figured it couldn't hurt to ask. I mean, if it were any other time, you'd be my go-to guy. You know? Even now, with all this..."

He waved a vague hand over the lagoon-shaped pool with its man-made waterfall.

"...I'd *really* like to hire you, you know. Even now," he said again.

Cal paused, briefly flustered as he seemed to realize how that sounded.

"Do you not do that kind of work at all anymore, man? Is that it? I know the building still says P.I., but maybe you get your flunkies to do that kind of thing, now that you're a big celebrity and all?"

Cal smiled awkwardly, like he was trying to pass off his words as a joke.

I watched Black give his friend a faintly annoyed look.

Internally, I rolled my eyes, but not at Cal.

You can find out what it is, I scolded Black.

My mind gave his a sharp prod.

It's not like we're going anywhere for a few weeks, I reminded him.

That vampire doc said probably two more weeks before Nick would be coherent. And you could use the distraction. Really, both of us could.

Black glanced over his shoulder at me, his mirrored sunglasses reflecting my face back at me in the New Mexico sun.

Grumpy, I accused softly.

Horny, he shot back. *Deeply fucking horny. And yes, grumpy about it. Pardon the fuck out of me for wanting to go on my honeymoon with my wife.*

I scowled, folding my arms.

Even so, his words brought up a ripple of separation pain that tightened my jaw.

I refrained from reminding him that waiting on sex was *his* idea, not mine.

I heard that, he muttered.

You were meant to, I retorted.

You're going to blame me for this now? he grumbled.

I'm not blaming anyone for anything, I pointed out. *I'm just saying we should help Cal. He's your friend. And both of us are climbing the damned walls.*

The three of us sat by the pool, under a dark red sunshade by a glass table littered with three fruit smoothies we'd just gotten from a waiter wearing a white tank top.

The sun was just now coming up from behind the Sangre de Cristo Mountains.

The bowl-like sky already shone a bright blue, and I watched hummingbirds pull nectar off the flowers around the pool, while chickadees, warblers, and different-colored finches hopped around on patches of lawn, and flitted between bushes.

I watched Black take a sip of his peach-colored smoothie.

Each of our drinks was a different color from the specific concoctions we'd requested.

Mine was bright blue from algae and blueberries mixed with banana.

The resort waiters also laid out several trays of solid food, for whoever else from our party might wander out to the pool area.

I glanced over the bowls of sliced mango, watermelon chunks, cantaloupe, cottage cheese, strawberries, blueberries, bananas, tangerine slices, not to mention yogurt, granola, muesli, two steaming platters of bacon and scrambled eggs, another plate of sausage, a basket of rolls with butter, jam and honey, several bowls of salsa, a heated pot of black and pinto beans, another portable warmer with tortillas.

Cal grabbed a piece of bacon while I watched, crunching on it with his back molars.

We'd gotten pretty informal with our meals here.

And wake-up times.

And going-to-bed times.

Most of our party hadn't shown their faces yet this morning.

Granted, it was only seven o'clock, but for this group, that was practically noon.

Black and I had our own reasons for avoiding the bedroom right then.

It was getting harder and harder to be alone with him.

For the same reason, I got up the second I opened my eyes that morning, used the bathroom, threw on a bathing suit and flip-flops, and headed for the pool.

I put my hair in a ponytail on the elevator ride down.

When I finally stopped swimming, gasping a little under the diving board on the deep end of the pool after doing over a hundred laps, I found Black waiting for me.

I'd started my swim before the sun came up, under the light of a waxing moon and a sea of New Mexican stars, but by the time I stopped it was getting light out, even if the sun hadn't yet made it up over the mountains. I watched it warm and illuminate the desert landscape, casting soft rays over the deck and pushing Black to don his sunglasses.

I knew that the desert sun would be a lot less gentle in a few hours.

When I first saw him that morning, Black had been sitting at the same table where we were now, in the same chair, under the same dark red umbrella.

He hadn't spoken at all when I first swam over to the pool's edge.

He hadn't even wished me good morning.

He just stared at me in my lime-green two-piece bathing suit, wearing the same damned scowl on his face he wore now.

He watched me hoist my body up out of the water with my hands.

He watched me walk over to him, dripping all along the blue-tile deck.

He never stopped scowling.

He scowled at me when I stuck my toes in my flip-flops.

He scowled at me when I wrapped a towel around my waist.

He scowled at me when I sat down next to him.

He scowled at me the whole time I ordered my blueberry smoothie from the waiter.

He was still scowling when Cal poked his head out of doors, and walked over to join us, his mobile phone clutched in one hand.

You should hear him out, I prodded again. *Distraction. Remember?*

I watched Black think about my words.

I felt him agree, well enough that I turned to Cal, one of Black's army buddies who'd come out here for the wedding, and the man who happened to own and operate my absolute favorite Italian restaurant in San Francisco.

Just thinking about it made my stomach rumble.

We weren't in San Francisco now, though.

We were sitting by the pool of The White Eagle Spa and Resort in Santa Fe, New Mexico, and Cal had been in our ridiculously large wedding party.

We were still waiting to have the rest of that ceremony, meaning the seer portion of our nuptials.

Which is why we were still there, and why Black hadn't yet reopened the White Eagle to the public. His friends, work colleagues, and other assorted other seers, humans, and vampires in our orbit filled nearly all of the resort's rooms, anyway.

Reopening would have been pointless.

I lifted a hand to Black's bare back, stroking the skin there gently.

He still had bruises there from his fight with that other dragon.

Bruises that Black, incidentally, neglected to tell me about. I would never have known about them at all if I hadn't seen him in a bathing suit the next day.

At the time, he'd insisted that transforming back to a human had "healed" him.

I grunted at the memory, annoyed in spite of myself.

"Did you say it was your brother-in-law?" I queried Cal politely, shielding my eyes with a hand. "He's gone missing, you said? Can't the police find him?"

Cal shook his head.

"No." Still thinking, he shook his head a second time. "...I mean... *yes*. And yeah, sure, the police are on it. They've been on it for a while now. And maybe they can figure this out without any help from me or you, or Quentin here, or whoever else. The lead detective, Cassavetes, seems pretty good. But I told his sister I'd ask, at least. I told her I'd try and get some bigger guns. She's pretty freaked out. She and her brother are really close..."

He hesitated, looking between me and Black.

"Also, there were some, you know... *weird* things. Things I thought maybe the cops couldn't handle. Not because they're stupid or scared or anything. They just might not know enough to look in the right direction."

Black gave him a flat look.

He made air quotes with his fingers.

"'Weird' things, Cal? Really?"

"Well... yeah." Cal shrugged. "You know. The kind of stuff you do. The kind of cases you took even before all the dragon stuff. The detective said there's some weird things with this case, too. They didn't elaborate, but from what they told me, I don't know the half of it. But *you* could find out for me, Black..."

He trailed, as if not sure whether he should go further with that.

Or maybe he wasn't sure if he should go further with that *yet,* when Black hadn't agreed to hear about it, much less take the case.

Then something else seemed to occur to Cal.

"Say, if you can't do it, what about that vampire?" He looked between me and Black, his brown eyes faintly hopeful. "He used to be a cop, right? Homicide? Someone told me he was decorated and everything, like a war hero. Some kind of super-sleuth, Columbo-type. Does he do any private, P.I.-type work?"

I stifled a snort.

Slowly, Black turned his head.

I couldn't see his gold eyes through the mirrored shades.

I imagined I could feel the death stare he aimed at Cal, anyway.

One thing I knew Black would *not* do, and that is let Nick show him up. Their rivalry might have fizzled with everything that happened recently, but it wasn't dead.

I wondered if Cal even knew that.

Whatever the truth of it, I suspected the worsening separation pain with me had Black's testosterone-fueled responses to things on even more ridiculous overdrive than usual.

"Is this guy murdered?" Black growled. "Or missing?"

"Not anymore," Cal said. "He *was* missing, but as of this morning—" He held up his phone, showing it to both of them. "—now he's not missing."

"What the fuck does that mean?" Black's eyes hardened on his friend. "All of this cagey, vague shit isn't making me want to help you, brother."

I touched Black's back, a faint warning in my fingers.

I turned to Cal.

"What do the police know?" I asked. "Were they able to tell you anything?"

Cal's gaze met mine, his eyes holding a faint relief.

His mouth and voice remained grim.

"Well, they won't tell me much," Cal admitted. He gripped the phone tighter in his hand. "I've got a few friends on the force, but I'm not *technically* family, so they're pretty close-mouthed with me. They aren't telling Nina much, either."

Glancing down at his phone with a grim look, he added,

"Nina has to go down there this morning, to the station. It's too early there now, but she says she's going in first thing, and she'll call me when she gets out."

He grimaced, combing a hand through his brown hair.

"I hate that she has to go down there alone," he muttered. "I wanted her to go with a lawyer, at least, but I couldn't find anyone with this late of notice. I might have my own brother go down there to meet her, just for moral support. Or maybe Manny, if you can spare him for a few hours. She's really freaking out, like I said."

"Ask Manny," Black said. "Not me."

"Sure. Okay. I'll see if my brother can get the work off."

He still held his cellphone in his hands, between his knees.

Like Black, he wore swimming trunks, sunglasses, and not much else.

"Her sister's totally useless," he added, shrugging.

"I thought you said he was your brother-in-law?" Black frowned, staring at him. "Wouldn't that make you family?"

"Well. He's not *exactly* my brother-in-law yet. Not technical-ly," Cal clarified. "He's my girlfriend's brother."

I saw Black's eyebrows go up. "Oh. I thought it was your brother's wife."

"No."

"So what *do* you know?" I pressed.

Cal looked at me.

Relaxing marginally when he met my gaze—and, more likely,

when he wasn't fielding Black's aggressive questions—the human exhaled, combing another hand through his hair.

I could practically feel the tension vibrating off him.

I also caught glimpses of him trying to soothe a hysterical woman over the phone. I saw her crying on the screen of a video chat in his hotel room that morning—a tall, fit-looking, dark-haired woman with glasses and green eyes he obviously deeply cared about.

Cal plucked another piece of bacon off the platter, and crunched it with his back teeth.

The waiter approached us in that silence, carrying a tray with three coffee drinks, and I could have kissed him.

Instead, I took my four-shot cappuccino with chocolate sprinkles out of the waiter's hand with a shit-eating grin on my face and hugged it to my chest. I thanked him profusely as I clutched the giant mug in both hands like it was some kind of illicit treasure.

Black shot another scowl in my direction.

I had no idea what brought that one on.

You look adorable, he growled in my mind. *Holding that damned coffee. I want to bite you. I swear to* gaos, *I think you're doing it on purpose at this point.*

I blew him an air kiss.

His scowl deepened.

I'm definitely going to bite you, he vowed. *...Hard.*

Cal went on talking nervously as the waiter walked away.

"Okay... so here's what I've managed to get off the cops and Nina so far," he said, exhaling. "It was her brother's birthday. They had this whole party-thing waiting for him at some fancy *tapas* place in downtown San Jose. She and a bunch of his Silicon Valley bro-buddies and other friends were supposed to go club-hopping after. It was kind of an 'event' thing, with one of his rich friends lining up access to all these exclusive places. He's been talking about it for weeks. It's a big birthday, the big four-oh, so they were pulling out the stops. Most of her family lives in the East Bay now, but her brother's got a mansion somewhere in Los Altos or Saratoga or Palo Alto or wherever. He's some big tech, money guy, like I said—"

Black motioned him on impatiently with a hand.

Cal began speaking faster.

"—Okay, so this guy never shows. *Weeks* of planning and prep and him bragging to anyone who'd listen about late-night parties, exclusive clubs, strippers, maybe flying to Cabo, or Vegas, or even St. Barts before the end of the night... and *poof!* Rodney disappears. Gone. No one can reach him on his phone. He says he has to stop by and see someone, that he'll meet up with his birthday crew at that *tapas* place, but he never comes. That was almost two weeks ago now—"

"Where was he going?" Black cut in. "Who was he going to see?"

Cal shook his head, exhaling.

"No one knows for sure, but Nina thinks it was some guy he went to high school with. According to her, her brother said something about it the day before the party ... that this friend asked to see him on his fortieth birthday."

"No one's talked to him?" Black growled. "The friend?"

"I don't know." Cal shrugged. "Maybe the police did. Nina says it *couldn't* be that guy. She thinks Rodney must have disappeared either before or after he went to see the friend. She says the friend is a loner... and a total weirdo. He's also, like, afraid of his own shadow. He lives with his handicapped father and barely leaves the house."

"Yeah, nothing serial-killer-y about that..." Black muttered.

"What?" Cal frowned.

"Nothing," Black said. "So what's so weird about any of this?" He sounded impatient now, borderline annoyed. "This sounds like a run of the mill missing persons case to me. Let the cops handle it—"

"No!" Cal shook his head, brow wrinkling. "No, man. They

found him. Sorry... that's the part I forgot to say. They found him. Just this morning. Early."

Black scowled for real. "What the fuck, Cal? Why is this—"

"He was cut in half. Like... *in half.*"

Black and I fell silent.

"Well, assuming it's him," Cal added, looking between us and gripping his phone. "Assuming the body they found is Rodney. But the cops think it's him. Nina needs to be there in the morning to ID him. It probably won't be official until she does that. But the detective I spoke to, Cassavetes, says it's him."

Cal used one hand to make a straight line across his waist.

"*In half,* brother," he repeated. "And it's probably him, right? The cops wouldn't call her if they weren't pretty sure?"

Black and I both blinked at him.

The scowl returned to Black's lips.

"So... gross. But still not *supernatural,* Cal."

"He was also drained of blood. Like... *entirely* drained of blood. In a way the medical techs couldn't explain."

That made me and Black exchange looks.

Black aimed his scowl back at his friend.

"Any puncture wounds?" he asked. "Bite marks?"

Cal shook his head.

"No," he said. "Nothing like that. That's the weird part. My one friend down at the station says it's not like those vamp kills in NOLA or any of the others they've seen. The blood's just... gone. They found some symbols carved on him, weird occult-type shit. But that was all done post-mortem. None of that explains the blood."

"Sounds like a ritual," I murmured.

Black gave me a hard look. "So?"

That brief pricking of my husband's ears on the vampire question seemed to dissipate.

His voice grew blunt once more, borderline indifferent.

"I mean, sure, it still *could* be a vampire," Black said. "But I don't know why they'd bother to get all elaborate with the blood-extraction thing, much less a bunch of airy-fairy symbols. Sounds like regular old human-murder to me. Weird. Gross. A bit melo-dramatic. But human. Probably one the media will have fun with, which will annoy the police. But not anything to get worked up about—"

"Black," I murmured.

He glanced at me.

Seeing my face, he fell silent, as if only now realizing what he'd said.

He glanced at Cal.

Taking in his friend's expression, he cleared his throat.

"Sorry," he said, gruff. "I mean... *obviously*... your girlfriend cares. I didn't mean to be a prick. I just don't really see how you need me for this."

"Well. I mean..." Flustered, Cal motioned around at where we were. He didn't indicate anything in particular, really, but his point was clear. "...That's pretty obvious, right?"

"Do you want me to ask one of the vamps?" Black asked.

He was using his polite voice, I noticed.

In his mind, he'd already decided the case wasn't for him.

Something about that voice made me want to kick him.

"I mean, he's not the most helpful guy in the world, but I could ask Brick," Black added. "He's sort of the head vamp around here. Really, he's sort of the head vamp in most of the world these days. He's definitely in charge of most *official* vampire-related things."

Pausing at Cal's frustrated frown, Black added,

"Honestly, Cal, the vampires wouldn't thank me for getting involved, even if it *was* one of theirs. They like to police their own. And I doubt it's a vampire, anyway. They just don't put that much effort into killing one random human. They don't even bother to kill their food most of the time, despite the myths. Not if it's just for food. Not unless it's personal."

"What if that vampire's psychotic?" I asked dryly.

Black looked at me.

He knew what I was referring to.

Dorian.

Dorian was dead now, but he couldn't be the only psychotic vamp out there.

"Sure," Black said, his eyes and voice skeptical.

He gave me an annoyed look, one that clearly conveyed, *will you just let me talk my friend off the crazy supernatural conspiracy ledge please?*

"...I mean, sure," he repeated, looking back at Cal. "Anything's possible. But generally speaking, it's more likely to be a human who goes off the deep end with this stuff, not a vampire. Vamps tend to kill the unstable members of their kind—"

"They missed a few," I muttered.

That time, Black frowned at me openly.

Still staring at me darkly, he went on, aiming his words at Cal.

"—Because of exposure threats and whatnot, they're generally too dangerous to leave alive," he explained. "Brick told me he barely managed to keep Nick alive long enough for him to transition out of being a newborn. He broke a number of their laws, killing at random and risking exposure in both Paris and San Francisco. The possibility of eliminating Nick was debated several times by the local enforcement arms where Nick committed crimes. It's generally up to the sire to control them, and if they can't..." Looking at Cal, Black drew a line over his throat with a finger. "Well, you know. The other vamps deal with it."

"Could this be a newborn?" I asked.

I admit, my interest was piqued by Black's explanation.

I had no idea he'd been chatting with Brick about vampire legal codes.

Black looked at me.

"Possible," he admitted grudgingly.

Looking back at Cal, Black exhaled.

Then he frowned.

I found myself thinking he'd just realized some part of him was already on this.

He turned, giving me a death stare.

Well, you're more or less making me, aren't you, doc? he grumbled.

Yes, I answered promptly. *I am. I think you should help him.*

Exhaling again, Black returned his gaze to Cal.

"I'll talk to Brick. All right? See what I can find out?"

Cal nodded, looking relieved. "Thanks, man. Thanks. I really appreciate it."

Black reached out a muscular hand.

He patted Cal on the shoulder, pausing long enough to aim a dark look at me, one that let me know in *no uncertain terms* that he would one thousand percent blame me if this ended up going sideways.

I felt him soothe his human friend with his light, even as he continued to glare pointedly in my direction.

"Don't mention it, brother," Black said. "Happy to do it."

His eyes never left mine.

Clearly, I would be hearing about this later.

3

JUST THE FACTS

"So, what I'm hearing is," Black grumbled over the line. "No one can confirm whether this Rodney Gallows guy went to see his weird fucker friend at the strip club or not. Is that right?"

Glen Frakes, Nick Tanaka's old partner in homicide, cleared his throat.

"Yeah," the fifty-something detective admitted. "That's more or less where they're at. According to the detective I talked to in SJPD."

"No CCTV picked him up?" Black frowned.

"None that they've found."

"Nothing at the club? I thought sex clubs were wired to the rafters, usually."

"The place is kind of a shithole," Glen conceded. "One room. A lot of tables shoved around a rinky-dink stage. A crapola bar that mostly serves watered-down shots and maybe two kinds of domestic beer. It's possible they didn't have any working surveillance—"

"So no cameras. Not even in the back?"

Glen shrugged. "No one got him on camera at the stripper place. According to my buddy down there in homicide, facial-rec is still going through everything they could get in downtown San Jose. Traffic cams. ATMs. Gas stations. You know the drill."

"What about wits? Anyone show his picture around at the club?"

"Not during the initial investigation into him as a missing person, no," Glen said. "From what I heard, a lot of people thought he might be out of the country. He had a lot of money. He was fighting with his ex. He just turned forty—"

"So everyone blew it off," Black grunted. "Thinking he was drunk as a skunk in a stripper club in Thailand. Perfect."

"My buddy said they're heading down there again tonight. To the club where he was going to meet his friend. I guess they called, and management told them it would be better to come in for the night shift. No one there now would have been on the floor. Anyway, it was like two weeks ago now. They see a lot of faces in a place like that."

Black frowned. "They didn't get names of the staff there before? Call anyone?"

Frakes exhaled, letting his annoyance grow audible.

"I don't know, Black. I wasn't on the case. It's not my department. It's not my precinct. Hell, it's not even my police force. This happened in San Jose, remember?"

"You didn't ask him when you called just now?"

"You know they just found the body like eight hours ago, right?" Glen said, exasperated. "That it was found by a homeless guy in the middle of the night? They're kind of busy right now, Black. I didn't really want to keep them on the line for twenty questions. Not when I know they're pounding the pavement right now."

"But they aren't the ones *actually* pounding the pavement, right?" Black countered. "That's what uniforms are for. They probably pulled in some foot-soldiers for that end. Isn't that what you jokers in homicide normally do? Delegate the boring crap?"

"Black—"

"I'm just saying. You could call them back, right? They aren't *that* busy?"

Frakes didn't answer for a beat.

He might have been biting his tongue, from what Black could feel on the middle-aged detective.

"Two weeks, Black," Frakes repeated. "The trail is already cold, and they'll have a lot of pressure on them from upstairs to solve this in a hurry. I wouldn't count on them using uniforms for the legwork, not for a case that might blow up as big as this. Given the type of crime, and the vic, and the way the body was found, there's going to be a lot of media interest. The dicks down there will probably want to talk to any potential wits themselves—"

"You say this is a buddy of yours on the case, right?" Black cut in. "What kind of detective is he? He any good? Or is he the phone-it-in type?"

"*She's* good," Frakes said. "Definitely not a phone-it-in type."

Despite his usual unflappable nature, Black could tell he was starting to wear on Frakes' nerves. Glen sounded faintly annoyed now.

Black didn't let that deter him.

"How good?" he pressed.

"Good enough to kick your ass if you pull this crap on her." Frakes let out a disbelieving grunt. "Jesus. What's your interest in this, anyway? You still doing this kind of work? Because I thought those days were behind you, Black."

"Why would you think that?"

"You seem... busy," Frakes said.

A dry humor lived in that last word.

Black's mouth hardened.

Thinking about the question, he exhaled.

He'd been using some of his talking time with Frakes to read him on details the homicide detective's "friend" in San Jose had shared with him about the case so far.

He hated to admit it, but he was intrigued.

Slightly.

Slightly intrigued.

Anyway, Miri hadn't given him much choice.

Besides, Cal was a friend.

"It still says 'private dick' on my damned business cards," Black retorted, his mouth curved in a faint frown. "So I guess I must still be in the business, Glen."

"Is Nicky around?" Frakes said. "He helping you with this?"

Black's frown changed into something closer to a scowl.

He hesitated, trying to decide how to answer that.

"Can I talk to him?" Glen prodded. "He's still in Santa Fe, right?"

Black continued to stare out over the pool deck.

Telling Glen that one of his oldest friends, ex-homicide cop, Nick Tanaka, and Glen's ex-partner, had been shot in the face by one of his best friends with a wooden bullet after being turned into a vampire, and was now being looked after by his mate, a five-hundred-year-old, military-trained, and now quasi-homicidal male seer with abandonment issues and the looks of a thirty-five-year-old human movie star—

"Black?"

Black didn't think.

He hung up the phone.

"You *hung up* on him?"

I fought not to laugh.

It wasn't really funny. I mean, it *shouldn't* have been funny at all probably, but it hit my dark humor funny bone anyway for some reason.

"You hung up on Glen? Seriously?"

"Not on purpose."

"Not *on purpose?*"

"I may have panicked," Black muttered.

I folded my arms under my bikini top, looking at him bemusedly.

"You don't think *maybe* you should have told Glen his buddy Nick got hurt?" I said, amusement leaking into my voice. "You don't think maybe Glen would want to know that? That Nick got hurt badly, but he's going to pull through okay?"

Black looked at me in disbelief. "No. Fuck, no."

I arched an eyebrow, smiling faintly.

Black blinked at my expression, then scowled.

"Seriously? Doc, I have *absolutely no idea* what Nick's told him about the last six months, or anything after our time on *Koh Mangaan.* Where do you want me to start with the explanations? Even apart from the fact that it would seriously piss Nick off, do you really think it would be remotely my place to tell Glen *any* of that?"

I nodded, still smiling.

I admit, I might have been yanking his tail a little.

At the same time, I found myself wondering if I should talk to Nick's parents, Yumi and Hiroto, about who they'd contacted about Nick.

I knew Nick's parents were still here, somewhere on the resort.

Funnily enough, Black invited them to the seer portion of our wedding, space cakes and all. Funnier still, they'd accepted—even *before* Nick got shot.

"Do you want to hear this?" Black growled. "Or not?"

I blinked. "Why would I need to hear it? Don't you want to tell Cal?"

"I'd rather run it past you, first," he said.

Sighing a bit under the increasingly hot Santa Fe sun, I refolded my arms, nodding.

"Okay. Lay it on me."

"Guy's birthday," Black says. "Rodney Gallows."

"This is Cal's girlfriend's brother, right?"

"Correct. Big Silicon Valley douche, from what I can tell. Everything Cal told us checks out. His sister, Nina, and one of her brother's closest, douchey, work-buddies planned the whole big night out. They were taking him for an extravagant, ridiculously-expensive, drug and alcohol-fueled, midlife crisis event that involved at least one private jet, and started at that *tapas* restaurant in downtown San Jose Cal told us about—"

"But the guy never shows," I said.

Black nodded, once.

"The guy never shows. Tells his sister Nina he has to visit an old high school friend first. Nina says this friend is weird but he and Rodney have history and the friend asked Rodney to come by *specifically* on that night for some kind of surprise. According to the sister, the friend definitely knew it was Rodney's birthday. They grew up together. And it's on the way to the restaurant, so Rodney agrees to the meet—"

"And did he make it to see the friend?"

"No one knows that yet."

"So no one's talked to the friend?"

"They *talked* to him," Black said. "The disappearance was two weeks ago, so they've talked to him a few times. No one knows for sure if he's telling the truth."

"But they have no proof he *isn't* telling the truth?"

"Correct," Black said. "And the body might change things, of course... but can I finish this timeline, or what?"

I snorted a little, but shrugged. "Sure. So are we assuming Rodney visited the friend?"

"We are. For now."

"Okay. So he goes to see the friend, and he's a no-show for dinner."

"Correct," Black affirmed. "But then things get weird."

I grunted. "I more or less figured that, since the guy was cut in half—"

"First weird thing," he said, cutting me off and holding up his thumb. "All the surveillance is out, all around the establishment where Rodney, our douchey and eventually bisected hero, is meeting his reportedly weird and antisocial friend."

"*All* of the surveillance?" I frowned, refolding my arms. "Are they sure?"

Black nodded, once. "All of the cameras... wiped. Even the traffic cams. Everything inside the club... which is surprisingly well-surveilled for such a small place... also wiped. A few cameras were even broken."

I frowned.

All right. I was intrigued.

I could feel that Black was, too.

"What was the establishment?" I said. "Why were they meeting there, exactly? Some kind of small club, you said?"

"Shitty little strip club. And his friend worked there."

I grunted. "His friend *worked* there? His shy friend, the one the sister says is afraid of his own shadow and who takes care of his elderly father... he worked at a strip club?"

"Yup."

My mind turned over this detail, along with the wiped cameras and missing video.

"Mafia?" I ventured. "Was his friend in deep with someone? Was it about money? Drugs? Wrong place, wrong time?" Still thinking, I added, "...Wrong person?"

Black made a dismissive gesture.

"If his friend is in deep with the mob, or drugs, or any kind of black-market scheme... hell, if he has access to money of *any* kind, legit or not... he's hiding it exceedingly well. That, or he's working deep undercover for the F.B.I. or some other entity."

Black shook his head, lips pursed.

I watched his flecked, gold, tiger-like eyes focus inward.

"I haven't talked to him yet," he added. "...or read him, obviously... but frankly, the idea of the high school buddy being some kind of crime boss or even a crime flunky strikes me as highly improbable. From reading Cal's girlfriend, the guy's a real oddball. They basically grew up next door to one another, and the two boys were best friends. She remembers him being at their house a lot when they were kids... and even through most of high school. Family pool parties. A few camping trips. Weird friend and her brother in the garage for hours, working on computers or making movies together on an old video camera..."

The gold eyes clicked back into focus.

He looked at me.

"She told me she had no idea Rodney still spoke to him. She had no idea Rodney had any contact with the childhood friend at all. The weird friend pretty much fell off the map after they graduated... Rodney didn't."

"So *not* another Silicon Valley douche." I lifted my eyebrow. "Was he just in town for a visit?"

Black shook his head.

"He never left. He never even went to college."

"Oh." I blinked. "He stayed in the Bay Area but him and Rodney didn't speak? At all? No meeting up for the occasional beer or coffee or whatever?"

Black shrugged.

"I imagine they didn't have much in common, doc," he commented dryly. "Silicon douche is Silicon douche. Weird and significantly less-successful high school friend lives with his disabled father in his childhood home in the hills of Saratoga, buying food and Lottery tickets with his dad's social security checks. Both him and his father collect food stamps... and his dad gets some kind of disability from an old job that covers most of the taxes on a house that's practically condemnable—"

"In Saratoga?" I said, bewildered. "Where a walk-in closet costs a mil?"

"I guess they've owned the house outright since the seventies."

"Still," I said, frowning. "Wow. I bet they aren't popular with the neighbors."

"I doubt most people even notice they're there."

I frowned. I had my doubts.

Black blew past my facial expression.

"In any case," he went on. "His douchey friend, Rodney, *did* go to college. And he's quite wealthy now, with a mansion in Palo Alto near Stanford. Not to mention a second house on Maui. And a third house in the Italian Alps."

"Ah," I said. "I'm beginning to understand how the sister is surprised they were still in touch. Does the weird friend really work at a strip club? That's his only job?"

"I doubt he works at all," Black said. "Not at anything that pays. He gets some money from the government, I believe, for being his father's caretaker."

"But you said the weird friend worked there, right? At that club?" Frowning as I thought about this, I realized how irrational it all was. "*Why* would he work there? Driving all the way from Saratoga to downtown San Jose? Why was he really there?"

I refolded my arms, frowning as I continued to think.

"You sure he's not there as a customer? Stuffing a few saved-up dollars in G-strings?" Still thinking, I mused aloud. "Could he have a girlfriend who works there? Someone he keeps away from dear ol' Dad?"

"All good guesses, doc. But no. None of those things."

My eyebrow lifted in a silent question.

"He was there to do a magic show."

"A *magic* show?" My eyes opened wider. I admit, I hadn't seen that coming. "That's still a thing? Doing magic shows? Outside of Vegas?"

"Apparently. And get this, doc... you'll never guess what trick our odd little friend performed for the finale that night."

I frowned.

For a few seconds, my mind stayed utterly blank.

Then there was a click, and everything he'd just told me came together.

A wave of nausea hit me.

Seeing my expression, Black nodded, once.

"Exactly." His voice turned grim. "Fucker sawed a man in half."

4

THE FIRST

I glanced around the curb outside the arrivals and baggage claim area of San Jose International Airport.

A very familiar-looking armored, black Bentley Bentayga SUV pulled up to that same curb, right as I reached the middle of the sidewalk.

An even more familiar face peered at me from behind the wheel.

Lester grinned at me, giving me a two-finger salute once he saw me looking at him.

He'd been one of the unlucky members of the crew who got stuck holding down the fort in San Francisco while the rest of us went to Santa Fe.

Black told me he was mostly able to leave behind relatively new employees and recently-recruited (but thoroughly vetted) seers, but he needed a few people he could really trust to keep an eye on everyone else. Even with Yarli and the others watching things long-distance via the Barrier, he needed at least a core group on site he could trust.

Lester picked the short straw.

So did Nancy and Johnson, two more humans who'd worked for Black for decades.

I'd just broken out in a grin at Lester's bearded face, when the person sitting next to him turned her head. She gazed at me through the passenger seat window, her eyes wide with recognition.

Then, after that bare beat, she smiled at me.

The look on her face was probably intended to appear humble or shy, but it just came across as manipulative and insincere.

My smile immediately faded.

Christ.

Maryn.

Black was going to shit a brick when he saw her.

As far as I knew, he hadn't spoken to his biological sister once, not even on the phone, not since that time he ran into her in the middle of the island resort on *Koh Mangaan.*

Who the hell sent her here, to pick up me and Black?

Why was she working with anyone at the California Street Building at all?

Last I heard, Black flat-out refused to use her in operations.

I glanced up and down the curb, frowning faintly.

Did I need to be worried about this?

It struck me as strange, suddenly, to be back here, in California.

It was stranger still to be back here alone, just me and Black, without a crowd of military-trained seers guarding our every move. I couldn't remember the last time we'd traveled with so little back-up, and so few of our people around us.

Black already got stopped a handful of times in the airport for autographs from gushing fans, and I'd caught a number of people snapping our photos and sneaking video as we walked through the terminal from the concourse where his private jet landed.

I hadn't wanted to go through the main airport at all.

Black told Cal we'd meet him here, though.

Cal left a few hours earlier than us on a commercial flight

he'd booked to get back here for his girlfriend. Black offered to take him on the private jet, but Cal couldn't get a refund for the ticket, and in the end decided to fly on his own. Because we could go straight to San Jose with no stops, and because we could leave more or less when we wanted, we timed our flight to arrive at San Jose International roughly when Cal's did.

Knowing Black, he also wanted to gauge the temperature of our reception, just to get a sense of how people were reacting to us these days.

Meaning the public.

Meaning the human public... which also meant the social media sphere.

I got the logic on all of those fronts.

Still, somehow, I thought there'd be more of us going.

I expected a bigger group to join us on Black's private plane.

Cowboy, at least. Angel.

Kiko. Ace.

Maybe Mika or Jax, or one of the other seers.

I even thought Black might order Dalejem to come along, if only to keep Nick's mate from trying to murder Dexter the minute we were gone.

But no one else came.

Everyone except for me and Black opted to stay in Santa Fe. Angel told me apologetically she needed the time to decompress after the insanity of the wedding. She also didn't want to leave Dex... or Nick... or Dalejem, for that matter.

I knew Cowboy wouldn't leave without Angel.

Yarli and the others had gone to San Francisco already.

They were working, so it was unlikely we'd see them. They'd been tasked with the aftermath of what happened at the resort. At this point, that mostly entailed setting Charles up in his own private holding cell under the California Street Building, separate from all of the other seers we were still holding in sight-restraint cages.

That left me and Black on our own.

It also meant it was only the two of us on the plane.

Black grumbled about that, too.

"I would have bought his damned ticket," he muttered. "Stupid to cram yourself in coach. Stupid to deal with a layover if you don't have to. Stupid when he could go in the back and sleep on a damned *bed* if he wanted. We wouldn't have bothered him. Even if he swallowed the cost of the fare, he could be drinking a beer and eating caviar on here... not chewing stale pretzels while Mitsy from Tennessee shows him photos of her naked grandson..."

I let him grumble.

I figured Cal probably wanted the thinking time an anonymous flight afforded.

That, or he felt weird taking Black's money.

In any case, I suspected Black was more offended than annoyed.

He could be touchy about some things. He could be especially touchy when friends didn't want to accept gifts from him for whatever reason.

Regardless, the flight was quiet.

Really, it felt more like Black and I were both flying alone, too.

Black spent most of the flight on the phone and bent over a screen, coordinating logistics with Yarli and the others based out of San Francisco. I suspected that had to do with Charles, and how they were securing Charles, and the security risks posed by Charles.

I didn't ask to verify that.

I sat across from him, curled up in a leather seat instead, reading a spy thriller.

I wished I was doing it on a pool lounger, next to Angel, holding another of those amazing coffee drinks, but really, maybe this was better.

Maybe it was good for both of us, Black and I.

Maybe we both needed the distraction right now.

"I'm not getting in that fucking car."

I jumped.

Turning, I felt my eyes go a little wider when I saw Black glaring at the Bentley. The sheer violence in his voice, and in those gold, tiger-like eyes startled me. Even knowing what I knew about Maryn and Black's history with his parents, it took me aback.

"I'm. Not. Getting. In. That. Fucking. Car."

If I'd been thinking Black might be calmer this time, dealing with his sister when he wasn't in the midst of a full-blown bonding psychosis with me... I would have been wrong. I looked between him and the woman he was glaring at, the woman who still sat shotgun in the Bentley SUV, and tried to decide what to do.

I didn't decide fast enough.

Black turned, aiming that glare at me.

"I'm not getting in that *fucking* car," he snarled.

"Cal's in the back," I protested. "We're just going to the police station, right?"

"We're taking a cab. *I'm* taking a cab. You're coming with me, doc. I don't want my sister whispering any of her fucking *poison* in your ear. If she tries to talk to you, to bond with you in any way, I'll kill her. Do you hear me? I will *kill* her, Miriam."

I blinked. "Okay."

"Tell them," Black growled, motioning angrily at the car. "Tell them right now. I'll stash the bags. Then I'll be finding us a different ride."

He bent down to snatch my carry-on bag off the curb by my feet.

I watched as he slung it over one shoulder, then stalked away, rolling a suitcase with the rest of our things behind him. He took all of the bags to the back of the Bentley, and pounded on the metal, indicating he wanted it open.

Exhaling in frustration, I looked at Lester.

When he quirked an eyebrow at me, I held up my hands, and

he laughed, shaking his head. He bent down, hitting the button to open the back hatch and the trunk. I watched Black as he tossed our luggage into the back of the vehicle.

"Brother?"

I heard Maryn call out to him and winced.

"Brother! Just come with us! You are being ridiculous. Get in the car with—"

Black slammed the back door to the SUV.

I watched him as he stalked away, his handsome face a hard mask.

I also saw people staring at him.

No one asked him for autographs that time, though.

Instead I saw their eyes widen once they took in his face, right before they moved *the hell* out of his way, practically leaping out of his path.

I sighed a second time, only now I felt angry.

Not at Black.

I wasn't angry at Black at all.

I turned to look at Lester.

When I motioned for him to roll down the window, he did, hitting the electric controls from the driver's side.

I didn't look at Maryn as I stepped forward.

"Really?" I said. "Was that necessary, Les?"

Lester smirked a little. "Just a little fun with the boss, doc."

I folded my arms, biting my lip.

I thought of a few dozen things to say regarding what I thought about their little "joke" at the boss's expense. After running through all of them in my mind, I decided to voice none of them out loud. Instead, I exhaled again.

"Okay," I said. "We'll meet you there."

Lester smirked a second time, glancing at Maryn. "Okay, doc."

I shook my head, clicking at him.

That time, I didn't really hide my anger.

"You're a braver man than me," I told him drily. "...or else a much bigger idiot. I'm betting on the latter, honestly. I'm not sure what you fools find funny about this."

"Maybe a few of us were a little annoyed we had to miss the wedding," he said, winking at me. "Maybe some of us felt a tiny bit of payback was due."

"It wasn't nice," I said more seriously. "Really, Les. Not cool."

"Hey, she insisted!"

"Did she, now?"

I didn't look at Maryn. I kept my eyes on the male human, mouth pursed.

"Okay then," I said after a pause. "I'll let you explain that one to Black. Good luck pulling the plum assignments in the future, friend."

The tattooed boxer chuckled, shaking his head.

"Oh, I'm sure," he remarked ruefully. "And I'll be having words with Wu and Davis, who put me up to this. You can watch all three interactions if you want, doc... all the while eating popcorn and thinking I TOLD YOU SO as loudly as you possibly can."

"Something like that. Yeah."

He laughed louder, gripping the steering wheel in one hand.

"Hey, the least I can do is give you the inside scoop on the betting pool," he offered. "I had money down on this interaction, and it went down more or less *exactly* the way I predicted. So I figure, even if I get reamed by the boss, I still might come out ahead."

I snorted, shaking my head.

"Whatever you say, brother."

Taking a breath, I finally glanced at Maryn, who, up until then, I'd studiously avoided looking at directly, despite how close I stood to her. She opened her mouth, intending to speak to me once she saw me looking at her, but I held up a hand.

"Nope," I said. "I'm not getting involved."

"But you're my *sister* now," she protested.

I blinked at that. I refocused on her for real.

"Excuse me?"

"You're my *sister* now," she insisted. "Not figuratively, but in reality. It's not only *him* who gets to decide things now, Miriam. You *both* are family. You *both* have just as much of a say in this as the other one does. It's *not* only him. And I'm not the only one who thinks so!"

I think my jaw might have hit the ground if I'd been a cartoon.

As it was, I shut it with a snap.

For a few seconds, I could only stare at her in disbelief.

"If you could just *talk* to him—" Maryn began.

"Wow. You are nuts," I said. "You are also one hundred percent on your own."

My voice came out a few shades colder.

"If you think I would *ever* speak to my husband on your behalf," I warned. "Or in any way *act* on your behalf, or take your side over his, or defend you in any way, you are *delusional,* Maryn. If you think I'd be on *anyone's* side but my husband's, including in any matters regarding his family, you're even *more* delusional."

"Side?" She frowned. "What *side?* There's only one side in this, Miriam. We're family. *That's* the side. The family side. That's it. It's as much your family as his, and all of us are in this together, don't you see?"

I didn't bother to ask her what any of that meant.

I also didn't bother to tell her she was in for a treat, if she tried to gaslight Black into thinking he had any sort of obligation to her, or that he owed her in any way.

It definitely wasn't my place to say any of those things.

Nor did I *want* to say anything to her.

Black had pretty full-on reasons for resenting his family.

Reasons I fully sympathized with, and would not touch, soft-pedal, or massage in any way, for any amount of money.

Black wasn't a client; he was my husband.

I had zero desire to tell him to take the high road in this.

I had zero desire to tell him he should face his childhood issues head-on.

They'd sold him into slavery.

His own family had *sold him into slavery.*

Maybe Maryn herself hadn't done it, but her utter callousness about it now told me she still had no comprehension of what their parents had done to him. Nor had she tried to find him and buy him back as an adult. Black had been beaten, raped, terrorized... owned.

He'd been *owned* by other people.

As a child.

So no, I wasn't going to tell Black shit.

I also had zero intention of attempting to unpack her absurd claims that we were all somehow on the same side now, and bygones be bygones, and family overcomes all, and whatever other manipulative bullshit she wanted to toss my way.

Truthfully, I could have punched her in the face more easily than I could have talked to her.

I definitely would *rather* punch her than try to argue with her bat-crazy logic about who we were to one another.

Rather than do any of that, I walked away.

I aimed my feet in the direction of the taxi queue, and my husband, and I didn't look back.

THE BOSS

"I don't give a *fuck* what you do with her," Black growled into his headset.

I jumped, glancing over.

It didn't take a rocket scientist to guess he was talking to Lester.

"Leave her downtown somewhere. She can Uber her ass back to the city. She can get on the train. She can *walk* for all I care. I don't *give a fuck*. Understand?"

He fell silent briefly, listening to the person on the other end.

I could faintly hear Lester now.

I couldn't hear him well enough to make out words, but my seer hearing picked up his voice growing louder through the headset, even from where I sat.

"I. Don't. Care." Black hammered each word. "I'd be okay with you stripping her naked and kicking her out with a literal boot to her ass. How she gets wherever she goes next isn't my problem. She shouldn't be in a company car at all..."

He trailed again, listening to Lester argue.

I heard Lester's voice rise more.

"Fuck you. Fuck all of you," Black's voice held anger, but I heard a thread of hurt there too, enough that it brought a pain to my heart. "Next time you feel like pranking me, leave my goddamned family out of it. Or you're fucking fired. All of you. That includes Yarli and whoever else was in that goddamned betting pool..."

My eyebrows rose at that.

Yarli? Was Lester saying Yarli was cool with this? I found that seriously difficult to believe.

I looked over, but Black didn't return my gaze.

"Like I said, I don't care. However you have to do it, I want her gone before you get to the precinct building. I mean it, Les. I'm not joking. I don't want to see her face..." He paused, listening. "...Then drive around the goddamned block! I'm telling you, if I see her, it's off. You can explain your little joke to Cal. Explain it to him, Les... in detail... Marine to Marine. Tell a guy I served with in two wars, who saved my life at least twice, and his grieving girlfriend who just lost her brother to *murder* that you chose my self-absorbed asshole of a sister over both of them..."

I flinched.

I was puzzled, though.

What the hell was going on? Why was this conversation even happening?

Why was Lester giving Black a hard time?

"You're not hearing me," Black said, cold. "If I see Maryn with you, I'm taking my wife back to New Mexico..."

I could practically feel Lester roll his eyes.

Jesus. Did he really think Black was being dramatic? From what I could feel through the line, Lester *did* think that. He thought Black was just angry, and making an empty threat.

I knew Black wasn't.

I couldn't believe Lester didn't know that, too.

I clicked on my headset, in spite of myself.

"Lester?" I said. "What's the problem here? Why are you arguing with Black?"

There was a silence.

I realized I'd gotten him in mid-sentence.

"Don't waste your breath," I said, not waiting for him to answer me. "The joke bombed. Badly. Black one hundred percent *isn't* bluffing, and he will *absolutely* take both of us back to Santa Fe. You need to do exactly what he said. Now. Drop Maryn off before you meet us at the station. I can't believe I even have to say this—"

"But doc, we're already here!"

"Black told you how to handle that."

"But doc, I can't do that—"

"So now you're arguing with *me*? Really?" My mouth curled in a hard frown. "Les. You're a friend, but you're crossing a major line right now. On multiple fronts."

Still, more than anything, I was puzzled.

I'd never known *any* of Black's people to buck the chain of command, for any reason. Yet I could hear the agitation in Lester's voice. He really didn't want to do what Black was asking him to do.

I made my own voice an open warning.

"You got your orders, Les. Twice. More than twice. And you've now gotten them from both of us—"

"*Di'lanlente a' guete...* fucking CUNT."

I jumped, turning towards Black in shock.

His gold eyes were out of focus as he stared straight ahead.

He cursed loudly in seer a second time.

"Black? What the—"

"She's pushing him." Black clicked loudly, looking at me, his eyes glowing with rage. "My bitch of a sister *pushed* them to get access. She must have gotten some of the humans alone. I should have realized, but I was so fucking angry about their 'joke,' I didn't see it..."

He touched his earpiece.

"Lester. Stay put. Don't do anything."

"Boss, I—"

Black had already clicked off the line.

Before I could react, he opened a second channel, inputting a new number for that line.

Without asking me, he connected me to that second line, as well.

"Hello?"

Black scowled. "Hello? Yarli? Is that how you greet me? Really?"

"Here, boss," she began, a little breathless. "I'm here. Sorry. Manny and I were just—"

"I'm not interested in your goddamned sex life," Black snapped. "Did you know my bitch sister is *pushing* humans on our team? That she somehow managed to coerce Lester and a few others into granting her access to me, via the pick-up in San Jose?"

There was a silence.

The line crackled.

I didn't hear Yarli so much as breathe.

When her voice rose next, she sounded almost as furious as Black.

"Dealing with it now, brother."

"I think you'd better call me 'boss' right now," Black growled. "I think *everyone* better call me that for a few days. Or they might get unfairly punched in the face—"

"Understood. Dealing with it now, boss—"

Black didn't let her finish.

He hung up both lines.

Our taxi was already pulling into the parking lot in front of the police station.

I saw the Bentley parked in one of several slots located directly in front of the steps leading up to the main entrance. As I watched, the SUV's tail lights came on as the Bentley's engine rumbled back to life.

Lester slammed a foot on the gas, accelerating out of the parking spot and skidding to a stop in front of us, fast enough to leave marks.

I watched Black scowl and slide over on the seat.

Once close enough, he snapped the latch on the car door, and briefly I worried he might be going after his sister himself, maybe to strangle her with his bare hands for screwing with his human employees. But once he stepped out of the car, he only buttoned his suit jacket, moving back and out of the doorway to let me through.

I watched him stare at the SUV.

He watched it idle for a few seconds more, probably while Lester spoke to Yarli on his headset. Black tugged down his shirt sleeves, arranging his jacket over his shoulders and the collar of his shirt, all without taking his eyes off the Bentley.

It was already warm out here.

Really, it was edging into hot.

In direct sunlight, with no shade against the early afternoon sun, it almost felt like being back in Santa Fe.

I exited the taxi and stepped into that same sun.

We hadn't left Santa Fe until roughly eleven in the morning, but with the time change, it was still only one-thirty in San Jose. Of course, it didn't hurt that we took Black's jet, which was not only fast, it didn't have to make any stopovers along the way.

Cal, who left two hours before us, landed in San Jose ten minutes later, since his plane stopped over in Phoenix.

The back passenger door of the Bentley opened.

I watched Cal as he stumbled out, catching his balance on the door frame briefly before he turned, nodding to someone inside. Then the chef with the stunning green eyes and dark brown goatee shut the door and backed away from the SUV.

Lester peeled out of the parking lot, hitting the gas even harder that time.

I saw his face briefly in the side mirror, the mask of absolute fury he wore as he straightened the car, aiming it for the driveway leading back to the main road. All the humor in his expression had gone. The smirk had gone.

The eyerolls were gone.

I highly doubted he still thought either me or Black had been "overreacting."

I got a brief glimpse of Maryn, Black's sister, as well.

She was still riding shotgun, but now, her stony expression held nothing but contempt.

I watched her fold her slim arms. I glimpsed her pursed mouth and those cold eyes, and figured she was probably getting reamed out by Yarli via the Barrier.

I strongly suspected Yarli wouldn't be done for a while.

I also suspected it wouldn't just be Yarli who would be angry about this.

Black had been crystal clear about the rules regarding his human employees.

No seer was allowed to touch their minds.

Ever.

For any reason.

Before I could ask Black what they would do with Maryn now...

...a dark-haired woman got up from the steps leading up to the main entrance to the police station. I watched her throw herself at Cal, wrapping her arms around his neck in obvious relief. Once he had ahold of her, her body seemed to crumple, sagging into him where he held her, as if she'd used the last of her strength just to reach him.

I felt a flicker of grief, watching them.

Maryn didn't matter.

This mattered.

Cal and this woman mattered.

6

DOPPELGÄNGER

Black and I stood there a few seconds more, waiting for Cal and his girlfriend, Nina, to finish. When the woman finally pulled away from his embrace, and began talking to Cal expressively, gesturing with her hands, I started a little.

I blinked, staring at her face.

Once I noticed it, I had difficulty *not* noticing it.

I looked down her body, her legs... her shoes.

Frowning faintly, I went back to studying her facial features, especially her eyes.

I wasn't imagining things, was I?

No. Black murmured it in my mind. *You're not imagining things, doc.*

Black gave me a cynical look, nudging me playfully with an elbow after he walked up to stand next to me. His eyes trained on Cal and his girlfriend, a frown forming on his perfectly sculpted lips. I could feel him trying to find the humor in it, trying to pass the whole thing off as a joke. I could also feel he wasn't quite succeeding.

It wasn't all the Maryn thing.

I could feel that the thing with Cal's girlfriend genuinely irritated him.

You're definitely not imagining things, he repeated. *She looks like you. She looks a LOT like you, doc. Believe me... I noticed. And I'm not the only one.*

Like him, I fought to shrug it off.

I mean... a little, I conceded. *It's not that noticeable, Black—*

Bullshit. Not noticeable, my ass. Every male member of my team who's seen her made a crack about it. Cowboy and Angel, too.

I turned, staring at him. *When the heck did they see her?*

Wedding planning lunch. You were in London already. Cal brought Nina along when we were planning the food and some of the other details.

I nodded.

Now I was biting my lip.

Well? I shrugged deliberately. *I mean... shit happens. It's a coincidence.*

Black scowled, glaring at Cal as the dark-haired woman began to cry.

Coincidence my ass. He went out and found himself a doc-lookalike to fuck. Black's mental voice grew quieter, but no less irritated. *She even dresses like you, doc. She's probably a damned shrink. Who studies martial arts. It's like finding your wife's photo in your friend's porn collection. Only worse.*

Folding my arms, I glanced at Black, eyebrow quirked.

He glared back at me.

His expression didn't soften.

I knew he thought you were hot. Black's mental voice remained angry. *But that's some seriously blatant, next-level incestuous bullshit right there. He brought a clone of my wife to my own damned wedding. I'm beginning to wonder if he had Dex steal some of your blood so he could have you cloned for real—*

I let out an involuntary laugh.

I clapped a hand over my mouth when I saw Nina look over, her lips pulled in a frown.

They just found her brother's dead body.

We shouldn't be talking about this.

We definitely shouldn't be talking about this here.

She doesn't look that much like me, I told him. I folded my arms. *And even if she does look that much like me, it's probably a coincidence. Everyone has a type, Black. Even you. I'm sure he didn't do it deliberately.*

Black aimed a hard stare at me.

Clearly, he disagreed.

But Cal was motioning us over now, so I made my expression as neutral as I could.

When Black didn't move, I jabbed him with an elbow.

"Come on, grumpy," I murmured. "We can argue about your strange, uncomfortable feelings about Cal's new girlfriend later."

"Fuck you." He glared at me openly. "That's not the damned point, doc. At all."

"So you say."

"Guys!" Cal called out. "Are we going in? Or not?" He tapped his watch with a finger, looking between us like he was trying to figure out what the hell we were doing. "They're waiting for us. The detectives are here now."

That time, I didn't wait for Black.

I pushed past him instead, making my way towards Cal and his doppelgänger girlfriend, even as I told myself it didn't bother me.

It *didn't* bother me.

I mean, why would it?

That would be irrational. Not to mention immature.

I was ninety percent sure it didn't bother me.

That would be ridiculous.

From behind me, Black grunted, expressively.

I know he knew I heard it.

I didn't look back.

7

TOO MUCH NICE

I caught Nina staring at me as Black and I approached, her mouth pursing in puzzlement as she wiped the smeared make-up off her face with her fingers.

I saw her eyes flicker down the rest of me, taking in my figure, my hair, my clothes, my posture, my overall demeanor and appearance.

I could almost feel her thinking what I'd been thinking.

Wondering if she was imagining things.

Knowing she *wasn't* imagining things.

Wondering if she should take it personally.

She glanced at Cal in the same set of seconds and frowned.

I found myself annoyed with Black all of a sudden, too.

Don't get pissy with me, doc, he muttered in my mind. *You were the one who pushed me to take this case, as I recall.*

You could have given me a head's up, I muttered back.

I thought you didn't look anything like her? he retorted.

The woman, Nina, seemed to make a decision to move past it.

Tentatively, she stepped forward, sticking out a hand.

She offered it first to Black.

"Thank you," she said. "Thank you, Mr. Black. Thank you *so much* for being here. I can't tell you how much I appreciate you looking into this for me."

I saw her too-bright, light-green eyes drinking in Black's face, and felt my teeth clench. I had no reason to think she was batting her eyes at Black, or that she meant anything at all by looking at him for that long, but I wasn't entirely unfamiliar with the wounded bird game a lot of women played with men.

I knew that was insane of course.

It wasn't just unfair, it was bat-shit insane.

She'd just lost her brother. She was grieving.

Cal was her fiancé.

But Black was Black.

Not only did he look the way he did, he'd always had that weird magnetic pull, both with women and men. Unlike when I'd met him, what felt like a thousand years ago now, Black was a damned celebrity now, too.

Maybe I'll enjoy this after all, Black murmured in my mind.

He stepped forward, smiling at the dark-haired woman in the low-cut blouse and tight jeans.

Watching him, I bit my tongue hard enough to draw blood.

"Not a problem at all, Ms. Gallows," he said politely, taking her hand and shaking it in return. "Anything for Cal. He's probably told you we've been friends for years."

"Of course," she said, smiling wider. "He talks about you all the time."

Black released her hand.

Craning her head and neck to look past Black—no mean feat for a lot of reasons—Nina Gallows smiled at me next, her expression tentative. Her eyes darted more nervously over mine, studying me cautiously.

I couldn't help noticing all over again that she was a younger, possibly more insecure, and right now definitely more sad version of me.

Probably less of a pain in the ass, too, Black murmured.

I knew he was teasing.

I knew he was enjoying getting my goat, that seers got a perverse thrill out of making their partners jealous, and from what I could tell, it was a species-wide tendency. But for some reason, that comment stabbed at me, enough that I unexpectedly blinked back tears.

I don't think any of it showed on my face.

Even so, I held my calm expression with an effort.

"Hi," Nina said, as I accepted her outstretched hand. "You must be Miriam."

I had an irrational urge to tell her *that's Dr. Fox to you.*

Instead, I smiled back. "I am. Nice to meet you."

"Thank you so much for coming." Like with Black, she sounded heartbreakingly sincere, verging on breathless. "Cal tells me you're a highly-respected forensic psychologist. That you work for your husband to help him on cases?"

I felt another glimmer of amusement off Black.

I knew why he was amused.

Technically, we owned *Black Securities and Investigations* together. I didn't work for Black, not on paper, but I didn't correct her.

Anyway, it *was* Black's company, whatever it said on the masthead.

Bullshit, Black growled in my mind. *That's utter fucking crap, Miri.*

That time, he sounded actually annoyed.

I didn't look at him.

"Yes," I said, speaking only to Nina as I released her hand. I kept my voice light. "He poached me off the SFPD a few years back, if you can believe that. I used to do some consulting work for the homicide division there—"

"Now she owns half the fucking company," Black cut in, his voice as irritated as his thoughts. "She's co-owner. She's my partner. She's also my wife. *Not* my employee. She's just being polite... or something..."

Cal chuckled.

I ignored the "or something" jab.

Nina looked up at Black, a little wide-eyed.

Her green eyes returned to me.

She smiled, tentatively at first, then more warmly as she studied my face.

"Homicide," she beamed. She seemed to make sense of my words on a slight delay. "You said you worked in homicide before this? That's just... wow. That's perfect. That's really great, I mean it. I can't believe my good luck in having both of you here."

Again, she sounded like she meant it.

I hated how hard I was having to work to like her.

Black still exuded annoyance, and now puzzlement.

I practically felt his eyes boring into me when I refused to return his gaze. I felt him on the verge of thinking something at me, and blurted out words to Cal and Nina before he could.

"We should go up, right?" I said. "Speak to the detectives? Or have you already done that?"

"No." Nina shook her head. "I've been waiting for all of you."

Her breath caught a little as she looked at Cal.

"I ID'd the body," she blurted. "It was definitely Rod. They brought me to the morgue for that. I told them I would come in here later. That I'd be bringing other people with me."

"I bet they loved that," Black muttered.

I didn't look at him, but I knew he was right.

The police wouldn't love having some hotshot, celebrity, talk-show-circuit P.I. poking into their case. Especially not one as high-profile as Black. Especially not one that was splattered all over the news and rumored to turn into a dragon in his spare time.

Black let out a half-amused grunt.

I still didn't look at him.

I felt his irritation ratchet up a few notches.

Then I felt it tip into concern.

Hey, doc. I was just yanking your tail a little. You know I'm not myself right now.

It's fine, I sent.

Which means you're ready to stab me, he muttered back. *You never say "it's fine" unless I'm about to get kneed in the crotch*—

"Well, let's go up," I said, with all the cheerfulness I could muster. "All they can say is no, right? At least we would have tried."

Behind me, Black's mind fell totally still.

❧

"Hey." Black knocked on the plastic edge of a gray, cloth-covered cubicle wall, his mouth tight. "You Cassavetes? Detective Cassavetes?"

I was standing behind Black, so I didn't see the detective's face until she pushed her rolling swivel chair backwards to stare up at who addressed her.

She took one look at Black and her eyes grew wide as saucers.

Then she beamed at him.

Unlike with Nina, there was nothing vulnerable, or flirtatious, or wounded-bird, or remotely tentative about that grin. She beamed at Black like someone had just handed her a Christmas present.

"Whoa. You're him." The grin broke wider on her thirty-something tanned, sharp-featured face. "Holy crapola. You're really him!"

Before Black or any of us could react, Cassavetes turned her head.

She bellowed, loudly, to someone on the other side of the cubicle wall.

"HEY BARRY! CHECK THIS OUT!"

"WHAT?" he yelled back, his irritation obviously put on. "WHY ARE YOU YELLING NOW, CASSAVETES?"

"LOOK!" she shouted. "LOOK UP HERE, YOU LAZY BASTARD! WE GOT A REAL CELEBRITY HERE!"

A head popped up over the wall.

A man's dark blue eyes widened even more than the woman's had, appearing almost cartoonish even before he raised his head higher, revealing a handlebar blond mustache and a cleft chin.

"Whoa! Guess our case made the big time!"

"Connections in high places, eh?"

The woman grinned, looking at the male, presumably her partner, before glancing back at Black and grinning even wider. She remained tilted casually back in her chair, her short leather boots planted solidly on the floor.

Her dark-brown hair was cropped fashionably short in front, giving her severe but jagged bangs over a shoulder-length bob. She wore a well-fitting dark blue suit and a pale blue blouse that was open at the neck.

Her throat was decorated with a large turquoise pendant.

I didn't see any other jewelry.

No wedding ring. No earrings.

There was something weirdly likeable about her blatant delight in seeing Black there.

At the same time, I felt a less-rational side of me bristle all over again.

Black, as usual, didn't help.

Taking a half-step back, he wrapped an arm around me, yanking me up so I stood beside him. Then he clapped me on the shoulder.

He did it hard enough to nearly make me stumble.

"What'd I tell you, doc? You're too pessimistic about people..."

He grinned at the detective and her mustachioed partner.

"...and here the doc thought you'd be *unhappy* to see me, detectives. That you'd be all 'jurisdiction' this, and 'no-press' that, and 'let me see your license you phony carnival barker media whore' about the whole thing."

Cassavetes laughed.

She exchanged looks with her blond partner, who also chuck-led, shaking his head.

Cassavetes' eyes swiveled back to Black.

"You're here to help us?" Her sharp eyes slid past him, to Nina Gallows and Black's army buddy, Cal. "...On the Gallows' case?"

"We were hoping we might be able to help, yeah," Black said.

He shrugged his big shoulders, still holding me almost possessively.

"We were hoping to collaborate, really."

Detective Cassavetes' eyebrows rose, nearly to her spiky, short bangs. She exchanged another look with her blond partner, who raised his own eyebrows in return.

"*Reaally?*" Cassavetes said, drawing the word out somewhat.

"Really and truly," Black confirmed.

"You're going to *help* us with the case?" Cassavetes repeated.

"We've done some work with police departments before," Black explained, his voice taking on a more serious, businesslike, negotiations-type tenor. "I have contacts at SFPD who will confirm that my company, Black Securities and Investigations, fulfilled private contracts for SFPD homicide in the past four years. Not that we're asking for payment..." he added more hastily, holding up a hand.

"We've agreed to the family's request that we provide assistance, that's all. Really, we're just hoping you don't mind us interviewing some of the same people and running a parallel investigation, within certain limits, of course. We'll share anything we find, detective. Certainly anything relevant, anything that might help you to build a case—"

"You want to work *parallel* to us?" she said, her eyebrows still kissing her hairline.

"More or less. Yes," Black said. "Again, we're happy to work out ground rules for how we interact with your team and inves-tigators."

There was a silence.

The two homicide detectives had gone back to exchanging looks.

If they'd been seer, I would have thought they were having an intense discussion somewhere inside their minds.

As it was—

"So let me get this straight," Cassavetes said, turning to look up at Black. "You want to help us solve our case?"

"Well... yes. Ideally."

Cassavetes laughed, looking at her partner.

He laughed with her, again shaking his head.

Cassavetes swiveled her chair back around to stare at me and Black.

"And you thought we'd be *unhappy* to see you?" She scoffed, looking first at Black, then aiming her grin at me. Her dark brown eyes returned to Black. "World-famous detective agency? Famous for his success rate in solving multiple, complex crimes, including murder? Not to mention, pretty much the only known *seer* detective agency on record? And a damned resource-rich one at that, with its own agency and staff and military-grade intelligence service?"

I blinked.

I'm pretty sure Black did, too.

"...Why on Earth would we be *unhappy* to see you?" She grinned wider. "I mean, Jesus Christ, we hit the jackpot, didn't we, Barry?"

"The goddamned jackpot," Barry concurred.

"I mean, you're psychic, right? *Really* psychic? As in, *actually, for-real* psychic?"

Black blinked again. "Well. Yes. I am."

"So you can talk to perps for us and tell us if they're telling the truth?"

Black blinked. "Well. Yes."

"Great!" The woman stood up, clapping her hands together, and both of us jumped. She straightened to her full height, which couldn't have been more than five-one, although her personality made her roughly six-feet, especially with those heels. "Let's go talk to that friend of his, right? The weird one? With the magic show?"

She was already swinging her jacket off her chair and shouldering it on.

"Unless you had another place you wanted to start?" she queried politely.

Black looked at me.

I looked at him.

Both of us were at a loss.

In the end, Black looked back at Cassavetes.

"No," he said. "No other place. Weird magician friend makes the most sense to me, too."

"Wonderful!" the detective crowed, flipping her hair out from under her jacket collar and winking at me. "With the two of you there, we'll have this sucker cracked in no time."

Black looked at me, his expression bewildered.

Then he let out a delighted... and surprised-tipping-into-shocked... laugh.

He clapped me on the shoulder a second time, shaking me a little at the end.

"See, doc?" He aimed his shark-grin in my face, winking one of his gold, flecked, tiger-like eyes. "I told you. People love me!"

8

THE UNSPOKEN THING

I honestly had to bite my lip to keep from doing the knee-crotch thing he'd mentioned earlier when he grinned at me like that.

At the same time, I knew I was wrong.

I was wrong, and he was right... or at least less wrong.

This was good news.

The San Jose homicide department actually *wanting* us on their high-profile, rich-victim, weird cause-of-death murder case? Given all the baggage and other potentially bad attention we could potentially bring to their precinct and their homicide division?

That was *more* than good news; it was a flippin' miracle, really.

The fact that Cassavetes seemed delighted to meet seers, particularly seer detectives, just made it that much more unbelievable.

Still, something was nagging at me.

It wasn't Cassavetes.

Honestly, I liked Cassavetes, pretty much instantly.

I didn't think it was her partner, either.

Whatever it was, it was getting harder and harder to ignore.

There was something more complicated going on here. I had no idea what it was, but I could feel it, pressing on some back part of my mind.

Unfortunately, I couldn't tell what it was about precisely.

The case?

Me? Black?

Me and Black?

I couldn't help but be hyper-aware of the issues going on with the two of us, and our seers' light, and our marital bond, but I didn't think any of those things were the off-note I was picking up on. Those things definitely weren't *helping*, but they didn't feel like the main source of my unease. I knew my strange hyper-reactivity wasn't all about me and Black's personal problems. I knew it wasn't all about Cal's girlfriend looking like me, or the weirdly happy detectives, or the fact that Black seemed to be even more hyper-sensitive than I was.

Something was wrong.

I didn't feel right.

Let me know when you figure it out, Black murmured in my mind. *Because it's starting to hurt my feelings, doc.*

I looked over at him.

I'd honestly assumed he was kidding, or giving me shit.

When I saw his eyes, however, there was no humor there.

We were waiting for the detectives to bring in their suspect.

We stood just inside the observation area adjacent to the interrogation room, both of us leaning against a low table right below the one-way mirror.

I was still looking at Black, studying his gold-flecked eyes, when the door inside the interrogation room itself, on the other side of the one-way mirror, abruptly opened.

I watched two uniforms walk in, escorting a tall, rail-thin man with strangely large, strangely liquid, strangely *deerlike* brown eyes.

They sat widely apart on his face, strengthening the association with deer.

Something about those eyes unnerved me.

I knew that probably wasn't his fault.

The size of them alone gave him a kind of fish-like, lifeless, blank-eyed stare.

Overall, he unnerved me in a way that almost made me feel guilty.

I knew I was reacting to things about him he could not control. That reaction came through as visceral, and purely instinctual, what verged on a kneejerk, "uncanny valley" distaste for how he presented himself—meaning, that strange disorientation many humans experience when something looks human but *not quite human enough* to pass some base threshold in our minds. I fought against that reaction, and felt worse when I only half-succeeded.

I fought to catalogue his appearance more objectively.

Late-thirties to early-forties.

Wispy, thinning, brown hair.

A precise center part that looked like it might be smeared with hair gel.

A face that went from a narrow, pointed chin up to a more bulbous head, decorated with those strangely large eyes.

A thin, almost disappearing mouth in pale, pinkish skin.

He wore a threadbare collared shirt, light blue with small checks on it, over badly-fitting jeans that were a few inches too short. Blue, bargain-bin running shoes decorated his feet with white tube socks. His watch looked like one of those old digital watches from the seventies and eighties. His hair looked like it had been cut for closer to eight dollars than eighty.

Everything about him evoked pity and revulsion in me simultaneously, and I didn't feel good about either reaction.

I also didn't understand the intensity of those reactions.

I didn't usually care how people looked.

As a counselor, I'd seen clients who spanned the gamut of physical appearance, with all different types of developmental and genetic variations.

I imagined him growing up in middle school and high school and actually winced.

If ever someone could have worn a sign reading "bully magnet" on their chest, it was this guy. Some part of me actually felt *scared* for him, and depressed when I tried to imagine what life must have been like for him over the years.

This was our murder suspect? Really?

I was beginning to understand why Nina thought it was impossible.

I glanced at Black and saw him grimacing as he stared through the glass.

"It's pretty hard to believe," he murmured, agreeing with me.

Something in his voice made me refocus on him.

"But you *do* believe it," I said. "You think he's our guy."

I didn't really voice it as a question.

Even so, Black didn't agree with me really.

He frowned, thinking instead.

After a few seconds, he shook his head, rubbing his jaw.

I didn't get a "no" from either the gesture or his expression exactly. I didn't really get a "yes," either. I saw doubt in his eyes as he stared at the man on the other side of the glass. He watched, silent, as the two uniforms guided the suspect to one of the four metal chairs, and indicated for him to sit.

The man, still looking like a deer in headlights, complied.

He sat down clumsily, knocked his knees on the underside of the table and visibly winced. Once he'd recovered, he didn't try to get up, but he wasn't particularly still, either. He stared around the featureless room. His eyes found the red lights of two different cameras, then the one-way mirror itself.

He fidgeted, both his hands and his tapping feet.

His mouth twitched. So did his cheek.

"Black?" I prodded.

"No," he said, that doubt in his voice. "Not exactly, doc. I wouldn't say I 'believe' he's the guy. But there's *something*... I don't know. Something off."

He fell silent, once more frowning in thought.

"Something dark," he added, slightly more cryptically.

I frowned, wondering what he meant by that.

I didn't ask.

Instead, I watched him look at the man handcuffed to the table.

Black stared at him silently, his eyes slightly out of focus.

I could tell he was reading the guy, or trying to, but I had no idea what he saw. When I looked at Jacob Mulden, unemployed magician, I got a big, blank wall... a whole lot of nothing. From my perspective, Jacob Mulden didn't appear to be thinking about anything at all. His light didn't emit anything approaching an emotion, not even fear.

I got nothing. Zilch.

"Yeah," Black muttered. "About that."

He didn't go on.

I watched him stare at the suspect for a few beats more.

"About what?" I pressed.

"That blankness. The *emptiness* there. That's part of it. That's part of what I was trying to tell you before, Miri. There's a darkness there..."

He trailed, frowning.

For a few seconds, I thought he might finish that thought.

He didn't.

He continued to stare at the lone man sitting at the metal table.

After a few seconds more, the two uniforms finished checking his cuffs and walked out of the lit interrogation space. Still, the detectives hadn't yet appeared. No one was in there with him now; Jacob Mulden was alone, and looking around like a coyote with its foot in a bear trap. Nothing about him was calm. Nothing about him appeared to be practiced.

Yet, I still didn't feel a single emotion off him.

I wondered where Cassavetes and her partner were.

I wondered if they were sweating out Mulden on purpose,

letting him react to being in custody, letting him deal with the reality of an interrogation room that looked like something lifted right out of a television cop show.

My eyes kept returning to Black.

It hit me again that I wasn't okay.

I was going through the motions of work, of my old job, what I used to do for Nick and the SFPD, and later for Black on his private cases.

But I really wasn't okay.

I found myself looking at his shoulders, at his arms.

For some reason, just looking at him, letting myself really *look at him,* letting myself feel the distance between us, had me fighting tears.

"Hey."

Worry reached his voice.

He walked up to me, his gold eyes on mine.

When I backed off, he came to a dead stop.

"Miri." He sounded at a loss. "Doc. What's going on?"

"Why are you avoiding me? Why? What's the real reason?"

I blurted the words.

I didn't plan to say them at all.

I didn't even know consciously that I *wanted* to say them, and once I had, I realized I didn't remotely want his answers to those questions. I wished I'd kept my mouth shut. I wished I could take the words back now. Of course, I'd had no idea I was going to say anything, not until it all came tumbling out.

Black blinked.

Then he stared at me, real shock on his face.

I watched him pale, and his expression brought my separation pain up so intensely, I really thought I might black out. I wrapped an arm around my chest, gasping.

"Miri—"

"Don't deny it." I shook my head, clenching my jaw. "Don't lie to me, Black. Please. Just tell me. Tell me the truth. Tell me now."

There was a silence.

Black looked at the door to the small observation room.

He looked back at me.

I could feel him not wanting to talk about this here.

I could feel him wanting to be alone with me first.

I knew he was right about that, too.

I could feel his unease at us doing this here, in the middle of a police station, and while my rational mind understood, while every sane part of me understood Black's perspective entirely, I didn't seem to have any control over the part of me that formed words. I also knew I was going to flip the fuck out on him if he tried to brush me off.

I'm not going to brush you off, doc... Jesus.

He stared at me, his eyes incredulous.

"Jesus, doc. I would never do that. No matter where we were."

He said the second part out loud.

Somehow, hearing his deep voice only made it worse. He sounded both utterly at a loss and utterly disturbed at the same time.

"Doc."

He reached for me, but I again stepped back.

Fear rippled off him in a dense cloud.

"Doc! Listen to me! I would never just brush you off on something like this! Never. I would *never* do that to you. I want to talk to you about this. More than anything."

"Then answer me."

"You know why!"

I stared at him.

Something about him admitting it, about hearing him admit out loud that he'd avoided being intimate with me, that he'd been using our wedding as an excuse, felt like being hit in the chest. Maybe with a mallet. Maybe with something a lot closer to a sledgehammer.

Tears rose to my eyes before I could stop them.

"Why?" I asked. "And why didn't you tell me before? Why did you wait so long?"

"Before what, doc?"

"Why did you do it?" I demanded, squeezing my arms to my chest. "Why, Black? Why the fuck would you *do* that, if that's how you felt?"

"Do it?" His expression grew even more bewildered. I felt the agitation in him rise. I saw and felt his light reacting to whatever he saw on mine. "Do *what,* doc?"

"Marry me," I gasped. "Why did you marry me?"

The silence that time felt physical.

Something about my own words, heard out loud, combined with the shocked, nearly devastated look on his face made me want to crawl into a hole and fucking die.

I knew I wasn't acting right.

I knew my words probably sounded insane.

I wasn't okay.

I knew I wasn't, but it didn't seem to make any difference.

It didn't seem to matter at all.

"Doc." He swallowed, holding up a hand. He took a step towards me.

He looked at me like I was a wild animal he was trying to calm.

I took another step back, unable to help myself.

I folded my arms more tightly over my chest. It felt like a shield.

Even so, it didn't shield much.

I hadn't felt like this with him since we'd first met.

I hadn't felt this sure he would rip my heart out and stomp it to nothing right in front of me since we first started having sex. He hadn't felt so completely *not mine* for months, for years, since the earliest part of our relationship at Angel's house above Divisadero.

Maybe not even then.

"Doc." That time, he said it so gently, it made my eyes sting all over again. "Doc, that's not what this is. It's not *you*. I swear on my fucking soul it's *nothing to do* with you. It's never had anything at all to do with you, Miriam. It's him."

"Him?" My jaw clenched. "Who? Who are you talking about, Black?"

"Coreq," he growled.

I stared at him.

Black exhaled, worry coming off him in a cloud.

He subdued his voice, again holding up a hand.

"I'm talking about Coreq, Miri," he said, quiet. "It's because of *him*. It's always been because of him. Don't you see?"

I stared at the gold eyes of my husband.

I was still fighting to catch my breath, still feeling strangled by that pain in my chest. I couldn't comprehend what he was saying. I couldn't make sense of it.

"Coreq?"

"Honey, yes," he said, even more gently. He took another step towards me, still holding up his hands. "Honey. Coreq *wants* you. Don't you understand that? He *wants* you—"

I shook my head. "So what? What does that have to do with—"

"It feels *wrong* to me," Black growled. "It *should* feel wrong to you."

I stared at him.

Again, I felt like he was speaking some other language, something my brain couldn't quite wrap its way around, or make sense of in a way that was meaningful. I fought to understand what he meant. It felt really important to me, to understand what he meant—

Coreq isn't me. He's not me, Miri...

The words tumbled out of Black, swimming through my mind.

I felt fear there, anger, worry, a near panic as his thoughts came faster.

He's not ME. You get that, doc. Right? He isn't me. He feels foreign to me. He feels dangerous to you. I don't know what he wants from you, but his obsessive, insane focus on you scares the shit out of me. It feels wrong. I'm trying to protect you until I can understand it better. All right? Without pissing him off. Without letting him take over my consciousness entirely. Because I've felt him thinking about doing that, too. Getting rid of me, so he can have you to himself. So he doesn't have to SHARE you...

Black's mental voice trailed.

He swallowed visibly, still gauging my eyes, but I could feel the fear on him now. I realized some part of me had been feeling that fear for a while.

In the cracks he made about Coreq.

In the aside comments he made about Coreq being "a little too gung-ho" about their honeymoon, a little too focused on the fucking part of their marriage.

In his own way, Black had been bringing this up with me for months.

Some part of me hadn't wanted to know.

Some part of me didn't want to feel it before.

Some part of me didn't *let* myself feel it, maybe because I couldn't see a solution.

Now, it seemed to surround me, like a dense energy field.

It felt like it might suffocate me.

"He's not me," Black repeated aloud, still holding up his hands. "He's not. I know we've been pretending he is, both of us. We've been talking about him like he's some imaginary friend of mine that occasionally likes to take over my body and light... that likes to turn me into a dragon now and then... but that's not what this is, Miri."

He swallowed, studying my eyes, looking for comprehension.

"He's a foreign presence, Miri. You understand that. I know you do. And before, I was able to pretend that didn't matter, but he's getting stronger in me now. That presence is getting stronger all the time. And he's way, *way* too interested in you. He gets jealous of me, doc. Like he wants me out of the way... like he's biding his time."

Black paused meaningfully, watching my face.

He looked like he was trying to determine if I was hearing him yet.

"He wants to be married to you *without* me," Black said. "He isn't at all interested in sharing, regardless of what you or I want."

My mind was slowly gearing into what he was saying.

That freaked out, unmoored part of me still fought not to tilt off the playing field altogether, but another part of me, a deeper part, was starting to understand.

I felt a stronger core of me start to stabilize around that understanding.

"You're losing control over him," I said.

"I never *had* control over him, doc," Black growled.

"But it's getting worse."

Again, it didn't feel like a question.

Slowly, Black nodded.

"Yes," he said. "It's definitely getting worse. And he's getting possessive. And threatened by me. And angry at you for preferring me."

Feeling my jaw tighten, I nodded.

"Okay," I said. "Okay. I see that. I can feel that, Black. That makes sense."

Both of us stood there, absorbing our mutual understanding.

I fought to think about it without letting the reality of what it meant, the fear it evoked in me, overwhelm the part of me that needed to look for a solution.

I didn't really succeed.

"Miri," Black said. "Do you really want me to *give* you to him? Because that's what he wants. He pretends he wants us to 'share' you... but that's not how it feels. And what kind of fucking husband would I be, if I agreed to that?"

He swallowed, his jaw hard, his gold, tiger-like eyes overly bright. "I don't want to share you. I don't want to *share* you, Miri. I'm not okay with it. Even if you are... I'm not."

I stood there, staring at him.

He was right.

This had been hanging over us for months.

At least since *Koh Mangaan.*

Probably a lot longer than that.

We hadn't talked about it.

We maybe did, a little bit, while we bonded in Thailand.

Then our people got kidnapped, and we had to cut the bonding short. Then the thing with Nick happened. Then we were coping with what Nick had done, and that pulled us away from the problem of what to do about Coreq.

Then we needed Coreq.

We needed "Black's Dragon," as we thought of him, as we called him when we spoke about him. We couldn't afford to have a conversation about getting rid of Coreq then. We couldn't beat Charles, or that other dragon... not without Coreq.

Coreq was our ace in the hole.

Now I realized how selfish that was, how unfair to Black.

I could feel Coreq listening to this, even now.

We had been pretending Coreq wasn't there, somehow between us as a third presence in our marriage. He'd always been there, from the very beginning, but Black was right. It was different now. It was worse now... exponentially worse. Since Black had been turning into a dragon, Coreq was in Black, able to be felt, more or less all of the time.

Coreq was taking up more of Black's life.

Coreq was taking up more of Black's mind.

Coreq was taking more and more of Black, period.

He was inserting himself in our marriage.

He was cannibalizing my husband, body and soul.

"Fuck," I muttered.

I looked up at Black.

He watched me, fear making his gold eyes nearly glow. I saw that fear mixing now with a near-relief as he saw me begin to understand, to absorb what he was saying.

He saw me understanding all of it—what we'd been avoiding talking about, what we'd been avoiding facing, why Black would be more and more nervous about sharing a bed with me, given that "Coreq," the dragon, shared his skin and light.

Coreq was actively trying to bond with me now.

"Yes," Black said grimly, still watching my face. "Exactly. That's exactly what he wants, Miri. He's told me that's what he wants. He's more or less demanded it of me."

Black swallowed, his gold eyes bright.

"He's waiting now, Miri. I managed to stall him, to get him to agree to wait for our seer wedding ceremony and our honeymoon. But I may not be able to put him off after that. I may have played the last card I have left to play."

There was another silence.

"We should have talked about this," I said.

"I know."

"Before the wedding, Black."

"I know." He stared at me, swallowing. "I didn't want you to back out. I told myself... *gaos,* Miri... I told myself we both *knew* this already, that we could fix it after. That the marriage would only help us maintain our commitment to stay together."

"You thought I might leave you." I stared at him, incredulous. "Jesus, Black. You really thought I might *leave* you. Why? Why would you think that?"

"You just accused me of the same," he growled.

"Because you've been avoiding me for months!"

"I've not been *avoiding* you, Miri," he said, exasperated. *"I'thir li'dare...* do you not see what he is doing to us? Even now? *Neither* of us are ourselves right now, doc. Don't you feel this? He's screwing with the bond. Something about me becoming this 'dragon' thing has made our bond less solid than it once was. He's *fractured* it somehow. It's what they warned us about, those other seers... my cousin and his wife. We're basically only half-bonded right now. That's the *real* problem with us. It's making the lack of sex worse, but sex isn't really our problem."

I nodded, biting my lip.

Everything he said felt right.

All of it felt true.

Unfortunately, I didn't have a solution to any of it.

"We'll go to that other dimension," I said. "We'll see if your cousin and the holy people there can help us, Black. Maybe they know a way to fix this—"

There was motion on the other side of the glass.

Black and I turned.

The two detectives were entering the room now, accompanied by the two uniformed cops. The woman, Detective Cassavetes, stopped a few steps into the room. She turned to the officer, saying something to him I couldn't hear.

Then she stepped back, and clapped the same uniform on the arm, grinning at him in thanks. The black man with the bald head winked back, shaking his head and smiling at her.

Then he looked to the other uniform and motioned with his head.

The two of them began heading for the corridor.

I had to get my head back in the game.

I had to.

This thing was about to begin.

9

WALLS AROUND LIGHT

T he way the uniform cops looked Jacob Mulden up and down, eyebrows raised, told me they were likely thinking along similar lines as me. I suspected they were having very much the same thoughts I had when I first laid eyes on the man.

This guy? Really?

None of us could quite believe that *this* might be our guy.

Even so, Black's words from before stuck with me.

That blankness. The emptiness *there... there's a darkness, Miri.*

I fought to focus on the job, why we were here.

I tried to calm that part of me that was on the verge of freaking out, that had my seer's living light, or *aleimi,* sparking and flickering around my body in disconcerting waves. I did everything I could to bring back my "doc face," as Black called it. I fought to embody the part of me that could hold a poker face in front of unruly clients, not to mention mass murderers, rapists, and child abusers I'd interviewed for the police.

I used to think I could keep that poker face through just about anything.

For now, I had to hope I could at least do it temporarily, while we were here.

I felt Black watching me.

Every part of him exuded caution, wariness, concern.

More than anything, I felt the worry woven into that unease.

Was he worried about me? Or was he worried about what I might do?

I tugged the shield more tightly around me, receding further into myself.

Gaos, Miri... wife. I love you. I love you so much that looking at your face right now might just fucking kill me. He paused as if with an effort. *I swear to the gods, doc... I'm trying to protect you. I'm not doing ANY of this because I want it. I only want to keep that fucker from hurting you... or taking you away from me... or harming our marriage...*

I nodded.

We'll go see them after this, he sent. *Revik and Allie. Those holy people who taught you how to use the inter-dimensional thing. You're right. We should have done it before. They talked to me a little about it, but not enough.*

I nodded again, swallowing.

His words made sense. It was a good plan.

The rational part of me agreed with that plan wholeheartedly.

That less rational part of me could barely think, however.

I wanted Revik and Allie to cut that thing out of him.

I couldn't stand the thought that I might be losing more of him, day by day.

You're not, he murmured, tugging on me softly with his light. *I promise you're not, wife. I promise you I'm still here. I'm not leaving you. Not ever. And we'll go for help, Miri. Right after this. We'll go somewhere and find someone to talk to who can help us. Then, when we get it fixed, we can come back. Maybe spend a few weeks at the beach house in Santa Cruz.*

He swallowed, still pulling on and playing with my light. *You're right. We have to deal with this. We should have talked about it a long time ago.*

I nodded again.

Taking a deep breath, I nodded a third time, just for good measure.

The door to the observation area opened to my right, and I turned.

Cal stood there, along with his girlfriend, Nina.

I watched them walk into the room.

I heard their murmured voices. A minute or so later, I heard as Cal and Black talked about what happened when they brought the guy in, how he'd reacted to seeing Nina, how he'd seemed mortified that Nina had seen him in handcuffs.

I only heard bits and pieces as Nina came over to stand next to me by the window.

"He had a huge crush on her when they were kids," Cal murmured to Black. "We told the cops that. I think they were hoping that seeing her here might knock him off balance a bit. Make it easier to get something out of him in questioning."

"It's not a bad idea," Black admitted.

I felt more than saw him glance at Nina where she stood next to me by the window.

"The detectives are good," Black added. "That Cassavetes is smart. I'm not even sure you need us here, brother. I suspect they'll do fine without us—"

"No!" Cal's voice sharpened, growing louder in the small space. "No, man. Stay. You heard those detectives... they want you here. Anyway, even if they're good, all the more reason, right? Why not give them a little push with the psychic stuff? Maybe that's a relationship you'll want reciprocated at some point."

I looked over at that.

In the silence after Cal spoke, Black and I exchanged looks.

I had already wondered if Black would tell his friend we couldn't read this Jacob Mulden guy, or admit the same to the two San Jose homicide detectives.

Whatever he intended to tell Cassavetes and her partner, he didn't tell Cal.

"We'll stay a while longer," Black assured him. "Long enough to hear them interrogate this guy. Long enough to talk to Cassavetes and her partner after."

I could feel the impatience on Black, though.

He wanted to go talk to his cousin now.

I felt the urgency vibrate through his light.

I looked back at Jacob Mulden, our suspect, staring at his face as the two detectives took their seats on the other side of the table.

I found myself reorienting around him for real.

He really was an enigma.

His light, his mind... I really couldn't see any of it.

I couldn't see anything. Not a damned thing.

No hum of thoughts.

No whispers of emotion or anxiety, which I normally would have gotten from a human without even trying, without deliberately reaching out to read them. That would only be *more* true if that human had just been picked up for murder.

A human who'd just been picked up from murder, especially one who already had psychiatric issues, or social interaction dysfunction of one kind or another, would be broadcasting their emotions even *more* loudly.

In my experience, it was usually difficult to block them out.

With this man, Jacob Mulden, there was nothing.

His *aleimi,* or living light, lived behind a thick, black wall.

"Yeah," Black agreed.

I looked over.

He'd walked away from Cal.

He stood next to me, and I felt that urgency on him again.

We'll do this fast, he murmured in my mind. *We'll go tonight. Okay?*

I nodded, feeling a faint relief.

Good, I sent. *Yes. Tonight.*

Meeting my gaze briefly, Black took a breath, seemingly with an effort.

I felt him trying to relax, too.

He glanced at Nina, who still stood to my right, then Cal, who now stood on Nina's other side. Without changing expression, he aimed his stare back through the glass at Jacob Mulden, childhood friend and across-the-street neighbor of Rodney Gallows, murder victim.

Still standing next to me, in a way that felt almost protective now, Black sank down to sit on the table, right next to where I stood.

Remaining close to me without touching me overtly, he arranged his weight and the angle of his body so he could see both the monitor displaying the CCTV image and the direct view through the one-way window. He folded his arms. Without looking at me, he reached down to click an orange button on the console, which immediately lit up.

I heard a crackle overhead as the speakers came to life.

A low hum filled the observation cubicle, right before the sound of shoes and moving clothes from the other room filled the small space.

Black folded his thick arms over his chest.

I moved a little closer to him.

I felt a faint relief from him when I did.

The monitor sat on the same long counter where Black perched, directly between me and Nina. The view from the camera gave us a different angle on the interrogation room and the three people seated at the metal table. Due to the tilt of the camera, it also focused more on the suspect than the two detectives, giving us a near close-up view of Mulden's face.

Inside, Cassavetes folded her hands on the table's metal surface.

"Can we get your name?" she said politely. "For the record?"

"You're recording this?"

Mulden's voice was low, tremulous.

Cassavetes smiled. "You are in a police station, Jacob. Of

course we are recording this. Everything you say here will be official. On the record."

He seemed to wince when she said his name.

"Am I a suspect of some kind?" Mulden looked between them. "Why?"

"Right now, you're a potential source of information for us."

"But I already told you everything! What else can I do?"

Cassavetes quirked an eyebrow, her gaze steady on his. "Don't you want to help us find out what happened to your friend, Jacob?"

"Of course!" he snapped. "But that's not what this is, is it? You think it's me. You think *I* did something to him? Are you crazy?"

The male detective with the blond, handlebar mustache, the one Cassavetes called "Barry," cleared his throat, glancing at his partner.

Then he faced Jacob directly.

"Where were you the night Rodney disappeared, Jacob?" he asked.

"I told you that. I told the other cops *all* of this. Weeks ago. The day after it happened."

"So tell us again," Barry said.

"Why?" Mulden leaned forward, gripping the edges of the table. "Why would you want to hear it all again? Is this a test? Are you *testing* me?"

Barry and Cassavetes exchanged looks.

Then Cassavetes looked back at Mulden.

"Part of this is to check for consistency in your story, yes," she said evenly. "Does this bother you, Jacob?"

"So you think I'm a liar?"

Cassavetes' shrewd eyes never stopped examining his, but her lips rose in a warm smile. I couldn't help noticing how disarming it was, that smiley, disarmingly open and friendly expression. It almost entirely camouflaged the sharp scrutiny that lived behind it, and the even sharper mind.

"We would like you to tell us again, Jacob," she said brightly. "This is okay, yes? We ask every witness this... to tell us their story more than once. It is a standard procedure, as I said. It is not personal. We will ask everyone we speak to these same questions. We will ask them to repeat their stories a second time, just like you."

Cassavetes' words carried a faint accent.

I realized I'd noticed it before, but my mind hadn't tried to catalogue it.

It struck me as European, but I couldn't quite pinpoint the country.

"Things have changed," the detective went on, smiling, holding out her hands. "When things change, we must review the facts differently. We must be sure we did not miss anything the first time we spoke. There is a different significance to these things—"

"I didn't hurt Rodney," the man blurted. "I would never *do* that. He's my best friend."

"Was," Barry said flatly. "He *was* your best friend, Jake—"

"I would *never* hurt him," the man snapped, turning to glare at the man with the handlebar mustache. "NEVER. The idea is preposterous. Jacob was my brother. I spent *weeks* working on his present. Why would I—"

"Okay," Cassavetes said, holding up a hand. "Okay, Jacob. We understand. He is your friend. But you had not seen your best friend for a very long time, yes? For some years, at least? So it is interesting, yes? That you would suddenly want to see him this night? Why would you ask him to come meet you *now?* Right before he disappears?"

"He was turning forty."

"I understand."

"Clearly you *don't* understand!"

"There were birthdays before this," Cassavetes said patiently. "Surely some of those were important, too. Why wait so long?

Why not invite him over to see you sooner? Why not invite him to the magic show sooner?"

There was a silence.

In it, Jacob looked between them, biting his lip.

Then, seemingly making an effort to calm down, he exhaled in a sigh. He combed a hand through his wispy hair, slumping deeper into the metal chair.

"I don't know."

"Did you want to see him before now?"

"Of course! I *always* wanted to see Roddo. Always—"

"So this is your friend's fault, maybe? Rodney? He is not available to you before?"

There was another silence.

Then Mulden, seeming to think about the question, pressed his lips together. After a few seconds more, he shook his head.

When he next spoke, he sounded defeated.

"Maybe. He's busy. He has an important job."

Cassavetes nodded sympathetically. "I understand."

"No... you don't!" The man's lightbulb-shaped head turned. His complexion darkened, gradually turning a brighter red. "You *don't* understand! You're pretending you do, but you don't. Rodney was my *brother.* He was *family.* Time doesn't mean the same for family. We could go *years* without seeing each other, and it wouldn't matter—"

"Or decades," Barry muttered.

Mulden glared at him, eyes cold.

"I would *never* hurt my family. Never. For any reason."

"Yes. Well, that may be," Barry said.

Holding up his hands like Cassavetes had done, the male detective shrugged.

"The thing is, Jake, a lot of families don't feel the way you do. We get calls about families all the time here. Mothers. Brothers. Fathers. Aunts. A lot of families beat the shit out of each other, Jacob. A lot of families kill each other."

Barry held up his hands a second time, raising his shoulders in a shrug. "In fact, families can be downright vicious, Jake. You wouldn't believe the stuff we've seen, me and Detective Cassavetes here, when it comes to families—"

"Not me. Not Rodney."

"And yet, you don't seem all that interested in helping us figure out what happened to him," Barry said. "Or who might have done it. Do you, Jakey?"

Jacob Mulden visibly flinched.

I suspected it was the "Jakey" that made him flinch, not the detective's actual question.

Of course, I couldn't know that for sure, since I still couldn't read Jacob Mulden at all.

There was a silence.

In it, Jacob looked between the two detectives, his deer-like eyes holding a faint thread of panic. The brown irises reflected pale green from the overhead florescent lights, in a way that made them look like they glowed with their own internal illumination.

The combination managed to make him look even more like an animal.

I watched him, frowning, trying to figure out why I couldn't read him.

He was clearly human.

He had to be human, right?

"I honestly don't know, doc," Black murmured. "I think so, too. But this..." He motioned vaguely towards the glass. "...This isn't human. There's no human explanation for what is going on right now. Or how blank his living light is."

Cal looked over, frowning.

"Human?" he said. "What does that mean? There's no human explanation for what?"

I didn't answer Cal.

Neither did Black.

I watched Black's face instead.

I felt Cal and Nina watching him, too. I felt a whisper of

Nina's puzzlement, but Cal felt more annoyed and less surprised. I suspected Cal was simply more used to Black's long silences, and his indifference to questions he didn't feel like answering, at least not yet.

I could feel Cal and Nina so clearly. I could read all of their emotions and a good chunk of their thoughts without even trying.

Being able to feel the two humans in the observation area so easily only made the contrast with Jacob Mulden more acute.

I refocused on Black.

I watched him frown at the man on the other side of the glass. My husband's expression remained difficult to read, but I could see more there now.

I could see the frustration in his eyes almost clearly.

Something about Jacob Mulden was bothering him.

Something about that wall around Mulden's light was bothering Black a lot.

I almost wondered if whatever he felt on Jacob Mulden was familiar to him.

As I thought it, I realized that wasn't what I wondered at all.

No, I wondered why it was so damned familiar to me.

10

SOMETHING OR SOMEONE

B lack didn't look over when I spoke inside his mind.

Do you think he's a seer? I sent.

I don't know.

Vampire?

Black's frown deepened. *Highly doubtful.*

I gazed at Jacob Mulden through the glass.

Cassavetes and Barry were still playing tag-team, not letting up on the odd man with the thinning brown hair and lightbulb-shaped head.

"So you didn't see Rodney that night?" Cassavetes pressed.

When Jacob Mulden didn't speak, Cassavetes prodded him again.

"That's what you told our officers here, when your friend first went missing. We need you to answer us again now, Jacob. You told Officer Julia Nguyen, who was initially assigned to the missing persons case, that Rodney never showed up at the club that night. You said Rodney was never there. Is that still the answer you want to give us, Jacob?"

She paused.

When he didn't speak, didn't stop staring off, she pursed her lips.

"Is that still true?" Cassavetes asked.

"Of course it's still true." Jacob's voice pitched higher. "Why wouldn't it be *true?*"

Clearly, the strain was getting to him, which was likely what Barry and Cassavetes intended. Jacob Mulden now sounded openly defensive, verging on combative.

"Why *wouldn't* it be true?" Jacob asked again. "Do you think I would have 'forgotten' whether or not I saw my friend two days after he disappeared? Only to suddenly *remember* two weeks later? Do you think I have amnesia, officer? Or are you just going to keep accusing me of lying?"

"Stories change," Barry said, his voice expressionless. "And that's *detective,* Jacob. You'll address her as *Detective* Cassavetes. I'm *Detective* Wood."

Jacob blinked.

From his expression, he didn't comprehend a word of what Wood said.

I'd been noticing that throughout the interview, though.

Jacob Mulden only paid attention to things that were about him. As soon as the topic shifted to someone or something else, it's like his brain just fuzzed out.

Like now.

Of course, I couldn't know that for certain. I couldn't read him.

But from his body language and the things he said, Jacob Mulden was deeply uninterested in the vast majority of people who weren't him.

He glared at Cassavetes now, then back at Detective Wood.

"My story doesn't change." Jacob glared harder, for emphasis, then looked back at Cassavetes. "Rodney didn't show up. I invited him, but he didn't come. He didn't show up to see my show that night. I didn't see him. Okay? I don't know how many times I need to say the same exact thing to you people—"

"You're sure?" Cassavetes pressed.

"Of *course* I'm sure. I *know* he didn't come!"

"Maybe he came but he didn't stay for the show?" Wood suggested. "Maybe he came back to see you, just for a few minutes? A quick hello? A birthday drop-in? Maybe he joined you in your dressing room and you just forgot?"

"No. No... I told you that. I told you I didn't see him. Why wouldn't I *tell* you that, if I'd seen him before my show?"

"The bartender says he brought *someone* back to see you," Cassavetes said. "He says he brought in someone who asked about you. He also says he never saw that someone come back out again."

My eyebrows rose.

This was the first time I was hearing that about the bartender.

Her words didn't seem to affect Mulden, though.

Jacob only shook his head, eyes angry.

"No. That's not possible."

"It's not possible you forgot?" Cassavetes pressed. "It was a few *weeks* ago, Jake."

"You people came by when it happened," the man snapped. "I *told* them this. I told them *all* of this then. More than once."

"Don't think about that, about what you already said." Cassavetes advised. She lifted a hand, smiling at him in a friendly way. "Do not think about what you answered before, Jake. Just try to remember that night. You really have no recollection of this person the bartender told us about? The person who asked to see you?"

"No!" Jacob's jaw jutted. "I *really* don't have *any idea* what he's talking about. None whatsoever. I'm telling you, there was no one else there—"

"He seemed pretty sure," Barry cut in. "Also, we showed him a picture of your pal, Roddo. He seemed even *more* sure when he saw that. He told us the man he saw that night was *definitely* the same guy as the one in our photo. Definitely. That's a direct quote, Jacob. He seemed really, *really* sure. He was able to describe Rodney's car—"

"Well, he's lying."

There was a silence.

Barry and Cassavetes exchanged raised eyebrows.

Cassavetes focused back on Jacob first.

Leaning over the table, she re-clasped her hands, staring up at his dark eyes.

"Why would he lie?" she asked, pursing her lips. "Can you think of a single reason why he might lie to us, Jacob?"

"I don't know."

"Why would you say that, then?" Barry pressed. "That he's lying?"

"I don't *know*."

"Put yourself in our situation, Jacob," Cassavetes said, her voice persuasive now. "What would sound the more plausible to you? What would *you* think happened, if you were us?"

"I have no idea. But then, I'm not paid to play super-sleuth. Am I?"

Jacob sounded peevish.

Significantly more peevish.

Sulky on steroids.

He leaned back in the metal chair, folding his arms as he glared between Barry and Cassavetes.

"He doesn't like me," he snapped. "Okay? He's *never* liked me."

"The bartender doesn't like you?"

"Yes." Jacob sniffed. "It's hardly unusual. A *lot* of people don't like me."

Cassavetes held her poker face better than Barry did.

"I see," she said diplomatically.

"I'm sure you do," Jacob snapped.

"So you think he'd lie?" Barry interjected, drawing Jacob's eyes to him.

From the male detective's expression and the dubious note in his voice, Wood didn't think the bartender was lying. He thought someone was lying all right, but definitely not the bartender.

Barry pressed his point.

"Again, Jacob... why? *Why* would he do that? He'd risk interfering with a police investigation, obstructing justice, simply because he doesn't like you?"

"I don't know." Jacob's pale lips pursed. "Maybe he saw a chance to cause trouble. Maybe because you're police, and you were poking around, asking about me, he thought he'd cause trouble for me. Who knows why people do anything? Who knows why someone might want to screw with someone? *I* never know. People are shitty. That's the truth of it."

His lips tightened in a harder frown.

He looked between the two detectives, and for the first time, he sounded worried.

"You really haven't found him yet? Rodney?"

There was a silence.

Cassavetes and her partner exchanged looks.

Black and I exchanged looks, too.

It struck me that I hadn't heard them mention the word *murder* up until now. I'd only heard them talking about Rodney's disappearance. Feeling Cassavetes' light, I found myself thinking the two detectives had done this on purpose.

They'd wanted me and Black to see Jacob Mulden react to the news, so they held off on telling him until they got him here.

"No one told you?" Wood asked Mulden.

"Told me what?"

Cassavetes and Wood looked at one another again.

Then Cassavetes leaned over the table, exhaling in a sigh.

"We found Rodney, Jacob. We found him last night."

"You did?" Jacob blinked. "Where is he? Is he all right?"

Cassavetes shook her head.

"No, Jacob. He is not all right. Your friend, Rodney Gallows, is dead." Cassavetes' voice managed to convey a genuine-sounding sympathy while remaining wholly matter-of-fact. "I'm very sorry Jacob. Detective Wood and myself, we're with homicide. We're no longer investigating this as a missing persons case. This is a murder case now."

The silence stretched.

When Jacob broke it, he nearly spat out words.

His voice rose a few octaves.

"How would *I* know why people lie about me? All I can tell you is what happened. I didn't do anything! No one came to see me! No one! Anyway, I still have the present. Why would I still have the *present* I made him, if Roddo came to get it?"

I blinked.

Had Jacob even heard her?

Was this some form of denial?

A refusal to grasp the basic fact that his friend was dead?

Or was Jacob Mulden just a psychopath too stupid to pretend he cared?

For the first time, I felt genuinely angry I couldn't read him.

"Did you hear me, Jacob?" Cassavetes frowned. "I just said Rodney is dead."

"I *heard* you. Did you hear me?" He glared at her over the table. "You're not going to pin this on me! I made him a *present.* Why would I do that, if I was going to kill him? I still have it. Why would I still have the present if I'd seen Roddo that night? Why would I?"

"Maybe because the bartender's right?" Barry remarked drily. "Maybe because 'Roddo'..." Barry made air quotes with his fingers. "...never got a chance to *leave* with his present, Jake?"

There was another silence.

"Why don't you tell us about the cameras in the club, Jacob?" Cassavetes said next. "Did you ever tamper with any of the cameras there? For any reason?"

Jacob stared at her, then at Detective Wood.

"I want a lawyer," he snapped. "I want a lawyer right now."

I frowned, still trying my damnedest to read behind Jacob Mulden's dark eyes.

That blankness was really starting to frustrate me.

At the same time, none of the explanations my mind tried to come up with sounded remotely plausible.

Can we get them to do a DNA swab? my mind muttered to Black's. *"Accidentally" cut his finger on something, so we can test his blood?*

Next to me, Black grunted.

I extended my seer's light further.

For the first time, I really attacked Jacob Mulden's light with mine. I tried to understand what was blocking me from seeing his thoughts.

I felt all around the blank spot where his living light should be.

I still came up totally blank.

Which was even weirder given how completely expressive his face and eyes were, not to mention how emotional his voice sounded.

"Either he's some kind of Academy-Award deserving actor," I said, folding my arms and exhaling in frustration. "Or there's something seriously hinky going on here."

I ignored Cal and Nina's questioning looks.

Exhaling, I looked up at Black, still speaking out loud.

"Could someone be protecting him?" I asked.

Black nodded slowly, but more in thought than what felt like agreement.

His eyes remained slightly out of focus as he gazed through the glass.

"Yeah, maybe someone," he muttered. "Or maybe something."

"Some*thing?*" My eyebrows went up. "What kind of something?"

Somehow, I didn't think he meant a seer or a vampire.

"I really couldn't say, doc."

"But you have a theory?"

"I really don't."

I bit my lip. *"Why* would someone be protecting him?"

It was mostly a rhetorical question.

I found myself trying to answer it, anyway.

"Maybe they wanted Rodney dead?" I guessed out loud. "He's some Silicon Valley power broker, right? A finance guy? Maybe it's some corporate espionage thing. Or a competition over cutting-edge tech thing. Something to do with something new coming out, something with potential to make a lot of money."

Still thinking, I shrugged.

"Or maybe it's something a lot simpler," I admitted. "Maybe Rodney just got in with the wrong people. Maybe he took money from the wrong people?"

Before I could get any further, Nina cut me off.

"Rodney wouldn't do anything illegal." Her voice grew angry. "He wouldn't, Dr. Fox. Rodney would never do anything shady at all. He wouldn't be that dumb. He had too much to lose, for one thing. He had kids. And a good life."

Black and I exchanged skeptical looks.

Nina must have seen it.

She shook her head, raising her voice.

"No. I can see what you think, but no. He wouldn't have done it, not even if he knew he wouldn't get caught. He would talk all the time about how stupid people were, to jeopardize their lives for that kind of thing. He wasn't that kind of person."

To be honest, I ignored that, mostly.

Everyone wanted to believe that about their families.

Everyone came up with odd theories about why their family member was different. No one wanted to believe someone they liked could do anything wrong. Most people wanted to believe that all human behavior was rational.

Like people only stole when they needed the money.

Like people wouldn't be reckless if they had something to lose.

Like people weren't hypocrites and liars.

The little bit I'd picked up about Rodney Gallows from the

two detectives told me "Roddo" might have been one of those guys who cut corners now and then. He had a lot of money. He had a huge ego. He had power, an outsized sense of entitlement, and a chip on his shoulder. He felt the world had tried to screw him, and lost.

From what I could tell, no black and white explanation for Rodney Gallows existed.

The story of his life was likely a lot more complex.

I suspected his ex-wife would have a very different take on him, too.

Black didn't so much as glance in Nina's direction.

Still thinking, he nodded slowly to my words.

"Maybe."

I continued to run scenarios in my mind, staring sightlessly at the glass.

"Maybe they picked this guy, Jacob, as a patsy of some kind?" I frowned, still thinking, working the scenario out loud. "Could they have used vamps or seers to brainwash Jacob Mulden into committing the murder? Could they have pushed him to kill Rodney, after luring him to the club? It would explain why Mulden is so sure he didn't see Rodney. It would explain the cameras, and how long it took them to find the body."

"Why?" Nina demanded. "Why would they do that?"

I glanced at her, shrugging. "Deniability. So it couldn't be traced back to the people who were actually behind it."

"It's more likely they paid off the people at the club, doc," Black said. "Some of them, anyway. They missed the one bartender, obviously. But it would explain the cameras."

I nodded.

Human murder. Right.

A part of me was too used to looking for more elaborate, supernatural-type explanations for death and mayhem.

This might end up being a lot more simple than that.

That might even be true in regards to his blank, impenetrable aura.

Maybe Jacob just had weird living light.

Maybe us not being able to see Jacob's *aleimi* had nothing to do with his race at all. That would be a first, but that didn't make it impossible.

I thought about the possibility that all of this really was just human-on-human crime.

That nothing about it was supernatural at all.

That made Jacob Mulden sound a lot more guilty.

"It does," Black agreed. "But I'm a little skeptical that he's got nothing protecting him, doc. Maybe they have tech. Some kind of blocker."

I nodded, exhaling. "That makes more sense."

I knew my uncle had things like seer light-blockers under development.

It wasn't totally inconceivable that one of the human companies got their hands on a prototype. Maybe Rodney knew too much. Maybe he stole tech for them. Maybe he bought stolen tech off someone else. Maybe he bought illegal tech on the black market.

Or maybe they simply got him out of the way. Maybe the wanted to steal tech or resources from him, or from someone he represented.

As for the grisly death, maybe there were more people involved.

Maybe they'd been sending a message.

None of that really explained why neither Black nor I could read the guy, but that could be a completely separate issue. Jacob Mulden's weird light might have nothing to do with what happened to Rodney Gallows.

Still thinking, I frowned.

"So who's likely to have had access to Charles' tech?" I said. "And why would they be protecting Jacob at this point? If they lined him up to be a patsy, wouldn't they want him to take the fall? Protecting him only calls attention to him at this point, especially with us involved."

I glanced at Black.

I could see from his eyes that he didn't like my explanation.

It didn't ring true for him.

That, or he wanted a lot more evidence and a lot less speculation.

Of course, I couldn't read Black all that well, either.

I definitely couldn't read him well enough to know what he was thinking about everything I'd just said. He didn't appear to be overly eager to share his thoughts with me, either. I'd more or less been talking to myself up until now.

He hadn't offered any theories of his own.

He still wasn't offering any theories.

He didn't even bother to tell me why my theories were wrong.

My frustration keened into something a lot closer to anger.

I forgot about Cal. I forgot Nina was standing there.

I found myself looking at Black.

I stared up at his inhumanly handsome face, his broad shoulders, the muscular hands now resting on his waist as he frowned at our suspect through the one-way glass.

Studying my husband's expression, I realized I couldn't read him any better than I could Jacob Mulden. Really, Black lived behind an even thicker wall, because I couldn't read his face, and with Mulden, at least I had that. I could see the panic in Mulden's eyes. I could read the twitching muscles of his cheek, the flushing, the sweating, the panting, the white knuckles.

The wall around Black felt impenetrable.

It felt deliberate, too.

Not to mention the fact it felt personal, and hurt me like hell.

Miri... please. Please, *baby. It's only for right now. Just let us get through this damned case. We'll go see my cousin after. We'll go the second after this is done* —

A noise from the speakers made me jump.

"I CAN'T HELP YOU WITH THIS! I CAN'T! *I CAN'T!!*"

My eyes jerked to the glass.

I stared into the interrogation room, bewildered.

Jacob Mulden gripped the table with both hands, clenching his long, pale fingers around the scuffed metal.

He leaned forward, screaming into Cassavetes' face.

I'd known it was Jacob's voice that was yelling.

I'd known that before I turned, but those few, screeched words were barely recognizable as him, despite all of his earlier peevishness. Jacob's deer-like eyes widened further, until they swallowed most of his strangely chinless and jawless face. That lightbulb shape of his skull, with his wide forehead and thinning hair made me think of old cartoon depictions of aliens.

Or possibly old cartoon depictions of birds.

Jacob was breathing harder now.

He was panting.

He sweated profusely under the florescent lights, staring between the two detectives like a cornered animal. His skin looked waxy now, nearly gray. He gripped the table until his knuckles turned white. He shook his upper body violently, rocking and shoving and shaking his entire person with both hands, back and forth against the metal table.

He never stopped staring at Cassavetes.

He looked like a man losing hold of his reality.

He looked dangerous.

"...I CAN'T HELP YOU!" he screamed. "I CAN'T! I CAN'T I CAN'T!"

"Calm down, Jake—" Barry said.

"I CAN'T!"

"You need to calm down. This isn't acceptable—"

"I CANNOT DO THIS!"

"JAKE!" Barry Wood's voice grew openly warning. "Calm down. Right now. Or we'll have to call someone in here—"

"FUCK YOU, CALM DOWN!"

Spittle decorated Jacob Mulden's thin lips.

His eyes widened as he seemed to be trying to see through

Cassavetes' eyes to her very soul. Those dark sockets turned his face into wax-covered bone.

"MY BEST FRIEND IS DEAD! MY *VERY BEST*, OLDEST, DEAREST FRIEND RODNEY IS DEAD! RODNEY IS DEAD! SOMEONE MURDERED HIM! SOMEONE *MURDERED* HIM!"

"Jacob! Calm down!"

I swallowed, disturbed in spite of myself.

Jacob Mulden barely seemed to hear Wood speak.

He gasped, as if his own words pained him.

"NOW YOU'RE ACCUSING *ME*!" he screamed, shaking his body harder. "YOU'RE SAYING *I* DID IT! ME! ME??!!"

More spittle flew off those thin, pale lips.

Cassavetes remained calm.

"No one is saying that, Jake." The female detective held up a hand. "No one. We did not say this. You are afraid."

Her voice exuded calm.

After her partner's threats, it also came across like a command.

Her partner threatened to have him committed.

Cassavetes merely ordered him to remain still.

Her words somehow conveyed an inescapable authority.

Even so, I could feel the unease vibrating her light, even as I saw it writhe through her pale blue and pink aura. Unlike Jacob Mulden and my husband, I could feel the two detectives in that room as clearly as I could feel Nina and Cal.

Both Cassavetes and her partner were spooked.

They exchanged bare looks, and from the alarmed flickers there, they were likely wondering if they needed to have Mulden committed to a hospital, and forcibly sedated.

"We just want the truth," Cassavetes repeated, exuding more of that calm. Her voice remained authoritative, no nonsense. "The truth is good, yes? For you? For your friend, Rodney? For us? It is good for everyone. The truth is what makes the world right, Jacob."

I looked at Jacob.

I couldn't tell if her words were even reaching him.

Contemplating the truth certainly didn't seem to be Jacob Mulden's priority right then.

Her commands didn't seem to be reaching him all that well, either.

I watched his face turn a darker red, until it was nearly purple.

I watched his lips move in and out with his labored breaths.

I braced myself, prepared for him to start screaming at Cassavetes again.

I wondered if he might be on the verge of a violent seizure.

Or maybe actual violence, maybe aimed at the female detective.

When suddenly, out of nowhere...

Jacob Mulden disappeared.

Jacob Mulden, as a distinct and separate, albeit *weird* personality, completely vanished.

THE NEW JAKE

T he person who replaced Jacob Mulden was someone none of us had ever met.

I'd certainly never seen them before.

I doubted the detectives had, either.

When I say Jacob vanished, I don't mean he *literally vanished,* the way I do when I jump dimensions, or when Black turns into a dragon.

Jacob Mulden didn't disappear physically, as in his body.

Jacob's body remained exactly where it was.

What I mean is, the man who had been there, sitting at that table, screaming and spitting and rocking back and forth, gripping the metal slab... that *person* vanished. Every shred of emotion I'd seen in his eyes, every twitch and spasm and bloom of color on his oddly-shaped face, every contortion in his body, every bloodless knuckle...

All of it got wiped clean.

It happened so fast, I blinked a few times.

I felt actively disoriented by the change.

I could still read nothing on him, but the physical transformation alone was unnerving to the point where I actually felt a flicker of fear.

Jacob Mulden's fingers relaxed visibly around the edge of the metal table. His shoulders unclenched. His chest slowed its manic breaths. The bloom of red in his cheeks transformed into a beige-tinged white. The blotchiness I'd seen on his skin, even before he flipped out on the questioning officers, smoothed.

His eyes... his eyes looked so strange.

It took me a few seconds to realize his pupils had dilated. They went from near pinpricks in the brightly-lit interrogation room to wide, deep black spheres that nearly swallowed his irises.

That blankness borne of panic was gone.

The blankness that replaced it couldn't be more different; it was indifferent, bored.

The fear was gone.

A silence remained, one that went beyond his physical body. He sat so still, he could have been made of stone.

If I'd been watching a recording, I would have assumed that recording had been paused.

"Jacob?" Cassavetes' voice turned openly wary. "Jacob? Are you all right?"

"I wish to speak to them."

Cassavetes flinched.

It was the first time I'd seen her lose her unswerving calm.

She looked at her partner, and he looked at her.

I understood the utter disbelief in those exchanged looks.

More than that, I saw the fear.

"Who, Jacob?" Cassavetes said. "Who would you like to speak to?"

"The one on the other side of the wall. And his wife," the thing inside Jacob Mulden said.

His eyes flickered away from the detectives.

They focused the one-way window.

I swear, it looked like he stared directly at Black.

Barry sounded angry, but I felt his fear.

"Jacob, *we* are the detectives here. You must speak to us. You don't get to dictate terms, or tell us who you want to interview you—"

"I won't talk to anyone else." The thing inside Jacob Mulden remained utterly calm. "Only them."

☙❧

"All right." Cassavetes walked briskly into the dimly-lit observation area. She held a manila folder in one hand, her mouth set in a grim line. "We have gotten permission for this. We even had a temporary contract written up. To avoid any sense of impropriety on the case. Legal thought you should get a version of our standard consultant's contract, if you are okay wth signing this. My captain wasn't happy—"

"Waive the fees," Black said.

He glanced at Cal, then looked back at Cassavetes.

"This is a *pro bono* thing. I'm helping out a friend."

Cassavetes shook her head.

"Absolutely not," she said. "You will be paid. It looks better for us. It makes this official, and your relationship to us becomes one of professionalism."

Cassavetes' mouth lifted slightly at the corners.

For the first time since she left that interrogation room, I saw a glimmer of that mischievous smile she'd worn when we first met.

"...Of course, I imagine we are getting you at bargain-basement prices, Mr. Black. Compared to your usual fees. We are only a humble police precinct, after all."

Black grunted, but returned her smile.

I could tell he liked Cassavetes, just like I did.

Even so, I noticed his gold eyes remained hard. He hadn't slipped out of that tense, quasi-military persona since the interview with Jacob Mulden first began. Now he looked positively dangerous as he scanned through the fine print of the contract she'd handed him.

I don't know how carefully he read it.

He did read it though, and at the end, he nodded, once.

Cassavetes handed him a pen, and I watched him sign on the line at the bottom.

"Does that allow only him in there?" I asked Cassavetes. "Just Black?"

She shook her head. "No. Not at all. I had it made up for Black Securities and Investigations. We do not hire him. We hire his P.I. firm. Anyone who is an employee of that firm can be used at the owner's discretion, Mrs. Black."

"She's not an employee," Black growled. "And that's *Dr.* Black."

For the first time, he sounded angry at her.

"She doesn't work for me," he warned. "She's a goddamned equal partner. And that's *doctor* to you, detective. *Doctor* Black. Or Dr. Fox, if she prefers... since I'm reasonably sure she's on the verge of divorcing me again."

Cassavetes blinked.

Like before, she held her poker face remarkably well.

After that slightly-too-long pause, she looked at me.

"You will go in with him, Dr. Fox?" she queried politely. Her eyes rose to Black. "Both of you? Together, yes? I am thinking the psychologist and the military man... this is a good team. Especially since you do not have access to your, ah, usual... well, advantages."

We'd told her we couldn't read Mulden.

Black told both of them that our "psychic powers" were useless against their suspect. Interestingly, that information seemed to reassure Detective Barry Wood, even as it disappointed Cassavetes. That had been when they first came into the observation room to debrief, and only a handful of minutes after Mulden demanded to speak to us.

Now Black looked at me.

I could see in his eyes that he didn't really want me in there.

He didn't want me anywhere near Jacob Mulden.

Despite the wall around his light, I could practically *see* the restraint there, a flicker of Black fighting himself to keep from saying as much in front of the others. Knowing him, it was taking every ounce of his willpower to stop himself from *ordering* me not to go in.

Which would have been more than a little ironic, given the speech he'd just given to Cassavetes.

I turned to the female detective.

"Yes." I gave Black the barest warning look. "Both of us will go in. We'll go in together. We should probably do it soon, before something changes again."

Cassavetes didn't hide her relief.

"Excellent. Thank you so much, Dr. Fox."

She exhaled a second time, one of those infectious smiles brightening her face. She clasped her hands in front of her chest, giving us both a slight bow, also in thanks. Already, she was backing towards the door, subtly leading us out of the observation area.

As she reached for the handle, she beckoned openly.

"I agree with Dr. Fox," she said, glancing at Black. "Now that the paperwork is signed, we should proceed at once. Before he changes his mind and asks for a lawyer to be here, or gives us some other condition before he will talk. This is usually when they realize that maybe yelling at us is not such a good idea for them."

I smiled at her politely.

Even so, I found myself thinking she didn't really believe her words.

She didn't think Jacob Mulden would call a lawyer.

She didn't think Jacob Mulden had a lawyer to call.

She also didn't think Jacob Mulden was likely to be making the same sort of practical calculations as most murders suspects.

No, she wanted to see what Mulden would do when me and Black entered the room.

She probably also wanted my opinion as a psychologist now,

too. I strongly suspected both detectives wondered if Mulden might be about to try for an insanity defense, given the odd changeover in personalities.

I doubted any of this would be that simple, though.

"I'll do the best I can," I assured her. "But remember, we can't read him. So anything I'm able to tell you as a psychologist will likely be preliminary and theoretical. At least until I'm able to spend more time with him... or Black's people figure out how to read him."

Cassavetes nodded thoughtfully.

"I understand." She gave me a shrewd look as she pushed open the door, holding it ajar so we could walk past her. "We appreciate you being open with us about your inability to use your psychic gifts on him," she said. "However, neither of you have told us *why* this is. What would cause this?"

"We don't know," I told her truthfully.

She quirked an eyebrow, looking from me to Black.

"Is this common?" she asked.

"No," Black said, blunt. "Not remotely."

Cassavetes nodded, exchanging looks with Detective Barry Wood, who stood in the corridor just outside the door, holding roughly twenty ounces of name-brand coffee in a cardboard cup. He'd clearly been listening to Cassavetes when she asked us about the psychic stuff. He'd just as clearly heard both of our answers.

"Well," Cassavetes said brightly. "Maybe Mr. Mulden will tell you this, yes?"

I smiled back.

Not a single one of us believed he would tell us anything of the kind.

Still, it was as good of a way to break the silence as any.

‹❧›

B lack walked in ahead of me.

He stalked across the tile floor, his leather, designer, motorcycle boots making almost no noise as he glided across the fifteen or so feet to the metal table. I recognized that tread. He was definitely in hyper-alert, predatory mode.

He took the far chair and sat, without taking his eyes off Mulden's face.

Even so, despite Black's unwavering stare on our suspect, I felt his focused awareness fully on me. His living light felt nearly claustrophobic as I followed him into the interrogation room, walking over to sit in the chair next to his, the one Barry had occupied.

After I sat, that hyper-vigilance of Black's only grew more intense.

The shield of light he threw around my body felt nearly physical.

Briefly, it disoriented me, making it difficult to see Mulden at all.

This seems a bit... paranoid... Black, I muttered in his mind.

He didn't answer.

He stared at the man with the deer-like eyes, his expression cold, immovable. If that quasi-violent stare intimidated Mulden, I didn't see any evidence of that intimidation.

Mulden's returning gaze remained bland, borderline empty.

"Who are you?" Black growled. "*What* are you?"

Mulden's lips curved in a faint smile. "Hello, brother."

Black and I exchanged looks.

Seers called one another "brother" and "sister."

It could be a coincidence. I could tell Black didn't think so. Before he could continue his line of questioning, I turned to Mulden next.

"Who are you?" I asked, mirroring Black's question. "Are you going to tell us? Or is this some kind of game? Did you deliberately draw us here for some reason?"

Mulden's eyes never left Black's.

"I am here to obtain what is mine," he said calmly.

"Which is what?" I said.

But Mulden practically ignored me, and my words.

"We were scattered, you and I," the thing inside Mulden said.

From his eyes and focus, he spoke only to Black.

"...Scattered to the wind. The creator. The primal matter behind all things. There are so many of us now, brother, diluting all of us. We have been stolen. Our power... our wisdom. It is stolen. Yet these are the very things that the many dimensions all need."

He paused, that faint smile still toying at his lips.

"I would like to unify us," he said. "I would like to rectify this wrong."

He looked at me, and I felt a jab of fear.

His eyes had changed again.

I gazed directly into those coal-black, fathomless eyes, and it felt like looking into the end of all life as I knew it. They hadn't been that black before, had they? They hadn't contained so much. They hadn't felt like falling into a black hole in space, a place lacking light, lacking time, lacking any kind of grounding in reality whatsoever.

They hadn't been like that before, had they?

"No," Black said.

I honestly wasn't sure if he was speaking to me or to the thing across the table.

The other being leaned back in his chair, shrugging easily.

"You cannot blame us... brother." The thing inside Mulden emphasized the word a touch harder that time. "It is your wife who called to all of us. It is your wife who made us all aware of one another again. Your wife gave us focus. Gave us desire."

I felt sick to my stomach.

I couldn't help but weave different elements of his words together, to make sense of them. A part of me couldn't help but piece together his vague riddles, especially since I'd worried about something similar ever since the last dragon crash-landed here.

Ever since that thing tried to kill my husband at my and Black's wedding.

"We do not wish any ill upon you, brother," the creature emphasized.

Those coal-black eyes bored into Black's face, holding a hint of sympathy.

"We simply want what is ours. You have borrowed it long enough. And it was never really yours to begin with... was it, brother? It was always borrowed. Always belonging to another. It was really only the worst kind of luck that it landed with you..."

He turned to stare at me.

"You too, sister."

I hated the vagueness of his words.

Even more than that, I hated that I half-understood them anyway.

The man leaned over the table, placing his forearms on the scuffed, burnished metal.

"Now you have two of us," the creature said. He looked at Black, then at me. "I would like us back now. I can only promise you that the priest you have here... the one who first tried to summon us... he will not control the direction of our history. He is a very small prawn in a world much bigger than he seems to comprehend."

The thing inside Mulden cleared Mulden's throat, leaning back in the chair. It folded Mulden's hands across the center of Mulden's chest.

"But the priest is inconsequential," the creature said, making a vague, dismissive gesture with one hand. "It is the two of you who matter. For it is the two of you who have stolen fragments of the whole."

The black eyes shifted to me.

Well, his mind said into mine. *Three really.*

I flinched violently as that presence filled my light.

The thing in Mulden must have seen me flinch. Its eyes remained indifferent.

It looked back at Black. "Since you swallowed our other brother, you are responsible for all three things. Do you understand? Two parts of a whole. A whole. This is three. So this is not a threat. It is a mere statement of fact."

I looked at Black, feeling my heart leaping sideways in my chest. Under the table, he took my hand, clasping it in his, holding me almost tightly enough to hurt.

"Take it, then," Black growled, staring into those fathomless eyes. "Take it and get the fuck out of here..."

The creature smiled, winking.

"Oh, I will," he assured Black. "But I have a few more magic tricks to perform for you, first. I made a promise to the priest. I must fulfill my promises too, little brother."

Something about the way he said that brought my heart up to my throat.

I felt a panicked, irrational fear.

Before I could speak, before I could begin to really react—

—the creature's hands darted out, fast as lightning.

He moved like liquid light.

It was too quick, too blurringly fast, for me to track the motion with my eyes.

All I knew was, he suddenly held my and Black's wrists.

He gripped us tightly, one in each hand.

He grinned. That grin injected another jolt of adrenaline into my blood, even before I realized how maniacal it looked, how animalistic. It looked like he was baring his teeth, or maybe like an upside-down scream.

I imagined him lunging for my throat, tearing it out with his teeth.

Instead, he leaned slowly, deliberately over the table.

His pale face filled my view.

His deep-black eyes widened until they eclipsed everything

else. They eclipsed my view of the interrogation room. They eclipsed my view of Black.

I wanted to scream.

I fought to scream.

I couldn't.

I wanted to grab Black, to jump us out of there.

Both of those things went through my mind in a millisecond.

I struggled to move, to gear into those structures above my head.

I felt tears come to my eyes.

I felt Black's light gear up, exploding up out of him like a volcano—

—then, nothing.

Then, everything disappeared.

OPPORTUNITY

Angel had just taken her first sip of real coffee.
Letting out a half-orgiastic sigh at the heavenly taste,
she leaned her head back on the lounger under a dark blue
umbrella, and thought about horses.

Maybe she could talk Cowboy into taking her horseback
riding tomorrow morning.

Maybe they could go to Ship Rock.

Maybe they could go up to the Rez and check in on the farms
there, make sure everything was okay with so many of the usual
residents staying here at the resort.

Maybe Magic and some of the others might want to come
with them.

Then again, maybe she'd rather be there with Cowboy alone.

She was still running the idea vaguely around inside her head,
considering various options, when Cowboy appeared above her.

He wore clothes that might have made her blink... even
before she saw the look on his face.

Normally, Angel's new husband was a T-shirt and worn jeans
type of guy. Today, he looked like he'd been raiding Nick's closet,
or possibly Dexter's. A dark blue and gray, Hawaiian-style short-
sleeved shirt with green and blue flowers hung open on his

shoulders. The unbuttoned front displayed a lean, muscular chest and abdomen.

Half of that bare skin was covered in tattoos.

Angel couldn't help but stare at that stretch of flesh.

Her eyes went there before she'd had a chance to pick up something was wrong.

Cowboy cleared his throat.

"Darlin', you see the news? Out of California?"

Angel frowned.

Her eyes drifted up to his face.

Now she saw it. Even with his gray eyes shielded by sunglasses, she could see the worry on him. His mouth looked tense. His shoulders looked tense. His jaw looked hard. His dirty blond hair was tied back in a half-ponytail, like he'd been working out.

She could already feel he was wound up.

Possibly even angry.

She had on her darkest pair of sunglasses, but still held up her hand, shielding the glare of sun hitting her off the mirrored pair he wore.

"What news?" Her tone was already wary. "Am I going to want to know this news?"

"Probably not," he said grimly. "I'd recommend looking at it anyway."

She grunted. "Of course you would."

Without asking, Cowboy sat down on the lounge next to her, inserting his body in the space left him by the curve of her waist above her hip. He raised the computer tablet he held in one hand and swiped the screen with his fingers.

After swiping and tapping through a few more things, presumably to find the *exact* thing he wanted to show her, he turned the tablet around, and more or less thrust it into her hands.

"Sounds like our boy. Wouldn't you say?"

Angel scooched backwards on the lounger, pressing her leg into his.

She scowled a little as she raised her sunglasses to the top of her head, using them to pull back her braids. She tugged the tablet onto her sun-warmed thighs. A video news bulletin took up most of the screen, with a short summary in text she didn't bother to read.

Cowboy had queued up the video.

Now he leaned over and hit the "play" symbol, then tapped on the volume control to make it louder.

"...explosion of unknown origins. There is no official word as to the cause, but, as you can see..." A blond, male reporter stepped to one side, motioning towards a smoking building behind him.

White and gray columns billowed smoke up into blue skies, creating dark clouds.

"...it more or less leveled the central San Jose police precinct," the man said, his voice tense. "We've been told by emergency responders and a representative of the police that the incident has injured approximately eighty people, with forty of those hospitalized and two possible deaths currently being reported. Those aren't official numbers yet, as they continue to conduct rescue operations in the rubble. We were told about at least ten people who were rushed to the hospital and are in critical condition..."

Angel swore.

"...No official cause of the building's destruction has yet been given," the reporter continued. "The police are not sharing any information they have about what happened at this time. It's possible they don't yet know the cause..."

"What in God's name happened?" Angel burst out.

"Listen," Cowboy said grimly.

He tapped on the screen, raising the volume a few notches more.

"...while we have been unable to get a confirmation," the

reporter continued. "At least five witnesses outside the police precinct building have reported a large, black *dragon* was sighted in the immediate aftermath of the destruction..."

Angel felt her chest constrict painfully.

The reporter emphasized the word "dragon," his cultured voice holding a kind of blank incredulity even as he said it.

Angel could relate.

She couldn't quite make herself say that word normally yet, either.

Even with everything she knew, some part of her choked on it.

"Further reports have Quentin Black's private plane parked at the San Jose Airport at this time," the blond reporter went on grimly. "He was witnessed leaving the airport at roughly noon this afternoon, and arriving at the police station at approximately one p.m. Witnesses all claim he was accompanied by his wife, forensic psychologist Miriam Black. While all of this information is circumstantial at this point, the combination is leading to speculation by many that the infamous billionaire investor, private detective, and defense contractor might have been the cause of the accident here..."

Angel let out a dismayed sound, biting her lip as the video clip ended.

She scanned through a few more of the headlines.

She clicked on and watched a few more of the videos.

They all pretty much said the same thing.

"Anyone try to call him?" she asked, still scrolling through news briefs.

"I did," Cowboy said at once. "I tried Black's private number. Miri, too."

"What about Cal?" Angel looked up from the tablet, still frowning. "Has anyone tried him? He was with them, right?"

Cowboy blinked, then scowled.

"Damn." He shook his head, obviously annoyed with himself

for forgetting. "Ayuh, he's with them... I totally forgot. I'll call him now."

Cowboy rose to his feet.

He yanked his phone out of the breast pocket of the dark blue and gray Hawaiian shirt. Angel watched as he scrolled through a series of contacts, then hit a button and put the phone to his ear.

Angel watched him listen to the phone ring, his mouth firm.

"No one's picking up?" she said.

Cowboy looked at her, shaking his head grimly.

He hung up the call, then dialed again.

Angel didn't bother to ask, but just waited, watching him pace back and forth across the front of the lounger as he held the phone to his ear.

She had to assume it was ringing on the other end.

That time, someone picked up.

"Lizbeth?" Cowboy sounded relieved. "Y'all watching this? The news?"

There was a silence while he listened to the woman on the other end.

"Yarli, too?" he said.

Nodding at whatever the person on the line said in response, Cowboy exhaled, half in frustration, half in relief.

"I shoulda known they'd be on it," he muttered, glancing at Angel. "All right. Yeah. Well, let us know what they figure out, once they've got a good look at things..."

He trailed, listening again.

"Ayuh. Sounds like the best thing. Did Yarli think they'd be able to piece together what happened?" he asked next. "We're just getting the regular news reports here."

Angel watched him listen for a few seconds more.

"That's all I got, too," he said. "Ayuh. We'll let you know. Call me or Ang if anything changes. And let us know about it, if Cal and his missus check in. I imagine they'll be wanting to talk to someone if they can't reach Black or the doc."

He hit the button to hang up the line.

He stuck the phone back in the same breast pocket.

For a few seconds, they only looked at one another.

"Do we need to go out there?" Angel said.

There was a silence after she asked the question.

Well, not a *real* silence.

Jax and Kiko could be heard laughing, splashing one another from the other side of the pool. A handful of humans and seers were talking around the buffet table. Dishes and glasses clinked where they sat and ate at tables a dozen or so yards away. Angel heard birds in the bushes and trees around the pool. Someone piped melodic, Native American flute music through the outdoor speakers, making her feel like she was in a health spa.

She didn't want to leave.

She could have stayed there forever, in that New Mexico paradise.

At the same time, she felt a suffocating kind of foreboding.

Almost like he heard her, Cowboy exhaled.

He looked at her, hands resting on his slim hips.

From his expression, she already had a pretty good idea what he would say.

They were going back to California.

⚜

"Cowboy called in?" Manny looked over from where he and a handful of others stood in front of the large wall monitor.

They were all in the main conference room at the flagship offices of Black Securities and Investigations.

Yarli nodded, her expression grim.

"Lizbeth talked to him. He also just texted me the flight details for him and Angel. They're on their way."

"How much does he know? How much does Angel know?"

Yarli frowned, thinking.

"Probably as little as we do. Maybe a little less," she admitted. She let out a slightly discouraged sigh. "I'll send them what we have so far."

"That won't take long," Reuben commented dryly.

Yarli heard the sarcasm in the human's voice.

She was too agitated to really answer it, at least not directly.

"We can send it encrypted," she said to Manny, still thinking aloud. "At least they'll have the basics. They obviously know Black's transformed into a dragon, and may not be able to transform back. We can tell them that Miri's disappeared... and the suspect in the murders has, too. We can also loop them into the regular communications as this unfolds."

"What about Cal? His girlfriend?"

"Injured," Javier said, looking over from where he'd been listening to something on his headset. "Supposedly the girlfriend, Nina, is mostly fine... but that hasn't yet been confirmed. They tell us Cal has a broken collarbone and is at Kaiser Permanente Hospital in San Jose. She might be there too, under observation, at least. One of the two detectives on the case was injured, too. The man, I think. The police are looking for the suspect—"

"Where is Black?" Luce asked. "Now, I mean?"

Unlike Reuben, the Filipino-American, ex-Special Forces vet looked openly worried.

Yarli gave her what she hoped was a reassuring look.

"Last I heard, they'd spotted him over Alcatraz Island," she told Luce. "He doesn't seem willing to leave the Bay Area... but he also appears to be avoiding places with a lot of civilians. That's done a lot to calm the Pentagon and the military down. It also suggests he wants to transform back, and is likely waiting for help to do so..."

"Miri," Jorji breathed.

Yarli gave the other seer a grim look.

"Yes, Miri," she agreed. "Most likely, he's waiting for her to find him. He might not even know she's disappeared."

She saw Larisse and Luric exchange glances.

"And still no word on where she is?" Luric asked.

"No." Yarli shook her head, once. "She disappeared. We managed to tap the police footage inside the interrogation room, and caught the very beginning of Black's transformation. Miri disappeared just like she does when she's doing those interdimensional jumps of hers. We have to assume that's what happened."

Again, Yarli caught Larisse and Luric looking at one another.

Something in those exchanged looks made her pause. She found herself wondering if the two of them were dating.

Come to think of it, they did seem to know one another well.

There was *something* there, in terms of a connection between them. She had no idea if it was sexual, but it was difficult to unsee, now that she'd noticed it.

They almost looked like they could be related.

Something in the eyes, and the shapes of their mouths.

Yarli cleared her throat.

"As for Black," she continued. "In addition to Alcatraz Island, he's been spotted over a number of state and national parks, and just generally less populated and more rural areas. Reports we've intercepted have included the following places: the Santa Cruz mountains, Mount Diablo, parts of Napa, Mount Tamalpais. Fremont Peak. The Pinnacles. No one's seen him threaten anyone, or do anything aggressive. He's actively avoiding people, and only seems to move on when people or planes approach. It's probably the only reason we've been able to keep things from escalating. Even the military can tell he's avoiding anything even approaching a confrontation... although I imagine they're following him closely on radar and via satellite."

"We need Miri," Manny muttered. "If he's stuck, she's the only one who can do anything about that. We need Miri to get him back. To help him transform back into Black."

"Well, there's not much we can do about that, my love," Yarli said drily.

She heard the edge in her own voice.

From the surprised glances she got, so did most of the seers and humans standing there. It was pretty unusual for Yarli to get sharp at all, with any of them.

It was a lot *more* unusual for her to get sharp with Manny.

Her mate didn't take it personally.

When she looked at him next, his eyes shone nothing but calm. Reaching out, he took her fingers and squeezed them briefly, warmly, before letting her go.

He didn't say anything, but she could almost hear him thinking at her.

It'll be okay, honey. Miri will come back. Then Black will come back, too.

Exhaling, Yarli nodded.

She nodded to her human mate, almost like he'd said the words out loud.

"Sorry," she said.

Manny smiled.

Something in that smile warmed her to her core.

"You know I have a tendency to voice the obvious, love." Manny raised her hand to his lips, giving her fingers a kiss. "I get how that might be irritating right now. So don't apologize. I should keep my rambling, old-man thoughts to myself."

Yarli laughed.

Luric, the medic, glanced between them, his eyes almost suspicious. From his expression, he might have been wondering if Manny and Yarli were speaking together like seers, like Manny wasn't who he claimed to be.

Still watching them both suspiciously, Luric folded his arms across his chest.

It hit Yarli that she didn't like Luric particularly.

She'd never really liked him.

He was a damned good medic, but his bedside manner was shit. He was rude, condescending, and came across as racist to most humans, at least to her.

He also struck Yarli as a uniquely un-empathetic person.

Most of the seers and humans currently standing in the conference room had come back to San Francisco from New Mexico at the same time Yarli and Manny did, as part of the small team helping to transport Charles and secure him safely under the building.

Jorji, a more recent recruit, volunteered to help; he'd originally been in the employ of Charles before he escaped to Black's side due to "ideological differences" with the anti-human cult. Javier, Luce, and Rueben, all humans on Black's team, had come back with them from New Mexico to help with security, as well. All of them planned to return to the White Eagle Resort and Spa as soon as they got the word that the rest of the wedding would be going forward.

The female seer, Larisse, wasn't one of those who came back from New Mexico. Unlike the group who came here from Santa Fe, Larisse hadn't been present at the wedding at all. She'd stayed in San Francisco along with a few unlucky others who missed the wedding because Black needed to maintain a presence here.

Yarli didn't really know her.

They certainly weren't friends.

In fact, most of Yarli's knowledge of Larisse came from *Koh Mangaan*, when the female seer pissed off Black and a few others by constantly hitting on Miri.

Wu, one of Black's senior tactical guys, had come back with them from New Mexico. So had Michelle. Both were human members of Black's team.

Luric also rode back with them from Santa Fe.

The medic seer more or less had to; they needed him to monitor Charles' vitals after he'd been knocked out by the mercenary group, Archangel. They also needed him to make sure Charles was physically cleared to be imprisoned with the others.

Anyway, Nick was their only real health concern in New Mexico, and Nick was a vampire. He was best seen to by vampire medical experts.

Luric was definitely not that.

In fact, Yarli had gotten the strong impression, more than once, that Luric was no fan of vampire-kind, any more than he was of humankind.

He didn't seem to like much of *anyone* who wasn't seer.

He didn't like seers getting involved with non-seers, either.

He didn't like seers mating with humans.

He *definitely* wouldn't approve of seers mating with vampires.

For the same reason, she strongly doubted Luric would willingly treat a vampire like Nick, who was sleeping with a seer, and had in fact *mated* with that seer. She doubted Luric would want to treat *any* vampire, much less be tasked with keeping one alive, but he would have a particular hostility to doing so with Nick.

Yarli had little doubt Luric was Team Dex, all the way.

When it came to Dex shooting Nick with wooden bullets, Luric would definitely be cheering for the bullet, and for Dex himself. Like a number of others on the team, especially those close to Kiko, Luric likely only wished Dexter had succeeded in his attempt.

Of course, most of them would keep that opinion to themselves.

Regardless of her personal views of Luric, however, Yarli was confident that the curmudgeonly medic was solid.

Every seer and human on this team was solid.

They'd all been vetted and re-vetted for security purposes, multiple times over the past few years, usually without their being aware of it.

Yarli had dealt with the security breach with Black's sister.

She had Maryn under house arrest in Cupertino right now.

They had traces and other surveillance on all of the local vampires.

Charles' people were secure in their cages.

They had surveillance on the science team in Poland.

Miri would come back; she always did.

Once Miri came back, she would help Black.

They would deal with the Jacob Mulden problem then.

So why was Yarli so uneasy?

Why did she feel it wasn't safe to speak freely, even here?

She looked at Manny, and found him watching her carefully, his eyes concerned.

After the barest pause, she clicked over onto a secure channel, cutting everyone out except her mate.

"Mañuel, try not to show anything on your face. I want your opinion on something."

She waited until she felt his acquiescence.

Once she did, she spoke again. Like before, she used the subvocals.

"Do you wonder if maybe this is a distraction? Like something else is going on here?" She hesitated, watching his face. "Or maybe something else is about to happen? What do you think? Am I reading this wrong?"

There was a silence.

When Manny answered her, his mouth and throat barely moved.

"You think that's what this is? A distraction?"

She bit her lip. "I don't know. Something feels wrong. Something beyond whatever happened in that police station. I wondered if you felt it, too."

Manny was silent another few seconds.

From his expression, she could tell he was thinking about her words.

He was trying to put logic to what she was asking him.

"A distraction for what?" he said after another beat. "What kind of thing?"

Yarli frowned.

After a long-feeling pause, she shook her head perceptibly.

"I honestly don't know," she said, exhaling.

"You think this Jacob Mulden is working for someone else? Someone connected to Charles' people, maybe? Or the vampires? Brick's people?"

Thinking about that, Yarli frowned.

No. That didn't feel right.

It didn't even feel particularly plausible.

"I don't know," she admitted. "Maybe it's more that I can feel something coming? Maybe it's less about a distraction... more like an opportunity?"

"An opportunity."

Again, he didn't really voice it as a question.

Yarli watched her partner turn her words over in his mind.

Looking at him, she realized something else.

Manny felt it, too.

He felt the same, distant warning bells that Yarli did.

He wasn't just trying to convince *her* it wasn't real.

He was trying to convince both of them.

He was trying to convince himself.

Once she saw that much, Yarli felt that sick feeling in her chest worsen. She glanced around the room, pausing on every face. Like Manny, she tried to tell herself it wasn't real, that she and Manny were just wound up, that all of the events of the past few weeks, with Charles, battling dragons, the wedding, Nick... it was all just getting to her.

In the end, though, she didn't really believe it.

She knew Manny didn't really believe it, either.

13

LOYALTY

C harles' eyes opened.

He stared up blankly, his mind absorbing the reality of a buzzing, sizzling, writhing ceiling of light. It took him a few blinks more to recognize it as the glowing, green, semi-organic electric field of his cage.

His cage.

The cage Miri put him in.

The cage Black put him in.

It was irrelevant, really, which one had done the actual honors in the end. They were both culpable. They were both traitors to their blood and to their people.

He had to hope his people had done what he commanded.

He had to hope the contingency was in place.

Charles didn't know what woke him, not at first.

He sat up slowly on the twin-sized mattress. He looked around the dimly lit space. His body still hurt. He still felt like he'd been run over by a truck, or maybe a tractor.

He rubbed the back of his neck, wincing.

There wasn't much to see, whether sitting up or lying down.

His jailors had done something to make the glass-like walls opaque, presumably so he couldn't communicate with anyone

else, or get any ideas around escape. There was no chance of sign
language here, or even of knowing whether a physical escape
might be possible. He had no idea where his cage lived. This
silent, numb, blank-walled cylinder could be housed inside a
building, on a ship, underground, under the ocean.

He could be on Mars.

He could be imprisoned on another of Miri's alternate
worlds.

Clearly, his niece felt she had to take extra precautions this
time.

Charles couldn't feel anything useful with his seer's sight. He
could feel the living light of the Barrier, but only the parts of it
that existed inside his small cage. That cage was maybe ten by
ten feet on the ground, with a ceiling that stretched roughly
fifteen feet overhead.

He'd already begun to lose track of time.

He guessed he'd been in here for maybe a week.

He couldn't believe that with much conviction, however.

Maybe it had only been a handful of days.

Maybe it had been closer to a month.

He remembered standing before them on the pool deck of
Black's resort in Santa Fe, surrounded by Black and Miri's
wedding guests, their disgusting hangers-on, race-traitors, bloodsuckers, and worms.

He remembered the look on Black's face when he first saw
Charles there.

He remembered the anger in the young pup's eyes.

More than Black, Charles remembered Miri.

He remembered seeing his niece come for him... just like he
knew she would.

He remembered the warm satisfaction he'd felt, watching her
slam into that table after the dragon-seer threw her across the
deck. He'd seen her struggle to regain her feet, obviously dazed
after being tossed aside as though she were as weightless as a
rag-doll.

Then... after that flare of elation lifted him, all-too-briefly...

Nothing.

Charles remembered nothing.

Dimly, he had a remnant of a sharp stab of pain, but he couldn't think about that with much conviction. He might have made that up. He might have hallucinated the pain, hallucinated the unknown attack, simply to give his mind an explanation for what occurred.

He might have made the whole thing up *after* he first woke up here.

All he could say for certain was he lost.

He lost... again.

He lost Black.

He lost Miri.

He lost consciousness.

Everything grayed, went dark.

Charles knew he'd been knocked out in some way, but he had no idea how Black had done it, how he'd circumvented the sight-blocking device Charles wore, the one he got from the lab in Swinoujscie, or how Black managed to circumvent the bigger dragon.

Charles had no idea how Black battled the dragon's telekinesis.

Black *had* done it, though.

Black won. Again.

Charles lost.

Charles knew this because Charles woke up here.

Still, he could not be certain of the contingency. He couldn't be certain that all of his plans had been thwarted. The fact that he couldn't possibly know, that he had no way of knowing if it had worked or not, was maddening.

But it felt like too much time had passed.

The contingency should have taken effect by now.

He had to remind himself that he'd woken up with no idea of how much time had passed, no way of knowing where he was. If he was in another dimension, he likely wouldn't know if the contingency had happened or not. Worse, they might not have any way to bring him back. He had to hope they would. He had to hope they would figure it out. But he might wait here for decades, for centuries, waiting for them to find him.

After all, time worked differently in other worlds.

Could he really have miscalculated so badly?

He had honestly thought Miriam wouldn't take him to another dimension, not after what happened last time. Wouldn't she worry the same thing would happen again? That she'd be felt in those other dimensions, and inadvertently bring something back?

He had counted on her not wanting to risk that again.

Had he been mistaken?

No way of knowing anything now.

He's lost the first round, and he may have lost the second. He might not even know whether he'd won or lost for more years than he could stand to think about.

Charles stood up.

He stretched his arms, stretching his back.

He decided a dream must have woken him.

Nothing else could have reached him in here. The only disruptions he experienced were those created within his own mind. He wouldn't have felt a disturbance in the Barrier or in the physical world outside the cage, even if one occurred.

He stretched his back a few more ways. He did some yoga poses, a handful of sun salutations, some *tai chi*, a few *katas* and other forms from various martial arts he knew. He practiced a few moves and combinations in *mulei*, the main form of seer martial art from the Old World. He went into lotus position and repeated chants.

When he finished, he fell to his back, cushioning his head with his hands.

He did a few hundred crunches.

He did a hundred or so regular pushups.

He was doing knuckle pushups on the cement floor, when, for the first time since he'd found himself inside his silent cage...

Something changed.

Up until now, the only deviations in Charles' days and nights—which he had no way to distinguish, in terms of which were which—were those times he woke up to find boxes of food on the floor. Sometimes, that food was hot.

Soups, pastas, casseroles, hamburgers, French fries, baked potatoes, stir fries, fried chicken, grilled chicken, steamed vegetables, Thai food, goulash.

Sometimes, the food was cold.

Sandwiches, salads, fruit, raw vegetables, dried meat, cheeses, cold cuts, bread, crackers, olives, yogurt... once even ice cream.

Sometimes, the smell woke him.

Sometimes, they didn't leave only food. Charles had found second boxes and bags containing reading material: magazines, nonfiction books, paperback novels. They'd left him clean clothes. They left him soap. They left him toiletries. They'd left him puzzles.

They'd left him blank paper and charcoal so he could write or draw.

It gave him some hope he was still on the version of Earth he knew.

That same possibility also made him more and more certain the contingency had fallen through. Something had gone wrong. Somehow, Black had known. That, or Miri had been the one to figure it out. Somehow, either they or one of their race-traitor infiltrators had stopped things, before the final strategy could be implemented.

After all, no one had come for him here.

Nothing in his world had changed.

Until now.

Charles heard the difference first.

A faint humming, buzzing melody. He heard it grow louder, but only very *very* gradually. It started off like a distant whisper.

Then, slowly, it grew impossible to ignore, until the frequency began vibrating off the walls.

Charles came to a dead stop.

He hung there, supporting his upper body on his knuckles, panting, sweating lightly from exertion, balanced evenly on his fingers and toes. He looked up when the faint noise first began. He looked for the source, his eyes scanning the length of the walls after dismissing the ceiling and floor.

For a long handful of seconds, nothing happened.

Then, slowly, the visuals around him started to change.

The white-gray consistency of the walls began to shimmer and morph, to twist and grow shifting holes, blank spots where Charles swore he glimpsed fleeting images of the other side. It took Charles a few seconds to realize the hard, semi-organic substance of the walls didn't change at all. The glass-like tiles remained exactly the same.

No, what changed was the clouds that filled them.

The substance blocking his view of the other side began to clear.

The clouds were beginning to clear.

Charles pushed himself up with his hands. He knelt on the hard floor, looking around at every segment of wall around him. It wasn't just happening to the tiles on this segment of wall; it was happening to all of them.

He regained his feet slowly, never taking his eyes off the wall.

The clouds turned into vortices.

They thinned and thinned, allowing more and more light to shine through.

The color began to rapidly empty out.

It seemed to take forever before the last wisps finally evaporated, leaving the panes clear, slowly revealing the contours of a gray, featureless room outside that transparent wall.

The wall had turned into a window.

Charles saw two people standing there.

Two very familiar people.

"Luric." He choked on it, barely got out the name. His eyes shifted to the female seer standing next to him. "Larisse."

Brother and sister.

Two of the best infiltrators Charles had ever trained.

Loyal friends of the cause.

Family.

True family.

He looked between them, one face and then the other.

He had recruited and trained them himself, dozens of years ago now. He found them when they first arrived on this version of Earth, maybe ten years after he and his own blood sibling arrived. Back then, the humans had been relatively harmless still. They'd definitely known nothing about seers, or even about their own native non-humans, the vampires.

Now, Karlov (Charles) Andrey Vasiliev, seer name, Faustus ("Lucky") Lucifer, looked at two of his oldest friends, and his heart surged.

The emotion nearly blinded him.

Triumph. Love.

Rage.

Revenge.

A fierce will to finish what he'd started, what he'd spent his whole life fighting to attain, nearly blinded him of all else.

For himself. For his people.

He realized what them standing there really meant.

He hadn't been thrown into another of Miri's primitive, alternate dimensions.

He wasn't under the sea.

He wasn't even on a different continent.

He was in San Francisco, housed at the California Street Building alongside all of his loyal friends and self-created family. He'd been thrown into the same dungeon under Black's head-quarters as the rest of Charles' people—everyone Miri kidnapped in that cowardly way and imprisoned, just so she and Black could hand the world back to the damned worms.

He wasn't yet out of the game.

He wasn't yet dead, or consigned to a desolate wilderness, unable to come home.

He stared at his two friends, and saw them smiling at him.

That was when the full import of their being there really hit him.

The contingency.

They had found a window.

Someone or something had created a window for them, an opportunity to make everything right, to free those who should never have been chained. Whatever it was, it had distracted the seers and humans of Black Securities and Investigations well enough that Larisse and Luric decided it was time.

It was time to end this.

Charles was about to be free.

All of them were about to be free.

The contingency would save them all.

More than that, the contingency would allow Charles to remake the world.

14

OUT OF CONTROL

I gasped, fighting to breathe.

I couldn't pull air into my lungs.

I couldn't breathe.

I couldn't stop myself from falling.

I was already starting to black out.

I could feel my individual cells freezing, turning to ice crystals. I could actually feel it, with an intensity that burned under my skin.

I was dying.

I was really dying this time.

In the few seconds I could see with my physical eyes, before my vision began to blur out, a wash of scarlet, blue, red, yellow, white, and orange filled my view.

Stars shockingly, *shockingly* bright... shockingly beautiful...

Color so vibrant, it made me want to cry.

It was killing me, but it was so incredibly beautiful.

A nebula.

I was inside a nebula.

Those heart-shockingly plentiful and bright and colorful stars spun around me, rotating with my outstretched limbs. Fear blanked my mind. I was the one spinning in an airless sky, nausea roiling my stomach as I tried to breathe, to scream.

There was a flash...

...and I was somewhere else.

I gasped, staring out over a toxic swamp.

The sky was brown and red here, endless, with black clouds.

I looked up from a valley at the base of steep mountains, surrounded by blackened trees. Mold covered the trunks. I saw a lizard bigger than a dog, crawling and writhing over the ground. It looked up at me with bulbous eyes.

There was another flash...

...I was in a desert.

Shocking white sand blew around me and into me like snow and ice.

Eddies swirled into mini-cyclones. Dunes stretched on and on, as far as my eyes could see. I heard a screech. A shadow fell over the crystal white. I looked up, saw an animal like a pearl-white bat, circling overhead.

There was another flash...

...I was somewhere else.

Then somewhere else.

Then somewhere else.

Then somewhere else.

I remembered this.

Even though I hadn't brought those memories back with me at the time, I remembered most of these places now, my mind reacting with the same blank, mindless terror as it had back then. Somehow, I'd been thrown backwards in time, forced to relive how things were for me in the beginning, when I first started making inter-dimensional jumps.

In the beginning, I couldn't control any of it.

I definitely wasn't the one steering now.

I stood in another valley, looking up at mountains that felt vaguely familiar, even as I saw volcanic lava making its way inexorably down craggy, black, smoking slopes.

Pitch black smoke billowed out of a crater on top.

A thick gas filled the air, one I could barely breathe through. It was better than the vacuum of space. It was better than being eaten by an enormous white bat. It was better than the sea of toxic waste. It was better than the graveyard full of skulls and blood. I felt my body warming, beginning to thaw. My lungs were getting enough oxygen to stay alive, but my head pounded, I could barely think...

...another flash, and I was on a city street.

I stood there, naked, as people walked by.

They stared at me.

Their faces glowed under the florescent streetlights, ghoulishly pale, their bodies encased in black material from their necks down to their feet.

I looked up, gasping in smoke and chemical-smelling air.

The buildings stretched so high, they appeared to nearly meet.

I wasn't safe here.

I definitely didn't feel safe.

Even now, people were stopping to stare at me.

I saw lips moving. I heard voices murmuring into headsets, clicking and buzzing their lips as they stared at me with wide, too-pale eyes.

They were reporting me.

I was being reported to the authorities.

My existence here wasn't okay.

I was unauthorized...

...another flash threw me somewhere else.

I lost track of faces, landscapes, civilizations, living creatures.

I have no idea how long I was out there, jumping from world to world, time period to time period, dimension to dimension.

It went on until I felt sick, until I wanted to scream...

It would kill me.

The shock of the jumps alone would kill me.

Even as I thought it, abruptly, with no warning...

It stopped.

It took me a few minutes to realize it had stopped.

I found myself lying on something soft, panting, my body wracked with each breath.

I lay there, in a state of shock. Confusion, terror, an utter lack of comprehension kept me lying there, unmoving apart from those hitching breaths. I don't know how long I lay there. I don't know if I remained conscious for all of it, either. I don't remember any thoughts going through my head. I was sweating, nauseated.

At some point, I realized I was lying on a bed.

Then I realized what bed it was.

Some time after that, I tried to get up.

I crawled over a black and white patterned comforter, to the edge of the mattress.

I managed to crawl off it entirely, not sure how else to get to the floor.

Unfortunately, I landed hard.

I hit into the hardwood floor, landing on my side. About the only good thing I can say of that is that I managed to stop my head from hitting directly into the wood.

I lay there, panting, for a while longer. I don't know how long.

I was gathering myself, gathering strength.

Gathering oxygen.

Then I was crawling on my hands and knees, dragging myself over an expensive rug.

I made it into the bathroom before I threw up the first time.

I threw up on the tile.

Then I threw up in the toilet.

I threw up in the sink.

I threw up in the toilet again.

I think I was in the bathroom for a long time.

I crawled into the shower, and somehow managed to turn on the water.

That helped.

The hot water helped. I might have even dozed off, slumped and sitting on the white tile in the corner of the glass-encased shower.

Eventually, I managed to turn the water off.

When I pulled myself up to my feet, I nearly collapsed.

I opened the shower door. I gripped the edge of the wall, then pushed and launched myself towards the door to the bedroom. I lurched first to the bathroom counter. My body heaved again, wracked with spasms, but there was nothing left in me to throw up. When my stomach finally calmed down, I turned on the water in the sink.

I washed down my vomit.

Then I drank from the faucet.

I drank and drank.

I threw up some of what I drank.

I drank some more.

By then, I could almost think.

I had no concept of how much time had passed.

Using the walls, I stumbled and dragged my way back into the bedroom.

I went to the closet, fumbled for the light.

I managed to wrangle my way into a T-shirt and sweat pants. Both articles of clothing stuck to my wet skin. Still using the walls, I struggled into the living room. I needed to find other people. I needed to find Black.

Just the image of him, flashing in my mind, made me burst into tears.

Then I was screaming for him.

BLACK! BLACK!

Once I started, I couldn't stop.

BLACK! I NEED YOU! I NEED YOU! BLACK! COME HOME!

Tears ran down my cheeks. They blinded me.

I choked on them.

I couldn't remember the last time I'd felt so much.

I couldn't remember the last time I'd missed someone, even him, so much.

Every part of my body hurt.

I fought to calm down. I told myself I was probably scaring him. If he couldn't get to me, if he couldn't answer me, he would freak out. He would panic, and if he couldn't get out of wherever he was trapped, if he couldn't reach me to find out what was wrong, he might do something crazy. He might hurt himself.

Black... please come to me... please. I'm not hurt. No one is killing me, but I need you... I need you to come home... please come home...

Grief blanked out my mind.

It blinded me.

I needed to know where Black was.

I needed to know he was alive.

I needed to know he knew I was alive.

When my vision cleared next, I was kneeling on the pale carpet of the living room. My head was down, my eyes closed. When I opened them again, raising my head, another wave of nausea hit, half-blinding me.

I nearly passed out.

I bit my lip, refusing to pass out.

BLACK! I screamed into the dark. *BLACK! COME HERE! COME HERE! PLEASE BABY COME HERE NOW I'M SO SORRY...*

I felt other presences around me.

Confused. Scared.

They were scared of what they felt on my light.

I didn't care.

I just begged them to bring Black to me.

I couldn't even discern who they were.

I made it to the couch.

I curled up on my side.

I realized again I was in the living room.

Our living room.

It struck me that it was night-time now.

The view out the window was the city at night, showing the Bay Bridge lit up in the distance, and the Ferry Building lit up at the end of the street. I wanted to cry when it really sank in where I was. I was home. I was home in San Francisco, in the living room of Black's penthouse. Our penthouse.

Our home.

Even with how terrified I was, I was so damned happy to be there, I wanted to cry.

Maybe I did cry again.

Crying seemed hard. Exhausting.

Using voice commands, I turned on the television, putting it on the news.

I dragged myself back to my feet. That time, I made it all the way to the kitchen, and found a computer tablet on the counter.

Thank the gods it was plugged in.

I wondered how fried the long-term battery must be, given that the tablet had likely been plugged in for at least a few weeks. Black and I hadn't been back here in over a month. Somehow the tablet got missed. We left it here, plugged in.

Now the battery was probably fried.

Black was a billionaire.

I didn't have to care about this.

I didn't have to care about one tablet, but thinking about it bothered me anyway.

I scrolled through the apps until I found the phone... then Black's contact list. I punched in the front desk for Black Securities and Investigations.

It rang.

I don't know how long it rang.

My mind was still humming with static, still paralyzed with fear.

It rang maybe three times. Maybe one.

Maybe twenty times.

I nearly dozed off, waiting for someone to pick up. I

wondered if I'd accidentally hung up. I wondered if I'd forgotten to hit the call button at all. I started to think no one would be manning the desk, that I would need to find a number of someone here—

—when there was a click.

A breathless, achingly familiar, female voice rose.

"Black Securities and Investigations. To whom am I speaking?"

When I heard the voice on the other end, I finally burst into tears.

"Lizbeth?" I gasped. "Lizbeth...? It's me. It's me."

There was a silence.

"Lizbeth," I said again. "It's Miri. I'm Miri. Where are you? I need you—"

"Oh my God! MIRIAM! Are you all right? Where are you?"

"In the penthouse... I think. I've been trying to reach someone—"

"The penthouse?" Disbelief combined with relief in her voice, and it occurred to me she was practically screaming into the phone line. The call grew muffled but I realized I could hear her talking to someone else. "It's Dr. Fox... Miriam. She's in the penthouse... yes..."

Her voice grew louder.

"Miriam, are you hurt?"

I looked down at myself in the clingy T-shirt and what I now realized were Black's sweatpants. The eagle insignia decorated one leg.

They were dirty, and rumpled, and about four sizes too big on me.

They smelled like him.

"MIRI! Are you hurt, honey? Are you all right? Someone is coming. They heard you yelling for Black and were out looking for you. I had to call some of them back..."

"Black?" I closed my eyes. Pain rose in my chest. "Black..." I half-sobbed his name. "Is he okay? Where is he?"

"He's okay! He's *fine,* honey! He's turning back into a person again. They said he started to turn, not long after they heard you calling for him. They'll bring him back here, as fast as they can..."

"Where is he?"

But Lizbeth was yelling at someone on the other end.

I could feel it now.

She'd always been a one-person command center, but I could really *feel* that now. I could feel her jumping from line to line, coordinating different groups of people, different functions, different tasks, even as she alternated speaking with whoever was in the room with her.

"Miri, honey, they're looking for the doctor. Can you tell me if you're hurt?"

"No..." Fighting to think, I shook my head. "I mean, yes. Yes, I'm probably hurt... but I don't know how. I might not be okay. I can't see anything, though." Fighting to think, I looked down at myself again. "I'm not cut. I'm not shot. There's no blood. I'm weak. I'm probably dehydrated. I might be in shock. I need someone to look at me—"

"They're coming straight over now, Miri," Lizbeth broke in, still breathless. "Someone will be there soon. I'm going to unlock the door from here, okay? Just stay where you are. Someone is coming for you."

I nodded, feeling a relief I couldn't express in words.

I could already feel people coming my way.

"Black?" I gripped the edge of the bar in both hands, leaning all of my weight on the volcanic stone. I wanted to go to the couch, but I knew I wouldn't make it there on my feet.

I could crawl. There was carpet in there.

"Black," I managed. "When will he be here? Are they bringing him back now?"

There was a brief silence.

My heart rose to my throat.

"Lizbeth?"

"He's all right, Miri... he's fine. They've got him in one of the company vehicles. They're on the other side of the Golden Gate Bridge, near Napa. They're bringing him down now, but it'll be a little while. Just be patient, honey... he's okay..."

My heart sank and lifted at the same time, see-sawing violently enough that I felt nauseated all over again. I lost my ability to stay upright and sank down to the carpet, sitting underneath the kitchen counter.

I wanted to crawl to the couch, to pull the cashmere throw blanket Angel gave me for my birthday over me and wrap myself up in it completely.

I wanted Black.

I wanted Black to come home.

I'd never wanted anything so badly in my life.

I was cold. I'd never felt so sick. I must have a fever.

I needed sleep.

I couldn't sleep until I knew Black was okay.

I could still hear Lizbeth over the tablet.

It was the only reason I knew not much time had passed.

Barely any time at all had gone by.

"What happened, Lizbeth?" I said. "What happened to us?"

I heard the front door slam open.

"MIRI?" A voice boomed out over our living room. "MIRIAM! DOCTOR FOX!"

I recognized Manny's voice.

I started crying for real.

"I'll let them explain," Lizbeth said gently. "I'm going to hang up now, Miriam. I'll be over there soon. I'm going to bring you some soup, okay? And some crackers. And some soda. I'll bring you lots of warm drinks."

I nodded, still fighting to breathe through my tears.

"Okay," I said. "Okay. That sounds good."

When she hung up, I set the tablet down on the carpet.

By then, Manny had found me.

He came over and squatted down on the carpet in front of me.

Yarli was with him, along with Luce and Javier from Black's human team, and Jorji from the infiltration team. They stood around me in a circle, then Jorji walked up and he and Luce grabbed my arms. Luce slung a muscular arm snugly around my waist, and Javier caught hold of me from the other side. It felt like five or six people were holding me simultaneously.

They brought me over to the couch.

Then Yarli and Manny were with me.

They took my hands and sat on either side of me, warming me as I sank into the white leather. Someone grabbed the cashmere blanket and wrapped me up in it.

"She's in shock," Manny muttered. "Get another blanket."

He pointed.

"There. In that wall unit. Or check the bedroom."

Javier ran off, following Manny's pointing finger.

"Where the *fuck* is Luric?" Jorji grumbled. "Why can't anyone find him? He didn't go with Cowboy and Angel out there to get Black, did he?"

"No. He's not with them. Jax and Kiko went. They brought Wu, Rueben, and a few of the newer seers." Yarli that time, sounding tense. "I can't get a response out of Luric's headset. Not even on the emergency channel."

Luce sat down in front of me, on the coffee table.

I watched the Filipino boxer peer into my face.

Javier was with her, standing just behind her.

Before I could take a breath, Luric bustled into the room. He walked over to the couch and more or less pushed Jax and Manny out of the way.

Without asking, he began examining my light, checking my pulse, wrapping a blood pressure band around my upper arm. He used a hand-held thermometer to check my temperature, then yelled for someone to go into the bedroom and get me more blankets.

Javier, who was already back there, yelled that he was coming.

The whole time, Manny and Yarli were trying to talk to him.

I was also trying to reach Black.

Black? Are you okay? Answer me!

I could feel a shield around him.

I fought it, forcing my way through.

BLACK?

"Where have you been, brother?" Yarli asked.

I opened my eyes, confused.

Yarli wasn't looking at me, though. She was looking at Luric, her perfect, sculpted mouth set in a hard line. The male seer barely spared her a glance.

"I was downstairs."

"Downstairs doing what?" Manny asked from my other side. "We looked downstairs, Luric. We looked in a lot of places. What floor were you on?"

"What difference does it make?" the medic snapped.

"Why weren't you answering on the emergency line?" Yarli said.

"Do you mind if I do my *jurekil'a* job right now?" Luric half-snarled the words, turning to glare at her. "You can ask me your irrelevant questions later. After I've determined if Dr. Fox is out of danger—"

"I think you'd better answer them now," Manny said.

I fought to stay awake.

I was still trying to feel Black.

I wanted to believe Lizbeth that my husband was okay. I wanted to.

But I so badly needed to really know it.

I needed to hear him. I needed to feel his light.

Black? Please answer me. Please—

Miri? His presence flooded into me like liquid fire, and I could have screamed with relief. *Miri, are you okay? Where are you?*

I closed my eyes. *I'm okay. I'm okay. I'm waiting for you. They said they were bringing you here, I —*

You're all right, though?

I nodded. *Yes. I'm okay. They said I'm in shock. I'm cold. I'm really cold and tired. I threw up a lot. I made a mess in the bathroom —*

Wait. What's happening there? Black's mind grew alarmed, hyper-alert.

I could feel him in the space around me, looking at things, looking at presences, at people, at humans and seers, at where they all were in relation to me, at their living lights. Maybe he was reassuring himself I wasn't alone, that I was with friends.

Miri? Who are you with right now? What's going on?

It hit me how quiet it was in the penthouse.

Up until then, I'd been leaning back into the sofa, eyes closed, fighting not to doze off, fighting to stay awake long enough to talk to Black with my light.

Now that I could feel him, I couldn't make myself let go.

I held onto him with everything I had in me.

I don't know — I began.

Who's there? Is Yarli there?

He sounded panicked.

Something about his fear brought back my disorientation, closing my eyes.

I nodded, feeling sick from the motion.

Yarli, I told him. *Manny. Luce. Javier. Luric just got here. I'm in shock. Medicine. Luric is going to give me medicine —*

I felt Black think about this.

Something was bothering him.

Something was really freaking him out.

I could feel him trying to figure out what it was.

Luric. I felt panic spike in Black's light. *Oh my god, Luric...*

There was the barest pause.

Then Black's light exploded over mine, making me gasp.

GAOS MIRI! DON'T LET HIM DO ANYTHING TO YOU!

DON'T LET HIM! DON'T LET HIM! TELL YARLI STOP HIM STOP HIM NOW!

His words bled together.

Their intensity vibrated my light.

I opened my eyes.

Luric held up a syringe.

He tapped it with a finger as I watched, holding it up to the light.

It all felt like it happened in slow motion.

There was already a rubber strap around my upper arm.

MIRI! Black screamed from the dark. *MIRI STOP HIM STOP HIM!*

I didn't think.

I snatched the syringe out of the other seer's fingers—

—and threw it away from me as hard as I could.

15

A NEW REALITY

The syringe smashed into the wall monitor.

There was a hard *crack* as it broke the glass.

Then the needle fell to the carpet below.

Everyone stared at me.

Everyone stared at me, their eyes comically wide.

The monitor buzzed, fizzed into static... then the picture righted itself.

The news resumed its march along the now-cracked and slightly wet surface. I could hear a reporter talking about a destroyed police station, about people being hurt.

Listening to him made me feel sick.

I lay my head against the back of the white leather sofa, panting.

Adrenaline shot through my bloodstream, all the way to the ends of my fingers, making my voice shake, making my heart jerk sideways in my chest, beating in erratic pulses.

"Black said no."

I gasped out the words.

I looked at Yarli. I looked at Manny. I looked at Luce.

"Black said no. He said no Luric. Nothing from Luric. He said no..."

I felt every muscle in Yarli's arm tense where it pressed to my side.

I felt her move a fraction of a second before she actually did.

I never saw the scalpel until it rose, gripped tightly by Luric's hand.

I felt the protective shield of light Jorji threw over mine.

I felt his arm half-strangle me as he grabbed me from behind the couch. He yanked me up and over the back of it, even as Yarli leapt. All three things seemed to happen at the exact same instant—Yarli's leap, Jorji jerking me violently over the back of the couch, the older male seer with the wavy brown hair who slashed down with the scalpel he held.

I only realized afterward that he'd been aiming for my throat.

He got my arm instead.

He opened up a long line of flesh on my inner arm, making me gasp in pain.

It hurt so bad, I barely noticed Jorji half-strangling me.

I found myself lying on top of Jorji on the carpet.

I could feel him panting under me, even as I heard scuffling and shouting overhead.

Then everything was slowly growing dark.

I realized I was passing out. I fought it, trying with all of my being to stay awake. I didn't want to go unconscious. I didn't want to fall back into darkness.

I needed to know Black was all right.

I needed to talk to him. I desperately needed to talk to my husband.

I needed to stay awake until I could see him, until I could really *talk* to Black...

That was the last thing I remember thinking before I lost the fight.

⚜

P eople were talking near me. At least two people.
Maybe more.

Definitely at least two.

It took me probably ten or so minutes before I was actively listening to either one of them, much less piecing together the full meaning of their words.

"All of them?" a woman's voice asked.

"Ayuh," the male voice answered grimly.

"Can't they track them?"

The male sighed. "Yarli's got people on it now. But they found at least half the implants in sewers already, or crushed by various means. There were even traces of blood down in the basement, so clearly they knew we tagged 'em all when the doc brought 'em in. They cut out those sensors at the first damned opportunity."

"And the seers? They can't find them? Or the vamps?"

The male sighed.

I knew it was Cowboy by then.

I wanted to confirm that, to look at him, but I couldn't quite force open my eyes.

"Ayuh. They're tryin', of course," Cowboy said, exhaling a second time. "But it's a good bet they've already gone underground. We got that one lab in Swinoujscie, but there might be others. Black thought there might be at least one more, somewhere in Asia. We already know they've got some toys we haven't cracked, in terms of being able to shield. And not everything was accounted for, on that island in Poland."

Cowboy sounded tired when he added,

"Yarli seems to think we caught it all too late. They got too much of a head start. And because of that, it'll be damned hard for us to find a single one of 'em, now they've ditched the RFID. Not without some kind of breakthrough on our side. We should have probably done the nanotech thing. It was experimental, but it might've given us options."

There was a silence.

Then I heard Angel sigh.

She sounded even more tired than her husband.

"What about the police?" she said. "Did they find their suspect? Jacob Mulden?"

Another voice joined the other two.

I found I recognized that one as well.

"Not yet," Manny said, his deep voice sounding angry. "They're anxious to speak with Black. They've called four times this morning already."

"Should we wake him?" Angel said, doubt in her voice.

"Hell no," Manny retorted. "They can damned well wait."

There was another silence.

Then Manny spoke again, his voice more subdued.

"They managed to salvage a bit more of the footage from the last part of the recorded interview. The suspect grabbed the two of them, like we saw before, and it looked like something weird happened with his eyes. Like they flashed or something, filled with light. He didn't disappear like Miri, though. He ran for the door. The angle was cut off before, with Black's transformation, but they're now thinking he may have walked out. But no one saw him leave the precinct building... and surveillance didn't pick up anything either. There's been no sightings of him since. They've widened the facial-rec scans all the way down to L.A., and north of Ukiah."

"Could he be dead?" Cowboy asked.

"Possible, but they've been through all the rubble now. No one thinks so—"

Yarli spoke up, interrupting her husband.

"I have Jem conducting time jumps," she said. "From Santa Fe. I've got him on Charles now, but he spent a few hours looking at the scene of the explosion yesterday. When I talked to him just now, he didn't think Mulden was dead, either. He said the light signature flared, not long after Mulden left the interrogation room. He said the signatures felt eerily similar to some of the more complex structures in Black's light."

Yarli's voice grew grimmer.

"...They also felt a lot like that thing in Los Angeles."

"Great," Angel grumbled. "So another dragon."

"Maybe," Yarli said, noncommittal. "Even Jem wasn't ready to say that for sure. I think we need to wait for the boss and Miri to tell us that. No one else will know for sure."

A fifth voice rose.

I started to wonder just how many people stood over my bed.

"We can get a few others in the infiltration team to look at what Jem saw, do a couple more time jumps to verify," Jax said, his calm voice sliding in when Yarli took a breath. "But I find it hard to believe we'll find anything Jem missed. And what Yarli said is true. We need to prioritize Charles. Whatever happened at that precinct exactly, it happened too fast, with too much of the surveillance knocked out, for us to track him down that way. None of us can even get a lock on the suspect's light. With that other dragon, we could see the structures in his light. With this person... nothing. So he might be with Charles anyway. They might be the ones protecting him."

"Black told us the same thing last night," Angel affirmed. "He and Miri couldn't real Mulden, either. From what he said—"

Another voice rose, from a lot closer to where I lay.

"Can you all please shut the fuck up? *Gaos di'lalente...* or at least talk in the other room? You're like a bad dream that won't go away..."

Black's voice came out low, controlled.

At the end it turned into a near-guttural growl.

"Although maybe you don't need to bother with fucking off now," he added coldly. "Since you already woke up my wife, and managed to piss me off..."

Hearing his voice was the thing that finally got me to move.

It got me to open my eyes.

I hadn't realized until then that he was lying next to me.

Once I realized he *was* lying next to me, I felt sick.

Pain slanted out my mind, blanking out the room.

Was he blocking my light? Was he keeping his light from mine?

Was he avoiding me, even now?

Honey, no.

Strong arms wrapped around me.

They pulled me close, squeezing me up against a hard, muscular, blindingly familiar chest. He shifted the angle of his body, then tugged on me again, bringing me over the remaining foot or so of mattress so that most of my upper body rested on top of his. Once he had me where he wanted me, he squeezed me, snuggling me against him.

I hadn't felt so much off him in weeks.

Months, maybe.

I wasn't trying to keep you out, he murmured into my mind. He kissed my temple, then my cheek, caressing and gripping my hair in one hand. *Not like that. I was trying not to fuck with your light. I was trying not to wake you up. I wanted you to sleep.*

His thoughts were lulling, warm, infused with affection.

Not just affection... desire.

As he sent them to me, his light flooded into mine.

Cautious at first, then with more and more intensity.

It went from warm, affectionate, to hot, more liquid... infused with pain.

Gaos, he sent. *Miri. I've missed you so much.*

He held me so tightly I could barely breathe.

It still didn't feel tight enough.

I forced myself to turn my head, to look up at the people standing around our bed.

I saw all the people whose voices I'd heard: Angel, Cowboy, Manny, Yarli, Jax.

I also saw Lizbeth standing there, looking worried.

"She needs to eat something," she scolded, looking around at the others. "I'm going to get the soup I made. I'll just be a minute... don't let her get up until she eats. I want to heat it up again. It's probably cold."

I realized she was talking about me.

I turned over in the bed, so that I was lying more on my side. I was going to call Lizbeth back, tell her I wasn't hungry, but when I moved my arm, I banged it right smack in the middle of the bandage and sucked in a breath.

For a few seconds, the pain was blinding.

"Take it easy," Black murmured, kissing me again. "Lizbeth's right. You need to eat. Stop being so stubborn."

He turned to the others.

Instantly, his voice changed, dropping into that harder growl.

"So?" he said. "We have people looking for Mulden too, right? We're not putting that all on the cops?"

There was a silence.

Then Yarli exhaled. "We have people. Most of ours are looking for Charles."

"What about Archangel? Can we hire them again?" Black asked.

"We've got a message out to them. No answer yet," Manny said.

I could feel Black thinking.

I could feel how angry he was about Charles.

I could feel how angry he was about Luric.

I got glimpses of others who'd left with Charles and his people, including Larisse, who apparently was Luric's full blood sister. They might even be twins. In any case, both had been plants of Charles. Both had been spying on us, reporting back to Charles, for months.

I pulled all of this off Black's light without really making an effort to read him.

"What about the vampires?" Black asked.

That time, his voice sounded reluctant. From that one question I could feel he didn't want to go there, but didn't see us having much choice.

"...Has anyone informed Brick about Charles?"

"He's been told," Manny said somberly.

"And?" Black said.

"Let's just say, he wasn't overjoyed at the news," Cowboy said flatly. "There was a lot of cussing... some of it, I'd guess, from the seventeen-hundreds, or thereabouts. He got downright nasty. Even a bit accusatory. Wanted to know how we could let such a thing happen. How we could have missed two operatives among our people for so long—"

"Which is a damned good question," Black growled.

There was another silence.

Then Lizbeth bustled back into the room, this time holding a tray.

I could smell the soup in the enormous bowl in the center of that tray, even before I realized what she held in her hands.

My stomach growled so loudly, everyone looked at me.

Then they chuckled.

I was glad my empty belly could break the tension for a few seconds, but I knew it wouldn't last. It also didn't really fix anything.

Black helped me sit up against the headboard, and Lizbeth put the tray down in front of me, arranging it right over my lap.

I have to admit, that first mouthful was heavenly.

I'm pretty sure Lizbeth's homemade chicken soup was the best damned chicken soup I'd ever had in my life.

I was still sitting there when she brought me some crackers.

She came back a minute later with a bottle of ginger ale, and some ice. Cracking open the bottle, she poured it over the ice while I continued to wolf down her soup.

I listened to the others talk while I ate.

Really, they were mostly going in circles.

Everyone was feeling angry, disheartened, betrayed—

"Tell the cops I'm coming in," Black said suddenly, his voice blunt. "Tell them I'm up here, that the soonest I can come is probably two hours, but if they can see me then, I'll drive down to San Jose. I want to see his house..."

I swallowed the last mouthful of chicken soup.

"Me too," I said.

Silence.

I plucked a cracker out of the bowl on my tray, picking up my ginger ale with the other hand.

"No," Black said.

I looked at him, munching on the cracker. Swallowing that, I took a sip of the ginger ale. I already felt almost like a person again. I felt like enough of a person, I wanted a shower and clean clothes, and to wash my face.

"Yes," I told him. "I want to come."

I didn't say what I was thinking under that.

I didn't want to let Black out of my sight.

I felt him pick up on the underlying motive there, anyway.

I also felt an equally strong sentiment on him that more or less mirrored my own.

"Yes," he said. "All right."

He threw back the covers, sliding out from behind and under me, and it hit me that he'd acted as my cushion through most of that, holding me while I ate, pulling back my hair so it wouldn't fall into my soup, rubbing my back and the base of my spine.

"You're sure you're okay?" he said, gruff, now sitting on the edge of the mattress.

I finished swallowing my mouthful of cracker and ginger ale.

"I'm okay," I told him, plucking another cracker from the bowl. "I might want a burrito pretty soon. A big one," I added.

Black smiled.

I saw the worry in his gold, tiger-like eyes, right before he aimed a harder stare at the people watching us from the foot of the bed.

"All right, fuck off," he grumbled, motioning at them. "Go out to the living room. We'll be out there in a minute. And call the police," he added again. "Tell them Miri's coming, too. And ask them if there's anything we can do to help them find Mulden."

I heard murmured agreements even as their voices receded, heading for the next room.

Only when it was silent, only when the door had closed and I'd polished off the last of my crackers and ginger ale, did Black speak again.

"We're showering together," he said, gruff.

His fingers stroked mine, even as a flush of pain left his light.

"Then I'm going to change your bandage, okay?"

I looked down at my arm, then up at him, nodding.

"Okay," I said.

"I mean it. We have to be careful." He frowned, watching my eyes. "You could disappear again. You could go back to jumping all over creation... like before."

"You could turn into a dragon," I reminded him.

He nodded, his gold eyes on mine.

I felt him thinking about my words, about both of our words.

"We need to find Mulden," he said. "Before we worry about Charles, before we do anything else. We have to find Mulden. He's the key to all of this."

"And if Mulden's working for Charles?" I said dryly. "Like the last one was working for Charles? What do we do then?"

Black frowned, staring out the tall stretch of bulletproof glass that made up one of our bedroom walls.

He didn't answer.

16

THE SPANISH HOUSE

"Your partner's all right?" Black said, frowning as he glanced at me. He looked back at Detective Cassavetes, his mouth grim. "My people tell me he was discharged. From the hospital?"

"He's all right," she said, smiling at both of us.

"And you're all right?" I asked, frowning faintly.

I still felt a little light-headed, but I'd dozed on the way down from San Francisco, and felt a lot more like myself again.

"I am all right," she assured me. She smiled wider, winking. "I was very lucky, in terms of where I was when your husband changed. It was scary though. No?"

I had to fight not to smile.

I looked at Black, who was looking at the female detective like she might be brain damaged.

I was starting to like her, though.

Figures, Black murmured in my mind.

Oh, I already know you like her, too.

He nudged me with a hand.

Because she's a little like you, doc. And a little like Nick. All three of you pretend to be dingbats, and I'm pretty sure you're all smarter than I am.

I fought not to roll my eyes.

Before I could think of a response, Cassavetes spoke again.

"A lot of people in my precinct, they think I should arrest you," she remarked, that smile still playing around her lips. "But I think you are probably more helpful to me, if I do not arrest you. If we work together."

She paused, leaning down to ring the doorbell of the two-story Spanish-style house.

The three of us had just reached the end of the tiled courtyard leading up to the front door. The courtyard itself was choked with weeds. Half of the tiles were broken or cracked. An old, now-dysfunctional stone fountain had been filled with rusted tools and empty planting pots. Rusted chairs sat around a glass table crusted with dirt, decorated with an empty metal candle holder and a few clay pots.

The house itself wasn't in much better shape.

White paint peeled off the stucco walls in chips and strips. Clay tiles were broken on the roof. I saw holes in a few sections of the stucco, some of them big enough for small animals to go through, including mice, squirrels, snakes, maybe even raccoons.

The painted designs on the tile had been worn down by countless feet, and the finish on the redwood handrails had been worn off by weather. The matching wooden doorframe was pitted and looked like termites had gotten to it.

The screen door was trashed: the frame bent, holes ripped in the metal mesh that wouldn't have kept anything out, not even a large cockroach.

All three of us stopped, listening after Cassavetes pressed the buzzer.

No one answered.

I didn't hear any footsteps, either.

Honestly, the place looked abandoned.

The porch light flickered a sickly yellow color, but I didn't see any other lights.

Cassavetes leaned down to press the buzzer again.

"Can you tell me anything more about this?" the detective asked casually. She straightened, folding her hands neatly behind her back. "Is there anything you would tell me? About what happened in there? During that interrogation?"

"You mean besides the fact that I'm going to have to donate a lot of money to the San Jose Police Department to build you a new precinct building?" Black muttered.

The detective laughed.

Funnily enough, it sounded like a real laugh.

Her question still sounded like a real question, however.

"Besides this," she said. "Besides your inevitable generosity towards the city of San Jose. What else can you tell me, Mr. Black?"

"You saw it," Black grunted. "He touched us... and it turned me into a dragon."

"Outside of your control?"

"Outside of my control," Black affirmed.

"And your wife?" Cassavetes raised an eyebrow, looking at me. "What happened to her was outside of her control as well?"

Black glanced at me, and a worry skated briefly over his gold eyes.

"Yes," he said. "Mulden did something similar to the doc here. Only hers might have killed her. She's damned lucky to be alive. *I'm* damned lucky she's alive. And really, if I was a remotely decent husband, she'd be at home in bed right now, sleeping it off."

I have to admit, the conversation astounded me... on both sides.

I still forgot, sometimes, that we were no longer hiding the fact that we were seers.

Black's frankness surprised me.

The detective's frankness, her utter lack of fear or drama in regards to what Black and I were, might have been even more bewildering than the respectful and shockingly transparent way Black treated her. In the end, I honestly wasn't sure which thing stumped me more... the detective's matter-of-fact questions, or Black's equally candid answers.

"What does that mean?" Cassavetes asked. "What did he do to your wife?"

Black looked at me, his gold eyes clearly deferring the question to me.

Up to you, doc.

I stared at him, not hiding my incredulity.

Is it, though? I asked. *Is it really up to me?*

Who else would it be up to?

You know what I mean. I pursed my lips, staring at him. *Is it really all that safe for humans to know I can jump dimensions to alternate worlds? Not to mention there's a good chance I can time-travel, as well?*

You told that council of humans in Europe what you can do. Didn't you?

I thought about that.

Sure, okay.

In broad terms, I had.

Still, I wasn't remotely certain it was the kind of information we should be sharing with every human we encountered with a cheerful disposition and a matter-of-fact attitude towards our race. I was grateful Cassavetes was seemingly cool about the fact that neither Black nor I was technically human... but I was a lot *less* sure that meant we should induct her fully into the weirdness of the non-human world as we knew it.

At least, not without knowing her a little better first.

Still turning that over in my head, I cleared my throat.

"I have... a different ability," I said, refocusing my gaze on Cassavetes. "It's not like that of most seers. In fact, it's *extremely* unusual."

Cassavetes smiled, glancing at Black. "More unusual than turning into a giant, flying, fire-breathing lizard?"

I blinked.

Then I snorted a half-laugh.

"Okay. Maybe not," I admitted. "Maybe equally unusual, in a different way. Or maybe it really *is* more unusual, but in a somewhat less dramatic way. In any case, it's unusual with a different set of implications." Hesitating, I added, "Maybe the easiest way to describe it is to say I can do a form of teleportation."

Again, this didn't seem to faze her.

She nodded.

Her eyes grew thoughtful, serious, and it didn't strike me as an affectation.

"I figured it must be something like that," she said, still with that genuine-seeming frankness. "Teleportation. Maybe time travel... or some other form of dimensional phasing. Something that allows you to shift in and out of this reality."

I must have just stared at her.

Blankly.

"You disappeared," she explained, smiling into my silence. *"Poof.* If your husband turned into a dragon without his willing it, it seemed reasonable to think this Jacob Mulden must have done something to trigger your abilities, as well."

I honestly had no idea what to say to that.

In the end, I could only smile, exchanging wry looks with Black.

"You know he'll probably offer you a job at the end of this," I told Cassavetes, my smile turning wry. "If he does, and you want it, be prepared to aim high on salary... higher than you think you'll get. Ask for at least twice of what you'd consider reasonable."

Black smacked me lightly on the arm, scowling.

Cassavetes laughed.

It was easy to forget we were standing in front of the door to Jacob Mulden's childhood home, and his last known legal residence.

Maybe we were all just reasonably sure no one would answer that door, no matter how long we stood there, or however-many times we rang the buzzer.

Whatever any of us had been thinking, we all three jumped, stepping back sharply, when the door suddenly swung inward.

⊙⊱⊙

"Hello?" An older woman peered up at us, almost comically small inside the large doorway. She wore cat-framed glasses of pale green plastic, and squinted at our faces through prescription lenses I guessed must be a few years out of date.

"Who are you?" she asked with a raspy voice. "What are you doing here, coming so late at night?"

Everything about her exuded disapproval.

I pegged her age at maybe sixty-six, sixty-seven.

Possibly as low as late fifties.

Possibly as high as early seventies.

Cassavetes stepped easily into the breach.

She flashed her badge, smiling wider as she stepped directly in front of me and Black.

"Do you know a person by the name of Jacob Aaron Mulden?" she said, her voice exuding friendliness. "We apologize for the late hour, but we are here on police business. It is very important that we speak to him."

"Jakey?" The woman frowned. "What's he done wrong?"

"You do know him, then?" Cassavetes prompted.

"He is my nephew." The woman looked behind her, as if expecting someone to be listening to her in the corridor. She looked back at the three of them. "He's not here right now."

"I understand," Cassavetes said. "Could I have your name please, madam?"

"Amanda. Amanda Jean McComber."

"Thank you, Amanda Jean—"

"Amanda. Just Amanda."

"Okay." Cassavetes never lost her smile, or her bright tone of voice. "About your nephew, Amanda... about Jacob. Do you know where he is right now?"

"No. I don't know that." The woman's voice sharpened. "How would I know that? He asked me to come take care of my brother for a few days—"

"He asked you this? To come here?" The detective never lost her smile. "When was this, please? When did he ask you to come and take care of his father?"

"Yesterday?" She frowned. "Yesterday afternoon."

"Did he say why he wanted this?"

"My brother's sick. Jakey's a good boy. He couldn't be here, and someone has to be, so he called me. My brother can't be left alone anymore. Someone has to keep an eye on him... or he doesn't eat. Won't take his meds. I'm the only one close enough."

"Ah." Cassavetes smiled sympathetically. "That was very nice of you. Did Jacob say why he could not be here?"

"He said there was something he needed to do."

"He did not tell you what that something was?"

"No." Amanda's previous disapproval now sounded a lot more like anger. "No. He didn't tell me that."

"And you live in Saratoga, as well?" Cassavetes asked.

"Los Gatos. I have a house with my husband there."

"I see."

I couldn't help noticing the corridor behind her.

The white tile floor was tracked with mud and dirt from layer upon layer of shoe-prints, cat prints, and what could have been coyote prints for all I knew, or possibly a medium-sized dog. The surface looked like it hadn't been cleaned in years, either with a mop or a vacuum. The previously white-washed walls looked gray, and the floor was stacked with newspapers along the side, filling up maybe a third of the walking area.

Even in just those few seconds of us standing there, I could smell mold.

A small table was buried in fast food containers and dirty glasses.

I'd seen the signs of this kind of thing before.

Whether the shut-in father and son were full-blown hoarders

or simply dysfunctional in a combination of ways, they'd clearly been missed by caseworkers in social services.

I wondered how much of that had to do with living in a falling-down mansion in one of the most expensive suburbs of the Bay Area.

"How is your brother, ma'am?" I asked politely. "Is he well?"

Amanda's eyes jerked off Cassavetes and onto me.

"What business is that of yours?" she snapped. "I already told you he was sick."

"Could we speak to him, perhaps?" Cassavetes asked. "Your brother?"

The woman aimed her glare back at the detective.

"No. You can't. He's asleep right now."

Cassavates' polite smile never wavered. "It is not possible to wake him?"

"No. It's not."

My eyebrows rose a little.

If Jacob Mulden had been living in *this* for most of his life, that might explain a lot about why his personal accomplishments had been noticeably stunted, compared to his peers.

"Do you know Rodney Gallows?" I asked next. "He grew up next door to Jacob and your brother, didn't he?"

Amanda's stare grew deadly.

"Rodney Gallows was a selfish, greedy, *lying* boy who didn't give a damn about his friends once he became Mister Super-Duper Important."

I didn't bother to point out that both of these "boys" had recently turned forty.

"You know he's dead?" I asked. "Rodney?"

"I know." She tilted her head, her white curls catching the light in the dingy hallway. "I heard it on the news. Everyone around here knows. That doesn't make any of what I said less true. Rodney was a smooth-talker all right, but he was a liar, with no sense of loyalty. He never helped my nephew once... his best friend. He treated him like garbage once he no longer had any use for him..."

"I am sorry to hear that, Amanda," Cassavetes said, her voice neutral.

"Are you trying to pin that on my nephew? Are you trying to make it so Rodney's dying is Jake's fault?" The woman stepped closer, glaring into our faces. "Because Jacob would never hurt a fly. He's a good boy. He was nothing but loyal to Roddo, and Roddo threw him under the bus. The second he got some money in his pocket, he disappeared..."

She took another step forward, her dark eyes burning with anger, even behind the glasses.

"If I were you, I would look into Roddo's shady business dealings overseas. Everyone knew he was big into China. He would take money from anyone. Communists. Child traffickers. He likely deserved whatever came to him."

I glanced at Black.

I could see from his eyes that he was reading the woman in the doorway. His flecked gold irises were slightly out of focus. A faint frown toyed at his lips.

Anything? I asked him quietly.

This family is sad, Black remarked grimly. *Depressingly sad. Other than that, no. Everything she knows about Jacob aligns with the person we saw talking to Cassavetes and Wood before he changed into that other thing. Before he asked to speak to us. All of her memories align with the man we saw interviewed at the outset.*

So she never met the dragon?

I highly doubt it. From what I can tell, she hadn't noticed any change in him at all.

I nodded, more to myself.

That felt true to me, too.

Is there any point to us trying to find out more about Jacob Mulden? I asked next. *Meaning the human, non-supernatural version? I'm not sure anything we learn about that version is going to help us track him down. Or even give us any insight into Rodney Gallows' murder.*

I glanced down the dingy, newspaper-filled corridor, grimacing.

Clearly, this whole family needs some kind of psychiatric intervention. I felt a whisper of Black's sadness about the family when I added, *And a home visit by caseworkers to assess his father. But in terms of the murder, or what happened to you and me, I'm not sure we're going to get much that's useful out of the people who knew him before.*

I felt Black think about this.

Cassavetes was pulling out a business card now.

She handed it to Amanda with a smile.

"We might need to speak with you later—" she began.

Black cut her off.

"Could we see his room?" He blurted the question, his deep voice shockingly loud. "Jacob's. Could we see where he sleeps?"

Amanda looked at him.

I don't know if it was because Black is male, because Black is so strikingly, disconcertingly, annoyingly handsome, because Black was using his seer's light to push her, or if it was just some afterglow effect of the Black "aura" more generally, but for the first time, Amanda didn't look or sound angry.

She even softened her voice.

"What for?" She pursed her lips, gazing up at Black's gold eyes. "What do you hope to find in Jakey's room?"

Black rested his hands on his hips.

"We would like a better idea of what kind of person he is, Amanda."

Black's voice was as carefully polite as Cassavetes' had been, if several shades more serious and several shades *less* openly friendly.

If Cassavetes was a golden retriever, Black was a German Shepherd police dog.

"Jacob was very helpful to us earlier. Before the 'accident'..." Black added, giving Amanda McComber a knowing look as his fingers made air-quotes. "Frankly, we're worried the explosion may have been done to silence him. We really need to talk to him again. We're worried about him, Amanda. This is a *murder* investigation after all... and we don't know for certain if Jacob is safe. We want to get to him first."

I fought not to snort a laugh.

Trust Black to know exactly what to say to feed into her conspiracy-theory-loving heart.

"You think Jakey's in danger?" Amanda asked.

Her voice sounded alarmed, but I couldn't help but hear the excitement there.

"You think whoever killed Roddo might be after Jakey now?"

Black raised a hand. "We don't know that."

"But you think he knows too much? That he might be next?"

Her eyes widened more with each passing second.

I felt more of that excitement vibrating through her living light.

"Could we see his room, Mrs. McComber?" Cassavetes asked. "Please? Any clue we find could help us keep your nephew safe."

I had to fight not to snort a laugh that time, too.

But I didn't dare.

I kept my face serious. Impassive.

Like a rogue agent set to take down the Deep State.

I watched conflict roil Amanda's mind.

I watched her weigh family loyalties against her beliefs on how the world worked, who the good guys were and who the villains. Amanda McComber pressed her lips together, staring at each of our faces as she tried to decide whether she wanted to involve herself with us, if she wanted to help the police, how badly she wanted an audience for all of her personal theories on what happened to Rodney and why, and how her nephew fit into this story.

In the end, the temptation Black handed her was just too much.

She opened the door wider, stepping backwards.

"Okay," she said. "But not for long."

17

THE OTHER MAGIC

"Why did you want to see in here?" I murmured. I glanced over my shoulder to make sure Amanda McComber didn't hear me. "What are we looking for, Black?"

I wandered around the edges of the blue-painted room, occasionally leaning down to look at pictures or read the spines of books. Like the rest of the house, it was musty in here, but marginally neater than most of what we saw on our way to reach it.

Jacob had claimed the second-largest of four bedrooms, according to his aunt, who still hovered near the open door. It lived just off the inner courtyard with its algae-choked pool, and deck chairs that looked like they'd probably collapse if you tried to sit in them.

The house was big, which was about all I could say for it.

The one story, sprawling, Spanish-style ranch house had to be over three-thousand square feet. It might even be over four-thousand.

The aunt told us Jacob's father had been an engineer, one of the success stories in the first wave of tech engineers and defense contractors who built Silicon Valley.

She didn't tell us what happened to the money, but I could guess.

I looked up at the ceiling, which was covered with those tacky, glow-in-the-dark stickers of stars, along with a few holographic images of nebulas and planets.

I couldn't help but flash back to where I'd been sent when I first lost control of my abilities. The memory brought a shock of fear, coupled with a surge of nausea, that feeling of no control, of being lost. I remembered the certainty that I was dead... the unquestioning knowledge that my body and brain were already dying.

I grimaced at the memory, then tried to shove it away.

Jerking my eyes off a particularly vivid image of a nebula on Jacob Mulden's wall, one shaped like a giant eye in space, I fought against another wave of nausea.

"What are we looking for?" I asked again.

Black didn't answer.

I knew him, though.

He really did seem to be looking for something specific.

I glanced at Amanda McComber, Jacob's aunt, when Black didn't answer me. I wondered if he didn't want to say much out loud with her listening to us.

That didn't explain why he didn't answer in my mind, however.

Normally, he would have just answered in my mind.

I saw Cassavetes going through drawers in Jacob Mulden's desk, even as Black stood in front of a walk-in closet filled with props for Jacob's magic shows, including metal rings, a number of different-sized trick boxes, a trick mirror, lengths of rope and crepe flowers, not to mention a larger box, which had to be for—

"That's his 'saw a man in half' trick," Amanda said, grunting. "The police had an interest in that one already. They dusted every inch of that thing, and sprayed it all over, looking for blood." She gave me a suspicious look when I glanced her way.

"I thought you were police," she added icily. "Wouldn't you know that already? You would have all that stuff, wouldn't you?"

I glanced at Black, then Cassavetes, but neither stopped their intense scrutiny around the room, or their going through various drawers and feeling over the undersides of shelves and drawers.

The two of them seemed to be adopting the same strategy of selective deafness.

As for me, I still wasn't sure what I was looking for.

This felt mostly pointless to me.

I didn't like Aunt Amanda particularly, but she had a point.

The police likely would have found anything relevant in here already.

If Jacob had used that exact box to cut Rodney Gallows in half, there would have been at least trace amounts of blood and DNA on it still.

"Give me a profile on him, doc," Black said. He rested his hands on his hips, still standing in the doorway of the walk-in closet. "Tell me about the magic. Why magic?"

I frowned.

I glanced back at Amanda McComber, who scowled, folding her arms.

Looking away from her, I fought to think.

"Magicians are a subculture like any other," I told him. "I don't know a lot about magicians *specifically,* but like any subculture, their activities are chosen because they convey meaning to the participants. A sense of place in the world. A sense of distinct identity."

"A way of being special," Black said. "But why magic *specifically,* doc?"

I saw Cassavetes listening to us now, even as she flipped through more papers she'd found inside Jacob's desk.

"Usually magic is more about the prestige, about fooling people," I said, thinking out loud. "It's about being the smartest person in the room. At least when it comes to professionals.

People who take illusion work seriously, who make it a career, generally are very competitive. To be any good at it, you have to think a lot about manipulating people. About outsmarting them... but also how their minds work."

"Does that sound like Jacob Mulden to you?" Black said. "The Jacob Mulden we met? Before he turned into that other thing?"

"What 'other thing'?" Amanda asked from the door.

We all ignored her.

"Not really," I admitted. "But feeling powerless can be a strong motivator, even for someone who isn't particularly aggressive. His ego seemed healthy enough. He also seemed to be fairly entitled... even superior in some ways. He prided himself on having a certain code. It's possible magic was his way of feeling less invisible."

"Or it could have been more of a hobby, no?" Cassavetes asked, still bent over Jacob Mulden's desk. "A way for some fun?"

I nodded. "It could be."

"But you don't think so?" Black said.

"I didn't say that. I'm not sure what I think. But 'fun' didn't seem to be a big motivator for him. I suspect it was more than that." I watched Black's face. Studying his gold eyes, I frowned. "You have something in mind, though. You're not really asking me what I think."

"I *am* asking you," he said. "But yes, I have something in mind."

He was inside the closet now.

I followed him, venturing deeper into the musty space.

I could hear him knocking on the paneling inside the closet.

"What are you looking for?" I asked, moving closer so I could watch him explore the inside of Mulden's closet. "What is it you have in mind?"

Just then, Black hit one of the panels and it *thunked*.

I heard the deep, hollow sound, and flinched.

It was noticeably different from the others he'd knocked on.

He glanced over his shoulder at me, giving me a grim look, then felt over the edges of that panel until he found a latch at the bottom part of that piece of wood.

The top popped open.

Immediately, Black pulled it down.

Once he got that part open, he pulled down the panel next to it.

Then he pulled down a third one.

Cassavetes had moved over to the mouth of the walk-in closet by then, too. Now she whistled, staring at the opening Black had uncovered. She brushed past me to get a closer look, walking over to stand next to him as he stared into the dark.

"It's a door," she said, genuine wonder in her voice. "How did you know that was there?"

Black didn't answer her.

From behind us, Amanda's voice rose, growing shrill.

"Hey! You can't be in there! I said you could *look* at his room. I said you could *look*... not dismantle the walls to go on some kind of treasure hunt!"

Her voice grew more angry, but I heard a thread of panic there, too.

"You don't know when that was put there!" she snapped. "There's no proof Jakey did it! You can't be in there... no one gave you permission!"

"We can, actually," Cassavetes told her. "We can be here. We showed you a warrant for the house this morning. It covered the entire house. As you said, the police have been through all of this already... but them missing something does not mean it is not covered by the warrant."

"So why did you ask me then? Why bother if you're going to pull your government crap on me?"

"We were being polite," Cassavetes said cheerfully.

Amanda glared at her, but didn't seem to have a good answer to that.

She opened her mouth and closed it a few times.

Then, after standing there a few seconds more, she backed towards the bedroom door.

"I'm calling my lawyer," she snapped.

"You do that," Cassavetes said.

Black had already finished pulling the loose panels out of the wall, stacking them out of the way of the opening. Bending down, he angled himself sideways and slid through the opening. I'd moved closer by then, and I followed directly behind him. I felt and heard Cassavetes following behind me.

"Watch your step," Black warned. "There are stairs down here. It goes underground."

It struck me that Jacob Mulden was tall, too, and would have had to squeeze himself into that five-foot space, just like Black did.

"What can you see back there?" Cassavetes called to Black. "Is there a light? Do you need a phone light?"

"I can see. Use a light if you need to. I'm going down."

Black was already descending down the stairs.

Cassavetes turned on her phone light.

She aimed it down a short series of steep, cement steps. Out of consideration for me, she shone it past her own feet, in front of both of us, so I used the same light to walk down the maybe eight or nine stairs below the house.

I didn't stop until I reached the dirt floor at the bottom.

Just then, there was the sound of a match, and Black's fingers grew visible.

He held a wooden match in one hand, which he used to light a white candle on a low table against one wall. He lit another candle, then another, until he had seven of them burning over the wax-covered wooden surface.

The space opened up more than I expected.

Now that we were down the flight of stairs, I had plenty of space above me, and roughly eight feet around me, in the shape of a circle.

"Mind the floor," Cassavetes murmured.

I looked down at where she was still shining her phone's flashlight app, and realized a pentagram was drawn there, with the face of a dragon in the center. More candles had been positioned at each of the pentagram's points.

"Wicca?" I asked, frowning.

"There are a few different systems here," Cassavetes said. "I see some runes from Nordic religions, some Egyptian hieroglyphics. There is also that..." She pointed at a mark that might have been in blood, or possibly rust-colored paint. "That is from Aleister Crowley magic, I believe. And some of this is from Golden Dawn..."

Black glanced over his shoulder at her.

His eyebrows rose slightly at her explanation.

Then he motioned her over to the table where he stood.

Not table, my mind corrected.

Altar.

"What about this?" he asked her, motioning over the collection of artifacts that covered the painted wood. "What do you make of this?"

She walked up to stand next to him.

When I joined them, all three of us stood in a line, taking in the crystals, feathers, totems of various kinds, animal skulls and other bones, including something that looked like it had come from a human cadaver. I saw a canine fetus in a jar, maybe a dog or a wolf pup, and another fetus that looked distinctly human.

I grimaced, putting a hand over my nose and mouth instinctively.

"What the fuck?" I said.

"This is like the floor, only more so," Cassavetes said. "A hodge-podge of systems. Like the books. Some of this, I have never seen before. There are markings and characters that do not match any belief system or group I have encountered."

I hadn't noticed the books until then, but now I followed where Cassavetes pointed. The light from her phone illuminated a wide series of shelves, ten levels high, covered in books with leather spines. I scanned titles and authors, but only recognized about half.

I could have sworn some of those spines had seer writing on them.

They do, Black confirmed. *They are books of the old myths. I have no idea how a human could have come across something like that.*

I leaned closer, now using my own phone's flashlight.

"*The Clavicule of Solomon,*" I read aloud. "*The Book of St Cyprian. The Book of Shadows...*"

"That last is Wicca," Cassavetes said. "The foundational text."

"*The Book of Honorius,*" I continued. "*Psychic Protection Spells. How to Summon Demons. The Spear of Destiny. Ghayat al Hikam. The Origins of The Mythos Three. The Dragon Rouge. The Black Pullet. The Galdrabok. Jung's Red Book...*"

"He is all over the map," Cassavetes observed.

She moved closer to me to read the titles alongside me.

"I have heard of many of these," she explained. "But they do not come from the same systems at all. Some are generally viewed as entirely incompatible. And there are hundreds here, see...? How did he read all of this? Is this all he did?"

She aimed her flashlight to show me further stacks of books on the floor.

Some of the books looked like they were molding in the damp air.

"But this is not like magic shows," Cassavetes said, frowning. "It seems our friend Jacob is trying to do *actual* magic in here, yes? Not tricks to fool people, or to make himself feel smart. He is trying to perform spells... actual spells. He is trying to manipulate not only people, but reality itself. Possibly to conjure other beings."

She looked up at Black.

A thoughtful expression rose to her elfin face.

"That is what you meant before, yes, Mr. Black? That these tricks of his, what he performed at strip clubs and small cheap venues and children's parties... these were less his interest. His aim was more in the display of *real* supernatural abilities? He wishes to be Merlin, yes? The man who can create his own world?"

Black nodded, glancing at her.

He looked over her head at me.

I found myself understanding where he was going with this.

"You think he conjured this thing," I said. "Whatever it is that possessed him?"

There was a silence.

Then, almost reluctantly, Black shrugged.

"Maybe?" he said, holding up his hands. "Let's just say, I wonder if he left the door open for something a bit nasty to walk through. Something bigger than he could handle."

Glancing at Cassavetes, as if not sure how much he should say around her, he added,

"I've been kicking a theory around for some time now, doc. I've wondered if maybe these 'dragon' presences are more like a possession. Not like some intermediaries, where it's something you're born with, like my cousin and his wife... but instead something that *uses* us. Something that borrows our bodies and light for a set period of time."

He met my gaze, his gold eyes meaningful.

"What if the dragon isn't a real part of him at all? What if that presence simply *uses* corporeal beings as a means of manifesting in the material plane? Humans, seers, vampires... whatever it can habit. It uses us as a vehicle of sorts."

"So you *do* think it's a dragon?" I said. "Whatever's in Jacob Mulden?"

"Again... maybe?" Black shrugged his broad shoulders. "This is all just a theory at this point, doc. I honestly have no idea if it's got any merit to it at all."

"Is this true of you?" Cassavetes asked.

It hit me that she'd been looking between us, listening, as me and Black spoke.

"Did you attempt to conjure one of these things?" Cassavetes pressed.

Black looked at her, hesitating.

Then he looked at me.

Somewhere in there, he seemed to make up his mind.

He decided to just tell both of us everything.

"Not me," he said. "But someone in my life did. Someone who had power over me once."

Black looked at me, his expression grim.

"Johan," he said. "Back on Old Earth. He did a lot of rituals. They were considered religious on that world, but here, most people would probably equate them to conjurings, or spells. I thought it was all a bunch of superstitious hoo-ha at the time, but he was really obsessed with manifesting the 'One God,' as he called him. He was obsessed with the dragon spirit in particular. He also associated it with me in some way—"

"What is this 'dragon' thing you two keep speaking of?" Cassavetes asked. "Is this like a spirit? A demon? Is it how you transform into this animal you turn into?"

Black looked at her.

Again, he seemed to make up his mind.

"I honestly don't know," he said frankly. "I just know it feels foreign to me. It always has. And I have reason to believe it didn't start off as a part of me, but was something that became 'attached' to me later... when I came through the portal."

"The portal?" Cassavetes pressed.

"The door I fell through. What brought me to this world in the first place."

Cassavetes nodded, her brow furrowed.

I frowned alongside her, thinking about all of this.

I remembered my sister, Zoe, being into all this stuff when we were young.

I also thought about how alien that "Coreq" presence felt on Black.

He'd never really admitted to me before that he'd never felt that, that Coreq presence, before he came to this version of Earth.

At the same time, I worried it might be wishful thinking on his part. Was he trying to convince himself that "Coreq" was something he could separate out of his light? Or maybe he just hoped to learn to control it in some way, to keep it from harming either of us?

"Something like that maybe," Black muttered.

My eyes rose to his.

He met my stare, a faint frown on his lips.

After the barest pause, his eyes drifted away. He went back to looking at the wooden altar covered in wax, and all of the jars and parts of dead animals and humans encircled with crystals and semi-precious stones.

For a few seconds more, the three of us just stood there, taking all of it in.

Then Cassavetes broke the silence.

"So how does this help us find him?" she asked, frowning faintly. "This is all very interesting, do not get me wrong, and maybe good information on *what* he is... but how does it help us now? With *where* he is? With what he will do next?"

She didn't sound like she was complaining.

I more got the impression she really wanted this to be the key to finding Jacob, but she couldn't figure out how to use the information we'd just uncovered.

Black might have been thinking the same thing.

He turned to Cassavetes, then to me.

"Either of you know any witches?" he said. "Any good ones?"

He didn't sound like he was joking.

There was another silence.

Then, slowly, a smile grew over Cassavetes' face.

"I might, actually."

I was still thinking, when I nodded reluctantly as well.

"I might, too," I admitted.

Black stared at me a second too long, then nodded.

"I say we go with the vampire witch." He gave me an apologetic smile, still looking at me even as he addressed his words to Cassavetes. "What do you think, detective? Vampire witch? Or human?"

Cassavetes seemed to think about the question seriously.

Slowly, a smile grew on her delicate-featured face.

"I think vampire," she said, decisive. "Sounds like a two for one, to me."

"I agree," Black said, still watching me cautiously.

I didn't answer.

I also didn't tell them they were wrong.

18

OXFORD

B lack opened the driver's side door, jerking me out of my
doze.

I opened my eyes just in time to hear the tail end of his
phone call.

"...All right," he said, gruff. "See you down there."

He pressed the button to hang up his phone, sliding the
device into an inner jacket pocket as he climbed into the driver's
seat next to me.

His gold eyes studied my face, as if he was still trying to
decide how I felt about all of this.

Before I could say anything, he reached for me, leaning over
to where I sprawled in the shotgun seat. His fingers caressed a
few strands of hair out of my face, stroking my cheek.

He looked and sounded worried now.

"Were you able to sleep at all?"

"I'm okay, Black."

"That's not what I asked. Did you sleep?"

Black had more or less demanded I try and catch some zzz's
in the front seat of the car while he made the phone calls we
needed to make.

I'd tried. I really had.

I closed my eyes, trying my damnedest to do as he asked, but I hadn't had much luck, even inside the mostly-soundproof, toasty warm, and deathly silent car. Instead I watched him pace on the street in front of the parked Bentley.

I had no idea how many people he'd called.

I didn't try to follow any of the conversations.

That said, I could see him clearly enough.

Black left the SUV near the mouth of the quiet *cul-de-sac* where Jacob Mulden's house lived, right at the base of a wooded open space surrounded by golden cow pastures. He'd opted not to drive us anywhere until after he made his calls, so we remained exactly where we had been, parked at the very end of the mountain road that led up here, right under a streetlight.

Cassavetes had left in her own car nearly an hour ago.

"Honey?" he asked again. "Did you sleep?"

"Not really," I said. "But I really am okay, Black."

"You're not," he said. "I can feel it."

I considered arguing, then didn't.

Anyway, there was no point in denying it. Whatever Jacob Mulden had done to me and my living light, I was still feeling the effects.

I still felt pretty crappy.

Instead of insulting Black by lying about it, I changed the subject.

"So?" I said. "Did you get ahold of them? Are we doing this tonight?"

Black continued to study my face, worried, for a beat longer.

Then he must have forced himself to let it go.

He nodded, making the leather squeak as he leaned back. He combed a hand through his black hair and rearranged his bulk in the driver's side seat.

"Yeah," he said, sighing. "She's going to meet us in an hour. They gave me a location, here in Saratoga. A Japanese garden not far from downtown? She said it's pretty close to where we are now. It's closed, of course," Black added. "But Zoe claims it'll be quiet. And Brick said nothing's likely to be open right now, anyway... nothing suitable for this. He also offered up a cemetery... a bar downtown... and the local Dennys, which is twenty-four hours. I figured the Japanese Garden was the best of those."

I grunted.

A cemetery.

That sounded like Zoe, all right.

I was a little surprised my sister hadn't held out for that.

Black exhaled again, closing his eyes briefly.

"I offered to go back to San Francisco. But your sister said no. She didn't want to come to the California Street Building, not after the Nick thing, and I guess I can't blame her. Anyway, we should probably stay down here tonight, since we're working with Cassavetes. I'll have someone book us a hotel... unless you'd rather go to the house in Santa Cruz."

He gave me another piercing look.

"Speaking of which, I'm fucking *starving*. We have a little time. Want a burrito?"

I snorted a laugh.

He prodded my arm, half-teasing but mostly serious.

"Even more than me, you should eat something," he said. "We probably have an hour. Anyway, if it comes down to it, we can bring it with us."

"Aren't you worried that will make them hungry?" I joked.

"No," Black said, deadpan. "They're vampires. Real food won't make them hungry. It's more likely to nauseate them. Which I'm okay with."

I grunted a little, smiling, but my mind remained mostly elsewhere.

Zoe.

We were going to meet my little sister, Zoe.

Tonight.

To talk about black magic.

Black insisted on being the one to make the call.

Maybe that was weird, him calling my sister for me, but

truthfully, I was relieved as hell when he offered. I absolutely did not want to be the one to make that call.

Anyway, he'd really called Brick, the vampire king, at least initially. Brick and most of his entourage, as it turned out, were already in California. Apparently they'd all come back here after the wedding. Knowing Brick, he'd come back to make sure we did as we said, and imprisoned Charles in a way that he would actually *stay* imprisoned.

Which we'd failed at, as it turns out.

I knew Brick had argued for killing Charles on the spot.

Just cutting his throat... while he was still unconscious.

I knew he was likely still pissed we hadn't done that.

In all honesty, I couldn't even entirely blame him.

Either way, when he lost that argument, Brick opted to leave New Mexico with most of his people. He left a few vamps to watch over Nick, including his most skilled medical types, those who specialized in vampire physiology and medicine. He even left his own personal physician, or so he told me.

Then he gathered up the rest of his vamps, and all of them boarded a private plane with the windows blacked out at roughly three in the morning.

He brought his people here, to the Bay Area.

Which again, probably made sense.

It's not like they were invited to the seer portion of the wedding ceremony. As far as I knew, the only vampire going to *that* was Nick.

Also, come to think of it, Brick might have intended to kill Charles anyway.

He probably figured it was better to ask forgiveness than permission.

If that had been Brick's plan, he'd waited too long.

Pushing Brick's machinations, along with Charles and our missing seers out of my mind for now, I placed my focus back on Jacob Mulden, on what we'd be doing tonight.

I didn't know if Black had spoken to Zoe directly.

I didn't really want to know, so I didn't ask.

"Where's Cassavetes?" I said instead. "Is she coming to this?"

"Yes," Black said. "I told her to meet us there. That's who I was just talking to." He looked at me, his gold eyes careful. "You know, we don't have to do this with Zoe, doc. Cassavetes said we could go see her person tomorrow, if we ended up needing another witch. The person she knows, the one she thought might be able to help us with this... she lives in Santa Cruz. So it's just over the hill."

"Zoe's fine, Black."

"I'm just saying. We don't have to do it this way. We have options."

I nodded. "I appreciate that. But I'm fine. We can use Zoe."

Black continued to study my face, though, worried.

"What about Cassavetes?" he said. "Are you all right with her being there? With your sister?"

My sister the vampire, I thought, thinking the part he didn't say.

I tried to really answer him that time, though, to think through his question objectively. I thought about Cassavetes, who already somehow knew more about me and Black than a lot of people on our team. It struck me as odd, not for the first time, that we were trusting her so much. Black had more or less already inducted her into the seer-secret-handshake club.

But I didn't feel any red flags.

On the contrary, I didn't feel any red flags about Cassavetes at all, which is maybe what made it all so weird.

"I know." Black exhaled, staring through the windshield. He turned the key in the ignition, bringing the rumble of the SUV's engine to life, then paused, resting his hands briefly on the steering wheel.

He turned to look at me.

"That happened for me with Cowboy, too, doc. Even in prison." Thinking, he added, "Some people just have that, I guess. That thing. A *simpatico* thing."

"I like her, too," I agreed.

Thinking about that, I exhaled.

"But we should probably vet her," I added. "You know. For real vet her. Given Charles now being on the loose. Given Luric and Larisse—"

"I've got Yarli working on it. So far, nothing. She's clean."

There was a silence.

Then I snorted.

I couldn't help it.

"Of course you have Yarli on it," I murmured.

"Would you rather I *didn't* have Yarli on it?"

"No." I shook my head.

I was thinking about Zoe again, though. I couldn't help but think about Zoe. Zoe had been completely obsessed with magic and spells and everything to do with the occult as a kid. It was unlikely that interest had evaporated entirely, maybe especially given what she was now.

Maybe that was dumb, though.

Maybe this would be a waste of time.

It was entirely possible she no longer cared about such things.

"No. She does," Black said. "She was really interested in talking to us about this." He took the SUV out of park, glancing at me as he took his foot off the brake, easing us off the curve and aiming the Bentley down the hill. "She's been studying it for decades now, apparently. She even got a degree in it... a Master's. Oxford, I think Brick said."

I stared at him. "What?"

"Yeah." Black quirked an eyebrow. "Weird, right?"

I nodded. I couldn't help but frown a little.

Maybe her being more similar to how I remembered bothered me more.

Maybe her having a Master's degree bugged me.

After all, if she was the same, why hadn't she ever contacted me? She could earn a Master's degree at Oxford, but couldn't pick up the damned phone?

Black laid a warm hand on my thigh, massaging my leg.

Somehow, his touch only brought up the emotions more, though.

I closed my eyes. I fought to push it all out of my mind.

Tonight definitely wasn't the night to get into all of that.

"A burrito, huh?" I said, my eyes still closed. Leaning into the headrest, I thought about Black's suggestion. "I could do a burrito."

When I turned my head, opening my eyes, he gave me one of his killer grins.

It almost, but not quite, distracted me from the flicker of relief I saw there.

"Good," he said, deadpan, turning the wheel as he accelerated around a curve. "Because you're eating one, wife, whether you want one or not."

19

A WEIRD REUNION

I leaned against a curved wooden railing, at the top part of the arch on the Japanese-style bridge.

I took a bite of the *chile verde* burrito I gripped in my hand, wrapped in tinfoil and filled with cheese, black beans, guacamole, slow-stewed pork *chile verde*, and rice. I nearly rolled my eyes in appreciation as the taste combination hit my mouth.

"I'm remembering why I married you," I told Black as I chewed.

He grunted.

Nudging me with my arm, he took a bite of his own burrito, which was steak and cheese with big chunks of avocado, black beans, and sour cream.

I sighed as I took another bite and chewed, gazing down at the moon and clouds reflecting on the top of the Japanese koi pond. A few of the lights were on around the gardens, presumably for the security guys, but Black pushed them into leaving us alone, at least for an hour or so. Those lights made the cherry blossoms glow under a few trees. They also illuminated the redwood gate by the gift shop building, and the outside of the Japanese Buddhist temple.

Most of the garden itself was dark.

I was so lost in the still, moon-washed beauty of the garden we'd broken into, and the glorious taste of the burrito I was still savoring in satisfied chews, I didn't see or feel the vampires until they were practically on top of us.

A delicate clearing of a male throat nearly ended with me falling backwards into the koi pond.

I jumped, gripping the wooden railing with the hand not holding the burrito.

Then I cursed.

"Goddamn it, Brick—"

"I tried to warn you, my lovely Miriam."

"Bullshit," Black growled.

I barely realized Black had moved until he stood between me and Brick. I heard the rolling chuckle leave Brick as he realized the same.

"My, my... and here I'd nearly forgotten how *sweet* the two of you can be. So touching, even at the worst of times. And newly-weds now, to boot." The vampire king beamed, looking between us as he balanced his palms on a black cane with a silver handle. "I really *had* let it slip from my mind, you know, just how completely *adorable* the two of you are."

"Cut the crap," Black growled. "Did she come?"

Another voice rose from the darkness by the bottom part of the bridge.

The familiarity of it jerked my head around.

I turned completely, staring at her before I could stop myself.

"I'm here!" Zoe continued walking.

Her graceful tread was utterly silent up the wooden bridge. I didn't hear so much a squeak from the old planks, even as she appeared to bounce on her boots' high heels. She wore dark-red, clinging pants, a tucked in black blouse that was open in front, a gold watch, gold earrings, and a gold pendant that emphasized the cleavage showing on her ample chest.

Unlike me, she wore contouring make-up, eyeliner, eyeshadow, dark red lipstick to match her pants, rings with matching red stones, expensive shoes. Her hair looked like she'd had it professionally done, partly slicked back with dark, ringlet-like curls framing her face.

She looked like a fashion model.

She looked like she belonged at an art gala, not out here, in the dark.

"I guess we should have said something." Zoe grinned humorously. "I was hoping it wasn't you. I could smell those damned burritos out in the parking lot..."

"You're just jealous," I quipped.

I said it without thought.

It slipped out, part of the back-and-forth banter I might have done with her a million or so years ago, back when she was human.

The fact that I did it so easily now shocked me into silence.

It seemed to do the same to her.

For a few seconds, that silence stretched.

Then I heard Zoe smile.

"Damn. Zingers from the cocky living. I wasn't expecting that—"

"What can you tell us? About this Mulden character?"

I cut her off without thought, somehow blurting in the opposite direction that time. I felt my cheeks warm, but plunged on anyway.

"Black told you who and what we're looking for, right?" I asked. "That we need some way to track this guy? It's really important we find him, Zoe. Tonight, if possible—"

"Do not leave me out of this."

I flinched when the other voice spoke from behind my sister.

Cassavetes sounded cheerful as always.

I'd completely forgotten that she intended to join us.

I don't know if Cassavetes forgot what and who Zoe and Brick were, but the homicide detective walked right up to the top of that danged bridge like it was nothing. She joined the rest of us, not shying away from standing right between the two vampires.

Once she got there, she beamed, looking between Brick and Zoe.

She thrust out a hand to my vampire sister.

"Pia Cassavetes," she said. "I am a police detective with San Jose homicide."

I practically felt Zoe blink in surprise.

"Zoe Fox," she said after that loaded pause, shaking Cassavetes' hand back. "Amateur occultist, general lay-about, and vampire."

"Ah, yes. You are my very first, you know? Just like your sister and her husband are my very first seers in real life... the first I know about, at least."

Cassavetes grinned the whole time she spoke.

From my other side, I heard a disbelieving and delighted laugh out of Brick.

"My, my," he said. "Wherever did you find *this* one, Quentin?"

"Long story," Black muttered.

"Favor for a friend," I told Brick.

"Not that long of a story, as it turns out." Black gave me a faintly irritated look. "Can we talk about what we came here to talk about? Or did I break into this garden and push those very freaked out and frankly over-dramatic security guards for nothing?"

"Ah," Cassavetes said. "I had wondered."

"But it's not your jurisdiction," Black reminded her. "So you don't need to wonder all that much."

"Technically, we *are* here for a murder in San Jose, which *is* my jurisdiction... and we are here on murder business," Cassavetes pointed out. She shrugged as if in apology, holding up her hands. "So really, my new friend, Quentin, you are wrong—"

"I offered to go to Dennys," Zoe pointed out.

"I would like to know why we are doing this," Brick said, his voice a touch louder than everyone else's. "Before we begin, in fact, I would very much like to understand why this is a priority right now."

He looked around at everyone.

That faint smile still colored his expression, but I saw the hardness of his eyes. He rocked slightly on his heels, still balancing his body on the cane.

"Why are we wasting time trying to find one, single, solitary, utterly *insignificant* human? Now? Right after you let Charles go free?"

"We didn't *let* Charles do anything," Black growled. "And we have to deal with this first."

"Why?" Brick's voice came out a touch colder. "How can this one, slightly murder-y human possibly *matter,* in the greater scale of things? Compared to the threat posed by Charles?"

"Who is this Charles?" Cassavetes asked, confused.

She looked between Black and Brick.

No one answered her.

Brick and Black were still glaring at one another, when I exhaled in annoyance.

"Brick, we need to find Mulden first," I said.

He swiveled his head, aiming his gaze at me.

"Why?"

"Well, a few reasons," I said, exasperated. "But the one you care about is because if Charles knows about Mulden, or finds out about him, then he'll head straight for Mulden himself. If we don't get to him in time, Charles will take Mulden off the map. Probably somewhere we can't find him until Charles has him fully trained and indoctrinated."

Brick's dark eyebrows rose.

"And why is that, Miriam?"

"Because there's a damned good chance this Mulden isn't human at all," Black growled, answering before I could. "He's clearly got special abilities. Maybe more than me. Maybe more than Miri. Which means Charles will do anything in his power to acquire him. And exploit those abilities against all of us."

Brick looked between me and Black, his dark eyebrows raised.

"Just how many of you 'special abilities' seers are there out there?" the vampire king asked drily. "Didn't you just have one crash your wedding recently, Quentin?"

Black and I exchanged looks.

Brick had a point.

Honestly, it wasn't something I really liked thinking about right then, given all the implications for us, and not simply in regard to Jacob Mulden.

We'd had way too many run-ins with odd supernatural types lately.

It seemed like we'd been a magnet for that kind of thing, ever since Black and I first started "awakening" to whatever lived inside us, inside our own living light. I couldn't help but wonder if all or some of it came from my newfound ability to jump dimensions. A part of me wondered if I was screwing with the timelines in some way, or creating resonances with those other dimensions that we could not control.

It felt dangerous to me.

It felt unnatural.

I didn't like it.

Honestly, everything about what had been happening lately made me really uneasy.

Brick the vampire king must have been watching my face.

He let out another delighted laugh.

"You really have no idea what's going on. Do you?" He chuckled again, looking between us, resting his weight on that ivory-topped cane. "I should probably find that fact deeply unnerving," he added, smiling. "But strangely, I find it somewhat reassuring."

"You shouldn't," Black said.

"Perhaps not," the vampire conceded. "And yet... there it is."

But this was getting us nowhere.

I turned to my sister, Zoe.

"Can you track him?" I bit my lip, looking between her, and her vampire king. I felt agitated again, torn between irritation and a growing awareness of my own avoidance around what was going on. Now that I'd admitted as much to myself, it was difficult to un-see what I was doing.

Black must be avoiding all of this, too.

"Can you?" I pressed, looking at Zoe alone that time. "...Or not? Will you be able to use this occult crap to find Mulden? Or are we all just wasting our time?""

For a second, everyone just looked at me.

Then I saw them looking at one another.

In the end, Zoe shoved her hands into her pockets, and cleared her throat. I knew it was pure affectation. Vampires didn't need to clear their throats. Vampires didn't generally need to do much of anything with their bodies, not unless they wanted to. I also knew they did that kind of thing as a matter of course, after years of trying to blend invisibly with humans.

For some vampires, it could almost be a nervous tic.

After a pause where she studied my eyes, she nodded.

I noticed for the first time that my sister hadn't worn colored contact lenses to our meeting. The eyes that studied mine were vampire eyes.

Clear, cracked crystal, shining in the faint light of the moon.

I didn't see so much as a hint of that scarlet color that bloomed around a vampire's pitch-black pupils when they were hunting or aroused.

Still, it wasn't hard to imagine it there.

"Yes," she said seriously. Her voice held a vibrating confidence. "If he is who you say, if he's done the kinds of rituals you found in that room... I can find him, sis."

I winced at what she called me.

I winced, but I could feel the part of me that liked it, too.

20

A RESONANCE

"So, I believe you are likely right about Charles," Brick said conversationally, quirking an eyebrow in Black's direction. "About his interest in this Jacob person."

He glanced at me, favoring me with a wry smile.

I was watching Zoe, my sister, study the photos of Jacob Mulden's ritual space on her phone. I hadn't realized Black sent her all of that stuff while he arranged the meeting, but I watched her frown down at them now, zooming up different parts to look at details.

When I glanced at Brick, he was watching me look at Zoe.

His gaze flickered away an instant later.

His crystal eyes went back to studying Black's gold-flecked ones.

"We have reason to believe he has been looking for these creatures," Brick explained. "That he has at least some portion of his remaining team keeping an eye out for certain, shall we say, anomalies in the psychic space. Things that presumably your kind can feel. We are told it comes through as a kind of 'discordant note' against the usual living light of seers and other creatures to be found on this world."

The vampire king's voice had lost some of the sarcastic,

impish quality he tended to foist on us, even in life and death situations. I knew he adopted that quippy, trickster persona mainly to throw everyone around him off-balance.

Apparently, that wasn't what Brick was going for right now.

Rather than his usual cat-toying-with-mouse cracks, Brick now sounded almost sincere.

Of course, the vampire king employing his "sincere guy" approach had to be as much of a ruse as the trickster.

Still, it was a welcome change from his endless quips and cagey smirkiness.

That version of Brick could be exhausting.

"He is tracking this thing," the vampire king added somberly. "Charles. He became aware of Jacob Mulden before we did... at least a few days before Mulden caused you to destroy that police station. We have some reason to believe he knew of him even before this. Before he became embroiled in a murder investigation."

"What makes you think that?" Black asked.

Brick turned, staring at him.

His eyes held a puzzled inquisitiveness.

"Is that a real question?" he said.

Black only stared back, his expression unmoving.

In the end, Brick sighed, the affectation so dramatic I could have rolled my eyes.

"We have been watching Charles' people, of course," Brick said, as if that were the most obvious thing in the world. "We chose not to dispose of all of them, in the event something like this might happen. We wanted some idea of his ongoing machinations."

"Which people?" Black growled.

Brick looked at him again. "Mainly the scientists creating those weapons out of Poland and the Ukraine," he said seriously. "Oh, we tried to stop the weapons, Quentin. They are surprisingly well-fortified where they are. We did manage to get one person into their compound, but shutting them down was out of the question."

Black's eyes were murderous when he glanced at me.

I saw the fury there as he aimed it back at Brick.

"It didn't occur to you I might be able to help with that?" he growled. "They have been trying to kill me for the last however-many months, after all—"

Brick raised a hand dismissively.

"We planned to talk to you about this, Quentin. Frankly, you've had your hands full of late. We chose to monitor them as best we could, to avoid them doing something... well... apocalyptic. My inside source seems to think that if they really faced a threat, they would do something rather childish." His crystal eyes swiveled to Black. "...Something end of the world-ish. We worried your rather impulsive nature might not mitigate that danger sufficiently."

There was a silence.

Brick delicately cleared his throat.

"Anyway," he said, gesturing a graceful shrug with one hand. "Not *all* of them are working on weapons, Quentin. Following the arrival of that wedding-crashing dragon of yours, and Charles' subsequent capture, many of his people changed their focus to what you might call 'talent acquisition.' They spent a great deal of time monitoring the psychic space, apparently for anomalies like that posed by this Jacob Mulden. We saw them take an interest in Mulden himself, maybe a month before the murder of Rodney Gallows. The news stories really only confirmed our suspicions—"

Black grunted, giving the vampire a sideways look.

Still, I was surprised more at the relative calm in Black's eyes, not the anger that still smoldered there.

He definitely didn't look as surprised as he should have.

"I figured as much." Black refolded his arms, scowling at the vampire king. "I figured you would never have agreed to this meeting so easily, if you didn't already believe it might help you find Charles. You at least would have attached a shit-ton of conditions."

Brick shrugged, unapologetic.

"Of course," he said, his crystal eyes studying Black's face. "This is obvious, my friend. But it is good to see we are knowing one another better these days."

Affecting another delicate cough, he shrugged cagily with one hand.

"I am also glad to see that you are willing to speak to me openly about this, Quentin. I would like to be candid with you now, as well, if I may. I have some thoughts around a number of things pertaining to the life of your wife's 'Uncle Charlie.' There are many unanswered questions I have about him... especially in regards to the early years. Those years when he first arrived on this world. Things that happened before he became your uncle-in-law. Things we have never spoken about, you and I."

I looked up from where I'd been watching my sister draw symbols on the dirt.

"Things?" I said, frowning. "What kinds of things?"

We'd decided to do the ritual here, at Hakone Gardens.

A part of me had been tempted to drive everyone to the house in Santa Cruz, where we could be inside and could control the space better.

Surprisingly, Zoe had been the one to say no to that proposal.

Zoe insisted that being closer to Jacob Mulden's house, closer to where he'd conducted his own conjuring rituals, would make it easier for her find him.

We'd even discussed going back to the Mulden house, having Zoe do her magicks there.

Black asked her if we should just use Jacob's altar, Jacob's "witch trinkets," as Black called them, and Jacob's drawn symbols and "magic rocks." He proposed pushing the two humans living there, Amanda and Jacob's father, so the five of us could go back through Jacob's closet to his underground ritual space.

Zoe vetoed that idea, too.

She told us that Jacob would likely have protection spells on his own space, especially if he'd read all the books we told her about. She warned us that it could give us a false reading in the end, to use Jacob's space, since the magicks there would be loyal to Mulden, not us.

I just nodded to this.

To both things, really.

I was taking a lot on faith at this point.

I wasn't sure what *kind* of faith, but I didn't examine that too closely either.

It certainly wasn't faith in the vampires. It wasn't faith in the trustworthiness of the kind of magicks my sister claimed knowledge of, or faith that those magicks worked, or even existed in a real way.

I doubt it was faith in my sister herself.

As much as some part of me might want to trust her, I knew I couldn't.

I suspect it was more faith in the *rightness* I felt behind this approach.

I had no evidence or facts to support that feeling. I had nothing concrete at all that I could have pointed to, in order to justify or defend my gut sense. That feeling of rightness was all I had. I chose to trust it, because I couldn't find anything else.

I couldn't feel Charles.

I couldn't feel Mulden himself.

The part of me that felt we were on the right track, conducting some kind of mystical conjuring using my vampire sister as High Priestess of the Earthly magicks, was likely pure wishful thinking on my part.

Still, it was something.

"You are aware Charles is a large believer in mysticism?" Brick aimed the question at Black, his marble-like, and now scarlet-kissed eyes serious. "You went to at least a few of those rituals as I recall, while he had you working for him in Paris."

I flinched.

I hadn't thought about that in a *very* long time.

Black and I had only been "dating" then.

Well, if you could call it that. I hadn't been sure what we were, truthfully. We hadn't even slept together, not in terms of intercourse. That, and he disappeared for weeks, going to Paris without telling me and working for my uncle.

That had been Charles' doing.

When Black and I started developing feelings for one another, Charles intervened. Charles more or less blackmailed Black to get him to come to Paris. He'd forced a contract on him, kept him away from me for months, all so he could "evaluate" Black's suitability to be my seer mate. He tested him in various ways, abused him... raped him.

How had I forgotten all that?

How had I forgotten the sheer insanity of it?

It was amazing to me, really, that Charles managed to get me to forget those things about him, what he'd done to Black and to me, in the time since.

He'd always been evil.

Black and I both knew it.

What Charles allowed Ian to do in Bangkok was proof enough of that.

"Rituals," I said, frowning. "Are you saying Charles has been conjuring things, too? Things like what Jacob Mulden conjured?"

"I think he has been trying, yes," Brick said, aiming his serious look at me. "I think he has been trying to do this for a very long time." Brick swiveled his gaze back to Black. "It is possible, you know, that what has happened to you and Miriam is a result of those rituals. I am not saying I absolutely *believe* this to be true... but the possibility has crossed my mind."

I gaped at him.

I don't think Brick had ever said anything that surprised me so much.

Rituals? My uncle?

Brick thought Charles' rituals were behind what happened to me and Black?

Nothing like that had ever once crossed my mind.

Hearing Brick say it out loud didn't sound implausible. Yet it fell so far outside what we'd been made to understand before, not only here, but in that other dimension, with Black's cousin and his cousin's wife, that I was speechless.

They'd made it seem more... biological, I guess.

But now that I thought about it, I remembered them talking about our abilities as something that were "borrowed" from life to life, that we didn't necessarily take into the next life with us, but that might be passed on to another.

There was so much we didn't understand... whether about the dragon elements of Black's living light, the "Coreq" persona, not to mention whatever it was that allowed me to jump dimensional worlds.

The idea that Charles could have done this to us pretty much blew my mind.

"I don't know that he did it on purpose." Brick watched me shrewdly, almost like he guessed what I'd been thinking just then. "But yes, over the years, he did many rituals, most of them calling on powers and presences aligned with what he called 'the Old Gods' or sometimes, 'the One True God.' We were made to understand the image for this was a dragon."

I glanced at Black.

He frowned, looking back at me.

"He wouldn't have put that on Black, if so." Still frowning, I turned over Brick's words. "He would have wanted to wear that himself. Hell, he would have *demanded* that it come to him, and him alone. He would have believed no one else was worthy... certainly not Black, who he viewed as a kind of low-class, ex-slave hooligan with insufficient race loyalty..."

"Manners," Black murmured, quirking an eyebrow.

"Not my words, honey."

Black gave me a faint smile, then looked at Brick.

"She's right," he said. "I'm the last person Charles would have trusted with such a thing."

Brick's eyes remained shrewd. He held up his hands in a sort of apology.

"I don't claim to know everything." The vampire's voice held a faint warning. "However. As I said, he may have been playing with forces he could not fully control. It is possible he called on something, and that something chose its own targets..."

"Boy would that have pissed him off," Black muttered.

But I shook my head, frowning.

"No." I shook my head again. "No, that doesn't make sense." I looked at Black. "You said Coreq was a childhood friend, right? That they likely used him in some way for the organic machines? I thought you brought that Coreq presence *with* you through the doorway when you came from Old Earth. I thought you said you picked it up as you passed through..."

I could feel Cassavetes and my sister listening intently to all of this.

I found myself wondering what they were thinking about it all, then brushed that aside.

They would just have to deal with it.

Brick was right.

This was a conversation the three of us needed to have.

"I'm not saying I understand all of it," Brick cautioned. "But remember... Charles was calling for this thing long before your husband arrived here. It's possible there is some confluence of events that caused this. The door with Black's friend. Black's friend having a resonance with this 'dragon' presence, Charles calling on the dragon... Black himself having some resonance..."

"Johan." Black's mouth was grim. "Johan conducted rituals."

I looked at Black.

As his words sank in, I felt myself pale.

I'd totally forgotten about Johan.

Black had mentioned him before, but I'd forgotten to connect him to the conversation we were having now.

Johan had been a seer who owned Black on Old Earth. He'd been obsessed with dragon, with the One God. He'd been the one who put that dragon tattoo on Black's back. He'd called Black his "Little Dragon," and abused him horribly.

Until today, I hadn't heard Black mention Johan's name in a very long time.

I'd never heard him mention Johan in front of anyone else.

"He was a seer, back on Old Earth," Black told Brick. "He had me when I was young. Too young to fight back. He conducted rituals around the dragon. It's possible that caused some kind of resonance, like you said. Or maybe those rituals somehow combined with whatever happened to Coreq, along with whatever Charles was doing..."

I thought about that.

It didn't explain anything about me, of course, or my abilities, but it made a hell of a lot of sense in regards to Black. Coreq had always felt like a foreign element in Black's makeup. In many respects it felt like maybe it shouldn't be there at all.

I'd never fully viewed it as an integral part of Black himself.

Coreq controlled the dragon.

To Black and me, Coreq *was* the dragon.

"*Gaos*," I muttered. "So all this time—"

"—I might not have been the dragon at all," Black finished.

"Again," Brick cautioned, holding up a few fingers. "I have attempted to study this, at least in terms of what Faustus believes... and what the old seer religions claim in their texts. It is possible it is not so simple, not so black and white. It is possible that no one really is 'The Dragon' in the strictest sense. It is possible that this presence utilizes those who form a type of resonance with it. A bond of sorts. And you, Quentin, became the vehicle for this here, after Charles called to the dragon presence through his rituals."

Black frowned.

I watched him process this.

I fought to process it, too.

I was about to ask Brick if we could see some of these texts, when Zoe straightened back to her full height, brushing off her hands.

She smiled around at all of us, like she was pleased with herself.

"Okay," she said. "I think we're ready. I just need someone to help me light the candles."

"I can do that," Cassavetes said at once.

Watching the two of them bend down to do that, I glanced back at Brick.

"And what about me? Have you seen anything about the Dragon's mate in any of your writings?"

Brick smiled at me.

His crystal eyes flickered towards Black, then back to me.

"I do not know very much about you at all, lovely Miriam," he said, shrugging with that faint smile. "But yes, there is mention of the Dragon's mate. They call it the Tortoise, and talk about it as a master of time and space... which strikes me as a rather dramatic coincidence."

Black and I exchanged looks.

That's more or less what those seers in the other dimension told us.

I looked at Brick. "Those books. Would you share them with us?"

Brick smiled. He twisted his torso, without unfolding his arms, looking from me to Black and back again.

"But of course," he said. "Of course. In the meantime, however," he added dryly. "Before you delve into the tens, possibly *hundreds* of thousands of pages... pages that it took my people decades to find, steal, copy, translate, read, and attempt to interpret using seer historical texts and symbology... we can perhaps talk with somewhat less sophistication about what we think this presence *wants* with the two of you. And what it means that this otherwise unextraordinary human, Jacob Mulden, seems to have some power over it."

"Let's find him, first," Zoe said, looking up from where she was lighting the last of what had to be roughly twenty candles.

I glanced around where we stood, worried for the first time about someone stumbling upon us up here.

That was a lot of fire.

But Zoe didn't seem concerned.

She straightened to her full height, dusting off her hands.

"Maybe he can tell us himself," my sister added wryly.

21

A CASTING

W e stood outside the circular designs my sister had drawn.

It was so strange, watching her do this.

Maybe it was the fact that she'd been into all of the same things back in high school and college, but she seemed more human to me now than she ever had.

Well, that is, she seemed more human to me now than she had since I'd first found out she was a vampire.

She hadn't quite seemed real to me before.

Honestly, some part of me still thought of my sister as dead.

Now, watching her draw careful symbols in the air with her hands, listening to her chant and say words I didn't understand, it really felt, for the first time, like my sister was still alive. She was still the same person somehow, even though I knew she wasn't, really. Or maybe she was, but because I'd missed her growing up, in addition to missing her process of becoming a vampire, I was blurring the two things together somehow.

In fact, she was a lot less like the Zoe I'd known than Nick was from the Nick he'd been prior to his own transformation. Nick, after all, had been a forty-something man when he turned. He also hadn't disappeared from my life for years on end.

Nick hadn't missed my time in the war.

He hadn't missed my time working for the police.

He hadn't missed my time with Black.

Nick had been there when I first learned I was a seer.

We'd lost Nick temporarily, but he'd come back.

I wasn't sure about Zoe in that regard, if she was back in my life now or not, but watching her face as she recited words, switching between languages with a fluidity I found both impressive and strangely disconcerting, I found I wanted to know the story now. Before now, I'd been too angry to want to know, but now I did. I wanted to know where she'd been all those years, who she'd been with, what she'd been doing.

Okay, so maybe not all of it.

After all, she'd been a vampire.

She'd also spent at least part of that time as a newborn, like Nick. I could scarcely imagine how she must have dealt with that transition, given what it had done to Nick.

I doubted I wanted to know very much about that side of things.

But the rest of it? After Zoe became herself again? Where she'd gone and what she'd done after the newborn phase was over?

Oxford?

Those things, I wanted to know.

"Okay," she said. "I think that's it."

She put down the book she'd been reading from, setting it down in front of her inside the center of the pentagram.

Reaching into her pocket, she pulled out a red velvet pouch, and opened up the top of it. I watched her pour some of the contents into her hand, what looked like fine powder, or possibly a very fine sand. Whatever it was, it shone an iridescent, moonstone white.

"I don't know what you will be able to see," she said. "But I'm going to try it now."

I nodded, folding my arms.

From next to me, Brick the vampire king tilted his head. He leaned his mouth towards my ear, and murmured in his melodious voice.

"She is being modest," Brick said. "She is quite proficient in this. I use her for such things quite frequently."

I blinked.

I glanced at Black, who quirked an eyebrow back at me.

"Okay," Zoe said. "Here goes nothing."

She held the powder up to her red-lipsticked lips, and blew slowly and steadily.

Whatever that substance was, it floated upward in a cloud, lighter than air.

It began to glow the instant her breath touched it. Then it fanned out, creating a swirling cloud in the space just in front of where she stood. It glowed a pale white-violet, but I saw shimmers of gold and silver woven in, along with flashes of black and darker blue.

I watched in disbelief as it began to create a painting in the air.

Not just a painting.

A map.

"Can you see it?" Zoe said.

"We see it, my love," Brick murmured.

I glared at him, but he didn't bother to return my glance.

Zoe didn't react to his words at all.

She never took her cracked-crystal eyes off the increasingly complex topography in front of her. I saw buildings grow out of the glowing powder, towns, highways, cities.

Zoe looked at all of it intently, as if orienting herself.

Her dark hair flowed down her shoulders in a rippling wave, covering her chalk-white skin, somehow emphasizing how smooth and velvety it looked.

"That is his house," she explained, pointing to a particularly bright area.

I could see the faint outline of the dwelling, recognized the run-down Spanish-style house with its overgrown yard, and again, disbelief made me stare.

"*Gaos,*" I said. "I can see the underground shrine... his altar."

Zoe nodded. "Yes. I think he must have done most of his conjuring there. That kind of energy? That gold? That is what he pulled out of the ether... maybe what you would consider an alternate dimension. Or maybe it's more accurate to say it's a space of no dimensions at all, or quasi-dimensionality..."

I didn't really understand that, but I nodded.

"So the dragon came through there?" I said. "At his shrine? He opened some kind of portal?"

Zoe frowned, looking at the rest of the lit particles.

"No," she said, shaking her head. "I don't think so."

She drew a line with her finger, tracing a path through the lit air.

She stopped at another part of the map, and I realized that one had more of those lines of light, but they were different, darker in color. Most were blues and reds. I saw some deep greens as well, and streaks of violet and white.

"Here," Zoe said. "Here is where the presence first came to him."

"What is that?" Black said, frowning as he took a step forward. "Is that the police station? When he first asked to speak with me and the doc?"

Zoe shook her head again.

"No," she said, her voice surprised. "No, I think it's that club. The strip club... where his friend went to meet him. I think it was already there when his friend showed up. Maybe it wasn't Jacob there at all... maybe he was already possessed."

I glanced at Cassavetes, who pursed her lips.

"He might have been telling the truth," I ventured. "He might really think he never saw Rodney Gallows at all."

"Yes." Cassavetes nodded thoughtfully. "He might have been."

"If the real Jacob Mulden was 'not there' when his friend

arrived," I added. "It's possible that the 'Jake' part of his mind truly believes Rodney never showed up that night. It's possible he has no idea what he did while under the influence of that presence."

Cassavetes nodded again, but I could see from her eyes she wasn't convinced.

"I know this is pretty fantastical," I added. "And probably doesn't help you much, in terms of your actual case."

Cassavetes stared at the map of light.

She let out a half-humorous sound, almost a snort.

"I am a cop," she said, giving me a sideways smile. "From the perspective of a cop, if his body performed murder, Jacob Mulden is still guilty. If that thing killed while he was possessed... Jacob Mulden, human being, is still a murderer. It is up to lawyers and judges to decide if he was of sound mind when he committed his crime. And if he conjured the thing that killed Rodney, I'm not altogether convinced he *isn't* responsible."

We were all listening to her by the end.

Brick waited until she finished, then grinned at me and Black.

"Where did you find this delightful human?" he asked. Smiling, he rocked on his heels, using the ivory-handled cane for balance. "She is a miracle, is she not? *Tout à fait magnifique!* I must say, it is so refreshing and rare to come across a human with any amount of *real* sense to them, who is not blinded by stupidity and superstition—"

"Brick." I gave him a hard look. "Shut up."

Cassavetes didn't seem to care at all.

She never looked away from the map.

I turned back to my sister.

"What else can you tell us?" I asked. "Zoe? Can you see where he is now?"

Zoe nodded, her eyes and voice distracted.

"I was looking for that," she said. "This doesn't exactly show the present, more the past. But we should be able to extrapolate from where he's been. The idea is to look for a pattern of places. I think I've got a trail for him now..."

She pointed towards another explosion of light on the map.

That one was larger, made up mostly of dark greens, mixed with violent oranges, and reds. If that was the same thing he'd conjured at the strip club, it had grown.

"That's the police station," Zoe explained. "You can see a bit of you and Black there, but not very much... only the parts that interacted with him, since I did the conjuring on him, on the traces of magic remaining in his aura..."

She trailed, then looked back at the strip club.

"There might be another presence there."

"Charles?" Brick asked.

Zoe turned, giving him a grim look. "Possibly. It fells like it could be him. And Rodney Gallows' death took place before Charles was captured again. It was at least a week before the wedding. Right?"

I blinked at that, too.

I'd totally forgotten that Charles would have been free when all of this started. He might have been back in our dimension by then, too.

Which meant he could have potentially been messing with Jacob.

I nodded, refolding my arms. "And now? Do you feel Charles there now?"

"I don't know."

She continued to stare at the map, her eyes reflecting light.

"There is a lot of fear there," she said after a beat, frowning. She pointed at pale white streaks infused with black and dark purple. "You see that? He is afraid. He looks like he is fleeing at first. He ran from the police station in terror... possibly as Jacob once more."

She traced a snaking set of lines with her fingers.

I had no idea how she knew which threads to follow.

They all looked the same to me. But she seemed confident,

so I just did my best to follow the course of her finger with my eyes.

"Here," she said. "Here, he begins to calm down. I think the thing possessing him is talking to him here."

She frowned, cocking her head as if listening.

"You know," she continued. "I think it's really possible he has no idea what happened at the police station... or how and why the police station came down around him. I think he must have transformed back into his human self when the two of you lost control. That, or the thing possessing him left him for a time to deal with the two of you..."

She trailed, still squinting at the patterns of light.

"...He calms down here," she went on, pointing at a place where the lit particles turned from purple and red to a softer, more subtle violet. "He is calmer, you see? I think the thing is talking to him, explaining. After that, you can see he's heading this way. He was on foot before this point, but somehow he gets a car. Maybe a taxi? A ride share? He could have even stolen one. But he's moving too fast to be on foot now—"

"Where does he go next?" Black said, gruff. "Is he still in San Jose?"

There was a silence.

In it, Zoe continued to trace threads of light with her fingers, lines made of star-like particles that seemed suspended in space above the middle of the pentagram. Zoe inhabited that area alone, as if she'd created her own sphere of living light. She stood in the exact middle of the rings of salt, chalk, and flames from the candles.

"No," she said after another beat, shaking her head. "No. I don't think he's in San Jose now. After he got a car, he went to San Francisco."

"Where in San Francisco?" Black growled.

I heard the alarm behind his aggression.

I also felt the meaning behind his alarm.

Black was worried Jacob went up there looking for us. He

was worried Jacob Mulden would show up at the California Street building and unleash holy hell on whoever he ran into up there.

Zoe must have picked up on that, too.

"He didn't go to your place," she said, shaking her head. "He's all the way on the other side of town." Her cracked-crystal eyes remained out of focus. "He did stop somewhere fairly recently, though. Maybe only ten or so minutes from now. The imprints are fresh. I see him outside his car. He's walking…"

There was a silence.

I watched Zoe squint up at the glowing particles.

"He went to a club. I can see the outside of another club…" she said.

"A club?" From Cassavetes' voice, something in those words pricked her ears. "What club is this?"

Zoe frowned.

Slowly, she shook her head.

"I can't make out the name of it."

"Do you know *where* it is?" Cassavetes pressed. "What part of the city?"

There was another silence.

I saw Zoe's shockingly pale brow clear.

"It's in the Mission District." She sounded more confident now, like she'd somehow locked in on the location with more certainty. "I couldn't get the exact street, but it's off Valencia. The door is red. The place looks older than a lot of the surrounding businesses. It's painted black. It looks run down…"

I saw disbelief flicker in Cassavetes' eyes.

"You know this place?" I asked.

She shook her head slowly, her mouth grim.

I didn't exactly get a "no" off her answer, though.

"What kind of place is it?" Cassavetes asked. "What is the business?"

Zoe frowned. "I mean, apart from a club of some kind? I guess it could be a bar? Maybe a place where bands play? Maybe a gay bar? It looks like an old dive bar, but one hipsters go to now... I can't quite make out the sign."

"That's okay. I think I know where this is, where he has gone."

"You *do* know," Black said, sharp. "Where is he, Cassavetes?"

She held up a hand.

"I do not know this for sure," she amended. "I cannot know for sure, not without seeing. But we were told Jacob Mulden had another magic show booked for this week. That he and his act were picked up by a small place in the Mission District. A place I looked up... that is off Valencia, in an old building surrounded by newer things, in a gentrified part of the strip..."

She pulled her phone out of her jacket as she spoke.

I watched her tap through keys, using the map function to bring up San Francisco, then a specific place on the city map. I waited while she pulled up photos of the address, photos of both the inside and the outside of the club, photos left by users of the GPS app.

She handed me her phone.

"You see?" she said, her voice grim. "This is the club. And yes, it has a name. It is called *The White Rabbit.*"

"Another strip club?" Black asked.

"No," she said, looking at him. "A dive bar, like she said. They have musical acts, open mic, poetry nights, local bands, burlesque... and magicians, apparently. It is a hipster place, so there is some kitsch to what they do, with obscure and outdated entertainments."

I looked at the image.

It showed the outside of a small, black-painted bar. The building itself looked old, like any one of the historical buildings no one had yet bothered to have renovated. It also looked dirty and seedy, like it hadn't been maintained very well. A neon white rabbit danced across the front of the club, with pink and white tubes spelling out the name.

The bar's door was painted a dull, faded red.

I looked at Cassavetes.

"Shit," I said.

"Yes." Cassavetes gave me a humorless half-smile, taking the phone back when I offered it to her. "Shit is correct."

"When is his show?" Black asked in a growl. "When was he scheduled to perform there?"

Cassavetes frowned.

She went into her email, pulling up another few screens of notes and attachments.

I watched her check her watch and frown.

"Now," she said, looking up at Black. "He is scheduled to perform right now."

22

THE WHITE RABBIT

"We're not going to get up there in time," Cassavetes said, her accent coming out stronger as she frowned down at the clock on her phone. "We're going to be too late. And if this 'Charles' you speak of is tracking him also, he is likely already there."

"We'll make it," Black grumbled.

"Not unless he stays after his show," Cassavetes warned. "Would Charles risk that? We do not even know if he performed."

"We're almost there," Black said. "There's no point arguing it now. You should have said this before we got this far."

"I did say these things," Cassavetes reminded him. "Several times."

"Then maybe you should have figured out by now that I'm not going to listen to you about this," Black said.

"Maybe I should have," Cassavetes grumbled.

She was staring at her phone again, looking at the map.

I'd been listening to this back and forth with them for the forty or so minutes it had taken us to get this far. It seemed to be a nervous tic of Cassavetes', to tell Black they weren't going to make it, and for Black to grump at her that he was going anyway.

Black didn't even look over at her, I noticed.

Cassavetes didn't look at him.

She barely took her eyes off the map on her phone.

She sat shotgun with him.

I sat in the back with Brick and my sister.

I mostly did that for Cassavetes, too. I didn't want to make her sit in the back of the car with two vampires, whether she thought it bothered her or not.

I couldn't help but feel uncomfortable myself, though.

I picked the window seat behind Black. My leg was pressed against the door on one side, and the ice-cold, hard-as-cement thigh of my sister, Zoe, on the other.

I suspected she didn't *have* to be pressing into me so close.

She didn't make any effort to adjust her position so that we wouldn't be touching me, and I refused to say anything about it. I bit my lip instead, folding my arms across my chest.

"Is he moving yet?" I asked Zoe.

She frowned, then shook her head. "I don't have as clear of a view here. We don't have the circle... or the map. There's a lot more interference—"

"But you can feel *something*, right?" I cut in. "You're still connected to that presence, right? The thing he summoned in the ritual?"

Zoe hesitated.

Then, letting me hear her frustration, she exhaled.

That was pure affectation, too.

Vampires don't breathe.

"I can feel a little," she admitted, her tone openly grudging. "I can't promise you anything precise, but I *think* he's still there. I can't be totally certain... this isn't like a blood connection. Most of what I see, even in the ritual space, is the past, not the present. Definitely not the future. But I think he's still at the club. That, or there's such a strong concentration of that presence there, it *feels* like he is."

"Is anyone with him?" Black asked.

He didn't seem to care about her lack of precision, or her reluctance to guess.

I watched him turn onto Mission Street, then immediately swerve around a jaguar. He hit the gas, accelerating down a stretch of road past the streetlight, and weaving around two more cars, including a brand-new Tesla he passed like it was standing still.

We were on Valencia now.

"Zoe?" Black said.

I flinched when he said her name.

"Is he alone?" Black growled.

"I don't know."

"But what do you *think?*"

"He might be with someone else. If I had to guess, I'd say it feels like he's not alone. A few times it's felt like he might be talking to someone..." Frustration leaked into her voice. "...For all I know, he could be talking to *himself,* Black. That presence and the host body could be talking to one another again."

I flinched when she said my husband's name, too.

I glanced over at Zoe.

It was so strange seeing her, much less sitting so close to her, much less touching her. She looked so much like my sister, yet didn't look like her at all. The clothes were wrong. The eyes. The six-hundred dollar haircut, highlights, and styling. The red lipstick and dark eyeshadow. The ghostly-white skin. She *felt* all wrong.

Her mind was closed off from mine.

She was Zoe but not.

Or maybe she's more Zoe than you want to admit, Black murmured at me. *Or she's your sister but you're not sure if you want her to be.*

I turned, staring at the back of his head, at the shaggy black haircut that probably cost only a little less than my sister's.

It hit me, not for the first time, that in some ways, Zoe—the Zoe I remembered, at least—was more like Black than I was.

She'd always been the more reckless, adventurous one.

She'd been the clothes horse, the wise-cracker, the one who dated a lot of different men.

She'd liked cars more than I ever did.

She liked nice hotels, vacation resorts, expensive restaurants, expensive jewelry.

Charles used to joke I was his little scientist.

Zoe was the artist, spy, danger-hound.

I was the boring one.

She was the pretty one.

A ripple of separation pain went through me before I could stop it.

Gaos, doc. I'm sorry... I'm sorry, honey.

But Black apologizing to me right then didn't make it better.

Somehow, it only made the feelings worse.

Maybe because my emotions were all over the place, and I couldn't think rationally about any of it, I folded his apology into my fears. I knew that part of me was somehow stuck on my childhood and adolescence. Maybe it was because that was the last time I'd had any kind of close relationship with my sister.

Knowing those things didn't help me at all.

Also, since I wasn't even sure what Black was apologizing for exactly, my mind went to the bad place with it. That hyper-emotional, irrational, high school version of me decided he was sorry because everything I'd been thinking was right, or that he thought I was boring too, or that he was apologizing because the separation pain wasn't affecting him.

Doc, he murmured. *Gaos, wife. No.*

His light was achingly soft.

Something about the way he coiled it into mine, a vulnerable, soft tendril of light, cut my breath, making the pain in my chest exponentially worse.

Doc, listen to me, he sent. *I'm sorry for the insane shit you were thinking about her and you just now, and the fact that Charles encouraged a rivalry there. I'm sorry if I did anything to make it worse, since I always seem to do the wrong thing when it comes to your sister. As far as*

*the exact things you were thinking... I don't even know what the hell
you're talking about frankly, but I can feel kid stuff in it, and I know kid
stuff is horrible when it gets dug up like this.*

He sent me a pain-infused pulse of heat.

*Doc, I'm sorry because I can feel how much it's hurting you, seeing
her, without her making any effort to talk to you, to resolve anything... or
hell, even to fucking* apologize, *or say she missed you. I can feel how
hard it is, not being able to feel her light. I can feel how much you love
her... and I can feel how much the separation pain with me is making it
all worse. I wish like hell you didn't have to deal with any of this shit
now, when we can't even —*

"Stop!"

Zoe leaned forward, liquid fast.

She grabbed Black's arm, even as she inserted her body
between the front two seats. Still holding Black, and now with
her face right next to his, she pointed with her other hand.

"That's it. That's the sign. See it?"

"She is right," Cassavetes said, looking down at the map on
her phone. "I am sorry. The map makes it look like it is past the
next block. But that is the sign they have pictured here. That is
the red door I have in the photos."

Black swerved over, across two lanes.

A few drivers honked.

I saw one man yelling at him through his closed window.

Black ignored all of it.

A car was parked directly in front of the club's front door.

He managed to aim the Bentley into a space two cars ahead
of it, lurching the armored SUV to a stop and throwing the auto-
matic gear shift into park. I was already yanking on the latch to
open my door, my booted foot hitting the asphalt as he turned
off the ignition.

"Doc, wait."

I didn't look back.

Leaving the car door open, I headed for the red door.

"Doc! Wait up!"

No bouncer sat or stood outside, barring entry.

Two teenaged-looking girls dressed in seventies-style, carpet-like coats were in the process of going inside. The first one, who had long, curly, auburn-colored hair, threw her head back in a drunken-sounding laugh as she held open the door for her friend, gripping the brass handle in a small hand with blood-red fingernail polish.

Her friend, a Japanese-looking girl with black cat makeup on her eyes and stylishly severe bangs, was still telling the story that made her auburn-haired friend laugh, gesticulating with her hands, a big smile on her face.

I watched the two of them pass through the red door, which I now saw was padded with red vinyl.

Something about the insane normality of the two of them made me want to call out to them. I wanted to shout for them to not go inside, that it wasn't safe.

I wanted to drag them out physically, if necessary.

At the same time, that could have been me and Zoe, back when we were barely out of high school. I knew the two girls... young women, really... were probably closer to twenty-two than seventeen, but they both looked so damned young to me.

I gripped the handle of the same door, seconds later, and jerked it open.

Doc, wait. Alarm rose in Black's mind. *Doc, he could recognize you. Wait until the vampires get in there behind you, at least —*

I didn't slow my steps, or turn to look at him.

I passed through the same opening as the seventies-styled girls.

I found myself in a dim club with thumping music.

No one was carding guests or taking money at the door.

I walked towards the bar, scanning faces, taking in the club's basic layout.

Neon, black-light paint covered most of the walls, giving it a seventies-retro style, like an old acid hangout during the psychedelic years. The floor was sticky and painted red. Tables were scattered around the narrow main floor before the low stage.

The bar itself stood to my left, taking up most of the wall there.

I saw a large, stuffed, bleached jackrabbit that held center stage on the black-painted wood. It looked mangy, like it had been posed there, in the dank, smoky, stale-beer-smelling space, for longer than its shelf life recommended.

The dead rabbit's bleached fur was pure white.

Someone had dressed it in a little waistcoat and a top hat, and glued a monocle to its eye. A pocket watch had been glued to one of its paws, which was articulated so that the rabbit appeared to be looking at the time.

The White Rabbit.

I wondered how old the bar was, if that had been a play on the Jefferson Airplane song.

My eyes returned to faces.

I saw the two young women who'd come in ahead of me, leaning over the black-painted wood, speaking their drink order loudly to the bartender.

My eyes scanned through the rest of the people there. Most were smoking and drinking at the round tables scattered over the floor, but I didn't see Jacob there, either.

I didn't feel Black until he was standing right next to me.

"Damn it." He spoke loudly over the music, which I suddenly realized *was* Jefferson Airplane, playing the bar's title song. "Don't do that to me, doc. Or I'll start racking up spankings for you later."

He scowled, still looking around.

"I'll see if I can push them into showing us the surveillance... assuming those work..." he added, gesturing up towards the walls, where I realized I could see at least two God's eye cameras. "Maybe we can at least find out if he was really here. Not to mention when he left, and if he was here with someone else."

"Could he still be in the back?" I said, also half-shouting over the rising music. "Maybe he hasn't gone on yet?"

"His act was supposed to be at eleven," Cassavetes said, speaking even more loudly than me, and looking at her watch. "It is midnight now. A little after. I think we are too late."

She looked at me, her mouth grim. "And I don't think this place has much of a backstage, but I will go with your husband. Maybe with my badge and his psychics, we can get some more information, at least. Keep an eye on the door. Or have the vampires keep watch."

I watched her go to the bar with Black.

I considered following them, watching the door from there, but paused to look at Brick and Zoe, who were now casing the room with their vampire eyes.

"You have no idea where he could have gone next?" I asked Zoe, speaking loudly.

I'd forgotten how sensitive vampire hearing is.

Zoe flinched.

She looked at me, and I saw a flicker of... something... touch her eyes.

"No," she said then. "Like I said in the car... I could see the residuals of where the presence of that thing was really strong, but those kinds of spells aren't really that precise when it comes to timelines."

"But he was definitely here?" I pressed.

She hesitated. Her eyes continued to scan the bar's patrons as she nodded.

"He was here," she said.

"Do you still think he might have been here with someone else?" I pressed.

She hesitated again.

Her clear, glass like eyes met mine.

"I *think* so," she said. "I hate to sound so certain when I'm not, but it really felt like he was talking to someone. Or maybe that presence was talking to someone. I don't know if it was just the presence talking to Jacob, but if I had to guess, I'd say not. I think when that presence is in control, Jacob is generally just... not there. It doesn't seem that interested in the human Jacob at all..."

"But it resonated with him enough to possess him?"

"Yes." Zoe nodded, conceding my words. "Yes. It did."

"And you said it calmed him down before? After the police station?"

Zoe shrugged, her voice frank.

"I think it only soothed him that time because it needed him," she said. "It needed Jacob to do the practical things to get them out of there. And possibly to bring the presence up here, to San Francisco. It needed him to get them a car. To deal with money. Phone apps."

"So it can't fly?" I said. "It can't turn into a dragon, like Black?"

Zoe turned, looking at me with her vampire eyes.

"I have no idea, Miri," she said.

I flinched.

Before I could say answer, Black was waving at me from the bar, his mouth grim. He motioned for me to come join him, where he and Cassavetes were leaned over the wood to talk to the bartender. I saw the two women from before perched on barstools nearby, staring at Black with wide eyes, like he was a movie star and his presence there rendered them mute.

One of them was smoking what had to be a joint.

But then, that was hardly surprising.

Over half the people in the bar were stoned.

I walked to Black.

Zoe and Brick followed me.

It struck me that Brick was uncharacteristically quiet, but I didn't let myself dwell on that too much, either.

I reached Black's side and he wrapped an arm around my waist. He pulled me close, bending down to speak into my ear.

"He's got surveillance footage. In the back. But he says Jacob was already here and gone. He did the show, then left... leaving the bar maybe a half-hour ago."

"Was he alone?" I said, still speaking loudly over the music.

Black raised his head. He shook it, once, his mouth grim.

"No."

The bartender held a set of maybe twenty keys in his hands as he motioned with his head, indicating for us to follow him down the length of the bar. I saw a woman who'd been on the floor in an old-fashioned uniform for a cocktail waitress take his place. She began taking drink orders as he led us to the opening on the far end, the one furthest from the club's door.

He raised the old-fashioned, hinged segment of bar-counter, sliding through the narrow opening. Still fumbling through his keys, he led us to a black-painted door just past the bathroom door, which was painted red, the same color as the door outside.

He used one of the keys to let us in.

We all crowded in behind him after he turned on the light.

I found myself standing inside a small, cramped office with a single wooden swivel chair, a desk covered in receipts and other papers, an old-fashioned, plastic rotary phone, and a few stacks of metal filing cabinets.

The only semi-modern thing in there was a laptop computer, which sat on top of the stack of papers, looking weirdly out of place with the rest.

It smelled strongly of marijuana smoke in here, too.

The bartender-manager sat down in the swivel chair, and pulled the laptop over to him, flipping up the top. He used the track pad to click on an icon on his desktop, and a row of rectangular video screens opened up, showing different views of the club.

"You can go through any of it," he said, turning the laptop around to face us. "I got to go back out there, but you can look at anything you want in here."

"Can I rewind this?" Black said, scanning the program on the screen.

"Sure. Go back as far as you want. The sound pretty much sucks... you won't be able to hear much. I've never been able to make out conversations or anything. The music pretty much drowns all that out."

Cassavetes smiled at him. "Thank you. We shouldn't be long."

The lanky bartender nodded, his long hair hanging in a tangled, half-fallen-out ponytail down his back.

He slid and squeezed through our cramped group to get to the door.

There was a loud burst of sound as he opened it.

It cut off seconds later, when the door swung shut behind him.

Black was already sitting in the swivel chair, the laptop open on the desk in front of him. Cassavetes leaned over the chair behind him, gripping the wooden backrest as she peered down at the row of video screens.

"That one." She pointed at one of the camera angles. "Check that one. He said he was sitting at the bar after the show, no? With someone else?"

"I want to see the show first," Black muttered, using the laptop to click on something else. "He didn't say it, but I read it on him. He didn't perform alone."

I frowned at that, startled.

Who hadn't performed alone?

Jacob? Who the hell had been on stage with Jacob Mulden?

I walked over to the desk and behind Cassavetes. I stared down at the camera angles with them, squinting to make out the different views of the bar.

Black clicked on the rectangular view showing the bar's dinky stage, making it so it filled the laptop's entire screen.

He began to rewind the digital recording.

Zoe and Brick moved so that they stood just behind me.

I knew vampire vision was better than that of seers or

humans, so I was sure they could see everything more clearly than I could.

Even so, it felt like we all huddled within a few feet of the screen.

"There it is!" Cassavetes pointed. "That is him... that is the show."

"Who is that?" Black said, frowning.

He stopped the recording, pausing his rewind before he got to the beginning of Jacob Mulden's magic act. Hitting play, he let it go forward at normal speed.

Two people stood together on that stage.

I frowned.

Leaning closer, I stared at the face of the woman next to Jacob Mulden.

She wore a ruby and gold sequined costume, a high-cut leotard with high heels and fishnet stockings, like an old-school magician's assistant. Her black hair was arranged and piled high on top of her head, held up with rhinestone clips.

She wore dramatic makeup and heavy rouge, but I still recognized her.

"That's Nina," I said, dumbfounded. "That's Nina Gallows. Rodney Gallows' sister."

I looked at Black, the shock in my voice growing.

"..That's Cal's girlfriend."

23

HIGH SCHOOL BLUES

I watched Cassavetes scroll through more video recorded around different areas of The White Rabbit bar. I scanned the visuals alongside her, even as I listened to Black in the background, eavesdropping on his conversation as he held a phone to his ear.

"What time was that?" Black said, cutting someone off.

There was a silence while whoever he was speaking to answered.

"How the hell did they get past you?" Black asked.

He saw me glance over my shoulder at him.

He hesitated a split second, then seemed to come to a decision.

He pulled the phone away from his ear, and hit the button on the call screen to turn on his phone's speaker function. He held the device lower and towards me, so it was maybe a foot below his mouth, and we could all hear the person on the other end.

Cal's voice rose in the cramped office.

It echoed slightly, sounding vaguely tinny through Black's phone.

"...got back from the cafeteria a floor below, and she was gone. None of the hospital staff could tell me anything. They had no idea she was missing until I went looking for the night staff and asked anyone I could find where she was. I thought maybe they'd taken her away for tests or something. But there was nothing listed on her chart. No nurses knew anything about any tests, either, when I asked—"

"Wait." Black's voice was confused. "Why was she getting tests? They told us you were the injured one. They said you broke your collarbone, that you were in the hospital and she was fine. No real injuries."

There was a silence.

Cal sounded dumbfounded. "No. I was fine. No broken collarbone. I've been with Nina ever since the accident. Whoever you spoke to, they must have mixed me up with someone else, Black. Nina was the one who was hurt. She got knocked unconscious when the roof caved in. They've had her under observation for the head injury."

There was a silence.

Black, Cassavetes, and I all exchanged looks.

"So tell me again what happened?" Black said. "No one saw her leave?"

"No one," Cal confirmed. "But when they checked the cameras, they saw her walking out with someone—"

"Jacob?" Black asked.

"I don't know." Cal seemed to be thinking. "It could have been," he admitted, reluctant. "I saw the recordings. Whoever it was, he was tall. Thin. Yeah, it could have been him. It must have been, right? You said you saw her with him on those recordings there..."

Black and I exchanged another set of worried looks.

"Her head injury," Black said. "How bad is it?"

Cal exhaled, and I could almost see him there, pacing the hospital hallway.

"They honestly don't know. She was supposed to get a full evaluation from the doc tomorrow, since she'd only been awake for a few hours—"

"Wait." I spoke up without thought. "Only a few hours?"

There was a silence.

It hit me that Cal probably hadn't known I was there, listening to this.

"Cal, it's Miri," I said, making my voice matter-of-fact. "Black has you on speaker phone. There are a number of us here listening, including me and Detective Cassavetes. When you left to go to the cafeteria, was Nina conscious? Or had she fallen back to sleep?"

"She was asleep." Cal sounded strangely relieved to hear my voice. "Which was why I figured it probably wouldn't matter to her if I went and grabbed a coffee and something to eat. I couldn't sleep myself, and—"

"So she was sleeping normally?" I said. "It wasn't a coma sleep, was it?"

Cal's voice grew a touch more nervous.

"Well. That's the thing, Miri... they don't know. She was maybe more *out-cold* than asleep in the normal way people sleep when they're just tired, you know? She was awake and talking for a while, like I said. Then I looked over at her and she just... passed out..."

"What did the doctors say?" I asked.

"They really didn't know yet. They told me if she didn't wake up sometime over the next twelve to twenty-four hours, they would need to do a second round of scans to make sure she didn't have brain damage. They were really worried about the head injury. They said she could slip into another coma, which is why when I first got back to the room, I wasn't too worried. I mean, I was *worried,* but not about her being gone. Not that someone *kidnapped* her or whatever. I just assumed it was more tests—"

"This is Detective Cassavetes, Cal." Pia Cassavetes had gotten up from the desk chair and now moved closer to the phone, her slim hands resting on her hips. "What kind of relationship does Nina Gallows have with Jacob Mulden? Do you know? Were they close as kids, like her brother was?"

There was a silence.

Then Cal sighed.

I could almost see him through the phone. I could feel how exhausted he was, how worried he was about his girlfriend.

"I don't know if I'd say they were *close*... at least from what Nina told me. From what she said, they had a pretty one-sided relationship."

Black and I exchanged grim looks.

Black's eyes fell back to the phone.

"Explain," he said, blunt.

"Well, I mean, Nina didn't put it this way... but Jacob was more or less in love with her. In high school, he left her love poetry in her school locker. He left her flowers. He offered to buy her lunch and ice cream. Once, when he got a new camera, he would try to take photos of her all the time, saying he was 'practicing' his photography skills."

Cal let out a cynical grunt.

"Then there was the movies. Jacob was obsessed with making movies. He would always try to cast her in the home videos he and Rodney made as kids. He wanted her to play different roles in each production. She said she played the wife, the girlfriend, a reporter... even a stripper once. I think he tried to get her to go out with him in high school a few times, too—"

"I see," Cassavetes said.

That time, it was me and the female detective who traded grim looks.

"Did this 'one-sided relationship,' as you put it, extend into adulthood, Cal?" Cassavetes asked.

There was another silence.

I was reading Cal a bit now.

I felt him sigh, as much as heard it.

"Well, she went away to school," he explained. "She said Jake wrote her letters and emails for a while, but I guess it stopped eventually, when she never wrote him back. She didn't want to encourage him, she said, so she was polite when she ran into him, but she refused to give him her phone number, and she never called him when she was back in town."

Still thinking, he added, "She also said she was relieved when her parents moved to a place in the East Bay, where she wouldn't run into him every time she came home to visit. She said it sometimes got a little creepy before that. It was like he just stood there, at the window, waiting for her. She'd go out to get the mail... or she'd be helping her mom with groceries or whatever... and she'd turn around and find him standing there, giving her what she called his 'lost puppy' look."

There was a silence.

Cal sighed, like he was seeing all of this in a new light now.

"Was she afraid of him, Cal?" Cassavetes asked.

The silence deepened.

"Maybe," Cal admitted.

His voice grew audibly reluctant. Mostly, though, I heard the dawning understanding and guilt in his words as he put it all together.

"I didn't see it that way when she talked about it before, but yeah, she might have been afraid of him. She definitely took pains to avoid him. She did her best to take precautions against running into him around town in Saratoga when she'd go back there. She'd even ask if he'd been invited to certain parties and get-togethers, and skip the ones where they expected him. She seemed really frustrated with her parents when they wanted her to 'be nice' to Jake, implying she should take pity on him because of his bad circumstances or whatever. She said when she'd tried being nice in the past, it just made things a lot worse."

Cal paused again, thinking.

I was reading him deeper now, seeing Nina's facial expressions through Cal's memories. I watched her eyes as she explained to him about her weird neighbor, Jacob, who had a crush on her.

Nina had definitely been afraid of him.

Even reading her through Cal, even reading the *adult* version of Nina through Cal, I could still sense that childhood fear.

"He asked her to prom," Cal added. "I forgot about that... he asked her to go with him to the senior prom, and made kind of a scene when she went with someone else. I guess he threatened the guy. Threw a drink on him. Stomped on the flowers the poor kid bought Nina for the dance. Jake acted like she'd gone with the other kid as his hostage... like the other boy had taken her prisoner, and Jacob was there to rescue her."

I felt my jaw slowly hardening as Cal spoke.

It only got worse when I focused on Nina's face through Cal's memories.

I could tell Cal realized the depth of his mistake.

I could feel him reinterpreting all of Nina's stories about Jacob.

What Jacob had done to Nina wasn't just pester her with some harmless, high school, unrequited, puppy dog crush.

He'd stalked her.

He'd tried to force her into some kind of relationship with him.

What Cal was describing was classic, obsessive, stalker behavior.

That didn't mean Jacob had been *physically* dangerous to Nina in those years, not necessarily, but it definitely suggested he *could* have been.

It also implied he had serious issues with consent and boundaries, at least when it came to high school girls. It strongly implied he had at least a partially-formed delusion-based attachment to her, one that might have served as a kind of pseudo-"relationship" in Jacob's mind.

The story about Jacob believing he was "rescuing" Nina from her high school boyfriend definitely suggested that.

Those types of delusional attachments often came from a

fictionalized narrative in the predator's mind that re-imagined the nature of his relationship to the victim.

Given everything I'd seen of Jacob at that police station, not to mention what happened to Rodney, I'd say Jacob was definitely dangerous now.

The dragon presence—dragon spirit, demon, or whatever it was—would only exacerbate that risk. There was no way for us to know how *that* thing viewed Nina through Jacob's eyes, but we had to assume the worst. If any part of Jake's obsession transferred to the creature that inhabited him, the danger to Nina could be astronomical.

When I glanced over at Black, he frowned.

From his expression, he'd heard all, or at least part of what I'd been thinking just then.

I watched him turn over the scenarios I'd let play through my mind.

He exhaled, combing a hand through his black hair.

I think we have to assume high school isn't something Jacob Mulden ever got over, he murmured grimly in my mind. *His first victim was Rodney. Now he's got Nina. I think it's safe to assume that he's somehow harnessed the creature he summoned to "make things right" from those early years.*

I felt my jaw harden.

Make things right?

Yes, Black sent. *Including eliminating anyone or anything that gets in his way.*

I felt that tightening in my chest worsen. *Sawing his best friend in half is "making things right," according to this scenario?*

Maybe "Roddo" wouldn't play along, Black sent. *Maybe Rodney Gallows liked his life better now. Maybe he'd moved on from those years, and didn't want to reminisce with his buddy Jakey about the good ole days at Saratoga High. Maybe Rodney wouldn't play his part in Jacob's nostalgia stage play about those years.*

I grimaced.

That sounded frighteningly plausible.

I wondered if Nina was doing a better job, playing her part.

"We have to find her." That sick feeling worsened in my gut, the longer I turned over Black's words. "She might have convinced him for now, but if she's lying, he'll figure it out eventually. That, or the dragon will figure it out for him."

"Dragon?" Cal blurted the word through the phone. His voice pitched upward, alarmed. "What the hell does that mean? What *dragon,* Miri?"

My eyes never left Black's.

I could feel him agreeing with me, even before I saw the flicker of pain in his eyes.

"We don't have much time," Black said, blunt. "Cal? We need to assume Nina is a hostage. That she's with Jacob against her will... maybe even that he's threatening her with something specific. We have to find the two of them. Now."

"What?" Cal's voice grew openly panicked. "You think that asshole is threatening her? I thought you said she was in some kind of costume? That she helped him perform his magic act?"

"What did you think is happening here, Cal?" I asked, unable to hide my irritation entirely. "You really think she left the hospital to do a magic show? With a severe concussion?"

"I thought maybe she was confused," Cal said, sounding defensive. "I thought Jacob was nuts, and still thinks he's in love with her, and he came in there when she was conscious, and talked her into coming with him. I thought he was too stupid or too crazy to realize she had a dangerous head injury... and Nina was too dazed to do anything but go along..."

"Cal, Jacob Mulden is obsessed with Nina Gallows," I said, sharp. "And with high school... and probably with trying to re-write the past in the way he wishes things had gone for him. He's likely to hurt her if she doesn't play the part he's picked out for her. Do you get that? He might even kill her."

There was a silence.

I swallowed, realizing I was coming down pretty hard on Cal.

You think, doc? Black asked, sarcastic.

I realized he was actually annoyed with me, or maybe just annoyed with what I'd said to Cal. Sympathetic maybe, but annoyed, and wanting me to ease up on his friend.

Of course I want you to ease up, Black grumped at me. *You just more or less made it sound like Nina is probably dead... or raped... or both. And that it's Cal's fault because he left her side for two minutes to get himself a coffee.*

I felt my cheeks grow hot.

Not answering Black, I focused back on the phone.

"Cal, I'm sorry," I said, my voice subdued. "I'm not trying to scare you. I'm just very worried about Nina. I'm worried we don't have a lot of time. Where would he take her? Can you think of anything? Is there any place she might have mentioned, something that might hold meaning for Jacob? Any place he might have associated with the two of them—?"

"She's right," Black cut in, blunt.

He gave me an apologetic look.

He turned back to the phone, leaning closer to the micro-phone as he raised his deep voice.

"We need to try and narrow this down, brother," he said, gruff. "Miri and I can't track him the usual way... the seer way, I mean... and so far, I haven't been able to track Nina, either. We have to assume we won't be able to, that Jacob is doing some-thing to make both of them invisible to our seer sight. That puts her in a tough spot, so anything you can do to help could make all the difference."

He paused, maybe to listen to his friend think.

I was already doing the same, watching Cal scan through memories, trying to narrow it down to something specific.

Black went on after a beat.

"It doesn't matter how random it is," he said. "Just try to think. Try to remember if there's anything she said. Any family trips, neighborhood barbecues, holiday parties, community pools, maybe wherever they held that high school dance? Anything at all you can tell us that might narrow down the possible places he could have taken her—"

"They went to Yosemite once," Cal blurted. "Jacob went with them. She said he tried to sleep next to her in the tent."

"Good," Black said. "Anything else?"

There was another silence.

I felt Cal thinking, turning over every word Nina ever said to him about Jake.

I felt his rising panic as he scanned memories.

My guilt worsened as I mentally played back everything I'd said to him.

Then, I felt Cal mentally flinch.

He'd thought of something.

"The clubhouse," he said, exhaling. "There was a clubhouse the three of them made. They spent a lot of time there as kids, and even in high school. She actually showed it to me. We went walking up on that hill behind her old house... and she showed me the clubhouse, and where they used to play as kids."

That felt right.

I felt the rightness, deep in my chest.

"Go on," Black said, glancing at me. "Why there, Cal?"

"She told me it was a special place to him. To Jacob. It held significance for him, when it came to her. He found her there once, crying. She'd gotten in a bad fight with her father... who *is* kind of a prick, honestly. Nina told me she and Jacob had a really good talk, that he was really kind to her. She said she regretted it later, of course, when he acted like it made them boyfriend and girlfriend... but at the time, she felt really close to him."

Black and I exchanged looks.

I could see from his eyes he was feeling and thinking the same thing I was.

Black's focus shifted back to the phone.

"That's it," he said, decisive. "Do you remember where it was, Cal?"

"Yes... of course. Like I said, it's in the open space near their old houses. Past the end of the *cul-de-sac* where their two houses lived. In a grove of oak and eucalyptus trees. I remember her saying it looked really different than it had when they were young, but it was pretty obvious kids were still using it as a place to fool around and get high. They'd painted graffiti all over the walls, and it's kind of trashed, but there's a couch, and tables—"

"Could you send us directions?" Black cut in. "Any details you can possibly remember would help, Cal. Distances, landmarks, fences, unusual rocks—"

"Wait. You're going there tonight?"

"Yes," Black said. "We're heading there now."

"I'll meet you there—"

"No!" I said, alarmed.

When Black and the others looked at me, I flushed.

I addressed my words to Cal.

"Cal, you can't come. Stay in San Jose." Glancing at Black, I frowned, still speaking to Cal. "Honestly, I'm sorry again about what I said before. I really am. It's too dangerous for you to come with us. Jacob won't be rational if he sees you. In all honesty, I now think you going to get that coffee when you did probably saved your life..."

I saw Black's eyebrows rise as he took in my words.

"Miri," Cal began. "I can't *not* go there. I *can't*—"

"No, Cal... listen to me." I made my voice a command. "Your being there will escalate everything. Don't you see? He's going to see you as a direct threat to his relationship with Nina. He's not going to take kindly to being faced with any reminder *whatsoever* that Nina's had sexual relations with other men... but if he thinks you're there to take her away from him, that will make him *extremely* dangerous, Cal."

I bit my lip, watching through my mind as Cal thought about my words.

I felt the truth of what I'd said to him down to my core.

I could also feel Cal resisting me, wanting to be there.

He was scared.

He was scared to death for Nina.

He was scared of what Jacob might be doing to her.

"He killed Rodney, Cal," I reminded him. "He killed his best friend. He kidnapped Nina. We have to assume this dragon thing is making him increasingly unstable. And even *before* the dragon got him, Jacob attacked Nina's boyfriend back in high school. He did it publicly. If he was willing to threaten someone he perceived as a sexual rival *then,* we can only assume he's exponentially worse now."

"He'll be stronger, too," Black said, blunt. "The dragon energy will make him strong. We have no reason to think he'll hurt Nina, Cal, but he'd be more likely to do it with you there. Miri's right. You can't come to this. I'll call you as soon as we know anything."

"Black, goddamn it... no!" Cal snapped. "At least let me come up there and wait for you down the street. I can wait in the car—"

"No," Black growled. "You hired me to do this, so let me do it."

Without waiting, he hung up the phone.

He paused long enough to glance around at the rest of us, his gold eyes grim.

"We have to go," he said. "Now."

24

NOT ENOUGH INFORMATION

"Fuck." Black pulled up to the curb, killing the engine.

The mouth of the *cul-de-sac*, of Old Oaks Court, the street where Rodney and Nina Gallows, and Jacob Mulden grew up, was quiet.

It was also dark.

High clouds blotted out most of the stars overhead. The half-lit moon we'd seen a few hours earlier, at the Japanese garden, had disappeared behind the same.

There were no streetlights illuminating this stretch of road.

It looked abandoned.

I'd been talking to Yarli, getting the latest update while they tried to find Charles, but now I looked up, following Black's gaze to a Jeep parked on the stretch of road in front of us.

We were on the last segment of road before the *cul-de-sac* where Jacob Mulden and his father still lived. I could see the tan-and-dark brown, sixties-style ranch house, the one located directly across the street from the Spanish-style house belonging to the Muldens.

It didn't look exactly the way I'd seen it through Nina Gallows' memories.

Even so, I could still see the bare bones.

The same triangular window peaked over the front stoop.

The same cement steps and red clay tiles led up to the front door, bisecting a manicured lawn rimmed with hibiscus flowers, purple agapanthus, red-leafed plum trees, white-skinned birches, and newer-looking rose bushes and snapdragons.

The row of cherry trees on the other side of the driveway were still there, although more mature than I'd seen them in Nina's memories.

They had a different fountain now, a new mailbox, and the garage and trim were painted dark brown instead of white.

The Gallows had lived there, when Jacob Mulden was a child.

I had no idea who lived there now.

The new owners didn't have a single light on in their house, but there was an Audi parked in the driveway, and I saw a row of new-looking succulents arranged in glazed pots on either side of the walkway up to the front door. The house still looked a bit dated, but the roof looked new, and they were obviously caring for both the yard and the house's exterior.

The same couldn't be said for the Spanish-style house where the Muldens lived.

Their weed-choked yard still made the house look abandoned to me.

Really, the house looked condemned.

Somehow it looked even worse to me now than it had the first time I'd seen it.

Chunks of the tile roof decorated the yard. A dry fountain was overgrown with plants. The stucco's paint was peeling all along the side of the house, and the steps leading to a side gate were barely visible in the dandelions and mallow weed.

It had to be around two o'clock in the morning by then.

I didn't see a single light on, in any of the houses.

"Did she find Charles?" Black asked me, staring at the back of the Jeep. "Yarli?"

I felt my mouth pinch at the question.

"No," I said. "She says they're all too well shielded still. She suspects they're heading for a safehouse, or even taking turns sleeping while they build a construct that will provide more permanent protection."

Black nodded, but didn't speak.

He leaned on the steering wheel, staring down the dark *cul-de-sac*.

We hadn't found any sign of Charles or his people in the recordings from the surveillance cameras of the White Rabbit. I hoped that meant Charles was still behind us, in terms of tracking Jacob Mulden. I still held out some hope (probably wishful-thinking) that Charles didn't know what Mulden was, and wasn't yet tracking him at all.

I didn't believe it, though.

I could feel the connections there, somehow.

Truthfully, ever since the conversation with the vampire king, I could feel the connection between Charles and "Coreq," too.

There was definitely something there.

Something we'd completely missed.

It made me wonder too, how much the seer adepts on that other version of Earth had picked up about me and Black, when it came to our "powers."

They'd always seemed more nervous about our gifts than anything else.

I'd thought at the time they were worried we might somehow destroy our version of Earth, the same way Old Earth got destroyed by its seers.

I thought maybe they considered us too young to wield that much power.

I thought they distrusted Black, especially, as too young, too reckless, too uninterested in spirituality, too much of a smart ass, too emotionally immature, too aggressive, too feckless, and too ungrounded to be all that trustworthy with the enormous amount of power he'd been given.

Now, however, I wondered if it was something else that made them uneasy.

After all, if we'd only ended up with these abilities due to some kind of dark spell that Charles had been attempting to cast for years... even decades... then these gifts likely were never meant to come to this version of Earth at all.

It also made me wonder what Charles' endgame had truly been.

One thing I knew: I needed to read up on seer religion.

I needed to understand more about this "One God," and what Charles believed.

I felt Black's eyes on me and turned, meeting his gaze.

I was in the shotgun seat now. Cassavetes insisted on sitting in the back, and the few times I glanced back at her, I saw her sandwiched happily between the two vampires, seemingly without a care in the world. She'd spent most of the drive from San Francisco back to Saratoga chatting with Brick, about everything from New Orleans (she recognized his accent), to Paris, where she was originally from, to the nature of vampire newborns.

I glanced back at them now, wondering at the silence, and saw the three of them looking down at something on the human detective's phone.

"They just announced it on the news... that Nina has been kidnapped from the hospital," Cassavetes explained, glancing up at me. "It just came through as breaking news, after someone reported it on social media."

I frowned.

Looking at Black, I motioned with my chin towards the Jeep.

"Are you worried that's Charles?" I asked.

Black frowned back at me.

"No," he said.

Without waiting for me to ask him anything else, he reached for the driver's side door.

He snapped the latch of the Bentley, not looking at me as he climbed out of the car.

I got out on the passenger's side in time to see him checking the gun he wore on a holster under his jacket. I realized he wore two guns when he checked the second directly after, which hung on his opposite side in an identical holster.

"You're going to shoot him?" I said. "Jacob Mulden?"

He gave me a sideways look.

He didn't answer me beyond that.

Still, I got my answer.

❦

I looked at the Jeep as we walked by. I tried to peer inside the tinted windows, but couldn't see much other than a parking sticker and a compass on the dash.

Somehow, nothing about it struck me as remotely Jacob-like. It didn't look at all like a car I could imagine Jacob Mulden driving, but it was the only car on the desolate street apart from the Bentley SUV and the Audi in the driveway that used to belong to the Gallows.

I had my doubts the Audi belonged to Jacob, either.

Really, the idea was laughable.

I doubted Jacob had a car parked in his own garage.

The falling down, Spanish-style house at the end of the *cul-de-sac* barely had a driveway, and the garage doors looked like they hadn't been opened in years.

Someone had parked a wheelbarrow right in the center of the cracked cement, and a pile of bricks covered another few feet of driveway next to a pile of gravel and another of dirt. Enough grass was growing in the pile of dirt that I found myself thinking those piles had been sitting there since Jacob and Rodney and Nina were all in high school.

Maybe they'd been sitting there since Jacob's mother had died.

Maybe they'd been there since his father got MS, and could no longer finish the garden project he'd started, all those years ago.

However long they'd been there, whatever event caused them to go neglected there, blocking most of the driveway, something about the presence of those three piles seemed to encapsulate so much about the Mulden family and Jacob Mulden in particular, I found them deeply depressing.

No, there was no car.

If Nina and Jake were here, they must have been dropped off.

The Jeep had to belong to someone else.

"Do we know where we're going?" I said.

From behind me, the vampire king answered, his Louisiana accent lilting in the cold night air, strangely loud out here, almost jarringly so.

"I can smell them," he said.

When Black and I turned to look at him, he motioned towards the end of the *cul-de-sac*, where a fire break lived between the old Gallows' house, and the house owned by the Muldens. The dirt and gravel road traveled between two wooden fences, likely built by the city, or possibly the neighborhood association, assuming there was one.

No neighborhood association would allow the Muldens to keep their house looking like that, doc, Black murmured in my mind. *I'd guess the city or county fire department.*

I found myself agreeing with him.

The Muldens probably would be harassed and fined daily if they had to deal with a real home owners association, especially in a town as expensive as this.

The two vampires, Brick and Zoe, walked ahead of us now on the path, walking soundlessly on the gravel, even though Zoe's boots had heels on them at least a few inches high.

I found myself watching her in the flowing pants she wore, the high heels, the expensive-looking blouse with the leather hip-belt cut at an angle to emphasize her hips and their contrast to her small waist. She really did look like a model.

Then again, she always had to a degree.

Like Nick said, the vampire thing had a tendency to exaggerate parts of yourself that were already there, meaning before you got turned. Most of what a vampire was, they'd already been as a human. Being turned didn't generally invent a new person out of whole cloth, although it might seem that way if the person in question repressed a lot as a human.

The thought of having to shoot Jacob Mulden made me feel sick.

At the same time, I knew Black was right.

We likely had no choice.

I glanced to my right, where Cassavetes paced me and Black.

She was a little louder than me and Black, and a lot louder than the vampires, but still quiet for a human. She walked on heeled boots through the gravel as well, but her heels were probably a good inch and a half shorter than my sister's.

She saw me looking at her, and gave me a wry smile.

"Cal sent us detailed instructions on how to get to the clubhouse," she said in her accented voice. "We should probably be looking at them, no?"

"We don't need them, Detective Cassavetes," Black said. "We have vampires with us. They've already said they can smell him."

"They know *his* smell? Specifically?"

I'd wondered that, too.

I looked at Black, who frowned faintly.

"I don't know," he admitted. "I suppose I was thinking that humans give off a particular smell, and they were just following that."

"There are humans in the houses, too," Cassavetes pointed out. "There are humans all around us. I am human."

"Perhaps they're combining that human smell with their knowledge of the rough location of the clubhouse."

I frowned a little.

I knew Brick and Zoe could hear every word we were saying.

Vampire hearing was exponentially better than that of seers, and seers tended to hear significantly better than humans.

They knew we were talking about them.

They'd heard Cassavetes' questions.

Still, they'd chosen not to answer.

They have their own motive here, Black murmured in my mind. *But you knew that already, doc. You've known from the beginning.*

Black paused deliberately, glancing at me.

Which is another reason you aren't really letting yourself go there with your sister, he added, softer. *You're waiting for the other shoe to drop, in regards to their motives here.*

I did know that.

He was right about me with Zoe, too.

They're hunting Charles, I sent, quiet.

Yes, Black affirmed simply. *They are hunting Charles.*

Do they really believe they'll find him out here? I asked. *Do they think Charles and his people have made contact with Mulden already?*

I don't know. Black's thoughts remained neutral. *All I know is, that Jeep doesn't belong to Jacob Mulden. I highly doubt it belongs to Nina Gallows, either.*

You think the Jeep belongs to one of Charles' people?

I don't know. Black hesitated, then added, *I'm more worried it doesn't.*

Meaning what?

Meaning, I'm worried Cal beat us here.

At my silence, Black turned his head, looking at me. His gold eyes glowed in the dark as he paced silently next to me, almost as soundlessly as one of the vampires. When I still didn't speak, he reached for me, sliding his fingers into mine.

You're forgetting. I served with Cal, Black sent softly. *I've known him for over twenty years, doc. You've only ever known him as a chef, but that's not how I met Calvin Eduardo Verago. I know what he's capable of. There was never any possibility he would wait for us in a hotel in San Jose.*

I swallowed, thinking about Black's words.

That felt true.

His words felt completely true, which made me wonder how I hadn't seen it.

Maybe I had seen it, though.

Maybe I'd known Cal would come out here, looking for his fiancée, even while I'd been talking to him on the phone. Maybe I simply hadn't wanted to know, so instead of confronting him directly about it, I'd yelled at him for getting a cup of coffee in a hospital cafeteria while he was worried about his girlfriend.

I hated how blind I felt in all of this.

Never had being a seer felt so useless.

The fences and the fire-break road ended on a field dotted with oak trees.

I saw elms and eucalyptus mixed in with the oaks in the most densely wooded area ahead of us. A wild growth area lived in what looked like a slight gully at the base of the hills. There might even be a creek down there, or simply runoff from when it rained.

It should have been completely dark among those trees.

It wasn't, though.

I glimpsed light there, a faint glow that somehow made its way through the undergrowth and mass of thick trunks.

"Yes," Black said to me. "It's there."

He turned to the vampire king, and my sister.

"How many?" he asked. "How many can you smell? And of what race?"

Brick turned from where he'd been staring at the same section of wood.

Meeting Black's gaze, he lifted one eyebrow.

The sky was pitch black from the high clouds, which may have been why it was so easy to see that distant light in the woods. It was the only real light out here.

Even so, Brick's vampire eyes seemed to glow with some invisible, caught light, like a cat's eyes in a lightless room. He smiled, holding Black's gaze.

"Two humans," he said.

"Any seers?" Black pressed. "Apart from me and my wife?"

Zoe answered him that time.

"We don't know," she said.

She turned her pale face towards ours, and like Brick, her eyes seemed to glow. She gave me a faint smile, then turned to face Black.

"You are much more pungent to us," she said, lifting a hand in a kind of half-apology. "We can't smell anything but you out here... at least in terms of seers."

I fought not to roll my eyes.

Zoe must have seen the skepticism in my face, even without the eye roll.

"It's true," she said, a touch more defensively.

"You must have an opinion." I looked between her and Brick, my voice flat. "In fact, I'm absolutely positive *both* of you have an opinion... together and separately. Just like I'm sure you've been talking about it via the blood connection you no doubt reinforced a few times since you first met us at the Japanese Gardens."

Brick smiled.

He opened his mouth, about to answer me—

—when a muffled yell came out of the woods in front of us.

A woman's yell.

All of us froze.

Then, seemingly all in the same fraction of a second...

...all of us began to run.

25

THE CLUBHOUSE

We all ran straight to the grove of trees where we'd seen the faint light.

I couldn't keep up with the vampires.

They ran like ghosts, like flickers of wind, first over the sun-bleached grass, then between the dense tree trunks. They ran so fast, I couldn't even follow them with my eyes.

Black ran fast, too.

I followed his retreating form, doing my best to keep up with him.

Behind me, I could hear Cassavetes gasping, fighting to keep the rest of us at least partly within sight.

I saw flickers of a jumping, jostled light behind me, and realized she'd also turned on the flashlight app on her phone, probably so she wouldn't do a nose-dive into the dirt, which was pock-marked with gofer and snake holes, thick roots, clumps of grass, cow patties, not to mention larger dens for jackrabbits and foxes, and even more for ground squirrels.

I did my best to dodge around and over those as well.

Once we were all among the trees, it was even darker where we were, but even lighter up ahead. I focused on that orange glow, still following Black's back, although he'd widened the distance between us.

When I finally burst out into the clearing that held the plywood cabin, I stopped so fast I nearly fell.

Luckily, Cassavetes was far enough behind me that she didn't run into me.

Within a handful of seconds, she stood beside me in the clearing, panting, sweating, fighting to control her breath and her galloping heart.

I saw Black had stopped as well, but he only stood still for a bare handful of seconds.

He walked directly up to the off-kilter door hanging on the front of the structure. The plywood clubhouse stood in the middle of a small clearing, beneath two massive oak trees.

I lurched after him.

"Black, wait—"

"Stay out here, Miriam!" he growled.

If anything, I started walking faster.

"Like hell..." I muttered under my breath.

There was no way I was letting him go in there without me.

Even so, I got through the opening a few seconds behind him.

I walked in without hesitation, managing to catch the door before it could swing shut after Black tried to pull it closed.

When I turned around, I found myself in a surprisingly large space.

There wasn't a lot inside.

The furniture was sparse, but worked for a kid's clubhouse.

A bar-height table made of an old rain barrel stood in one corner, decorated with wine bottles filled with white taper candles. All of those candles were lit.

A water-destroyed couch sat against one wall; it looked like it had no springs left in it at all. The frayed fabric sagged so low in the middle, the bottom rested on the ground. Most of the mold smell probably came from that thing, but it looked dry now. The fabric had faded, but I could still make out the faintest hint of the stripes that had once made it two different colors, maybe purple and pink, or red and blue.

The style, the stripes, the shape, everything about it evoked a different time.

Rugs and mats covered different sections of floor, half-buried under dirt.

Tattered magazines and comic books were stacked by the couch. Doll heads and plastic animals decorated the wooden sill of the shack's one window. Like Cal said, graffiti covered the inner walls, including a few crude pictures of genitalia, a few tags with initials, and comic book characters, a few of which were surprisingly well done.

A lot of that graffiti didn't consist of tags, though.

A lot of it evoked the symbols I'd seen on the walls and floors of Jacob Mullen's underground shrine. Some I recognized from the symbols Zoe drew around the pentagram she made in the dirt at Hakone Gardens.

I found myself looking at Nina.

Nina stood directly in front of me.

She was slightly off-balance, gripping the arm of a man who held her around the throat and most of one shoulder.

Another blink from me, and I comprehended the whole scenario.

It was Jacob, and he held a knife.

The blade dug into Nina's skin, causing a rivulet of blood to run down her neck, turning the white T-shirt she wore a dull red in the candlelight.

Black held up his hands.

"Don't," he growled. "We just want to talk to you, Jacob."

"You had that chance once," Jacob snapped.

He sounded like Jacob Mulden.

That wasn't the voice of the dragon creature I remembered from the police precinct in San Jose; it sounded like the forty-something man Cassavetes and Wood interviewed.

Jacob's eyes went past me and Black to the person who came into the clubhouse behind us.

"Of course, it's you," he said accusingly, glaring at Cassavetes. "I should have known you'd follow me. That you'd try to *spoil* this for me."

I had no idea where the vampires were.

I hadn't seen them enter the shack.

I hadn't seen them at all after they disappeared into the trees.

I didn't let my gaze drift towards the window, or to the half-ajar door behind me. I didn't dare look for them, not until we had the Jacob situation under control. I had to hope, whatever they were doing, they wouldn't actively try to get any of us killed.

I focused back on Jacob with an effort, and on Nina, whose eyes were wide, red with crying and what looked like terror. She stared at the far wall, tears running down her cheeks. Something about her face made me think she might be in shock.

Still, looking at Jacob, I felt a flicker of hope.

I really *didn't* see the dragon there.

I didn't see any hint of the creature we'd met before.

I saw the same sad, peevish man I'd watched Cassavetes and her partner interview at the police station in San Jose.

Like Black, I raised my hands in a peace gesture, taking a step forward.

"It's okay, Jake," I said gently. "We didn't come here to hurt you or Nina. We have absolutely no intention of taking her away from you, Jake. You can put the knife down—"

"Liar!" Jacob snarled. "All of you are *liars!* Her, especially!"

I bit my lip, watching his hand gripping the knife.

I continued to edge carefully forward.

"How do you know we're liars, Jake?" I asked. "What have we lied about?"

"She brought *him* here," Jacob snarled, jabbing the knife harder against Nina's throat. "She brought her dumb ape of a boyfriend here... even after I asked her *not* to!"

Nina let out a half-scream.

A sob broke out of her throat, cut off when Jacob pressed the knife deeper against her skin. The trickle of blood started to flow, the rivulet growing thicker.

"She brought that rapist goon *here,* to our spot," Jacob snapped. "She showed him our private place. He said they laughed about it... that they *laughed...*"

I saw Nina's eyes shift away from mine.

She stared at the other wall of the cabin, like before.

I watched her stare, her eyes bulging. She focused on a dark area of the floor, a part that lay outside the circle of candlelight.

For the first time, I followed her terrified stare.

A body lay there.

It had been left face-down in the dirt, its lower half sprawled over one of the carpeted mats. It wasn't moving.

I felt Black's heart leap, a ripple of intense emotion coming off him, before I'd even made sense of who it was.

Then I understood.

Cal.

Gaos... it was Cal.

I stared at him, feeling my heart hammer in my chest.

He wasn't moving.

He wasn't breathing.

I tried to look at him with my seer's sight, but I couldn't see anything.

I felt grief and rage spiral off Black in a dark cloud. I'd never felt anything quite like it before, not from him, not from anyone I'd ever known. I'd never felt so much love off him, twisted into a hard knot of disbelief, pain, a helpless fury.

I found myself wanting to touch him.

I wanted to wrap my arms around him.

Instead, when Black lunged forward, crossing the space in Jacob's direction, I clutched at him, gripping one of his arms in both of my hands.

I didn't do it so much to hold him back, but that ended up being what it did.

I did it just to be there for him.

It still hadn't fully sunk in that Cal was dead, even though I knew he was. I knew the body lying there wasn't coming back; I knew it with every part of my rational mind.

I just couldn't make myself believe it.

I didn't want to believe it.

"How?" Black's voice came out guttural, stripped of any pretense of friendliness. Every hint of that soothing calm I'd heard in him before evaporated.

So did any attempt by Black to deescalate the situation.

"How the *fuck* did you manage to kill Cal?" he growled. "And why?"

His voice broke.

"*Why?* Why would you kill him?"

Jacob blinked, staring at him.

From his blank, bewildered expression, I found I knew.

He hadn't done it at all.

The dragon had.

That presence inside Jake had sensed a threat, probably a deadly threat, and killed Cal to eliminate that threat. When I looked at Cal's dead body the second time, I saw a gun gripped in one of his muscular hands. I also saw his vacantly staring eyes, and the blood around his mouth and nose. He looked like he'd had a brain embolism.

Or maybe like he'd been hit with one of those sonic weapons, the ones that use high-pitched tones to explode blood vessels all through your brain.

"He tried to kill me!" Jacob screamed.

He pulled the knife off Nina's throat, brandishing it at Black.

"Don't come any closer!"

I gripped Black's arm tighter.

He's right, I told him. *Don't pull out the gun, honey. That thing will kill you, too.*

I felt the cold fury in Black's mind.

I also felt him absorb my words.

I felt him draw my meaning into the part of his mind that had gone full-blown strategic kill mode. That part of Black wouldn't do anything to jeopardize his chances to annihilate this thing for what it had done to his friend.

At the same time, the grief on him was so intense, I closed my eyes.

I gripped him tighter, fighting the pain that rose in my chest.

Honey, I'm so sorry. I'm so sorry, baby...

When Black spoke, next, it barely sounded like him.

He spat the words, his voice harsh, cold.

"What do you want? What do you want from me?"

Jacob glared at him, still holding out the knife, his face bright red as he continued to grip Nina around the neck. He looked like he might be about to answer Black.

Someone else spoke before he could.

"Don't bother asking him anything," a familiar voice said. "He knows even less than you do, I'm afraid. And you apparently don't know shit... as usual."

Black and I turned, moving so fast, and backing towards the wall so quickly, I half-stumbled, nearly falling into him. I caught myself by tightening the grip I still had on Black's arm. I continued to drag my husband back; I couldn't think about anything else at first.

I never took my eyes off the person who'd spoken.

My mind went utterly blank, lost somewhere between fury, disbelief, and a complete lack of surprise.

"Charles," I managed.

My father's biological brother smiled at me.

His pale green eyes looked white in the flickering light of the candles.

"Call me Lucky, my dear," he said. "Or Faustus. I do tire of the human name."

The false friendly note didn't resonate in the slightest.

When I looked at his eyes, when I caught flickers and glimpses of the living light around his lean, muscular form, I saw hatred. He hated me. The utter revulsion, disgust, violence, and cold fury he aimed at me, even more than what he aimed at Black, might have scared me at a different time.

Now, with Black's hurt and rage vibrating my light, it only brought up similar sentiments in me. I stared at the man I'd loved, the brother of my father, a person I'd looked up to more than any other, and I realized he had to die.

He had to *fucking* die.

Every day he drew breath, destruction and suffering followed in his wake.

He was malignant to the core.

His very existence was a cancer.

Lucky Lucifer laughed, throwing back his head.

"Oh, my dear." Open contempt filled his voice. "What a *child* you are. I cannot believe how much time I wasted, trying to help you to become anything else."

He looked away from me, still exuding that hate-filled contempt.

Turning his back on me, literally, but I suspect figuratively, too, he aimed his voice at the two people standing over the destroyed couch.

"Nina, darling... Jacob... that's enough..."

Charles' voice lilted melodically in the small space, vibrating with that strange, otherworldly accent I often heard from the mouths of Old Earth seers.

"...You can relax now, my loves. We don't need the charade any longer."

There was a silence.

Then the woman Jacob Mulden had been holding with one arm wrenched free.

Raising a palm to her cut neck, she staunched the blood. She aimed a glare at Jacob, but her words were one hundred percent meant for Charles.

"Can we get rid of these stupid assholes now?" she snapped

contemptuously. "Me and Jake did everything you wanted. We brought the two of them here. Isn't that enough?"

Jacob held up his hands. "Not yet, honey. We still need them—"

"Don't 'honey' me!" she snapped. "You didn't have to cut so deep. You could have sold it with just the knife... or used fake blood... you didn't need to scar me for life!"

"It *wouldn't* have sold it," Jake insisted.

"Bullshit! You're a sadist!"

"Trust me, honey. After tonight, you won't ever need to worry about scarring again..."

I listened to them argue.

As I did, I felt my mind tick down.

It sparked, slowed, like a lit fuse.

Tick, tick... tick...... tick...... boom.

Everything inside me went totally still.

I finally understood.

26

THE INEVITABLE GLOATING

S ome part of me recognized that quiet, deadly, immovable space inside me as the same one I'd felt in Black. That didn't matter to me, though.

Not now.

That space might have come to me from Black originally, but it felt like me, now.

It felt like mine, as much as his.

My uncle looked at me, that hatred still in his eyes, only now mixed with cold triumph, a cat-like satisfaction. I could feel the part of Charles that couldn't *wait* to tell me what he'd done. The part that positively *relished* the thought of telling me and Black all of it.

He couldn't wait to tell us how fucked we were.

He couldn't wait to inform us how gullible we'd been.

In his mind, Charles had already won. I could see it all over him.

I didn't care.

Not anymore.

"Gaos," Charles clicked under his breath, his voice full with that gloating contempt. "Did you really think this was a coincidence? That your friend's girlfriend would just *happen* to have a

strong, childhood connection to someone who worshipped an ancient seer god in his basement?" Charles scoffed. "...The *same* seer god who mistakenly got implanted partly in your arrogant *jackass* of a husband?"

Charles paused, looking between me and Black.

"Are you really that colossally stupid?"

I continued to grip Black's bicep in both of my hands.

I could feel the steel-like bands of muscle taut under my fingers, but his arm wasn't what I suspected would come out, when Black really let loose.

He wanted my uncle to talk first.

He wanted to know why all this had happened before he killed him in front of my eyes.

I wanted those things, too.

Both of those things.

"I found Jacob *years* ago," Charles informed us contemptuously. "By then I'd already determined the dimensional limitations of manifestations of this kind...particularly when they pertained to intermediaries. I already *knew* there had to be some human blood in any dragon manifestation here... or the being doing the manifesting would die."

Okay, that surprised me.

I looked at Black, and he looked at me, raising an eyebrow.

Both of us looked at Charles.

"It's a pity I didn't manage to perfect the rituals earlier, back when I lived on Old Earth." Charles' eyes and voice grew annoyed as he folded his arms. "Seers were a dominant species there. Here, they are not. I unfortunately learned this the hard way, in that the rituals only work with a being who carries the blood of one of the dominant species of a given dimension."

He faced me, his eyes cold.

"I wasn't about to give that kind of power to a godless vampire," he said. "That left me with only humans. If I wanted the One God to manifest here, I had to find some way to use a human to do it. Or, ideally, a human-hybrid, like you. But I wasn't able to breed with any of the human females I attempted this with. My brother was able to do it... fortunately... but he was killed by vampires before I realized how rare that ability was."

"*Gaos,*" Black growled. "How are you able to make even *this* boring? Get to the gods-damned *point,* Charles."

Charles gave Black a thin smile.

"I found this one had an aptitude for the right kinds of magick, at least." Charles motioned towards Jacob, giving Black a smile that made my teeth grind.

"Granted," Charles added sourly, still staring at Jacob. "He's not the most impressive of specimens on the surface... even for a human... but with a little training, he proved to be quite the quick study when it came to the old spells."

My fingers gripped Black harder.

It was taking every ounce of my willpower now, not to tell Black to do it now.

To wipe that damned smirk off my uncle's face.

To turn into a dragon and just *eat* the son of a bitch.

"What an interesting coincidence, that the girl next door looked so much like my niece, Miriam," Charles went on in that smug tone. "Of course, plastic surgery helped that along a bit more. And even before the surgery, Jacob here was so infatu-ated... it soon became the easiest way to control him."

Charles turned, aiming a flat stare at Black. "And extremely handy when I needed to draw the two of you to me," he added. "It was easy enough to arrange a chance meeting between my Nina and your pathetic friend with the crush on my niece..."

I stared at Charles, feeling sicker the more I put together his words.

He'd been working on this for *years.*

Probably ever since—

"Yes." Charles stared at me, his eyes pale green ice. "The vampires figured out what I was trying to do. I have to admit... that surprised me. It surprised me greatly. I never would have guessed in a million years that any of their kind would take the time to comprehend seer religion, much less our most esoteric magicks and mythological texts. I never thought they'd be smart enough to understand it, to be honest... much less smart enough to take it seriously..."

I glanced at Black; it was barely a look.

He did the same to me.

Neither of us took our primary attention off Charles.

"Konstantin?" Black asked. "Konstantin did all this? He figured out what you were trying to summon with all your twisted rituals? He's the one who killed Miriam's father? And ordered Zoe and Miriam changed into vampires?"

There was a silence.

Charles stared at Black through it.

Then he smiled, tilting his head sideways to concede Black's words.

"It was not Konstantin," he said, folding his hands at the base of his spine. "It was one of his lieutenants. A female vampire named Dahlia Marie. She was killed as part of the truce under Konstantin... to compensate me for the loss of my brother and my niece. As a part of that same truce, they agreed to leave my other niece alone... the one they *hadn't* managed to kill. But they warned me that if I ever went near you, Miriam, if I ever attempted to train you in the rituals, they would turn you into a vampire, too. Or simply slit your throat."

Charles' eyes and voice grew colder.

Colder than I'd ever seen them.

"The things I sacrificed, my dear... to keep you safe." He looked at me like he would like to have cut my throat, right then and there. "But I had no choice. Konstantin was not as clever as Dahlia Marie had been, but I knew he was surrounded by others who were smarter than him... who were more dangerous than him... and he, unfortunately, listened to those vampires."

"Are you ever going to stop talking?" Black growled. "We get the point. You trained up this psycho, and had him waiting in the wings in case you couldn't control me or your niece. You brainwashed the next-door neighbor sister and had *her* waiting in the wings, too... then arranged to bring her together with one of my oldest friends..."

Black's voice held even more contempt than Charles'.

"We get it," he growled. "You're an evil *fucking* mastermind. We're *soooo* very, very impressed, Faustus. Truly."

Black jerked his jaw towards Jacob.

"What are you going to do with this sad-sack now? Or have you figured out how to conjure up the dragon in him... like a good little lap dog?"

Charles gave Black a thin smile.

"Something like that."

"So your people are the ones who've been protecting him," I blurted. "You shielded his light. You made him invisible so we wouldn't know what he was."

I stared between Charles and Jacob, feeling the dominoes as they continued to fall, one by one, in my mind.

"You're the one who helped him learn those weird rituals," I said. "You gave him the books. You taught him the chants, told him what to say, how to draw the symbols, where to place the candles. And he went along with it because... what? You promised him Nina?"

Charles gave me an even more withering smile than he'd given Black.

"Why do you keep her around, Quentin?" Charles asked, his eyes still on mine. "She really isn't the brightest thing, is she? A pity, really. Her father was a genius. If there was anyone who deserved to pass his undiluted genes to pureblood offspring, it was Darius."

That thin smile tightened his mouth a few notches more.

"It must be the human mother's blood," he said acidly. "It was Darius's one real weakness, you see. I always told him he got too attached... that he'd do better to spend his nights rutting with barnyard animals than attempting to mate with that thing."

The insult didn't cut like it would have, even a year before.

Maybe even a day before.

I felt like I was seeing my uncle for the first time.

All of his bizarre, faux-paternalistic interest in me.

All of his supposed concern.

All of his brazen attempts to protect me.

All because I had something he needed, something he didn't have himself. Something he apparently couldn't fake, or find a way around, even with all of his sick genetic experiments and human trafficking.

Human blood. I had human blood, and he didn't.

He'd thought he needed me.

The vamps took Zoe from him, took my father.

I was all he had left to embody his gods.

Then Black showed up, and threw a wrench into all of it.

In all kinds of ways.

I still felt like I was catching up, still felt like I was missing pieces of all this, maybe because, unlike Black, I hadn't been privy to all of their weird underground church rituals, and I didn't know much about seer religion in general.

If I lived through this, I was going to have to remedy that.

Black, I thought in his mind. *I think we need to go. You know Charles. He'll have come here with overwhelming force. We need to get out of here. Regroup. Loop in the others. Maybe we should even go to your cousin and Allie, first... ask them what they know about all of this.*

Black's mind was grim.

I think it's too late for that, doc.

I swallowed.

I glanced back at Cassavetes.

You're closer to Pia. Grab her, and I'll jump us —

"You are about as stealthy as a wounded water buffalo," my uncle said, staring at me in open contempt. "Do you really think you can jump out of here? Now? As your husband just told you... it's far too late for that, niece. The ritual has already begun."

I stared at him.

I looked at Black.

I returned my gaze to my uncle.

Ritual?

I didn't want to understand.

From the way Black looked at me, he didn't want to understand, either.

UNFORTUNATELY DUMB

L ight rose abruptly outside the small cabin.

There was a loud *whump*, like a giant gas heater being lit.

I flinched, feeling the first wave of heat as I realized it was fire, that a high ring of flames completely surrounded the plywood clubhouse.

My uncle was right.

We'd been lured out here.

All of this... Nina supposedly being kidnapped, Nina taking Cal out to the clubhouse and telling him a story about how she and Jacob bonded here... all of it was planned.

Charles did all of it, just so Cal would tell us where to come.

Only now Cal was dead.

Black and I, and now Detective Cassavetes, were on our own.

I turned to Charles, only to see him dissipate, swirling into smoke.

"What the fuck?" Without thinking, I drew the gun I wore in a holster inside my coat, turning around, looking for my uncle.

When I looked at Black, he raised an eyebrow, a faint smile on his lips.

"You're armed," he said.

I scowled at him. "Says the guy with two Glock 29s on his person, and probably at least another two guns and a few knives concealed under those pants."

"Don't get testy with me, Dr. Black." Black smiled at me, despite the tension visible in his gold eyes. "Trust me... I approve."

He aimed a hand at Jacob.

"Can I shoot this son of a bitch now?"

"Where's Charles?"

"I suspect Charles was never here," Black said, speaking loudly over the sound of the roaring fire. "I thought he might only be a projection after he started goading us both like that. I lost contact with Yarli and Jem, which is never a good sign... also, once I realized he lured us out here, I knew he was pretty confident we couldn't leave."

"You knew he lured us?" I said.

"Not until he came and started gloating about it," Black retorted. "Did you?"

I lowered the gun I held, scowling. "No," I said. "Although in retrospect, we probably should have listened to the vampires."

I re-holstered my gun, glaring at Jacob and Nina.

Jacob was peering at Nina's neck where he'd cut her, and I scowled harder, realizing again that this whole thing had been nothing but bullshit. Jacob probably never harassed or stalked Nina in high school at all. He probably never threatened her prom date. Nina told Cal those things so we'd chase them out here, worried for her life.

The whole thing had been nothing but an elaborate act.

An elaborate act that ended with Cal being dead.

"Excuse me?" a voice called. "May I speak?"

I turned, blinking at Cassavetes.

I have to admit, I'd totally forgotten she was there with us.

Now, looking at her, I paled.

We were going to get our new friend killed, on top of everything else. All because she had the mistaken judgment to trust us, and to follow us out here in our search for Jacob Mulden.

"You said something about jumping," Cassavetes said, looking between me and Black. "Maybe that's something we should try now, yes? I know that man said it is not possible now, but maybe you could try? Maybe we shouldn't believe the psychopath who seems to want to kill all of us? The man who killed your friend already?"

I swallowed, looking at Black.

He returned my grim look, hands on his hips.

Some part of me had already heard it, of course.

The chanting.

I'd heard it in the background, but let it disappear into the sound of the roaring flames. When the chanting had slowly grown louder, I couldn't stop myself from hearing it, not entirely at least. I'd been trying not to acknowledge what it might mean, choosing to spend my mental energy trying to think our way out of this mess.

It was like the radio someone slowly turns up in the background until you can no longer ignore it.

I looked out the cabin's one window, staring at the wall of flame.

Whoever was chanting, I suspected they were on the other side of that.

"Boy, Nick would hate this," I muttered.

Black grunted, acknowledging my words with a vague gesture in seer.

I knew that particular gesture meant "yes" in seer sign language.

"Yes," Black repeated in English. "Nick would definitely hate this." His eyes grew serious when he looked away from the window, and back at me. "What about what Cassavetes said, doc? Can you do it? Can you at least try to jump us out of here?"

I'd been trying ever since Cassavetes mentioned it.

Really, I'd been trying since I first suggested it to Black,

while the projection of Charles had been holding court inside
the plywood clubhouse.

I couldn't access those structures in my light.

I couldn't feel them at all.

I assumed it was for the same reason I couldn't read anyone
really, the same reason I'd felt nearly sight-blind since we left
New Mexico.

"Yeah." Black exhaled, his hands on his hips. "They've been
blocking us this whole time. Probably since before we got on the
plane."

"You can't change into a dragon either, I take it?" I
asked him.

He shook his head. "No. Not a chance."

"Coreq?" I asked. "Did he tell you that?"

"I can't feel Coreq at all."

Black, Cassavetes and I all looked at one another for a few
seconds more. Then we turned, as if by mutual agreement, and
glared at Nina Gallows and Jacob Mulden.

"What the hell is this?" Black asked them. "What's the
chanting? What is this about?"

Jacob glared at us.

That glare turned into a sneer as he continued to study our
faces

I couldn't help but notice he held Nina's free hand in both of
his own, and that Nina seemed to be totally okay with Jacob
now. That was despite the fact that Nina still held her other
hand pressed tightly against the cut on her neck.

"You wouldn't understand," Jacob said. "This is bigger than
you, Black. You and your stupid wife. You're about to realize just
how *small* the two of you really are."

Black looked at Nina. "You let him kill your own brother."

She smiled, tilting her head sideways.

Holding up her hands, she shrugged, no guilt in her eyes.

"My brother was a prick," she said. "Just ask his ex-wife."

"He had kids," I said, disbelief in my voice.

Nina didn't so much as blink.

Instead, she rolled her eyes, not bothering to hide it.

"Trust me, that's not the worst thing I had to do for this," Nina shot back. "Those kids are better off without him. He was a controlling, sexist *asshole*. And he only had daughters. You really think those little girls needed *that* kind of influence in their lives?"

I could only stare at her.

I honestly had no idea what to say to that.

I looked between her and Jacob, completely at a loss.

Before I could ask them anything else, Cassavetes spoke.

"Why change your face?" She motioned around her own face, frowning faintly as she stared at Nina. "Why the plastic surgery? Why look like Dr. Fox?"

I blinked, staring at Cassavetes, then back at Nina Gallows.

Somehow I'd completely forgotten Charles said that.

He'd told us Nina got plastic surgery to look more like me.

"Is that true?" I asked her.

Nina rolled her eyes.

"Of *course* it's true," she said, her voice as contemptuous as Charles' had been. "Oh, sweetie. Do you honestly think the world works this way? With all of these fucking coincidences? I really didn't think the two of you could possibly be *dumb* enough to come out here, honestly. There was just too much. Too many things that were hard to swallow. Me looking like you..."

Nina motioned towards me.

"...Then you found Jakey's dragon shrine, and it seemingly *never occurred* to you what a totally insane coincidence that was. Or the fact that your buddy, Cal, asked for your help with a case that just *happened* to involve supernatural seer gods with similar powers as you and your mate. Or that Charles would be set free at the same time—"

"Are you going to answer the damned question?" Cassavetes folded her arms, obviously annoyed. "Or not?"

Nina turned slowly.

She stared at the detective with the spiky bangs.

Then she looked at me.

Then she looked at Black.

Her facial expression at each stare was more incredulous than the one before.

"Is that a real question?" she said.

All three of us stared at her, silent.

Nina let out a disbelieving and humorless laugh, throwing up her hands.

"For *Coreq,* of course."

Next to me, Black tensed.

Nina rolled her eyes, flipping back her straight, dark hair as she folded her arms.

"Jesus H. on a cracker. You both really are just fucking *stupid.* You know that?"

I didn't have a good answer for that.

Neither did Black, apparently.

Coreq. They'd made Nina look like me for Coreq.

My mind found ways to make sense of that, to make sense of the chanting and the fire, and what now appeared to be ritual symbols in paint and chalk all over the inside of the plywood cabin. My mind had answers for all of those things now.

None of them were answers I liked.

I also found myself maybe agreeing with Nina on the "stupid" part.

How had Black and I been led so easily into all of this.

It wasn't that easy, doc, Black growled in my mind.

I had my doubts. When Charles voiced it all out loud, the whole string of coincidences and strange events seemed obviously suspicious, too.

When Nina said it, it sounded downright laughable.

Then again, Black and I had been pretty distracted lately.

"What is this chanting?" Cassavetes said. "We are in a ritual, yes? Does this involve some kind of sacrifice? Are you going to kill us like you did Rodney Gallows?"

Nina gave the detective a faint, sly smile.

She flipped back her hair, and looked at me.

"See, I think Charles has it wrong." Nina smirked at me, raising an eyebrow. "Your friend Pia here is one hundred percent human, yet *she* seems to get it. Your husband doesn't have a fucking clue, and he doesn't have any human blood at all."

She held up her hands in a mock apology.

"I'm just sayin'..." She smirked wider. "I don't think it's the *human* blood or genes that make the two of you this dumb."

The chanting was getting louder.

Nina was getting more boring, too.

I was also realizing it was totally pointless taking to either her or Jacob.

They were both pawns of my uncle.

They were also both clearly psychopaths.

I didn't know if my uncle turned them into that, or if they were psychopaths already, before he found them, and my uncle just used that fact for his own ends. Either way, I wasn't going to get anywhere, trying to communicate with them.

Yarli's out? I sent to Black. *Jem, too? You can't reach anyone either in New Mexico or at the California Street Building?*

Black nodded somberly, looking around as the flames rose higher.

They were turning green and blue, sparking gold and black flecks off the top.

The chanting was so loud now, I'm not sure if Black would have heard me, even if I'd shouted at him.

What about Brick? I sent. *My sister?*

No way to communicate with them, doc. Anyway, depending on what Charles has out there, they might have split.

He gave me a hard look. Eyes flat, he shrugged.

You know Brick. He probably did *split. If he couldn't take out Charles with what he had, if he didn't like the odds, Brick would have just taken your sister and gotten the hell out of here. Before Charles or any of his henchmen found him.*

I couldn't disagree with that.

Honestly, I wasn't even sure Brick splitting with Zoe was the wrong thing.

It was definitely a logical reaction to whatever was happening here.

Hell, it's what I would be doing with Pia and Black, if I could get my dimension-jumping apparatus to work behind Charles' damned light shield.

There was a silence while we just stood there, listening to the roaring fire.

Listening to the chants.

I already felt weird.

I could feel my living light reacting to something, flaring and sparking in waves. It was making some part of me uncomfortably hot, even apart from the actual, physical heat coming off the fire around the shack.

I struggled to breathe, more and more nauseated.

I was sweating from the actual *fire,* too, which made it all worse, and made it that much more confusing, since I could also feel the structures in my *aleimi* going crazy under the rising chants, as they resonated with the painted symbols on the walls.

It was hard to track the precise effects of what was happening, much less the cause.

All I knew was, my seer's light didn't seem to be functioning right.

The structures in my light were overheating.

Whatever was happening, the reactions felt intense.

I wondered if they'd kill me by ripping out my *aleimi* altogether.

Maybe that's how they intended to kill me and Black. Maybe they planned on removing our living light, leaving the husks of our physical bodies to die.

It felt like a distinct possibility.

They were going to kill us.

They were going to kill me and Black.

In the process, they would try to lure the dragon part of Black, Coreq, to jump into Jacob. Simultaneously, I imagined they would try to lure the "tortoise" part of me into Nina.

That was my working theory, anyway.

It struck me as reasonably sound, given everything that had been said by Charles, Nina, Jacob, even Black himself.

It wasn't difficult to imagine what my uncle likely promised the two humans.

To be living gods? To be immortal? To fly?

To help him kill most of the humans on Earth?

Jacob didn't seem to like a lot of his fellow humans.

Neither did Nina, for that matter.

Maybe the two of them were reasonably okay with offing a whole bunch of them.

Maybe it seemed like a fantastic deal to the two of them. After all, being Dragon and Tortoise would likely make things nice and comfortable for the two of them. They could play house in a mansion in the California hills, drive any car they wanted, have as much money and power and fame as they wanted, scare the shit out of anyone they wanted.

Kill whoever they wanted.

Watching the flames change colors, growing so high I couldn't see anything past them, not even whether the forest was on fire, I felt like I might throw up.

I looked up at Black, my mouth grim.

Fuck, I thought at him.

Black returned my look, studying my expression.

Then he nodded, once.

Fuck, Black concurred.

He folded his arms, staring around at the rising flames, his gold eyes reflecting the rippling fire.

...Fuck indeed.

I could tell he was still thinking, though.

I just hoped he was thinking fast enough.

28

THE LAST DESPERATE
THINGS

Black, Cassavetes, and I split up the cabin after that.
I walked to the door, looking out at the fire.

Cassavetes coughed—a hard, dry, wracking cough—while she lifted up rugs on the floor, and examined all the wall panels, looking for anything that might be a way out. She examined every wall of the cabin, then turned her attention to the roof.

There really wasn't much of a roof, though.

It was just sheets of plywood nailed together, like the rest of the ramshackle structure.

We re-grouped back in the center of the clubhouse.

Now what? I asked Black.

"Now what?" Cassavetes shouted, looking between me and Black.

She rested her weight on her palms, resting those palms on her thighs. Looking up at the two of us, she forced a smile.

"Any bright ideas, my non-human friends?"

I shook my head, coughing a little as I held my sleeve up to my mouth.

"No," I managed, as I lowered the sleeve. "Sorry, Pia."

She smiled, shrugging like we'd just accidentally gotten her a parking ticket.

I'd totally forgotten I was wearing a headset, until a voice rose in my ear.

"Miriam?" Brick vampire voice was crisp, melodic, yet matter of fact. "Are all of you inside that structure still?"

"BRICK!" I more or less shouted his name, putting my palm over my ear to block out even more of the noise. "CAN YOU GET TO US?"

"No." He spoke in a regular tone. I could almost see him shaking his head, wincing away from my crazy and very un-vampire shouting. "Not right now. We're working on... well, *alternate* solutions. We unfortunately cannot reach the California Street Building using these headsets right now. We believe there may have been a breach there, to keep us from communicating. That, or there is some shield over the area, blocking the signal—"

"How many seers are out there?" Black cut in. "With Charles? Can you see?"

"Not as many as you might think, my friend," Brick said. "We may be missing some, but we've walked the perimeter twice... once before the ring of fire, and once after. Your uncle is not physically here, among the others. Only maybe twelve are here, total. All of them are wearing ritual robes. All of them are chanting. They don't look like fighters, but more like monks, or some other type of ascetic. We were considering taking them out, but—"

"Take them out," Black growled. "Now. Then get us the fuck out of here. I'll make it worth your while—"

An explosion burst out of the ring around the cabin.

It rocked the plywood walls, making chunks of ceiling rain down on us.

Cassavetes, Black, and I ducked.

I looked towards Nina and Jacob, but they were just standing there, holding hands.

It occurred to me that they'd been doing that the whole time we'd been frantically looking for a way out.

They'd just stood there, watching us.

Almost like they knew it was futile.

Almost like they knew we were wasting our time.

"What about them?" I asked Black, motioning towards the two humans. "Do we try to kill them?"

Black looked at them, then back at me, his expression grim.

"No guns," he said. "I don't know what they did to Cal, but he had a gun in his hand."

"I saw that," I began. "But maybe we could try something else. Instead of guns, we could all three try—"

Cassavetes cut me off.

"No!" The female detective shook her head, adamant. "No guns. No *anything*. Do not bother with trying to kill them. They are protected. That one with the blond hair and the green eyes... he would not have left us free to move around in here if they were in any danger. Clearly, he put a lot of effort into setting you up."

I knew she was right.

I already knew we wouldn't be able to kill Jacob or Nina.

I don't know how I knew, but I did.

Black nodded, looking at both of us.

"I know," he said, speaking in a near shout. "But we don't have anything else. And we can't unleash the two of them on the world... not with dragon powers. Not with Miri's ability to jump dimensions and timelines!"

I felt my heart sink, but in the end, I could only nod.

Black was right.

Even if it meant our certain deaths, we couldn't unleash the two of them on the world, much less on all worlds, across all timelines.

The damage they could do was beyond imagination.

Feeling my agreement, Black turned towards the ratty couch.

He made a running leap for the two humans.

I'd never seen him move so fast.

He wove low, darting across the small space, his entire being focused on Nina and Jacob. He crossed the now-burning floor of the cabin before I could suck in a breath to let out a yell. He launched himself off the dirt floor, straight at Jacob.

His timing was perfect, precise, utterly aligned.

I saw him reach for the male human, his hand and arm flashing out, even as he pivoted to deliver a kick from the momentum of his leap.

He never landed either blow.

He never touched Jacob at all.

I don't think he got within two feet of either one of them.

Something threw him back.

It *threw* him back.

Whatever it was, it was so violent, Black crashed through the plywood wall.

He landed in a heap outside the cabin.

I ran after him.

I ran out the hole in the wall and into the sweltering heat, gasping, fighting the pain of each breath into my lungs.

I found him at the base of the fiery ring.

I grabbed his arm, still struggling to suck in breaths, fighting to drag him backwards, to help him back to his feet. Blood ran down the side of his face. Splinters and a few larger pieces of wood decorated his neck and his jacketed arms. I started pulling them out, being careful of the ones in his neck, half out of my mind as I looked him over.

Cassavetes ran up to the two of us while I was still working on him.

"LOOK!" she shouted.

She pointed at the blue and green flames that cocooned us.

It took me a few seconds, but I saw what she saw.

For the first time, I noticed that the flames appeared slightly lower on one side of the cabin. It was an optical illusion, of course; the cabin simply wasn't level. It had been built on a gentle slope. A few yards past the back window, that slope slanted down at a steeper angle, becoming a short hill. Being on the highest part of the ground where we were now, I could almost see over the top of the flames.

I saw chalk-white, hyper-pale skin flashing through the dark trees.

I heard screams.

"THE CHANTING!" Cassavetes pointed at her ear. "IT'S STOPPED! CAN YOU HEAR THAT? IT STOPPED!"

I nodded, feeling a sick relief roil through my chest.

Of all people, Brick was coming through for us.

Brick might even save our lives.

He was getting rid of the chanting cult seers, and hopefully bringing an end to their dark magic before they could rip the raw *aleimi* off our still-living bodies.

Even as I thought it, that pain in my chest loosened a little.

I took Black's hand on one side, and Cassavetes' on the other, and the three of us tried to see past the flames to whatever the vampires were doing on the other side.

I looked up at Black, about to say something—

—when another explosion rocked the small clearing in the trees.

This one knocked me to the ground.

29

DRAGON & TORTOISE

I didn't know where I was.

I lay on something hard.

My leg hurt, badly.

I rolled on that hard ground, gripping my thigh in both hands, groaning.

My ears rang. I couldn't hear anything. I couldn't see past that blinding flash of white light, so bright it wiped out everything else.

I didn't know if I was alone.

I could feel people around me, but I was so confused.

Above me, I saw stars.

The stars shone so bright in that pitch-black night, it took my breath.

I felt a longing in those stars, a kinship unlike anything I'd ever felt.

I felt Black there... but not Black.

Above me, the stars reconfigured into gaseous streams, filled with color and light. I recognized them. I knew them all. I swore I could recite every name, every position. They were joined by other lights, other presences, and I swore I knew them, too. They swam through the stars overhead, and I watched them weave together, configuring and reconfiguring until they made up two distinct shapes.

Green and gold scales.

It breathed fire, wings outstretched.

It screamed into the night sky.

Glorious. Terrible. Bursting with primordial light.

It swam through the sky, so beautiful it brought tears to my eyes.

With it, floating on the wind, I saw...

God, a turtle.

Tortoise, a voice murmured next to me. *It's a tortoise, doc... see?*

An enormous, deep blue turtle... *tortoise,* the voice prodded... like something you might find swimming next to you in the crystal-blue waters of Hawaii. Only this massive, blue-green turtle (*tortoise,* he sent, soft) ...completely filled the sky.

This one swam through starlight and wind.

It didn't wade through water and sand.

I knew these beings.

Dragon.

Tortoise.

Together, they designed the world.

Together, they made it from fire and light.

I felt the pain of watching them go.

I felt some part of me saying goodbye to them.

I felt the longing there, the grief.

I also felt relief.

I felt a mind-crushing, soul-numbing, heart-filling relief.

I'd never felt so much relief in my life.

I felt Black next to me.

His fingers coiled into mine, but I couldn't be certain if he was physically there, if he was real at all. It felt like we were floating in the same sky as the Tortoise and Dragon, but they were going one way, and Black and I were going somewhere else...

Then I was standing in a room.

I recognized this place, too.

A long, high-ceilinged lodge, it reminded me of Native American lodges I'd been in as a child, but I knew it wasn't one of those. It was the prayer lodge from that other world, in that other dimension, with those other, beautiful, kind, *lovely* seers, who had done so much to take us in, who had tried so hard to help us.

A blue flame coiled up from the fire pit, and I saw an old woman's face.

I recognized that, too.

I saw Revik sitting there, Black's cousin. I saw his wife, the Bridge.

I saw their friends and other seers we'd met on our travels there.

They had tears in their eyes.

It's all right. Allie clasped my hand in both of hers. She smiled at me, her gorgeous green eyes, so different from my uncle's, swimming with tears. Her hands gripped me tighter. I realized her husband, the Sword, was crying, too.

We'll miss you, Miriam. Her voice was fierce. *We'll miss you both... my children will miss you... they will miss their blood cousins... but it's all right, my dear, dear friend. This is how it was meant to be. It's better this way. Your world was never meant to endure what those forces would bring...*

I didn't fully understand.

I wanted to, but I didn't.

I wasn't sure I understood at all.

How was I even here?

How did they know?

Yet already, the scene around me had begun to fade.

The high walls and ceiling of the prayer house were breaking up around me.

The faces of all those seers, all those people I'd grown to love, they were all growing insubstantial, like ghosts torn apart by wind.

Grief rose in me, a sadness unlike anything I'd ever known.

A part of me sobbed, howling out that grief.

At the same time, I could feel the part of me that agreed with her.

I could feel the part of me that exuded nothing but relief, nothing but peace.

I wanted Black.

I wanted Black desperately.

I wanted to tell him how sorry I was.

I wanted to tell him that this was for the best, no matter how badly it hurt.

I wanted to tell Black so many things—

But everything around me grayed out before I could say a single word.

LEFT BEHIND

I opened my eyes, wincing at the pain in my head when I did. My skull throbbed.

It felt like someone was hitting me in the head with a hammer, over and over again.

I made myself sit up, still squinting against the pain.

I looked around, and I remembered where I was, but I didn't recognize any of it.

The cabin was gone.

Everything had burned down. The ground around me continued to smoke. Blackened tree trunks filled the clearing. The grass was charred black, down to the root. Some of the higher branches were blackened and burned, too.

I gazed around at all of it, trying to remember.

Then, it hit me I could see.

It wasn't dark anymore.

The sun had come up... that, or it was just about to rise.

Light filled the small clearing, but it was early light still, tinting the sky pink and pale blue, without any rays of the star's light actually hitting me.

I saw Black.

Then I saw Cassavetes.

I crawled over to both of them.

I checked Black first, still blinking past my throbbing head.

He groaned while I was still trying to find his pulse, and I cried out in relief. I felt him all over, looking for blood, looking for injuries I might have missed, but I found nothing. He was cut from the pieces of wood. He had bruises and scrapes. His eyebrows were singed. His hair was singed. His jacket would need to go in the trash. He still wore his guns.

I crawled over to Cassavetes.

For the first time, it hit me that I was injured.

A chunk of wood stuck out of my thigh, and it hurt like hell whenever I moved that muscle. Staring at it, sitting over Cassavetes' still form, I considered trying to pull it out, then dismissed that and looked for homicide detective's pulse.

I found it, and closed my eyes in relief again.

When I opened them again, I saw her own eyelids fluttering. Then I saw her wincing in pain, and I leaned down, kissing her on the cheek.

"You're all right." My voice was hoarse with smoke. "You're going to be all right, Pia. Thank the gods. Or the vampires, maybe."

I checked her over again, just to make sure I didn't miss anything.

Then I looked over at Black.

"Doc." He groaned the word, lying on his back. "Miri... where are you?"

I crawled back over to him, and now I was gasping, feeling faint from the pain in my leg.

Black's eyes opened.

He winced at once, raising a hand to shield his eyes.

He never stopped trying to look at me, though.

"What's wrong with you?" Black held up a soot-stained hand, squinting at me. "You're hurt. I can feel it, so don't lie. What the fuck happened?"

He stared at my face, taking in my pained expression,

studying whatever else he could see there. He looked intently for a few seconds.

Then, without speaking, he started to feel down my body.

He stopped when his fingers brushed the chunk of dark, charred, bloodstained wood, and I winced violently, letting out an involuntary cry.

"Gaos." Tears came to his eyes as he stared down at it. "Miri."

"I'm okay," I assured him. "It hurts... but I'm okay."

I glanced at Cassavetes, watching her climb up to a seated position. She closed her eyes, wincing as she rubbed her temples. From her expression, she was dealing with the same skull-splitting headache I was.

She looked at me, her mouth tightened in a pained grimace.

"Are we all alone out here?" she asked me. "Are they all gone, Miriam?"

I realized both Black and Cassavetes were looking to me for answers.

Since mine was the first face they'd seen when they regained consciousness, they thought I knew more about what was going on than they did.

Sadly, I didn't.

I opened my mouth, about to tell them as much—

When someone else answered Cassavetes instead.

"No," a calm voice said. "You're not alone."

I looked up, sharply, biting my tongue when the pain in my head swelled.

I stared at two people I almost recognized, and almost didn't.

I knew what they'd been called before.

Those names didn't really seem to suit them anymore now.

Jacob Mulden.

Nina Gallows.

They'd grown up in Saratoga, California.

Yet I saw no hint of either human I remembered from before, when the blue-green flames rose around the plywood, and they both looked triumphant as they waited for us to die.

I saw nothing of either one of those people in the calm, far-seeing eyes that looked over the three of us now.

They were still holding hands.

Even that felt totally different, though.

They were also completely naked.

They barely seemed to notice their nakedness.

Before I could come up with words, they addressed all three of us.

"We apologize for any inconvenience—" the male began.

"—We are sorry you were not asked," the female added. "That your free will did not decide this question for you, that it was decided outside your control—"

"We are sorry for the violence of this, that it had to happen this way," the male said.

"—But we agree with you," the female finished, smiling at me.

I blinked, looking between those two faces.

It hit me again, they weren't wearing a stitch of clothing.

More than that, their actual features had changed.

They both looked ethereal, inhuman.

Beautiful.

Calm.

Filled with peace.

"This is not the right place for us," the male said, speaking as if he agreed with something no one had said aloud. "This place is too volatile. It is too young. It is too—"

"—Human," the female explained.

The male smiled at her.

Then he looked at me.

"Yes. Human. It is too human. And the non-humans are too volatile, too. But we believe we can still make our followers happy," he said.

"Very happy," the female who had been Nina smiled. "...But not here," she amended.

"Definitely not here," the male agreed.

"Somewhere else," the female said.

"So we will take them with us," the male explained. "All of them. Our followers. We will take them to a world that was built for their kind."

There was a silence.

The way the male had said this last thing, I distinctly got the impression it was supposed to reassure me, and to reassure Black.

I found myself remembering all the worlds I'd explored, the primitiveness of many of them, the innocence... and those that definitely weren't so innocent, or primitive at all. I had no idea what these beings planned to do on any of those worlds.

I did know one thing: the thought of Charles having any say in the evolution of any of those timelines made me feel sick.

The thought of Charles traveling to the world of the intermediary seers made me feel sick. The thought of Charles pulling together dragon presences from all over the multiverse and its varied manifestations and dimensions made me feel sick.

Some people shouldn't be given serious, long-lasting, power and influence.

Ever.

My Uncle Charles was definitely one of those people.

I looked at Black. He looked at me.

Then Black looked at the male, whose eyes glowed a pale white.

"Not Charles." Black's voice was respectful, but it came out low, commanding. "It would do great harm to the manifest worlds to bring Charles with you. It would be a mistake. A mistake you might not be able to fix." Black shook his head, decisive. "Don't take Charles. Don't use him to build your new worlds. Don't let him design your seer and human and vampire societies."

There was a silence.

Then Black cleared his throat.

"And please don't take me," he added, softer. "This is my home. It is my wife's home."

The silence deepened.

In it, I got the distinct impression that the two seers were speaking to one another.

As one, then turned, and looked at me and Black.

"Agreed," the male said.

"Agreed," the female said.

"You did not get much free will in this process," the male added apologetically. "So we would very much like to grant you this wish. As to who we will take, we will confine that to those who explicitly pledged themselves to the One God. All others will be allowed to stay."

But I'd thought of something else.

"The other dragons," I said, frowning. "Are you going to reunite them? Are you going to bring them all together into a single being?"

The male looked at the female.

The female looked at the male.

Both of them looked at us.

They shrugged.

That time, only the male answered me.

"Does it matter?" he said.

I looked between those two faces.

It was so strange, to see them like this, to know what they were, to realize how little I ever understood about either of them. It hit me that they could give me an answer to the question I'd asked, but the male was right... it really *wouldn't* make a difference. I didn't know enough to understand the good or bad ramifications of either answer they might give.

Asking was pure vanity on my part.

I didn't have the knowledge to comprehend the answer.

I nodded, letting it go.

"No," I said, feeling strangely relieved. "No. It doesn't matter."

The male smiled.

The female, who still gripped his hand in hers, smiled with him.

There was a brief flash of light.

I heard a faint pop.

And they were gone.

THE END OF A TIME

Black half-carried me to the Bentley.

After examining my leg, he opted to keep the piece of wood in it until he could get me to a hospital. The wood seemed to be keeping the wound from bleeding too much, even if it hurt like hell, every time I jostled it.

He was worried I might bleed out, and he wouldn't risk it.

We didn't spend long looking around the clearing.

We *did* look around, though. Or, more to the point, Black and Cassavetes looked around, while I sat on a boulder and watched them.

The plywood clubhouse was completely gone.

The only hints it had ever been there were the smoldering remains of the couch and rain barrel, some smoke-blackened wine bottles, and carpet mats that had melted into the ground. Cal's body still lay amid the wreckage on the dirt, just to the left of the smoking remains of the couch, and I saw Black stand over it for a long time, unmoving.

While he did that, Cassavetes did a quick sweep of the area.

"No other bodies," she informed us, when she came back. "I saw blood. I saw what might have been signs of a struggle, here and there... but not a single body." She motioned towards my head and ear. "Do those still work?"

I stared up at her blankly.

Then I realized what she meant.

I'd somehow managed to completely forget my headset again.

I touched it now, turning it on, but all that came back was static.

Looking up at her, I shook my head.

"Phones?" Cassavetes said. "Mine is out of juice."

Black and I checked ours dutifully, but ours didn't work, either.

I'd charged mine in the car on the way down from San Francisco; it should have had plenty of charge left, but I didn't say that out loud. There was even less reason I could think of why our headsets wouldn't be working.

The sun was up for real now, a glowing yellow orb in a bright blue sky.

Everything felt really strange.

I still felt oddly blind... underwater... maybe even more so than before.

I felt like I existed in the world with cotton wrapped around my ears.

It reminded me of how I'd felt after a bomb blast went off near my head in Iraq, and temporarily damaged my hearing.

Yet, that wasn't really right, either.

The truth was, every sound around me was more clear and more beautiful than I remembered it being in years. I could hear everything. Every bird, every creak of the branches overhead, every distant motorcycle or car, every frog croaking in the nearby creek, every bee buzzing, every airplane making a contrail above, headed for San Francisco.

The birds were awake with us.

I watched them dart from tree to tree as we walked.

More than any other sound, my ears picked out their various

calls, and I wished I knew all of them, which bird belonged to which sound. My mind recognized a handful, even with how out of it I felt: mourning doves, red-wing blackbirds, robins, blue jays, grackles, finches, mockingbirds, California quail, black phoebes, juncos, crows.

Towards the end of our walk, as we reached the fire trail, a pair of red-tailed hawks screeched down at us from the tops of tall eucalyptus trees.

I didn't realize how lost I was, in all of those bird sounds, until Cassavetes broke the silence, walking beside me and Black over the sun-toasted grass.

"Where are they?" she murmured, looking around as we reached the end of the fire-break road. "The ambulances? The fire trucks? Why is no one else here?"

I frowned, looking up the sloped street of the cul-de-sac.

I could just see the Bentley as we stepped onto the asphalt, with the Jeep parked half a block in front of it.

"I don't know," I said.

Black's arm gripped me tighter around the waist, but he didn't speak.

He brought me to the car.

Immediately, he used the car chargers to plug in two of our phones.

Once he had me settled, he went back for Cal.

I watched him walk back down the short road, a lone figure all in black as he headed back to collect the body of his dead friend.

For the first time, looking at him, I started to cry.

I must have fallen asleep at some point during the drive.

The next time I remembered being awake, I was in a hospital bed.

They must have had me doped up pretty good for the first

chunk of my stay; I didn't remember a damned thing after we'd driven down the hill and back to Highway 9 in Saratoga.

I barely remembered us driving through the small downtown area.

When I woke up, groggy and so thirsty I couldn't think straight, the first thing I saw was Black. I watched him pace back and forth across the foot of my bed, talking to someone on the phone. He barely glanced at my face when he hung up the line, and walked straight up to me, sitting on the mattress next to my arm.

He didn't speak, not at first, but stared down into my eyes.

I stared back at him.

His gold eyes caught pieces of sunlight through the window.

That same light highlighted the contours of his jawline and high cheekbones, the shape of his mouth. He looked so insanely beautiful to me, it caught my breath.

He didn't look real at all.

He smiled, and that only made the ache in my chest worse.

"One minute, doc," he said.

He rose smoothly to his feet, and walked to the door of the private room.

I heard him call out, telling someone I was awake.

I heard him say he needed someone to come check on me. Footsteps squeaked and pounded down the hallway. Then the door clicked shut and I heard Black in the corridor outside, talking to someone in a more normal voice.

I heard him talk to several someones.

When he came back inside the room, he carried what looked like a half-gallon, clear plastic pouch filled with pink-tinted liquid.

He brought it around to where I was, weaving through the jungle of flowers and plants that half-hid me from the door, until he once again sat next to me on the mattress. He held the container in both hands, angling it so I could reach the straw.

"Drink this, doc. They said even with the IVs, you're probably dehydrated."

He never let go of the container.

He sat there, holding it perfectly still. He watched me gulp down the entire contents of the bag, drinking as fast as the straw would allow me to get it down my throat.

"It's water, doc," he said, gentle. His hand caressed the hair out of my face. "They said there are vitamins in it. Electrolytes. Probably a pinch of salt to help with absorption. All that stuff." He watched me suck the last drop out of the bottom of the pouch. "I'll get you another one. All right? Just rest for a few minutes. Let this one settle a bit first, okay?"

I nodded.

I wondered how long I'd been in there.

I wondered that Black had trusted me to a human hospital at all.

Most of all, I found my mind struggling to comprehend everything that happened to us on that hillside in Saratoga. For some reason, I kept going back to the clarity of the birdsong as we walked back to the SUV, how different everything felt and sounded.

The world itself felt different.

It felt different even now.

When I looked up at Black, he was studying my eyes again.

He'd gotten up to set the empty drink pouch in the room's sink, but now he returned to my side, sinking his weight next to me on the hospital bed mattress.

I watched him look at me, his jaw hard.

"We have him," he told me. "Just now. That's who I was talking to on the phone. Yarli's people picked him up about an hour ago."

I didn't have to ask Black who he meant.

Black cleared his throat, gesturing gracefully with one hand.

"He was trying to leave the country," Black explained. "They got him attempting to board a plane to Moscow... but they were waiting for him."

I nodded again, still unsurprised.

Yet somehow, his words made it all real.

"Only him, though," I said. "Right? He was alone?"

Black held my gaze, studying my face as if trying to determine where I was with this whole thing, how I was doing.

"Yes," he said after that pause. "It was a hell of a lot easier to catch him, without his people to protect him. Really, we just had to wait for him to fall asleep. They tracked him to the airport and had people there, waiting to pick him up. We involved the human authorities too, this time. They want to prosecute him. Their first big seer trial."

I nodded slowly.

That made sense.

Really, it made a lot of sense.

"We could use that," I said, thinking aloud.

"I agree," Black responded. "So does Jem. He thinks it has the potential to help us start to build some goodwill. At least on the seer side of the house."

I nodded again.

I was looking around me now, frowning as I took in the sheer number of flower and plant arrangements around my bed.

Someone (*Black,* my mind told me helpfully) had arranged them artistically on tables of different heights, so that greenery and blooms nearly surrounded me, all while leaving a space around the window so I could see outside.

I looked out there now, taking in the park-like trees and grass.

A pond stood there, surrounded by pepper and willow trees, and dotted with ducks.

"Do you understand what happened, Miri?" he asked.

I looked back at Black.

Hesitating, he leaned towards me.

He kissed the side of my face, nuzzling me with a cheek, pressing his face into mine.

Both of us fell into that briefly.

We fell into one another's light.

We fell into each other's skin.

I couldn't believe how much it hurt; or how insanely good it felt. I felt like I'd been separated from him for months... years, maybe.

I was shocked at how much pain I felt.

None of it was pain from my leg.

It was all separation pain.

All of it.

My heart hammered in my chest as we fell into touching one another. My muscles clenched all over as I reached for him, stroking his hair, caressing the outline of his face, running my fingers over his collarbones, tracing small nicks and healing cuts he had, probably from the clubhouse exploding. Maybe from being thrown through that wall.

That pain felt different somehow.

It felt more bittersweet... and personal in a way that brought me to tears.

Before I could stop myself, I wrapped my arms around his neck. I clung to him, sliding my hands under his shirt to touch his back and chest, stroking his skin, pulling him deeper into my light. I couldn't believe how much of him I could feel.

I couldn't believe how much more *Black* he felt to me.

He opened his light to me unreservedly.

Sliding closer to me on the hospital bed, he wrapped his arms around my waist and back, clenching a fist in my hair as he pulled me against him.

Even in that, he was careful.

But I didn't feel any pain in my leg. I didn't feel any physical pain anywhere.

Everything just felt strange.

My body felt strange, but in a way that made it feel *more* familiar to me, not less. It felt like getting myself back, after months, maybe years, of not really knowing who or what I was. The sheer intensity of that familiarity, of feeling like *me* again, choked me up, catching in my chest in a way that brought tears all over again.

Black drew away slightly, but just enough that he could look at me.

"Are you okay?" he murmured.

His fingers still caressed mine.

I nodded, forcing a smile. "Yes," I said. "I think I'm very okay, Black."

"The Barrier will be different now," he said cautiously, watching my face. "You can't take that many seers out of the equation and not change the very nature of the Barrier itself. Just like it changed after Ship Rock... it's changed again, Miri. I don't think I fully realized the impact or the extent of the rituals Charles had his people doing, either."

I cleared my throat, looking down at his hands in mine as I nodded.

"Will that be a problem?" I asked.

"A problem?" Black frowned, thinking. "No," he said. "But the whole make-up of the non-physical space is in flux. Yarli and her people are working on mapping all of the differences, and reconfiguring all of our constructs, since the old ones were based on having a million more seers living on this world..."

A shock hit my heart.

I had understood this.

I really had.

I understood what happened, what occurred when those beings left this dimension, and this version of Earth, but some-how, hearing Black voice it out loud—it managed to shock me to my core, anyway.

"You and I, Miri..." Black swallowed, studying my eyes. "We're regular seers again, honey. Both of us. That ritual wasn't just to give the 'Dragon' spirit to Jacob. All along, Nina was meant to be a vessel for 'Tortoise' as well. She was meant to provide a body that would be mate to Dragon."

He shook his head slowly, still watching my eyes.

"You won't be doing any more dimensional hopping, *ilya*. As far as Yarli and Jem can tell, there are no interdimensional gates open *anywhere* on this world anymore. We're on our own, doc. Completely, now."

I nodded, taking all of that in, too.

I didn't remove my arms from around Black's neck.

I could feel him waiting, though, waiting for me to say something.

"Is it strange that I'm glad?" I said finally.

There was a silence.

Then Black exhaled, wrapping his arms around me tighter.

"No," he said, kissing my neck. He squeezed me tighter, and I felt a burst of love and affection from him, so intense it shocked my heart. His fingers massaged the base of my back, and I felt him open his light more. "No, *ilya*. It's not strange. I'm glad, too."

He kissed my face, exhaling in open relief.

"*Gaos,* Miri. I'm so happy to hear you say that. I was afraid... I don't know..."

He trailed.

In that silence, I found myself thinking about his words.

"You were afraid?" I mused.

Still thinking, I snorted, gripping his hair tightly in my fingers.

"You mean you were afraid that our marriage might be based solely on a prerequisite of us both being possessed by ancient, non-dimensional seer gods, Black? Gods who took over our free will occasionally, turning us into bizarre, not-very-helpful and often *disaster*-causing superheroes?"

Looking up at him, I lifted an eyebrow.

My voice stayed utterly deadpan.

"Yeah. I'm not feeling that right now, husband," I told him. "Are you?"

"Fuck no." He wiped his eyes, looking at me sideways with a look approaching his sharklike grin. Raising his head, he squeezed me tighter against him. "I'm not feeling that at all, wife. Not even a little."

He shook me a little, almost like he couldn't help himself. He didn't loosen his arms around me, and once more, I saw his eyes grow bright.

"I'm just relieved you aren't, either," he said. He kissed my jaw, nuzzling me with his face as he tugged on my hair. "That's good, wife. That's really, really good."

Gripping him tighter, again fighting tears, I kissed his mouth.

I felt his whole body react.

I felt him want to kiss me back.

I felt the desire rise in him so intensely he gasped.

Then, after a split second, I felt Black force himself to pull back. He closed his eyes, leaning his forehead against mine as a dense ripple of pain left his light, closing his eyes.

"So you don't want me less now?" he murmured, his eyes closed still.

"Pretty much the opposite, actually," I admitted, clutching him tighter.

Black nodded.

He raised his head, his gold eyes flickering towards the window. I felt a whisper of possessiveness in his light as he stroked my skin, his fingers tracing the bones along my spine under the hospital gown. He kissed my throat. He kissed the base of my neck next, his mouth so gentle where it brushed my skin, it made me shiver.

More than anything, I felt his restraint.

Right then, the sheer intensity of that restraint fascinated me.

His arms tensed where he held me, as if he had to stop himself from crushing me against his chest. His leg muscles were tense—his back, his shoulders. When I glanced up, he gritted his teeth, his jaw pushing out his cheek.

I felt him fighting to control his light.

"Yeah," he said after another beat. He leaned his forehead against mine, letting out a short gasp. His hands and thighs gripped me tighter. "Me too, doc."

For a few seconds more, we just sat together.

I had my hand inside his shirt, stroking his chest.

I barely noticed I was doing it.

I wanted to get out of there, though.

I wanted both of us to get the hell out of there.

"Can we go?" I asked finally. "Now, I mean? Can we leave here?"

I bit my lip, fighting the part of me that wanted to shake him.

"Can we just get the fuck out of here *right now*, Black?" My eyes stung as I gripped his hair in my hand. "I want to have the rest of our wedding. I want to go away somewhere. I want to spend some time with this. Alone."

Black held me tighter. He nodded.

"Yes," he said.

"To which part?"

"To all of it, Miri. To everything you just said."

I sat there a few seconds longer, thinking.

"What about Cal?" I asked. "Will there be a funeral?"

There was a silence.

Then Black exhaled slowly.

"We had one, Miri," he said, apologetic. "His family flew in over the weekend. We did it on Saturday. You were still asleep, but Cassavetes came. So did her partner, Detective Wood. A few of my army buddies were there, too."

I bit my lip, fighting tears.

"Oh. Okay."

"I'm sorry. I wanted to wait, but we didn't know when you'd wake up again." His voice grew sad. "I didn't want to drag things out too much for his family. They thought they would be going to a wedding for Cal this year."

Black winced, and I could see him remembering. "They're really messed up," he said, quieter. "His dad cried with me for hours. I had to use my light to get him to sleep in the end. It was horrible."

Remembering the smirk on Nina's face, I felt sick.

I was glad that Tortoise would call the shots for that particular soul from now on.

Then, thinking about something else, I frowned.

"How long have I been in here, Black?"

"A little under two weeks," he said promptly.

When I looked up at him, not hiding my surprise, he shrugged, caressing my face.

"You went into that seer stasis thing, doc," he explained, kissing my cheek. "So we weren't too worried. I had Yarli and Jem monitoring you the whole time."

"Was I really hurt that bad?" I frowned, trying to remember. "I didn't think my leg was that messed up. Did the shrapnel cut an artery or something?"

I looked down, flexing my thigh, moving my leg back and forth on the mattress.

"It feels fine now," I said.

When I looked up, Black slowly shook his head.

"No," he said. "Yarli doesn't think the stasis was about your leg. Neither does Jem. The structures you had in your *aleimi* were kind of intense, I guess. Yarli told me that before. When you first started those non-dimensional phases, she said she'd never seen anything like it, not even on the Sword. Taking all of that stuff out of you caused a major restructuring of your light. The 'Tortoise' stuff, the kind of living light you needed to do those inter-dimensional jumps... it was insanely complex."

He gave me a faint grin, winking.

"...Even more complex than the ones needed to turn into a dragon, apparently."

I frowned, looking around the room.

The small jungle of flowers and plants made more sense now.

The signs were all there.

I'd been here for a while.

Still, some part of me could scarcely believe it.

"Your sister came by," Black added, rubbing my thigh. "She came almost every night." He gave me a wry smile. "Even Brick came by once. He apologized that they weren't able to stick around that morning to ensure we were all right. Zoe got hurt in the fight."

At what must have been a startled look from me, he held up a hand.

"She's fine, doc. I've seen her, and she looks fine. Brick said she healed up in a day or so. But it was bad enough at the time, I guess, he felt he had to prioritize getting her out. He said he checked all of us, and we seemed to be all right. Other than your leg, he couldn't find anything *physically* wrong with any of us. He opted to get Zoe out and call the building at California Street as soon as he could reach them."

I nodded, feeling myself slowly calm down.

I looked out the window at the blue sky, the pond, the green field.

The ducks.

"I want to see everyone," I said, thinking. "Are they all back here now? In San Francisco? Or are they all still in New Mexico?"

"Just about everyone's in Santa Fe still," he said. "They're at the resort. Waiting for us. I sent Angel and Cowboy back. And most of the team I had watching over Charles' people in San Francisco got flown out, too. I didn't see any point in making them stay here, so I just told them to close up the building for a few weeks."

Grunting, he added,

"I even ordered Lizbeth to come out. She's sharing a suite with Luce and Michelle."

"Nick?"

"Nick's back to himself, I hear," Black said wryly. "I mean, as much as Nick ever is. Jem informs me that every single day, Nick argues with *someone,* usually Jem, about not being allowed to talk to Dex. He's furious, apparently, that he can't sit down and have a beer and a heart-to-heart with his buddy who tried to murder him."

I grunted, smiling in spite of myself.

"That sounds like Nick," I said.

"Yeah. I think Jem might strangle him." Black hesitated then, looking at me. "You know though, doc... I'm kind of with Nick on this."

I nodded without hesitation, meeting his gaze.

"I am, too," I said seriously. "Maybe we can talk to Jem."

The relief in Black's eyes touched me all over again.

"Well?" I said, as he stroked my fingers, caressing my hand. "Can we go?"

Black looked up.

Meeting his gaze, I realized he was crying again.

They didn't look like sad tears, though.

In fact, they looked like pretty much the opposite.

"Yes." Black nodded as he cleared his throat. He leaned over to kiss my cheek, wrapping his hand around mine, tugging it gently into his lap. "Yes, my darling, beloved, *insanely*-adored wife. We can definitely go."

❧

WANT MORE MIRI & BLACK?
Grab your FREE bonus epilogue!
Use the link or the graphic below!

Link: http://bit.ly/QB15-Epilogue

Normal cases. Human cases.

Black's hodge-podge band of seers, humans, and vampires might finally get what they want: for the races to co-exist peacefully, for everyone to embrace a new, less violent, less reactionary way of existence.

Funnily enough, it turns out Black is the optimist.

Even among his own people, however, who witnessed how badly things can go wrong between seers and humans on another, now-destroyed world, Black's idealistic wish for a "live and let live" society generates more than as small amount of resistance. Even to those who want peace, Black's goals of a transparent, world-wide racial nirvana strikes many as naïve in the extreme.

Black's wife, Miri, also worries things won't go the way her husband hopes... and that's before they take a case that tests Black's new world before it's even begun.

(Full, final description coming soon!)

PREORDER NOW!

WHILE YOU'RE WAITING...

Want to learn more about what happens to Nick Tanaka? Check out the **VAMPIRE DETECTIVE MIDNIGHT** series:

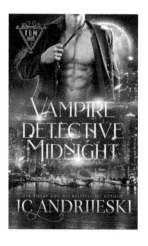

VAMPIRE DETECTIVE MIDNIGHT
(Vampire Detective Midnight #1)

Link: http://bit.ly/VDM-1

Nick Midnight, homicide detective, had his heart ripped out, stomped on, destroyed. It nearly killed him.

He doesn't talk about that. Anyway, things will be different in New York. No complications. No kids needing his help. No relationships. None of that human-vampire-psychic crap that got him in trouble in the past, or turned him evil for nearly a century. He'd toe the line, keep his head down, and do his job for the NYPD, where he works as a Midnight, a vampire who helps humans hunt down murderers.

Then Wynter James shows up.

A gorgeous, sexy, disturbingly intuitive, seer-human hybrid, Wynter treats Nick like she already knows him, like they've known one another for years. Nick wants her, bad, but he knows it's an absolutely terrible idea, and not only because they're not even legally allowed to date.

Everything's already going sideways with his first, big case—dead hybrids, a seer kid who needs his help, graffiti that tells the future, and Wynter, a woman he's so drawn to, it makes him actually insane. Oh, and a possible conspiracy involving the richest humans in New York.

In other words, it's Nick's worst nightmare. It's everything he swore he'd never do again.

Now he's going rogue, likely to get himself killed for a woman he just met—or end up back on the run, in that dark place he thought he'd finally left behind.

VAMPIRE DETECTIVE MIDNIGHT is a gritty, romantic new series set in a futuristic, dystopian New York populated by vampires, humans and psychics trying to rebuild their world after a devastating race war nearly obliterates the previous one. Written by USA TODAY and WALL STREET JOURNAL bestselling author, JC Andrijeski, it features vampire homicide detective, Nick Tanaka, who works as a "Midnight," or vampire in the employ of the human police department. Perfect for fans of paranormal mystery and sexy urban fantasy!

See below for sample pages!

FREE DOWNLOAD!

Grab a copy of KIREV'S DOOR, the exciting backstory of the main character from my "Quentin Black" series, when he's still a young slave on "his" version of Earth. Plus seven other stories, many of which you can't get anywhere else!!

⭐⭐⭐⭐⭐

This box set is TOTALLY EXCLUSIVE to those who sign up for my VIP mailing list, "The Light Brigade!"

GET MY FREE BOOK!

Or go to: https://www.jcandrijeski.com/mailing-list

REVIEWS ARE AUTHOR HUGS

Now that you've finished reading my book,
PLEASE CONSIDER LEAVING A REVIEW!
A short review is fine and so very appreciated.
Word of mouth is truly essential for any author to succeed!

Leave a Review Here:
https://bit.ly/QB-15

SAMPLE PAGES

VAMPIRE DETECTIVE MIDNIGHT
(VAMPIRE DETECTIVE MIDNIGHT #1)

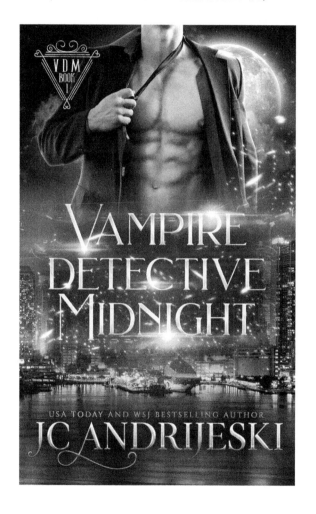

I / SMELLS TOO GOOD

HE SMELLED THE BLOOD, even before he turned the corner into the alley.

He heard them talking about him only a few steps after that.

That was the problem with working with humans.

One problem, anyway.

They had shitty hearing, so they assumed everyone else did, too.

"Where's Midnight?" he heard the lead detective say.

Nick heard the man's clothing move as he looked around, maybe making sure a random vampire wasn't lurking next to him already, or that he didn't see Nick himself walking towards him in the dark.

"I thought he was coming to this?" the detective muttered, taking a sip of something—something hot from the quick, cut-off way he sipped it, likely artificial coffee given that Nick could make out the faint, bitter-tinged odor of that, too.

Of course, no one called it "artificial coffee" anymore.

They just called it coffee.

But Nick remembered real coffee, well enough to know the bilge they drank now wasn't it.

It was an insult to coffee.

The lead detective glanced around where he stood a second time. He checked his watch again.

"Where the hell is he?" he muttered. "We could use a blood-sniffer right now. Christ. Look at this mess."

The man standing next to him grunted. "Fucking bloodsuckers. He's probably paying a blood whore to jerk him off while he drains her dry in a dark alley somewhere..."

The man trailed, mid-thought, flushing as Nick rounded the corner of the building.

Nick stepped deliberately into the light, right as he entered the narrow alley where they were all crouched, standing over something he could smell but not yet see.

He'd been right about the artificial coffee.

The detective standing closest to the scene, closest to the female tech leaning over the nearest body, collecting samples and photographing it from all angles, took another sip of the watered-down crap, gripping one of those semi-organic, morphing cups in his left hand.

Damn, Nick missed real coffee.

He knew it wouldn't taste right to him anymore, not as a vampire, but he missed it anyway.

Only the truly rich could afford real coffee these days. The few plants still in existence were tended meticulously in greenhouses run by boutique farmers who catered exclusively to the super-rich—the same handful of people who basically ran everything.

"You're late," the lead detective, a tall, scarecrow-thin black man with gray hair named Morley, declared neutrally.

Nick ignored the dig, looking around the scene.

Six. He smelled six.

He only saw five bodies, three female and two male, but he smelled six different types of blood, six different DNA imprints. The sixth, another female, could be one of the killers, but it didn't smell like it.

She smelled dead.

"Check the dumpster," he said.

He motioned towards the bin shoved against the wall to the left and a few meters behind where the techs and detectives were focused.

"You've got six bodies," Nick added, hands still in his pockets.

He continued to walk the scene, his nose wrinkling as he got closer.

As he did, he was even more sure of the sixth body.

He was still looking around, smelling the air, when he felt his fangs start to extend.

In reflex, he clenched his jaw, repressing it. Even as he did, he glanced around surreptitiously, checking faces, although the likelihood one of the humans might have noticed was pretty much nil.

Fuck, had he come here hungry?

Why was his stomach getting weird on him all of a sudden?

Shoving the thought from his mind before it started to affect his eye color, or his overall demeanor, he focused his attention back on the scene.

From what he could tell, apart from the woman they'd thrown in the dumpster, the killers didn't get near enough to touch any of the other five bodies. They didn't leave much in the way of trace imprints as a result. They definitely hadn't gotten into any kind of physical fight with the victims, not enough to leave blood, or anything with DNA.

At best, the techs might find some fibers or a few stray hairs in the mix.

Nick had his doubts they would.

Whoever these assholes were, apart from the anomaly with the woman in the dumpster, they seemed to know what they were doing. Anyway, if there *was* hair here, he likely would have smelled that, too, despite the overpowering smell of blood.

Sniffing the air again, he frowned.

The blood in the alley was really damned pungent, even for

how much of it there was. It struck him as somehow more pungent than usual.

It bothered him, how pungent it was.

Shoving the thought from his mind, he focused back on whoever had done this.

He smelled four of them.

He smelled someone else, as well.

Someone more recent.

"The scene's been contaminated," he commented sourly.

Without waiting for an answer, he walked past the other detectives, aiming his feet for the dumpster he'd motioned towards earlier. He wasn't thrilled with rooting around a dumpster that smelled like dead blood, or even being this close to a bunch of dead bodies, but the sooner he got his part of the job out of the way, the sooner he could get the hell out of there.

Like most vampires, he hated being around dead things.

The irony didn't escape him, which is why he didn't bother to mention that fact to most humans.

Most of them would look at him like he was nuts.

Well, that, and, generally speaking, explaining to a human how differently their blood smelled to him alive, versus how their blood smelled to him dead, tended to make most humans more than a little uncomfortable.

Donning latex gloves of his own, he lifted the lid of the dumpster gingerly once he got close enough, and stared down at the contents.

A clump of black hair greeted him, long and tangled over a back wearing a faux-leather jacket with a brightly colored, virtual reality (VR)-enhanced cartoon dog on the back.

Someone had thrown her into the dumpster, face-down.

The cartoon dog bounced around her back in the dim light, oblivious to its owner's death. When Nick lifted the lid higher, it triggered the VR sensors a second time, and the cartoon dog started barking at him, wagging its butt and tail playfully.

It didn't make any sound.

Something about that silent, dancing cartoon dog and the crumpled corpse smelling too-pungently of blood and death made Nick grimace.

Holding his breath, he lifted the lid higher.

Definitely a woman, from the curve of her hip in the form-fitting, shiny pants she wore, and the high-heeled, VR-enhanced pink and purple boots.

She smelled relatively young.

Twenties. Possibly early thirties.

He sniffed again and frowned.

It wasn't fake leather. It was the real thing.

He glanced down the rest of her clothes, taking a second look at her metallic-sheen pants. They fit her perfectly. The pants also had a more subtle virtual enhancement, one that sent shimmers of sparkles down her long, toned-looking legs and curve of well-exercised butt.

Her knee-high boots looked expensive, and shimmered with virtual cartoon dogs that matched the one on her real-leather jacket. The boots might be real leather, too, under the VR panels. Her hair, where it wasn't matted with blood, was silky and expensively cut.

Whoever she was, she had money.

He glanced around the rest of the dim space of the dumpster.

It was empty.

No purse. No headset, or armband.

The only thing in there was the woman.

So why had they bothered trying to hide the body?

He squinted down at her, tilting his head to see her from the side, to try and get a better look at her profile.

"They destroyed her face," he announced after another minute. "Her teeth, too, it looks like. They might have even removed them. I don't see an ident-tat."

Frowning, he leaned closer, squinting down at one of her leather-clad arms. He stared down at the hand at the end of that arm.

"...They took her fingers, too," he added.

"Fantastic," Morley muttered from behind him.

Nick carefully lowered the lid to the dumpster, stepping back.

"Better photograph it," he said. "Whoever she was, she had money. Someone's probably looking for her."

Three police techs in white, semi-transparent decontamination suits were standing at a safe distance behind him, presumably waiting for him to move away before they started photographing and taking samples.

One of them cleared their throat, speaking up.

"Those too," she said, blanching when Nick turned.

She motioned towards the bodies on the floor of the alley.

"...They have money, too," she clarified. "Expensive clothes. Manicures. Some plastic surgery treatments. At least one pair of diamond earrings—"

"They left all that?" the younger detective said, puzzled. "Why?"

The tech looked at him, then back to Nick.

She didn't answer.

Realizing he stood between the techs and the woman in the dumpster even now, Nick backed off to give them room. From the looks on their faces, they weren't about to approach with him standing there, no matter how fuzzy and cute he tried to make himself.

Frowning up and down the alley, he looked for signs of tampering with the scene.

Who was the contaminant? Did a beat cop walk through here?

It didn't smell like a cop. He couldn't quite explain that to himself, not in so many words, but cops had a particular imprint, and he didn't get it off this person.

He didn't like the anomaly of the woman.

"It's likely she was the primary target," he muttered, mostly to himself as he continued to scan the scene. "The others may have been incidental."

"Cause of death?" Morley said, his voice pointed. "They all die by plasma rifle? Or did the one in the dumpster die by something else?"

Nick glanced at him, then frowned.

"Plasmas, yes. The woman in the dumpster, too. They hit her in the face." He motioned towards his own face in rote. "That doesn't strike me as an accident. They tried to use the rifle to hide it, but the superficial damage to hide her ID all looked post-mortem to me."

Still thinking, he added,

"At least one of the killers carried an old-school projectile. He shot the one in the dumpster at least once, possibly twice. At least once in the head. That shot didn't go all the way through."

At Morley's puzzled look, Nick jerked his chin towards the metal container.

"I can smell the metal slug," he explained. "Smells different than blood."

Morley grimaced.

Turning away, he muttered something in Russian, sipping at his coffee.

Nick pretended not to notice the grimace, or the Russian, or that both things were aimed at him.

Stepping back into the main part of the alley, he went back to walking the scene. Using his eyes now, as much as his nose, he carefully skirted the pools of blood and smaller chunks of flesh to keep it off his shoes.

He frowned down at the next body he encountered, a male, adding,

"I don't think you'll find much DNA from the killers, not even with them having screwed around with the one body."

He motioned behind him vaguely, in the direction of the dumpster.

"This looks to me like a professional hit. At the very least, these are smarter than average killers. They wore gloves—real ones, the kind we use. That, or they've had their fingerprints professionally removed. I don't smell hair or skin fragments. I don't see any shoeprints, so they must have known to wear flatteners. That, or they had someone come clean up, but I don't see any evidence of a blower."

Nick motioned towards the walls, where the blood-spatter remained intact.

"See that? That's natural blood spray," he said. "A blower would have pitted all of that with dirt, and fucked up the pattern. I don't see any of that here."

He saw Morley and the younger detective follow his pointing fingers.

The younger one scowled, as if annoyed he hadn't noticed that yet, or, more likely, annoyed a vampire noticed it before him.

Nick blew that off, too.

"No," he continued, frowning. "It's more likely they didn't leave tracks to begin with. I would bet on expensive, untraceable flatteners, possibly full-prosthetics and blood patches, professional level non-residue gloves, at least one antique gun... maybe an old school sniper rifle, or even a shotgun..."

Again, he motioned vaguely in the direction of the dumpster.

"...the plasmas all look like close-contact hits, maybe after they had them cornered in the alley, or maybe after they felled some of them long-distance, using the antique rifle. It's the only reason I can think of for someone to use one of those... it's why I wondered if it was a sniper. Unless they're just attached to that particular weapon for some reason."

Thinking about this, Nick shrugged.

"The slugs will tell you for sure," he added. "...In terms of the weapon. Whatever the exact scenario, I'd look for pros. Which means either some kind of militia—maybe a political one, given the wealth class of the victims—or someone hired them. I don't know of any amateurs who could do that to a body and not leave more physical traces of themselves."

Again, Nick motioned vaguely at the dumpster.

"Most amateurs are idiots," he added, unnecessarily, given who he was with. "They stick around, touch things, step in things, leave bits and pieces of themselves everywhere. I don't see any stupid here. Plus, what they did to the woman in the dumpster, it was thorough. Which means they knew how to disguise her ident, and came here *planning* to do it."

Nick exhaled, still thinking.

The exhale was more show than need, since he didn't have to breathe.

He'd learned a long time ago, the more he could imitate human mannerisms and body functions, the more humans tended to relax around him. They probably didn't even notice he was doing it, but some part of them reacted to it anyway, animal-to-animal.

Of course, he learned some of that back in the early days.

Back then, it was more of an aid in hunting.

Now he used it to reassure his human coworkers that he *wasn't* actively thinking about eating them. He did it to reassure them they had something in common, that he wasn't so different from them... that he *wasn't* about to eat them.

Exhaling again, he added,

"Given where it is, and the exposure risk, it was likely a fast job, in and out. They didn't make chit-chat with the victims prior to the kill, or—"

"But why?" the younger detective asked.

Nick recognized him from his first day on the job, two weeks back, when he'd been first introduced to his new precinct.

His remembered his name, even.

Damon Jordan.

Like Morley, he was dark-skinned, what used to be called black or "African-American." He was about thirty years younger than the senior detective, though. This was the first time Nick had dealt with him on an actual case.

They'd mostly farmed him out to smaller jobs these first few weeks, probably to check him out since he was new.

"Why?" Jordan asked again. "Any idea of motive? What was the point of this?"

Jordan had been the one talking about blood-whores before.

Nick gave him another glance, looking over the man's muscular, broad-shouldered form. He looked like a fighter, like he spent a fair bit of time in the ring. He was young for a Detective II. He must have a decent mind on him, even if he was a racist fuck.

"How would I know?" Nick said mildly. "I just got here. Right now, I can tell you what I'm telling you. No tracks. Four killers, three males, one female. Probably three plasmas, and at least one antique combustion weapon, firing ammunition that used to be considered armor-piercing... although it wouldn't do much to the organic shielding we have now."

Exhaling again, if only to try to put them more at ease, he added,

"I'd guess a semi-modified assault rifle, probably something late 21st Century. That, or a shotgun, like I said. Something with some kick. Definitely not a handgun. Six victims, as we can all now plainly see, four female, two male. And there was an eleventh person who was here, who stepped in the blood..."

He pointed at the track he'd seen.

"...Male. Young. Maybe early twenties... at most. I can smell him, but I don't think he was involved in the killing. He's the only signature out here that left traces of himself everywhere. My guess is, he stumbled on the scene afterwards, walked around in it, maybe in shock, then bolted. If an anonymous tip brought you here, it was probably him. You'll want to run him down, though. If only to eliminate his DNA and other trace evidence from the scene."

Jordan stared at him with dark brown eyes.

They shimmered at Nick while he watched, almost in an amphibious way. That shimmer briefly illuminated a ring around the edge of the iris, a narrow line of pale blue.

Enhanced eyes. How had he missed that?

Those couldn't have been cheap.

"You telling me how to do my job, Midnight?" Jordan said.

Nick held his stare.

He knew his vampire eyes would unnerve the other man.

It was their instinct to be afraid of him... just as it was his instinct to view them as food. He didn't usually pull dick moves around that fact, but this time, he used it without thought.

"I'm giving you suggestions," he said. "Midnights are consultants. I'm assuming you want my opinion, or I wouldn't fucking be here—"

"Yeah, yeah, okay." The other waved him off in annoyance, looking away from Nick's eyes even as he clenched his jaw. "Whatever, man. And you're sure this 'contaminant' wasn't with the killers?"

Nick shrugged. "Reasonably sure, yeah. He smells more recent. Not a *lot* more recent... but maybe a few hours after."

Thinking, Nick glanced up and down the narrow alley.

Something still bugged him about the smell of all that blood.

Worse, it was making him aggressive.

Even as he thought it, he scowled at Jordan.

"...Unless you had another cop in here," he said. "Did you have another cop in here, Jordan? Someone too stupid to know not to fuck with a multiple homicide scene?"

The detective scowled back at him, his enhanced eyes growing hard.

"You sure this asshole was human, Midnight?" Jordan retorted.

"I'm sure he wasn't vampire, *Damon,*" he said. "Want me to explain how our blood smells different than yours? I can tell you... yours smells a lot better."

Jordan's pale-blue ringed eyes grew cold as metal.

Nick didn't flinch, but continued to hold his gaze.

That time, however, he found himself regretting his words, at least a little.

He was too new here to be picking fights, especially given how he'd ended up in New York in the first place. They'd have every reason to distrust him here. He was an involuntary transfer, sent over by his superior officers in L.A., who essentially "sold" him—sold his government contract, at least—to get him out of their hair.

No doubt, all the detectives here knew his history.

They knew he was essentially booted for being a problem.

He wasn't doing himself any favors, acting like an arrogant prick. He wasn't doing himself any favors projecting their worst stereotype of a vampire, either.

He needed to feed.

It was putting him in a foul mood.

That, and all this fucking blood...

Nick frowned, staring around at the alley floor.

It hit him again.

There was something wrong with this blood.

It smelled too fucking good.

It smelled *way* too fucking good.

That couldn't all be Nick's hunger.

"Anyway, that's what I can tell you so far," he said, making his voice deliberately casual. "Without knowing who the victims are, or what brought them to this alley, it's pretty hard to speculate on motive, but..."

Nick hesitated then, realizing something.

Frowning, he stepped closer to the pools of blood.

Nose wrinkling, he crouched down so he could smell it from closer, even though the scent was overpowering, even from a lot further away. Taking a few full whiffs, he felt his fangs begin to extend in earnest.

That time, he couldn't pull it back.

A flush of heat hit his gut and chest, burning in his throat. It was intense enough, he almost got hard, but he'd gotten pretty good at squelching that reaction, too.

He stood up at once.

Really, he lurched back.

It happened so fast, that smell and his reaction to it, Nick forgot to modulate his body's natural reflexes to accommodate the people around him. He was up and moving in a heartbeat, darting back in pure instinct, without slowing his movements at all.

He moved fast enough to make the humans around him freeze.

Instantly, they turned into prey.

Ignoring them, and ignoring their deer-in-headlights reactions to how he'd just moved, Nick backed away from the pool of blood with a scowl.

He backed away from the human detectives and tech team, too.

"They're hybrids," he said, emotion reaching his voice.

He turned around, staring at the humans sharing the alley with him.

The stared back at him, faces blank, eyes holding flickers of fear.

Frustrated, wanting to smash through that frozen prey look, Nick let his voice turn into a harder growl.

"Jesus fucking Christ," Nick said. "Did you hear me? They're all fucking *hybrids.*"

When they still didn't speak, he averted his gaze with a scowl. His eyes returned to the alley. Staring around at all of that blood, it sank in what it really represented.

Once it had, he couldn't help but feel sick.

2 / THE FIRST SIGN

NICK HAD INTENDED to leave, right after he gave his initial summary. He'd meant to give them the bare bones, then just leave.

Once he discerned the race of the victims, he found himself lingering, for reasons he couldn't fully explain to himself.

No one told him to leave.

Then again, no one asked him to stay, either.

Morley ended up being the first to break the silence after Nick told them what the victims were.

"Did you say hybrids?" The older detective blinked, then frowned, still staring at him. "The victims?"

Nick nodded without looking at him, grimacing as he stared at the lake of blood. He couldn't stop seeing it differently now that he knew what it contained.

He fought the reaction off his face. He knew he mostly failed.

"Yeah," he said, gruff. "I think all of them are. Were."

"*All* of them were hybrids?" Jordan said, speaking up from behind Morley. "All six? Are you sure?"

Nick turned, staring at the other male. "I'm pretty fucking sure, yeah."

Seeing something in his eyes, Jordan backed down. The anger in the human's eyes dissipated, shifting into something closer to fear.

Looking at him, it occurred to Nick that his irises had probably turned bright red—right around the time his fangs extended.

Right around the time he ID'd the hybrid blood.

Ignoring Jordan's reaction with an effort, Nick attempted to reassure Morley, who he more or less liked. As far as bosses went, and humans, Morley seemed to be okay.

But the older detective wasn't looking at him anymore.

Morley was staring down at the blood.

"Jesus." He whistled under his breath. "Six hybrids? And they just *happened* to be hanging out in this alley at the same time? That can't be a coincidence."

"No," Nick agreed. "It can't." Pausing, he added, "The woman in the dumpster. She had a human tat. The barcode was cut or burned off, but the 'H' sign was still there. Are any of the others wearing the marks? Have you scanned their ident-tats yet?"

Jordan shifted his attention off Nick. His face and neck remained flushed, either in embarrassment or fear or both, but he'd regained control over his expression.

He also seemed focused back on the job. He was staring at the blood with the rest of them, latex gloves on his hands, hands on his hips.

Now he shook his head to Nick's question.

"None of them had the mark for hybrid, I know that. They all had human tats. Pureblood. We're running the IDs now with Gertrude."

Gertrude was the artificial intelligence that ran most of the bureaucratic functions of the NYPD. Nick didn't know where the name came from. Probably someone's idea of a joke, unless it was named after the aunt of one of the AI's programmers.

Nick nodded to Jordan's words, but the frown remained on his face.

"Yeah," he said, when the silence stretched. "Well, I guess make sure the medical records weren't falsified under whatever Gertrude turns up. And yeah... make sure I'm right. About the hybrid thing. If they *were* all hybrids, and all of them are unreg'd, living under fake IDs, I'm guessing you have your motive. Part of one, anyway."

Jordan and Morley exchanged looks.

The female tech, who was still photographing the blood, stared only at Nick.

The three techs over by the dumpster stared at Nick, too.

Still fighting to get the cloying smell of hybrid out of his nose, Nick didn't look at any of them. He stared down at the blood, unable to remove the grimace from his face.

If these hybrids had human tats, that was more evidence they had money.

That, or someone sponsoring them had money.

Fake idents were no joke these days.

They took serious connections, people able and willing to pull strings, to procure fake documentation that would actually pass the verification process. To maintain a fake blood ident over time, they needed someone on the inside to alter the databases in the main registration banks, not to mention enough connections at a high enough level to get the street-level grunts to look the other way in random spot-checks.

That meant medical records, birth records, blood records, blood patches for random street and travel checks, fake fingerprints and usually fake X-rays.

The internal organs of hybrids rarely matched up closely enough to a full-blooded human's for them to pass through most check-points. Blood could be dealt with using fingertip patches, but only at the older checkpoints. The newer blood-draws were trickier to fool, but even so, generally-speaking, blood was the easy part.

Internal organs? Those were trickier.

Some of the newer checkpoint machines even had booths that scanned for organ placement, along with DNA strand checks on hair or skin. There were organic vests that could fool the machines, but those were damned expensive too, not to mention illegal to own, so only available on the darkest threads in the network.

Whoever these hybrids were, chances were, they didn't do a lot of traveling, at least not via commercial carriers.

What traveling they did, it was likely on private jets.

Nick was still staring at the ground when one of the techs by the dumpster spoke up.

"Hey! Could you come over here..." He looked at Nick, fumbling, maybe unwilling to use the moniker "Midnight," or maybe just uneasy about addressing him at all. "...Mr. Midnight," he finally settled on. "You should look at this, while you're here."

Glancing at Morley and Jordan, Nick began moving in the direction of the tech, careful to keep his footsteps slow and human-like.

He heard, felt, and smelled Jordan and Morley following him.

As soon as they got within a few feet of the tech, Nick saw where he was pointing.

Something had been painted there, on the wall.

It must have been exposed when they shifted the chrome dumpster. It didn't look like normal graffiti, even the more artistic varieties.

It looked like a painting.

Like a *real* painting.

Frowning, Nick stepped closer, studying the part he could see, which turned out to be a detailed depiction of a masked form, holding an antique-looking shotgun. It looked like an old Remington 870, like something Nick might have had in a black and white, years ago.

So... not a sniper rifle.

"What the fuck is that?" Morley said from behind him.

Nick shook his head, still staring at the painting.

"I don't know," he muttered.

"A confession?"

Nick turned and found Jordan standing just behind him, staring at the painting, his eyes narrowed. The younger detective didn't take his eyes off the wall.

"Some kind of signature?" he muttered.

Nick thought about that. "Could be," he admitted.

"Should we move the dumpster?" the first tech asked, the one who'd called Nick over.

He looked between Nick and Jordan, as if not sure who he should be addressing.

When no one else spoke, Nick did.

"This thing has wheels, right?" he said to the first tech. "Can these other two climb down and pull it away from the wall? Try rolling it sideways?"

The two techs working over the dead girl blinked at him.

Then they looked at Morley, as if for confirmation.

The older detective nodded, his mouth pursed.

"Do what he says," he said, taking another sip of the not-coffee.

The white-gloved techs with their white, raincoat-like lab suits exchanged looks, then, as if by silent agreement, climbed down carefully to the same side of the bright silver container. From there, with the first technician, the one who'd pointed out the painting in the first place, they each found clean parts of the dumpster to push with their gloved hands.

Slowly and carefully, and watching where they placed their bootie-covered feet, they rolled the metal dumpster sideways, exposing the wall behind it without running those wheels through any part of the nearby pools of blood.

Luckily, the dumpster wasn't heavy.

Even more luckily, those small wheels under the chrome dumpster still functioned.

Nick stopped thinking about any of that as the wall gradually became exposed.

The meticulously-drawn brush strokes, what he'd only glimpsed when the dumpster stood in the way, grew into a full, coherent image, unfolding into an elaborate painting that covered a few feet of the back wall.

Now, instead of the one masked face, Nick saw four masked figures, each of them holding guns. The other three carried plasma-rifles.

The figure holding the antique gun turned out to be shorter than the others, and drawn in such a way that Nick now wondered if his gunman was actually a gun-woman.

So, the female carried the shotgun.

A pretty weird choice in weapons.

A sniper rifle would have made more sense. Long-distance shooting was an unusual skill set nowadays, but still practical, even with the proliferation of drones.

The shotgun was just... idiosyncratic.

After the techs finished moving the dumpster, they walked back around to stare at the image along with the detectives and Nick.

For a long-feeling few moments, no one spoke, or moved.

The image was disconcertingly life-like.

Unlike most street art, it didn't appear to have been done either in that newer, metallic, VR paint, or even in old-school spray paint.

Instead, it looked like some more "classic" painting material —maybe acrylic, or even some kind of oil paint. Nick didn't know paint well enough to know for sure. It smelled pungent, which made him think it might be oil-based.

Whatever it was, the deep blacks and brighter colors stood out, giving it a strangely three-dimensional effect, even without the added dimension of virtual enhancement. That effect managed to add to the realism of the painting itself.

It showed the gunmen—with possibly one gun-woman—

aiming their weapons at five figures, two male and three female, who stood halfway down a narrow alley with a chrome dumpster. The dumpster stood against the metal-coated back wall of the alley, just like this one, only in the painting, the container was shiny and pristine, with no splashes of blood. The lid was open, and from the angle, which was slightly elevated, Nick could see black hair, along with the vague outline of a body crumpled inside the metal container.

If the image was right, the woman in the dumpster died first.

She may even have been killed somewhere else.

But why? Was she bait to get the others here?

And why destroy her face?

Nick's eyes flickered back to the killers.

He found himself examining the antique shotgun a second time.

It was such a strange choice, for this time period. Since the seer wars, guns like that had more or less disappeared. Ironically, it was probably worth a lot of money, as a bona fide antique, and if the painting was accurate, it was in good shape.

Still, it was strange to think of the weapon that way too, when such things had been a part of his everyday life, once upon a time.

From next to him, Jordan muttered under his breath again.

"What's the point?" he said. "I mean, fuck. Why go to all the trouble? Is it a warning? Some kind of taunt?"

Next to him, Morley grunted.

"Maybe we'll have a better idea once we ID the one in the dumpster," he said, his voice diplomatic. "DNA should give us a hit. Face or no face."

Nick didn't bother to point out the obvious fact that if she was really a hybrid, and unreg'd, all of her DNA and medical records would be bullshit, and might not tell them a damned thing about who she'd been before this.

Jordan glanced at Morley, his enhanced eyes openly skeptical.

From the look there, the same thing had already occurred to the younger detective.

Of course, they had other ways to track her down—including through the other victims—but if everything *legal* about her had been falsified, it might not be all that easy to ID her. The fact that she clearly came from money could either help them or hurt them, depending on who was behind this, and who wanted it covered up.

That wasn't what had Nick's attention right then, anyway.

The attempt to hide the woman's identity, while unusual, made sense.

What made a lot *less* sense, and was a hell of a lot more disturbing, was the reality of the painting itself—and what it meant once he'd glanced over the physical details more closely.

Blood spatter covered part of the image.

Parts of the painting had been worn away and discolored by dirt.

Other parts had been pitted and scratched, likely by street cleaners, or maybe by the prongs of the garbage truck as it emptied the chrome dumpster on its weekly rounds.

The painting wasn't done by a witness to the crime.

It had been here before the murders happened.

It looked like it predated the murders by at least a few days.

Possibly longer.

Staring at the painting, Nick felt a vague sickness grow in his gut.

He couldn't have said why, exactly.

The painting should have piqued his interest, like it clearly had the interest of the two human detectives. Nick should have seen it as a clue, perhaps even as proof of premeditation. At the very least, he should have been curious, the way he could feel a buzz of curiosity growing among the humans staring at the image alongside him.

He couldn't get onboard with any of that, though.

Truthfully, he just wanted to get the fuck out of there.

Maybe spend an hour or two inhaling bleach.

Anything to get the smell of that seer-infused blood out of his head.

Anything to wash the view of that painting from where it wanted to burn itself into the dark spaces behind his eyes.

3 / MIDNIGHT

"IDENTIFICATION, PLEASE."

The female-sounding voice droned the words from the other side of transparent, semi-organic shielding. It didn't sound like a question.

It really wasn't a question.

"Naoko Tanaka Midnight." Nick unholstered his sidearm, laying it on the round, greenish-silver plate in front of the speaker. "Homicide division. Ident tag 9381T-112."

"Year of change?"

"197 B.D."

The woman behind the organic nodded, once.

Nick honestly couldn't tell if she was an image implanted in his mind through his semi-organic headset, a hologram, or a robot.

He guessed a robot.

Maybe he just liked the idea of a robot best, of the three options.

"Stand for retinal and ident scan," the voice droned.

Nick froze in place in front of the scanner's multiple eyes, unblinking as the organic arm emerged from the wall by the transparent cubicle, its blue light flickering over his face, temporarily blinding his sensitive vampire eyes before sliding over the rest of him.

He held his inner arm out and flat, so the tattoo showed up easily, and the implant would be readable without multiple passes.

The bar code on his arm stood out on his pale skin, next to a dark red "V" about two inches long and painted with organic metal to counteract his skin's natural healing abilities.

For the same reason, his "tattoos" were really more like another form of implant.

Like his deeper implant, they were designed via organic tech to fool his vampire body into thinking they belonged there.

Both scanners flickered over every inch of his skin, then clicked off.

"You may enter," the voice said.

Nick grunted, watching his sidearm disappear into the morphing, full-organic metal of the round plate outside the registration cubicle.

Even now, after more than ten years of this gig, he never expected to get that gun back.

Hell, he never *fully* expected to be allowed to leave the building, not once he'd walked through one of those outer security doors.

He did it anyway.

He didn't have a lot of choice.

Well, he didn't have a lot of *good* choices.

The door buzzed then clicked, just like doors had back in the time when he'd been a human cop, in San Francisco, what felt like a million years ago now. Grabbing the unlocked handle, he jerked open the heavy, bulletproof, semi-organic panel after the buzz, and stepped inside before the sensor started beeping at him again.

Immediately, the sounds of the police station washed over him.

Those sounds were eerily timeless.

Letting the door fall shut behind him, Nick made his way down the featureless corridor towards the origin of those sounds.

His vampire senses of smell and hearing kicked in, telling him most of what he needed to know before he entered the main bullpen beyond the corridor.

He heard them talking about him again.

He was still the new guy.

This time, he got to hear about how the "new blood-sniffer" who'd recently transferred here from "fuckin' L.A." got in a few lucky hits out at that mess in the Bronx.

Some just called him "the new Midnight," which, honestly, Nick preferred.

In this new world, vampires got assigned government-issued surnames to make them more easily distinguishable from their human counterparts who worked roughly the same jobs.

Nick supposed it reassured humans, to make vamps as easily identifiable as possible.

There seemed to be some fear that random vampires could slip past them otherwise, maybe by wearing contact lenses over their crystal-colored irises, or long sleeves to cover the telltale "V" ident-tats and barcodes—as if vampires weren't segregated, regulated, tested, blood-checked and surveilled in every other fucking way, as a condition of being allowed to roam free.

As if vampires might start dating their cousin, or fucking their wife, and no one in the global or local interspecies enforcement bodies would notice.

The thought was laughable.

For the same reason, Nick strongly suspected a fair-few of these rules, including the name-tagging system, served more political functions than anything. Enforcement bodies did it to normalize the whole set-up, and render it more "polite."

Whatever the exact logic of the Human Racial Authority, or H.R.A., in coming up with the name-coding, vamps who worked for the police—at least those in homicide and interspecies relations, which was most of them—all got tagged with the surname "Midnight."

It was a better name than a lot of vamps got stuck with.

Then again, the H.R.A. had to pick surnames not in common use by humans.

Vamps working in medicine got tagged with the surname "Serpent," presumably in honor of the Rod of Asclepius and/or the Caduceus, both symbols of medicine and healing and both containing serpents.

Engineers were all "Machine."

Research and development got the moniker "Galileo," unless they worked in weapons, then they got "Supernova." Career military vamps, the only other option offered to Nick by the H.R.A. when they were assigning employment, were all "Centurion."

Teachers and professors got "Library."

Those pulled into think-tanks and strategy got "Chessboard."

Those in full-time sex and blood work were "Incubus," or "Succubus," the only surnames that depended on the claimed sex of the individual vampire.

Nick had most of the list memorized.

Then again, so did most people, human and vamp.

The Inter-Species Friendship Council, or "I.S.F.," as most humans called it—or "I.S. Fucked," as most vampires called it— was technically responsible for vampire code enforcement on United States soil. While the I.S.F. fell under the authority of the H.R.A., at least on paper, they also designed and rolled out policy, whether official or not, and far more quickly than the H.R.A., which tended to move at the speed of your average glacier.

Often, the H.R.A. adopted changes *after* I.S. Fucked was already enforcing those changes on U.S. soil. By the time the rule change was legally in the books, other countries were often already following the United States' lead.

Most of the vampire code surnames were country-specific, so

the I.S.F. likely had a hand in designing the specific names now in use in the States.

Supposedly, all of this worked out to make the system easier on everyone.

Nick didn't see a lot of "easy" in the system, though.

Well, not for vampires.

He couldn't exactly blame humans for taking the steps they did to ensure their safety. Despite their vastly superior numbers, humans were still, after all, *food,* to Nick and his people. That simple fact pretty much annihilated any basis for trust that may have existed between the two species. But the realities of the system meant to keep humans safe still kept vampires a semi-enslaved class.

At the very least, they were something significantly less than full citizens.

Of course, like most things, that relationship was complicated.

Organized crime and the black market were riddled with vamps.

A lot of those outfits were led by ex-military, too—with some of those vamps being shockingly well-connected, and closer to terrorists than simply crime lords. Some of those militias grew right out of the seer wars.

Even the whole hunter-prey dynamic got pretty fuzzy these days.

Plenty of humans *liked* being bit by vampires.

Enough of them liked it, in fact, that vampires could make a full-time living charging for the privilege, especially if they mixed bloodletting with sex.

And that was just pureblood humans.

Hybrids, back when more of those existed, got full-blown addicted to vampire venom.

They got addicted to the point where the I.S.F.—followed by the H.R.A.—were eventually forced to pass regulations forbidding hybrids from offering vampires their blood, or for soliciting vampires for sex, which was more or less the same thing.

Vampires were also explicitly forbidden from feeding on hybrids. The difference being, of course, that hybrids, if caught, would get hit with a fine and maybe do a stint in human jail.

Vampires, on the other hand, would be thrown in a government lab somewhere for what was politely termed "reprogramming." Or, if they were considered "incurable," they would have their hearts removed from their bodies with these claw-like, retractable tools the government created expressly for the purpose, called "alligators."

Nick had seen those things in action a few times, while he was still in L.A.

A few times, as it turned out, was more than enough.

It was gross as hell.

It still didn't entirely discourage vamps from biting, fucking and even dating hybrids, of course. It still happened. Meaning, hybrid and vampire sex and feeding still happened.

Even now, it still happened.

Hybrids were rare as hell, but they were still around, as the killing in the Bronx clearly demonstrated. But it was nothing like the early years, before the I.S.F. started passing regulations against hybrids and vampires more generally.

Seers, the other race that briefly shared a history with this world, had been even more vulnerable to the effects of vampire venom than their hybrid offspring.

Seers, well...

Seers lost their damned minds, when it came to vampires.

If a vampire wasn't too scrupulous, they could turn a seer into a literal slave.

A venom-addicted seer would do pretty much anything a vampire wanted—a difficult temptation to fight given how fucking amazing seer blood tasted to your average vampire, not to mention how incredible sex could be with one of their kind.

A seer's blood was Grade-A prime rib.

It was steak dinner, a fine wine... real coffee and chocolate rolled into one.

Compared to that, human blood was more like a defrosted tofu burger on soggy bread, covered in fake ketchup, with artificial coffee to wash it down.

Luckily, most vampires these days didn't know that.

Unfortunately for Nick, he did.

Shoving the thought from his mind with an effort, he didn't manage it successfully before a pair of pale green eyes rose briefly to the spaces behind his eyes. With that image of stunning, violet-ringed green eyes, came a flood of unwelcome memory, along with something that was nearly pain to his chest and gut.

By the time he forced the memory out for real, he was already in a foul mood.

He was also hungry.

Because of both things, his face was set in a hard scowl when he reached the end of the featureless corridor and the space opened up, revealing the main offices of the 17th Precinct of the New York Police Department.

He didn't want to be here at all, but he had no choice.

This was where the inter-species offices were located for Manhattan, and where Nick had to check in every night he was on duty. It was also one of only two precincts in the city that Midnight detectives were cleared to work out of, as of about six years ago.

They liked to keep everything pretty tightly controlled, when it came to vamps.

The wider jurisdiction for Midnights also gave them the freedom to assign him to cases in any part of the city, not just those that fell within a particular geographical area.

Very few vamps got cleared to work on the kinds of cases they gave Nick. For the same reason, he was under constant, intense scrutiny—too much scrutiny to let himself start thinking about food while he was on the job.

The very *last* thing he needed was some human cop getting jumpy because they happened to notice Nick's eyes were redder than usual, or his canines happened to be extended the slightest bit, just because his stomach was a little rumbly.

As for his food-obsession right then, Nick still blamed that damned alley hit, if only for putting the thought of hybrid and seer blood in his head.

Still, after what they found in that alley, he was interested enough that he couldn't help wondering if they'd gotten the lab results back on the victims yet.

Even more than the victims, he was damned interested in that painting.

He wondered if they'd managed to get anything on the artist.

Back at the crime scene in the Bronx, Nick stuck around the alley long enough to see the lab techs run spectrometer scans and take scrapings off the alley wall, hoping to pick up enough DNA or other trace evidence to ID whoever made the mural.

While he stood there, one of the techs told Nick that whoever it was, they'd spent hours on the damned thing. The tech pointed out the fineness of the lines and brush strokes, not to mention the detail in the faces and the reproduction of the alley itself.

Nick hadn't noticed on first glance, but the artist even included details of irregularities in the alley's cement floor, along with scrapes on the metallic paint of the walls, dirt smudges, steam coming off one of the pipes running the length of the right side of the alley. The level of detail made it look in parts more like a photograph than a painting.

The whole thing was bizarre, and not only because some whacko chose to paint the faces of professional killers and their hybrid murder victims as an act of vandalism.

Nick knew, from listening to them talk, that Morley and Jordan both thought the person who painted the image was connected somehow to whoever ordered the hit on the six hybrids.

They theorized the mural was some kind of message—either to the victims when they arrived in the alley and saw their likenesses there on the wall, or as a warning to someone else.

That, Jordan hazarded, or the painting might be a calling card of some kind, a message to someone else about who'd done the job.

Nick had his doubts.

About both theories.

He was still standing by the corridor entrance to the long, weirdly egg-shaped room, when someone called out his name.

Well, not *his* name exactly, but he knew they were talking to him.

"Midnight! Hey! Come over here. Check this out."

Gritting his teeth, Nick snapped out of his quiet little reverie, which hadn't exactly been pleasant but had the advantage of being... well, quiet.

Walking towards the small crowd he hadn't noticed clustered around Jordan's desk, he saw them all looking down at something that apparently lay in the middle of it.

Nick knew most of them by name already, despite only having been here a few weeks.

He'd always had a good memory for faces, even as a human.

Now, he remembered almost everything.

"Hey." The cop who'd called him over, a female homicide detective named Charlie, was hunched over what Nick now recognized as a liquid monitor on Jordan's desk. "You might want to take a look at this... since you were there with the others when they found it."

Charlie's full lips smiled at him as she said it, accentuating the curve of her cheekbones, and the almond slant of her eyes. Those eyes were a stunning, light-brown color, and looked almost too big for her face.

Charlie was some kind of Eurasian-black mix, and shockingly pretty.

Her round, muscular butt rested on the corner of Jordan's

desk, and as she glanced between Nick and that monitor, the smile on her face grew as she looked him over, appraising his physical appearance openly.

Nick couldn't help but see a second, more knowing quirk touch her full lips after she'd taken in the details of his body and face.

Christ. He hoped she wasn't another vampire groupie.

No way was he starting up something like that, not with someone he worked with; he didn't care how damned pretty she was. Being the vampire in the equation, if anything went sideways, as it eventually would, it would all come down on him.

Probably like a ton of bricks.

Unfortunately, the longer he watched her stare at him, the more he found himself thinking she had that look.

Something in those light-brown eyes just screamed, "I've never been bitten by a vampire before, but I bet it's really hot," and/or "I really want a vampire fuck-toy of my very own, and won't my friends be jealous if I brought him to dinner."

Not. Gonna. Happen. Lady.

"Well?" she said.

Charlie quirked an eyebrow at him, folding her arms.

It occurred to Nick that he'd come to a full stop, and was just standing there, staring at her.

"Do you want to look or not?" she finished, motioning towards the liquid monitor by her leg. "It's your case as much as Jordie and Morley's, right?"

Hesitating, he nodded, then stepped forward, wary.

Walking around her to get closer to the monitor from the other side, he craned his head and neck, doing his best to get a look at the curved screen without leaning too close to her.

He stared for a few minutes before something clicked, and he realized what he was looking at.

"That's security footage," he said, surprise reaching his voice. "You got the whole thing on surveillance? Is it a drone? Or stationary?"

Jordan looked up, frowning from where he sat just to the right of Charlie. Glancing at her, Jordan aimed his enhanced eyes back at Nick with a scowl.

Great, Nick thought.

Jordan wanted to get into Charlie's pants.

He now saw Nick as a sexual rival, on top of everything else.

If Nick was right about Charlie having a thing for vampires, that wasn't going to help his and Jordan's relationship any, either.

"Stationary," Jordan said, still scowling after that too-long pause. "It's owned by the warehouse on the right side of the alley, but subsidized, so it's also a government feed."

Nick nodded, not taking his eyes off the recording.

"They get the whole thing?"

"Not the murder," Jordan said. "Tapes were clean for that. The squad that performed the hit must have hacked in and disabled the cameras before they took out the hybrids."

Still frowning, he added sourly,

"But we got your Picasso. The system was still up and working when the painting was made, a few weeks earlier. We just got the footage from the Feds."

"A few *weeks?*" Nick stepped closer, interested in spite of himself. "Were you able to ID him? The artist?"

"Artist." Jordan grunted, giving him a disbelieving look. "No, Midnight. We weren't able to ID the 'artist.' Not yet."

Nick frowned, still staring down at the image.

He could only see the guy's back.

Whoever he was, he was big, with broad shoulders. He was also tall. He wore a threadbare, light-gray, sleeveless sweatshirt with the hood up, along with paint-splattered black pants, so Nick couldn't see his face.

"Did he have his barcode covered, or—"

"No barcode." Jordan pointed at the image on the screen. "See? You can see his left arm right there. You see any kind of barcode, Midnight?"

Nick frowned, refocusing on the man's arm.

Jordan was right.

The pale inside of his strangely muscular forearm was completely bare.

Jesus. That was completely unheard of.

Even weirder, the outside of that same arm, all the way up to his shoulder, was covered in brightly-colored tattoos. The arm on the right was completely unadorned as far as Nick could see. There wasn't a single design anywhere on it—or on his neck or face—official or not.

Nick wondered what lived on the parts of skin the sweatshirt and pants covered.

"Any chance it's prosthetics?" Nick said.

When Jordan didn't answer, Nick glanced at him.

"The arm. Could he have covered up the bar code?"

Jordan frowned a little, then shrugged. "It's possible, I suppose. I don't know why he wouldn't cover up all his ink, if that's the case. Or why he'd wear a sleeveless shirt unless he was signaling he had no reg number."

Nick thought about that, pursing his lips.

Then he nodded. He couldn't really disagree with Jordan's logic.

The clothes themselves were damned weird. Not only were they retro as fuck, but Jordan was right. Why bother with prosthetics when a long-sleeved shirt would have done the trick?

A shirt would have at least dealt with cameras, if not the scanner patrols.

And conversely, why would someone with no reg barcode wear a sleeveless anything? The guy hadn't even waited until it was dark out. He'd done it in broad daylight, while committing vandalism on private property. If he'd been anywhere in the world in the past twenty or so years, he must have known he was likely being recorded.

The whole world was under surveillance these days.

In a city as dense as New York, where there was still a fair bit of money and enough vamps to make people nervous, it was more or less a given.

"Were you able to follow him?" Nick said. "When he left? Were you able to see where he went?"

Jordan looked up at him, his mouth hard.

"We're working on it, Midnight," he said, his voice cold.

Making a show of checking his watch, he looked up at Nick's face.

"Aren't you out of here?" he said, his voice pointed. "Sun's coming up, Midnight. Don't you turn to stone or something, once it's daylight? I thought that's why they only had your kind working at night."

Nick frowned, then glanced at the clock on the wall of the bullpen in spite of himself.

He'd forgotten to check the time.

He'd had three crime scenes to walk before the one in the alley, starting at around 7 p.m.

It was almost 6 a.m. now.

Again, Jordan wasn't wrong.

Rather than waste time with words, Nick gave them all a brief bow of his head—without really thinking about where the mannerism came from, or even what he meant by it, exactly—and stepped back from the desk. He kept his eyes on Jordan, who watched him back away, until he was a good six feet from where they all huddled.

Turning on his heel only then, Nick headed for the elevator that would take him to the lower floors of the building.

Despite the time, he couldn't leave yet.

He was required to check in at the station every night, give a verbal report, then submit to a physical to make sure he hadn't been feeding while he'd been out on the job.

He was a Midnight, after all.

‍❧

WANT TO READ MORE?
Continue the rest of the novel here:
VAMPIRE DETECTIVE MIDNIGHT
(Vampire Detective Midnight #1)

Link: http://bit.ly/VDM-1

Recommended Reading Order:
QUENTIN BLACK MYSTERY SERIES

THANK YOU NOTE

I just wanted to take a moment here to thank some of my amazing readers and supporters. Huge appreciation, long distance hugs and light-filled thanks to the following people:

Shannon Tusler
Sarah Hall
Elizabeth Meadows
Rebekkah Brainerd
77Daisy

I can't tell you how much I appreciate you!

LIGHT AND DARK
LOVE AND MAGIC

JC Andrijeski is a *USA Today* and *Wall Street Journal* bestselling author of urban fantasy, paranormal romance, mysteries, and apocalyptic science fiction, often with a sexy and metaphysical bent.

JC has a background in journalism, history and politics, and has a tendency to traipse around the globe, eat odd foods, and read whatever she can get her hands on. She grew up in the Bay Area of California, but has lived abroad in Europe, Australia and Asia, and from coast to coast in the continental United States.

She currently lives and writes full time in Los Angeles.

For more information, go to: https://jcandrijeski.com

amazon.com/JC-Andrijeski/e/B004MFTAP0
patreon.com/jcandrijeski
bookbub.com/authors/jc-andrijeski
facebook.com/JCAndrijeski
twitter.com/jcandrijeski
instagram.com/jcandrijeski

Printed in Great Britain
by Amazon

78179494R00215